Bloodstorm

Dragon Wine Part Four

By

Donna Maree Hanson

About the author

Donna Maree Hanson is a traditionally and independently published author of fantasy, science fiction and horror. She also writes paranormal romance under the pseudonym of Dani Kristoff. Her dark fantasy series (which some reviewers have called 'grim dark'), *Dragon Wine*, was published by Momentum Books (Pan Macmillan digital imprint) in 2014. *Shatterwing*: Part One and *Skywatcher*: Part Two are now re-published independently in digital and print on demand. *Deathwings*, Dragon Wine Part Three and *Bloodstorm*, Dragon Part Four were published in 2017.

In April 2015, Donna was awarded the A. Bertram Chandler Award for 'Outstanding Achievement in Australian Science Fiction' for her work in running science fiction conventions, publishing and broader SF community contribution. Donna also writes science fiction romance, with *Rayessa and the Space Pirates* and *Rae and Essa's Space Adventures* out with Escape Publishing. *Opi Battles the Space Pirates* was published independently in 2017. In 2016, Donna commenced her PhD candidature researching Feminism in Popular Romance at the University of Canberra. Also, available is her epic fantasy series the Silverlands, *Argenterra*, *Oathbound* and *Ungiven Land*. Donna lives in Canberra with her partner and fellow writer Matthew Farrer.

You can contact Donna at her blog http://donnamareehanson.com

Or on Twitter @DonnaMHanson and Facebook

www.facebook.com/donnamareehanson

And if you like to keep in touch and hear about special offers, then consider signing up for her newsletter, Wing Dust.

Also by Donna Maree Hanson

The Silverlands (Epic Fantasy)

Argenterra, The Silverlands Book One

Oathbound, The Silverlands Book Two

Ungiven Land, The Silverlands Book Three

Dragon Wine Series (Dark Fantasy)

Shatterwing, Dragon Wine Part One

Skywatcher, Dragon Wine Part Two

Deathwings, Dragon Wine Part Three

Bloodstorm, Dragon Wine Part Four

Love and Space Pirates (Science Fiction Romance)

Rayessa and the Space Pirates

Rae and Essa's Space Adventures

Opi Battles the Space Pirates

Dedication

Dragons soar through the sky of my dreams…may they visit yours

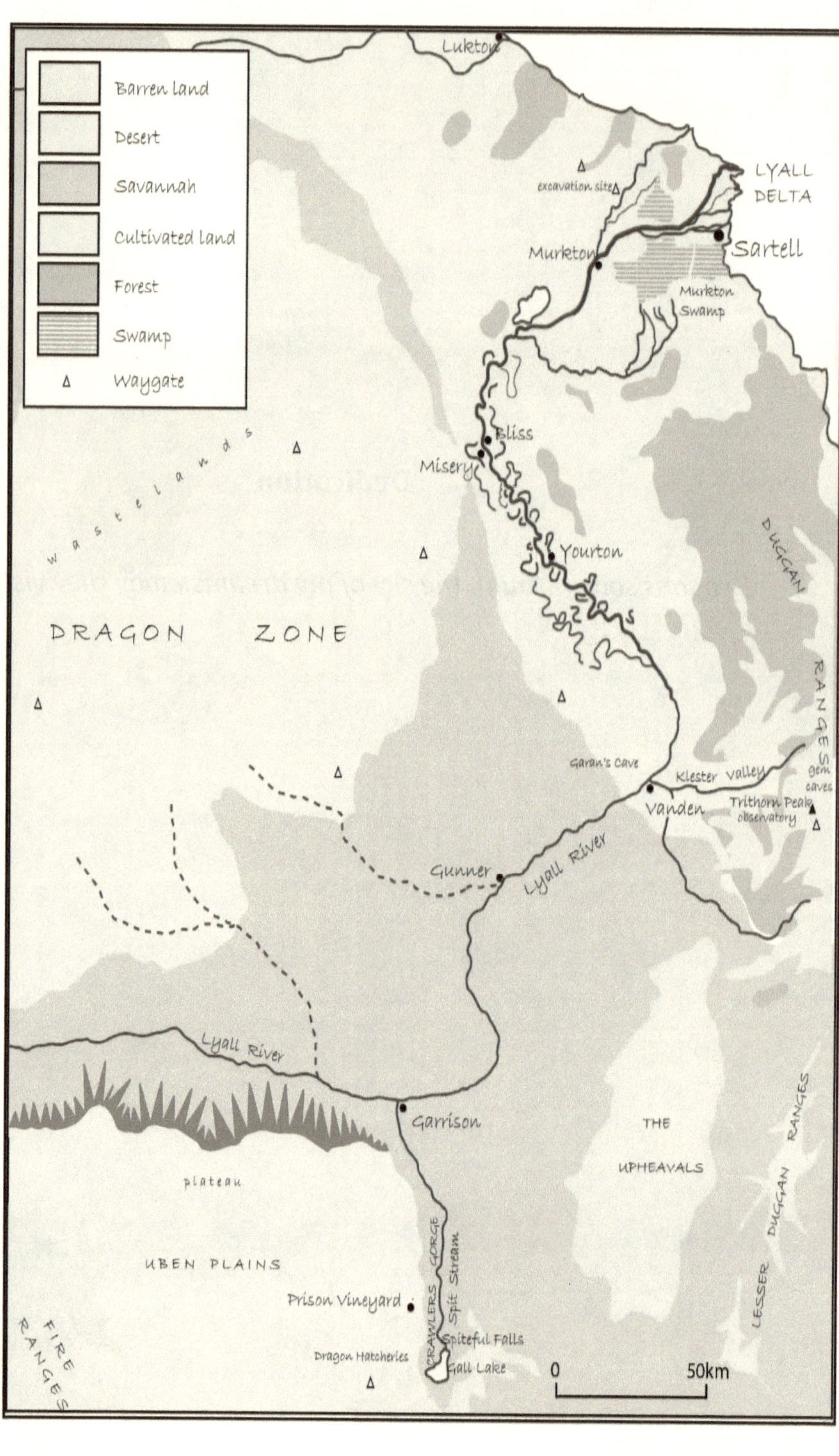

Barren land
Desert
Savannah
Cultivated land
Forest
Swamp
Waygate
Lukton
LYALL DELTA
excavation site
Murkton
Sartell
Murkton Swamp
Bliss
Misery
Yourton
Wastelands
DRAGON ZONE
DUGGAN RANGES
Garan's Cave
Klester Valley
gem caves
Vanden
Trithorn Peak observatory
Gunner
Lyall River
Lyall River
Garrison
THE UPHEAVALS
plateau
LESSER DUGGAN RANGES
CRAWLERS GORGE
Spit Stream
UBEN PLAINS
Prison Vineyard
FIRE RANGES
Spiteful Falls
Dragon Hatcheries
Fall Lake
0
50km

Prologue

Within Shatterwing, moon fragments shift and roll in tune to orbit and gravity. A lump of space rock blunders into a stable grouping, rocketing meteors off in tangential directions. Rueline and Ruelette exchange places to watch the dance. Fire trails streak the sky with violet-colored flares. Doom edges closer. And closer still.

Part 1

To live without dragon wine is to live without a soul

Chapter One

A FOOT UP THE LADDER

After returning from a long foraging trip, his belly full of a human snatched from a river, Gercomo saw the female dragon again, the one who had laid the eggs he had so enjoyed eating. She hissed at him as he drew near. Gercomo found her behavior amusing because with her bulk, she could do some serious damage to him. Jagged fangs. Razor-sharp claws. Yes, she could shred him without a thought. So why hiss? Why not strike? The fact that she hadn't intrigued him.

He angled his head toward her and drew his tongue slowly across her snout. It was a daring tease. Her body tensed but she didn't strike back, just hissed again and then turned away and ignored him.

Gercomo sauntered away to settle down into his burrow, belching up human aftertaste as he did so. He caught a glimpse of her scrabbling toward the egg pit.

Gercomo smiled inwardly, tempted to peer down after her to see her reaction to her empty nest. But that would require more daring than he possessed, and he had to be careful to keep his thoughts small or all would know that he had been the one to destroy the clutch of eggs. The dragons might not use sentences and concepts like humans, but they sensed strong emotions like guilt and fear. Gercomo would bet they could read intentions too.

A few minutes after the she-dragon had disappeared from view he heard a commotion. A few dragons who were slumbering among the rocks lifted their heads in response but were not interested enough to climb out of their burrows and investigate. Gercomo turned his head and noted that the head bull slept on, blissfully unaware of the female's distress.

More intense screeches echoed from the hatchery below. It wouldn't take long for the bull to react now, for it sounded like a fight had broken out. A grunt came from the bull's resting place.

It was time to distance himself from the action below, to remove himself from blame. Gercomo crawled out of the sand, which fell to the ground in a warm shower. The morning sun was strengthening as it rose and the scent of sulfur was on the air. Gercomo breathed deep.

Warm pools littered the area where he walked. Steam vents spewed vapor into the air, giving it moisture and warmth and releasing pungent aromas. He was tempted to lick the rocks for salt like the hatchlings did. He wandered further in. In the thermal area, he sampled different scents and tentatively tasted the mineral deposits that rimmed the ponds and vents. The purple salts were like hot spice and the yellow more like rotten eggs, or what he remembered of rotten eggs. Food did not taste as it once had; the crunch of bone and the slurp of blood gave him much enjoyment now, as did the quenching of the lilac-colored glow that centered on living things.

The sound of rock hitting rock alerted him to the presence of another dragon. He inhaled and knew it was her, the she-dragon who had so humiliated him and who he in turn had punished. She had come to challenge him over her eggs, the ones that had filled his belly with delicious energy.

Vengeance spewed from her mind. Turning her head sharply, she fixed her gaze on him, fangs dripping, ready for the kill. Gercomo could taste the hot emotion, like some strange sauce caught at the back of his throat.

She'd come alone, without her mate.

He had barely turned to confront her when she lunged for him, swinging her head to knock him down. Although he was taken by surprise, he was able to duck, avoiding the full force of the blow. Before she could strike again, he bit her on the neck, ripping the skin with his broken tooth.

Her screech near deafened him. She clawed at the ground and at him until he released her. He backed up and circled, trying to devise an attack strategy. She was a female, hence smaller than the bull, and yet larger than him by far. She lunged again, catching him a glancing blow across the head. Purple-tinged blood leaked down her neck.

He had wounded her. His grin could not be suppressed. How interesting. Although she was physically larger than he was, he could outmaneuver her, and he was smarter, of that he was sure. The blood glowed temptingly with that lavender-colored energy: her life force. His tongue lolled. He wanted to drink it.

He feinted left, she went to block, and then he was on her, overbalancing her so she fell. The blood on her neck drew him closer. He sniffed and licked tentatively, pretending at first to be considerate and caring. She did not throw him off. The taste of blood on his tongue sent ripples of ecstasy through him. What was that? He had to have more.

He licked again, savoring the blood, and then bit down hard into her leathery flesh. The female tried to break free but was paralyzed by his grip. He sucked the blood in, drew it down his throat. It burned its way into his stomach. Then the strength of it hit him. He let go of her and reeled, staggering backward.

Power. The raw power of dragon blood tore its way through his flesh and mind. The world tilted. He had a vague sense that he was on the ground before he lost consciousness.

When he came to, the female was sniffing his penis, gently probing it with her tongue. He growled a warning, but she put her foot on his torso and held him in place and licked him in earnest. Despite his revulsion, he was aroused by her ministrations. His cock hurt, though. Curling in on himself, he saw it was large, too large for his stature.

The power of the blood was still inside him, bursting to escape through his skin. He roared at the female. She withdrew her snout from between his legs and retreated. A shaft of pain hit as his hindquarters grew in size, first one leg then the other. It hurt but he was growing, stretching, becoming more. Giving himself a shake, he realized he was a good foot taller.

It must have been the dragon blood.

What else could account for this power roaring inside him and this sudden growth?

Climbing unsteadily to his feet, he checked himself out. He had definitely grown, but was still a runt compared to the rest of the herd. His tail swished across the loose stones littering the ground.

The female abased herself before him and whimpered. Alert, he studied her. Was she seeking to mate with him? He blinked and then she arranged her tail so that he could have access. Could he? Should he?

He circled her and her scent filled his nostrils, potent and overwhelming. Gercomo's erection quivered and burned in reaction to the chemicals hitting his brain. He wanted—no, needed—to copulate with her. It was all that was in his mind at that moment.

He climbed atop her and she opened for him. As he pushed into her, she moaned—a sound of pleasure. Gercomo just had to move, just had to ejaculate as fast as he could. The thought would not leave his mind. It possessed him, made him mad with lust. He thrust into her vigorously. She yipped and growled. The sound of their coupling echoed around them. There would be no doubt about what they were doing.

Unsought, he had made an impression on the female. Tactically, this was a good thing. Fucking a normal-sized dragon would give him status. As a normal-sized dragon, she would be a powerful ally, a powerful mate.

His seed spilled into her, though he wondered what sort of semen he had made with his stunted dragon form. Surely he could not fertilize dragon eggs. Utterly spent, he withdrew from her. His cock, now flaccid, was still large in comparison to his body. She turned and licked his snout, nuzzling him and nudging him gently.

Let the rest of the herd mock him, but this female was well satisfied with his performance. He growled at her, thinking pleasurable thoughts. It wouldn't hurt to keep her on side.

Ambling back to his nesting place, he burrowed himself in the sand, conscious of the other dragons' attention. The bull looked up and roared once. The female he had coupled with roared back. A sense of merriment filtered through his dragon sense. Had he unwittingly climbed up the pecking order by mounting that particular female?

The female grunted behind him. She had followed him to his burrow. He opened an eye and regarded her. Lowering her snout, she sniffed him and licked the top of his head. Then she turned to descend into the hatchery. Curiosity got the better of him. Disregarding his intent to hide away in his nest, he scrabbled across to peer over the lip of the pit. There she was, laying eggs. The process was stomach-turning. He was human enough to feel that. Yet, he wondered whether he had actually fertilized them.

What would his offspring be like? Would they be dragon or part human? It hurt his brain just thinking of it. He quieted his thoughts. No point in drawing attention to his strangeness. Not when everything was going along so well just now.

After pushing sand over her eggs, the she-dragon scrambled up the side of the hatchery. Before she emerged, Gercomo went back to his nest and feigned sleep. He had no idea what was going to happen next.

Through a crack in his eyelid he saw that she chose a piece of ground close to him and made the sand soft for her burrow. It appeared she had staked him out as territory. Odd, but it looked as though he now had a mate. As he dozed off, he realized this meant he had someone at his side, someone of normal dragon stature. If he kept her happy, she would do his bidding. Then he remembered the bite, and how her blood had tasted and the power that had surged through him. Her blood would give him greater power, make him stronger, larger. Maybe now he had a way to influence the herd and its head bull. Despite his misfortunes, everything was falling into place. Nice thoughts of revenge settled in his mind. Salinda. That blonde chit with her hidden power. *She will pay. She will.*

After a short rest, Gercomo shook the sand from his hide and lumbered off. He would fly about, test his luck. If there was prey to be had, it would be his.

Chapter Two

THROUGH THE WAYS

Laidan was gone and it was all Salinda's fault. Salinda clenched her fists and tried not to berate herself at this strange turn of events. She had to do her best to get the girl back. Closing her eyes, she let out a sigh and then shook her head.

Nils rested his serene silver-colored eyes on her, cocking his head to the side. "The boy has discovered Laidan's true nature and upbraided her about it. Is that not so? Then she has run off..." He closed his mouth and inclined his head as if listening to something far away. "Without much thought to where she was going, I suspect."

Salinda looked at him askance. "Yes, but..." Surely Nils had not spied on Laidan and Brill at the observatory. Yet his kind were known to have hidden in the spaces between the walls, noting things down and recording them in their archives. Had Nils known Laidan's secret all this time? If he had, why had he not spoken of it? She shook her head again. It was probably some kind of moral choice. Shaking the thought off, she began walking down to where Garan waited, urging Nils along with her. "Can you sense where she has gone, Nils?"

"With certainty."

Salinda let relief flow through her. "Good, then we must hurry after her." She grabbed hold of Garan and urged him to walk with her. To Nils she said, "Will any harm come to her within the Ways before we catch up to her?"

Nils walked behind them, the blue of his outer robe billowing with the speed of their descent. "The Ways themselves are not inherently dangerous, if she stays on the path. The peril lies more in the condition of some of the Ways, and the positioning of the Way Gates. She knows how to open them. Some lead to places that do not exist anymore. Others lead to places where something else exists. It is possible for her to open a gate onto a river, and thereby release a flood into the Ways."

"Wing Dust!" Salinda exclaimed and then continued to curse under her breath.

The girl had promised secrecy and had pledged not to enter the Ways. Salinda's Hiem mate would not take kindly to a breach of oath, just as Garan found it hard to re-live the girl's seduction of another man. The memory must have been very vivid indeed, and despite Laidan's flight, she was sorry for Garan and for Laidan too. While she had little respect for the girl, she acknowledged that it would be a hard thing to have someone see inside your head, experience your most private moments and your secret thoughts.

It did occur to Salinda that if the girl escaped, she would have no way of tracking her. Laidan no longer held the cadre, and so Salinda could no longer sense her. She hoped Laidan did not escape to a town, where the situation could only worsen. Salinda had a duty to return her to the protection of the observatory, hopefully unharmed. With Laidan's beauty, she would be prey to anyone with power. Hadn't that girl learned anything from being captured by Lenk and all the terrible events that had followed? A sudden dark foreboding flooded into her mind. There was danger, terrible danger for Laidan, for them all. Something bad loomed ahead. She could taste it.

"We must hurry," Salinda said as she quickened her pace.

Diverting to Salinda's abode, they gathered the things they would need for their journey. "Nils, can you track which Way she is in and then show us on the map the possible gates she could access? We have to think ahead of her."

Nils's expression was somber. "Yes," he replied. Taking a step toward the door, he gestured for them to follow. "Come, we will study the map. I can show you which one she has accessed."

Salinda thought Garan looked ready to burst.

"Why do we wait?" the young man urged. "If you know which Way she is in, why can we not follow straight away?"

Garan had not seen Nils's wondrous map. He thought charging after the girl through the Ways was the best and quickest solution. Where the heart leads, Salinda thought to herself, danger will follow.

"Calm yourself, Garan. We can plan better if we know what our options are," she admonished.

"But if we go now we can catch up with her before something happens." He gripped his head in his hands. "'Tis all my fault. I was overwhelmed by Thurdon's reaction to Laidan's deed. I was sorely hurt too, that was true, but…"

Salinda drew his hand into her own and squeezed. "It is not your fault. It's not Laidan's either, I think. It's just the consequences of things that have happened to her and to you. Don't worry. We will find her." She expressed more confidence than she felt. The cadre-fueled premonition could not be ignored.

Nils shouldered his way into his shroud. Unpowered, it was like a dull gray cape. She thought it best to test her assumption. "Nils, where were you when you sensed Laidan entering the Ways?"

"I was two levels below in my study, following a line of research. I did not feel her open the Way Gate as I was very distracted. As I returned a record to a shelf, I detected the vibration of her passage."

Salinda caught Garan's attention. "It has been hours since you spoke with her. She could have left straight away. It is likely she will exit before we reach her even if we leave now. Trust me. This way is better. Distance is distorted in the Ways; if we hope to head her off then choosing the best Travel Way is crucial."

Garan relaxed slightly, although he looked resigned. "If you say so. But please can we not move now?"

Nils was ready. "Yes. Follow Nils."

Nils led them through the city to the gate Laidan had used. It was the same one from which they had entered Barrahiem. It made sense, as it was the only Way Gate Laidan knew about from direct experience. Perhaps she sought to return to the observatory.

From memory, each Way started as a main thoroughfare and then splintered into smaller pathways. As they walked Salinda silently thanked the source that Nils had sensed Laidan's departure. He had told her that when the city was full of his kind, the traffic through the

Ways created vibrations, a thrum of life and energy that was part of the city, of everyday life. Now he was the last of the Hiem, one person using the Ways was like a light springing to life in the dark. They had not been walking very long when Nils announced that Laidan had found an exit.

"Show me," Salinda said.

Nils reached into his shroud and pulled out his hand-held map, a small metal ball. Garan gaped when Nils activated it. The device sent shining dots into the air to create a three dimensional image.

"She has reached here." Nils pointed to a spot on the map.

"Tell me, what is nearby? You found me in the town of Gunner, and the observatory is where?"

Nils pointed out the references on the map. Salinda frowned. "If that is Gunner, and that is the Uber plain, then Laidan has emerged somewhere near the dragon hatcheries. There are a series of them spreading from the prison vineyard to the base of the Fire Ranges. Nils, do you know if there is any geothermal activity in that area?" Salinda pointed to the spot where Laidan was thought to have exited the Way Gate.

Nils shook his head. "I cannot say. Too much of the surface has changed since this map was drawn. What once was a paradise could now be a wasteland."

Salinda narrowed her eyelids "In this case, it is. Do you think we could reach this Way Gate?" She pointed to the gate next along and slightly to the west of the one Laidan had used.

"Yes. If it is still functioning. Why, what is it?"

"If my bearings are correct, that will open very close to the dragon hatcheries and Plu's nest. He may be able to assist in the search." Hopefully the young dragon had returned to his nesting ground now that Salinda had entered Barrahiem. Plu had an uncanny ability to sense where she was and be there when she needed him. She hoped he would do so again this time.

Garan rubbed his chin as Nils turned off the map. "And if it does not?"

"Then we work on another plan. Laidan has stumbled upon an unpopulated area. It has been a while since I was at the vineyard. The government may have replanted and resettled it. If they haven't, then she will be alone and vulnerable. I imagine the dragons in the area have not eaten well in a while now that the prison vineyard no longer supplies them with burden beasts and old prisoners to eat."

"Dragons!" Nils and Garan exclaimed in unison, but their meaning was very different. By his expression, Salinda could see that Garan was horrified, while Nils fairly overflowed with excitement.

～～～～～

Garan could only shake his head in wonder at the magic of how Nils navigated the Ways. There was so much to learn about the present and the past. Nils was a treasure trove of information. Garan sympathized with Salinda. Knowledge was precious and, therefore, so were Nils and the relics of the Hiem.

The cadre he now carried seemed to expand with each new sight. Garan's mind was near to bursting. The cadre was a strange and awe-inspiring presence in his mind. One thing it had in common with him, though, was concern for Laidan. The agitation in Thurdon's presence only increased Garan's sense of guilt. He should have exercised more self-control instead of confronting Laidan and berating her for her actions. Actions that had been no concern of his. Laidan owed him nothing and he should have seen how it was with her and Brill, should have suspected Laidan's feelings went deeper than mere infatuation.

He had had no right to say anything to her about how she chose to live her life, and to whom she gave her love. He wanted to pound his head against a wall to expunge his ignorance and his arrogance. If only he had been better prepared he would not have yelled at her, upbraided her for something he could not change. It was her business who she gave her body to. She was not responsible for his feelings, even though she had toyed with them. She was too young to know any different.

They hurried through the Ways, desperate to catch Laidan but knowing that she was already out in the open. Nils told them he knew a short cut, and it did indeed seem only a brief time before he halted and studied the carved rock formation that identified the exit.

Nils pressed the recessed sections, chanting to himself as he did so. Some sort of ritual. Garan knew the gate would open without the words, for Laidan had once opened a Way Gate just by pressing the sections in the right order. Just in time, she had saved them, guided by the essence of Thurdon.

The Way Gate opened into a narrow crevice, its entrance fenced in by a single spear of bedrock. There was room for one person at a time to squeeze past it. Salinda begged Nils to stay behind and keep the Way Gate open so that they could return quickly if they needed to. Nils appeared reluctant but agreed when she stroked his hand.

Salinda edged out and turned sideways to step along the gap between the canyon wall and a solid upthrust of granite. The light glowed amber as the sun's rays reflected off the reddish streaks in the layers of earth that made up the canyon wall. Garan turned side-on and squeezed through, following closely behind Salinda. It was a tight fit for him. Once past this obstacle Garan smelled sulfur and slowed.

"Salinda, is that dragon sign?"

"Yes," she whispered. "But keep quiet about it. Nils would be out here in a second if he thought there were dragons close by, and I believe we are in the middle of the hatcheries. I won't know until we are clear of this rock formation."

Garan swallowed. Even with the cadre in his mind, he feared dragons. He couldn't help it. They were huge, savage beasts that ate people. He stopped where he was, sweating profusely, hands gripping the rock so hard his fingernails ripped.

Salinda asked, "You with me, Garan?"

He shook himself and sent her a nod before following. Straining to hear the normal sounds around him, he found his breathing grew hoarse. It was quiet here. There was barely any wind. If there were dragons, they were either out hunting or asleep. He prayed to the source that this was not a dragon hatchery after all.

Salinda disappeared from view as she levered herself up and around a corner. After a few anxious moments of scrambling to keep up with her, he drew abreast of her on a small ledge that gave them a wide view of the ravine that stretched out ahead.

His eyes widened at the sight below. Beyond the mouth of the craggy, eroded canyon walls, a brown plain stretched out to the left, and to the right, in the distance, was a charred ring of earth. There were signs of new green growth amid the charcoal black smothering the ground.

The *whoosh-whoosh* of dragon wings made his breath stop and his body freeze. Swooping from above came a dragon. Smaller than

Salinda's dragon, Plu, but impressive all the same. This one had a deep purple coat with a bright green pattern across its body. A hatchling, he guessed.

Salinda kept herself still after the hatchling disappeared from sight, obscured by the surrounding crest of the ridge. Garan drew in a long breath, not realizing he had been holding it. He made to move, but Salinda grabbed him by the wrist and held him there with a hard grip for a moment longer. In the distance, Garan caught a glimpse of another winged beast gliding over the plains near the blackened ring of earth. Garan suddenly recognized what the site was: the prison vineyard where Salinda had spent so much of her life. He wondered what she felt seeing it again.

Her hand released his and Salinda moved on, lowering herself carefully down from the ledge. Garan followed her. She picked a path between the rocks and boulders littering the way. She headed in a northerly direction. The walls of the ravine gradually cut away, opening up the land to the sun and sky.

Garan could not resist casting about for Laidan, eagerly searching for her and hoping that they found her before anything went wrong. Nonetheless his gut was heavy with foreboding. Positive thoughts did nothing to beat away that sense of dread. He tried to concentrate on details. That would help. What was she wearing? Had she changed from the Hiem gown back into her own? Garan found he could not remember what clothes she owned. He searched for blue, but nothing caught his eye.

About half an hour later, Salinda gestured for him to move closer to her. "We should be sufficiently sheltered here if any dragons come close. I'm going to call Plu. Do not be alarmed. He can help us scout around for her." They stood underneath a rocky outcrop, a large slab of stone forming a roof.

Salinda lifted her arms, angling them over her head. Her call went out and a thrum of power she used to augment it vibrated within him. The cadre he carried glowed with excitement. Garan suspected that the cadre he held admired the other cadre and its carrier immensely. Strange that he should think so. It was too soon to tell if that was fact; too soon to know whether the cadre had a personality or if it was his own wishful thinking.

At present, the cadre reminded him too much of Thurdon, even though the old man's presence had been subsumed into it. Even now Garan could still detect thoughts that had to be the old man's. Salinda had said that the cadre changed with each holder. That meant that they had to be careful who it was passed on to. Who could guess what damage would be done if someone evil or mad gained possession of it, someone like Gercomo? Perish the thought.

The sound of wings approaching heralded the arrival of Plu, who swept up from below to perch on the rocks near them. His claws crushed and jostled smaller rocks as he gained purchase. It seemed to Garan that the young dragon had grown. Plu's wings fluttered as he settled.

Salinda spoke to her young dragon. "Nier bach oon." *Find small man.* Garan found that the cadre understood Salinda. That raised his eyebrow.

The dragon aimed its head at her, as if readying for a strike. She leaned forward, maintaining a precarious hold by resting one hand on a boulder while using the other to stroke the creature's tongue. Garan lunged forward and grabbed her around the waist to secure her as she withdrew from the dragon.

Plu screeched once, then leaped to the stone slab above their heads before launching himself up to skim the canyon and the perimeter of the hatchery with long downbeats of his wings to keep himself airborne.

"Do you think he can find her?" Garan asked Salinda as he helped her down to the next level in their descent, a series of stone stacks with flat tops that were close enough together to serve as wide steps. He found he was extra anxious due to her pregnancy. The child she carried was precious, not only to Nils and Salinda but to all of Margra because it was the last descendent of the Hiem. He cocked his head, wondering where that thought had come from.

"Rest easy, Garan," she said, patting his hand. "I can manage from here." She shifted her attention from him to where her pet dragon flew. "Plu might be of use yet. Dragons have a different array of senses to assist them with hunting and even navigating the world. I can't say directly, of course. I am not a dragon."

Plu bleated in the distance. "Come on, I think he has spotted her," Salinda said, and clambered to a rough path that led down the slope, sending scree rattling ahead of her. Garan followed close behind, his feet sliding on loose pebbles. As he made his way after her, the skin of his fingers tore on the rocks and the rough, sharp-edged plants that clung to life in this barren place. In spite of her ungainly body, Salinda had managed far better than he.

Together they rounded a section of rock face and he thought he saw something in the distance: a flash of blonde hair and the flicker of a blue robe. "I think I see her."

"Good. We will approach her together. We may yet get her to safety before any dragons catch her scent."

Plu flew off, perhaps back to his roost. Conscious of the potential danger, Garan kept up a constant scan of their surroundings—not easy with tall boulders and rock fall as well as the curving ridge obscuring the view. On his second pass of the horizon, he saw a dark spot in the distant sky.

At first he thought it was a bird, but as it approached, it grew larger and more distinct and he realized it was a dragon. By her sudden burst of speed, he thought Laidan had spotted it as well. Then he realized she was running away from them and toward the dragon.

"Salinda!"

"I know, I see." Salinda bit her lip and shook her head. "Can't she see the danger?"

The guilt at what he had said to Laidan to precipitate this flight vanished as he watched her scramble, and fear hammered in his chest instead. Did she have no sense of the danger she was placing herself in? Probably not, he thought wryly. She was acting on emotions and was probably too desperate and upset to think straight.

With a shake of his head he realized that he could not throw off the cloak of blame. He had to acknowledge his part in her current state of mind. His gaze flicked up and around. The black spot had grown even larger. The dragon was zeroing in on them.

Up ahead, Salinda shaded the afternoon sun from her eyes with her hand. She watched in silence for a minute or two. Then, when she glanced back at him, his gut clenched.

"What is it?" he asked.

"It's him." Salinda bit her bottom lip, her eyes troubled.

"Who?" Though Garan immediately felt stupid for asking. It could only be the man he had tried to kill—the one they had transformed into a dragon. "Not...Gercomo?"

Salinda did not even acknowledge him, she just sped up. "Come on, we have to try to reach her before he gets here!" Her voice had a desperate edge to it, as if she was facing her worst nightmare.

What had that man done to her to rip away her confidence like that, Garan wondered. He was hard-pressed even to imagine what could rattle Salinda's calm. She was so serene, so quietly powerful in his eyes.

"I'll go," he said. "You stay under cover." He moved ahead of her, and when she did not answer he turned back, eyebrows raised in query. "Salinda?"

"Source preserve us!"

Garan turned around and squinted. Laidan was still out in the open. The urge to yell out to her, to warn her, burned in his throat. "Salinda, hurry."

She moved. "You don't understand, Garan. He can sense me." Salinda's eyes were wide and dark, her hands shaky, and even her complexion had paled. It was the first time Garan had seen her close to panic.

"You don't know that for sure. Stay down. I will go for Laidan."

As the creature drew closer he could see it better. It was definitely the one that had transformed at Trithorn Peak. It had the distinctive miniature build and an aura of menace. Gercomo came in closer and swooped over the rocks ahead of them. He had caught Laidan's scent or seen her, Garan suspected. Garan prayed he had not seen or scented them also. The only thing in their favor was the element of surprise.

"No, Garan. I must go with you. Only together can we fight him."

Partially obscured by their rocky cover, Salinda stood, her eyes never leaving the beast. She had recovered her composure and there was a sense of determination etched into her expression. He doubted she would panic again.

"But—" Why could he not fight this thing on his own? It was Laidan down there and she was vulnerable because of him. He caught another glimpse of her robe and realized she was running away from them, from him. His heart sank. *Gercomo!* He screamed her name loudly but it made no difference. She kept on running.

"Garan. With me," Salinda said. "We have learned much since our last encounter. We shall surprise him with our strength."

Seeing the now steely look in her eyes, Garan lowered his head and mumbled agreement. She was right. He had the cadre now as well as the power that resided within—and she had learned much about her own cadre.

Gathering her robe, Salinda leaped to the next rock and then the next, heading toward the menacing miniature beast. "First we must get into position and make sure we have a clear shot," she rasped.

He prepared himself mentally as he followed her steps. This would be the first time he had tapped into the cadre in this way. He had no crystal, but Salinda had said repeatedly that he did not need one. He hoped she was right about that. Then he remembered the power cells that had recharged at his touch. Was it the same thing?

Attacking Gercomo would give their position away, but would be worth it if he was distracted from Laidan. They took up their positions, and with a signal from Salinda, Garan called forth the flame as Salinda had shown him. Then he stretched it out between his hands and, freeing one end, he held it like a sword. Salinda mirrored him and then their flame blades joined. In sync, they put more force into the flame, building it up with hot power. As Gercomo came in for his next swoop, they released. A spear of light spat out.

Gercomo took the force of it head-on and faltered. He shifted tack, aiming in their direction, but they kept up the flame, and soon it engulfed the small dragon body completely. For a moment, Garan thought they had succeeded in obliterating the beast. He was ready to lessen the power he was feeding into the flame. Then Gercomo emerged from the fiery onslaught, shook off the residual flames and glared at them.

Salinda bit her lip and narrowed her eyes. "Not possible." She met Garan's horrified stare. "Again!" she commanded.

Quickly, he and Salinda re-aimed their combined power in a golden bolt, but Gercomo dodged and it hit the boulders behind him in an explosive shower of rock. Gercomo's wings danced as he climbed higher before swooping in for another pass.

Garan sweated and his heart raced. What if the beast had learned to throw flame? Garan was in the direct line of fire and Gercomo was one angry beast. Adjusting his stance, Garan put as much energy as he could into the next blast, reaching down into the cadre and the power within. This time their blast hit the beast square-on. Gercomo reeled, screeching, and then tumbled tail over head to the ground somewhere near the base of the hatcheries.

Garan stood on his toes and peered down the incline. Currently, Laidan was positioned between them and the Gercomo-beast. If they hurried they could reach her and escape. Garan hoped that Laidan had chosen to stay put and take cover, but he never had been good at predicting what she would do

Garan frowned into the silence. "'Tis too much to hope that the beast was killed or maimed by our attack," he commented to Salinda.

"Yes, it is too much to hope." She shook her head, her expression downcast. "He is not dead. He's like an ache in my mind. I didn't realize my presence would cause us so much danger. He can sense me, I am sure, and I can feel that he lives still. There is a connection between us."

"Hopefully he is badly wounded. Enough to keep him down until we get Laidan and get out of here."

Salinda huffed out a breath. "Yes, and may he fear us and not attack at all."

Garan's lip twitched. "At the very least, I hope it will give him pause before he tries to attack us again."

Garan climbed out of their shelter and gave a hand to Salinda, who scrambled up behind him. "We'd better hurry."

"I fear Gercomo will remember Laidan, remember that she held the cadre."

Garan swallowed. "Source preserve her!" He quickened his pace, heading to where he last saw Laidan. He knew there was danger for him, too, if Gercomo discovered that he now carried the cadre. Could that beast sense the cadre as he appeared to sense Salinda? Or was that some other tie, something to do with the dragon essence she had told him about?

Chapter Three

FIRE BURNS, FANGS REND

Laidan was so angry, tears coursed down her face and her nose ran freely. Why couldn't they leave her alone? Why had they followed her? She wasn't going back, couldn't go back. She was never going to look Garan in the face again. She had shamed herself and him. She had shamed everybody, and they hated her for it. She hated herself more.

Laidan had almost reached level ground at the base of the slope when she heard the sounds of fire blasts above. She ducked instinctively. Someone was attacking. What? Who?

There was a loud screech above her. She flattened herself against the ground but couldn't see anything. It would be just her luck to encounter dragons. Why hadn't she exited near a town or a city? Now she was going to be stranded unless she found another Way Gate. She thought of backtracking but they were after her. She couldn't face them. Not after Garan had seen it all and had surely told Salinda. *Damn you, Thurdon! Why did you ever shove that cadre into my mind? Why did you die and leave me all alone? Why did you leave me, Brill?* Another blast sounded. Were Garan and Salinda firing at her? Did they hate her that much? She lunged to her feet and continued on.

There was a pause. She heard the flap of wings and threw herself to the ground and rolled up against a boulder. A shadow passed overhead and she squinted. Definitely a dragon. Breath rasping and heart thumping, she climbed to her feet and ran to a gap between two boulders.

Then another blast lashed out, stronger and louder than before. She bolted from cover and tried to make the last dash into the open, tried to get away from them.

She had almost made it to the edge of the plain. Tongues of rock lay to either side of her, making a sickle shape on the ground already littered with jagged stone and scree. A noise sounded to the right and she jerked around, riveted to the spot. Her heart leaped in her chest and her breaths now came in heavy pants that left her throat burning. There in front of her, partially shaded by rocks, was a mass of twisting, convulsing flesh and scales.

Run! Run! her instinct told her, but her knees were locked together and her body refused to budge. The sense of dread grew steadily as she watched the mass writhe. *What is it?*

As she looked on, the shape of a man emerged, as excess scales and flesh fell to the ground and dissolved. Laidan backed away, searching around for the best path to take, the best place to hide. There was something too familiar in this.

Now she realized that Salinda had not been aiming for her at all. It was that man. The one who had attacked the observatory. The man who had nearly captured her. The man who had changed into a stunted dragon. No wonder she hadn't seen him, felt him. She'd been on the lookout for one of the massive beasts. What was he doing here? Laidan had imagined that he had died, not being able to live as a dragon. How wrong she had been.

The man's form kept changing, shrinking, forming into the semblance of Gercomo. His hands were claws still, bent over and sharp. His naked skin was red as if it had been burned. From the back a tail hung down and his erect penis looked over-large in his small frame. Gray and purple scales replaced the hair on his head. Yet he had legs and a body and he was heading right for her.

"You!" he shouted at her, making her flinch. His voice was different too—harsh, scratchy, unused to talking. "Where. Isth. Ittt?"

Laidan trembled all over and urine trickled down her legs. She couldn't move. A scream filled the air around her as she backed up, tripped on a rock and fell heavily.

Quickly, she scrambled on all fours trying to get to her feet. There were some boulders nearby; perhaps she could hide among them. She made headway, then next she knew claws slashed the flesh of her shoulder. She faltered and screamed.

Still desperate to make cover, she hunched over and put in a burst of speed. Gercomo reached for her again, his arm too long for a man. She stumbled, her head barely missing a rock jutting from the ground. Stunned, she could hardly breathe, and then he flipped her onto her back.

His snarling face loomed over her and his clawed hands anchored her clothing to the spot. "Githe me powerth." His voice rasped and saliva dripped from his mouth, smelling of sulfur. His slurred, mispronounced words took a moment to sink in. Laidan screamed again and covered her face with her arms, trying to hide from the horror of that face and the terrible deformity she could almost taste. He wanted the cadre!

"Giveth. Or Rip it. Frrommm youusth" The words came out slowly and rough, like his mouth found it hard to shape the words. He shifted his weight and the claws ripped her clothes, shredding them to strips. The sound of the fabric tearing went on and on. Terror more potent than any she had ever experienced took hold of her, sending her muscles into spasm. She could feel welts and cuts stinging on her skin where he clawed her robe.

Strange black eyes regarded her. She could see that they were barely a man's. A beast's eyes in a man's face. Up close, she could see the skin interspersed with scales. How could such a thing exist?

"Eats. Youusth!" The words grated out of his malformed mouth. He hissed, then spoke again. "Drink. Soul." A raspy cough sounded and she realized he was laughing. "Feel youusth. Die!"

His claws began to dig into her, piercing the flesh over her ribs. He dropped into a crouch between her legs and grabbed her hips. Pain speared through her. There were no more screams left.

Then he licked at her blood, nibbled on the torn flesh. *No!* was all she could think. He was violating her in every way possible. Laidan's hold on life, on consciousness, loosened. She could feel her life ebbing away as he continued to destroy her. His claws shifted to the sides of her head and gripped hard.

As he lifted her face to his, the rankness of him enveloped her. "Give me. It. Give." Over and over again, he repeated those words—lisping, grunting, spitting them at her. The claws ripped her scalp, putting pressure on the bone beneath as he squeezed. There was nothing but pain. She was going to die. A scream of denial left her throat.

♋♋♋♋

On their way down to the base of the slope, Salinda said, "We have to kill him. We can't let him get away."

Garan saw the truth of her words. Yet Gercomo's resistance to their power was worrying.

"That first blast should have taken him out," Salinda said, as if she understood the direction of his thoughts. "I can feel him out there, feel his malice. He is hungry for power."

Her words fed his urgency as he ran faster than he thought possible in this terrain. At the same time he kept his eyes open for dragons and other dangers. Laidan's scream reached him—a knife into his heart.

"There!" he said with a tremor in his voice as he sped past Salinda.

"Careful," Salinda shouted as she quickened her pace to catch him up. He jumped from rock to rock, desperate to find her before it was too late. As he drew closer to the level area where he had last seen her, the sound of a gravelly voice reached him.

Puzzled for a moment, he couldn't quite grasp what it was that he was hearing. Was there someone else in the area? Salinda called to him, and even from that distance he could tell her voice quavered with fear.

"Garan! Ware. That's Gercomo's voice. I know it."

"What?" Panic welled up inside him and squeezed his lungs. Gercomo was back?

Laidan's scream confirmed his worst fear. He leaped down from the rock he was on, nearly overbalancing. With a hand outstretched, he caught himself before he tumbled forward out of control. A loose rock shifted and he twisted his ankle. He limped on, fear for Laidan fueling his determination despite his pain.

Finally, he was out in the open. Standing there panting, he scanned the area, trying to gain his bearings. He let out a cry when he saw it. There was a large man-shaped form off to the right. It took a moment for him to recognize what he was seeing. A half-man half-beast, Laidan, and blood.

"By the Wing!" he cursed to himself. He lurched forward awkwardly on his twisted right ankle, ready to tear at the beast with his bare hands.

Drawing close, he gasped. Laidan wore a veil of red as blood ran from her head, her neck and her abdomen. He couldn't tell if she was alive. His impulse was to run to her and gather her in his arms. Garan stopped and, with tears coursing down his cheeks, drew upon his power and aimed. The blow dissipated off the man's hide in a flare of violet light. As if shrugging off a fly, the man-beast shook himself. Then slowly, as if becoming aware of Garan's presence, Gercomo lifted his head slightly and turned. The tail flicked once, and then Gercomo withdrew from Laidan's body. The man-beast faced Garan, engorged and bloody penis hanging near his knees. Scaled skin cut through reddened flesh and he had claws for hands. Garan's gut twisted in revulsion.

Garan swallowed a lump of cold fear as Gercomo raised an arm to reveal talons dripping blood and strips of flesh. Then, in spite of everything, Garan found himself mesmerized by the hybrid face. The nose was a snout, but the eyes were human-shaped, albeit with black orbs. A smile revealed jagged teeth. While Garan stood bound in horror, Gercomo lifted his talons to his mouth one by one and dribbled the gore down his throat, sucking each digit tip by tip.

Fighting horror and nausea, Garan floundered. Where was Salinda? She would know what to do. Locked in indecision, he was not sure if another burst of his power would have any effect. Gercomo took a step toward him. Instinctively, Garan threw everything he had within him at the creature: the power of the cadre and crystal combined.

The detonation threw Garan back against the rocks he had just climbed down. Dazed, he lay there for a moment. Shaking his head, he quickly searched for the Gercomo-beast. Groping his way to his feet, he saw that Laidan was lying prone on the ground, as still as death. From that distance he could not tell if she breathed.

Gercomo was not where he had been before Garan had thrown his power. Taking a few steps away from the wall of rock, Garan searched. There, about two hundred meters away, was Gercomo, climbing to his feet, shaking his head. So the blast had had an effect after all. But Gercomo was only stunned.

Behind him Garan heard Salinda call out. "Wait for me. I'll be there in a minute. Only together can we fight him off."

Gercomo came in fast, picking up his pace as he ran with inhuman speed.

"Hurry, Salinda. I cannot get to Laidan before he does." Garan lobbed balls of power and Gercomo dodged them and then halted.

Salinda's face was etched with worry when she joined him. "This is much worse than I thought. He is resistant to our power. Could it be that he used it to transform back?"

Garan gaped. "Transform? We made him change back!"

Salinda's eyes widened. "It's all my fault."

Gercomo hissed and Salinda balled her fist. "No…no…"

"Now is not the time for blame but action." Garan clasped her shoulder in reassurance.

Gercomo let out a hiss that set Garan's skin prickling. There was so much hate in his expression. Garan had never experienced such a sensation before. He had never experienced hatred or evil so strong that it climbed into his skin, his mouth, his nose. Suffocating.

Gercomo bellowed. "Youusth!" and then charged.

Salinda called to Garan, "Now!"

Garan wiped at his face as tears tracked down his face. They threw their combined fire. The energy glowed out in straight beams, then Salinda joined hands with him and the power wove together and hit Gercomo as one. He reeled and screeched, unable to fight back.

Inhuman cries pierced the air around them. They filled Garan with fear. Salinda put her other arm around his waist, holding and comforting him at the same time. He glanced at her face. She seemed unconcerned by the rage and hatred and visceral fear emanating from Gercomo. Yet even as they appeared to be gaining the upper hand over the beast, Garan was conscious that time was running out for Laidan. A sob in his throat escaped unbidden.

While they hurled their power, Garan could see that Gercomo was transforming again, enlarging, wings erupting from his back. The sight did not fill him with as much fear as it had the first time. Gercomo was much more fearsome in his human form, his evil somehow more cohesive and transmissible. A dragon was a beast, something to be feared, but without the directed evil that Gercomo had as a man.

Salinda and Garan stopped sending their combined power at him. They crouched, readying themselves to attack again if need be. Before their eyes, Gercomo's transformation halted. He remained half-transformed for a minute, two, and then three. Suddenly, with an evil grin, Gercomo shrugged and the transformation continued. Glancing at Salinda, Garan had the sick feeling that Gercomo could transform at will now. Gercomo lurched at them, feinting an attack.

"Again," shouted Salinda.

Garan put what was left of himself into the volley. He hummed, hoping the concentration would release more of what Salinda called his inner power. The blow bowled Gercomo over as stone and dust billowed into the air. When the air cleared and Gercomo climbed to his feet, he was as before, a stunted dragon. The dragon screeched, poised for attack. Both Salinda and Garan ducked instinctively. There was no flame. *Praise the source!* thought Garan. Yet the beast did not retreat.

Salinda stood up, apparently oblivious to all that was going on around her. She raised her hands by her sides, palms out. The dragon speech issued from her lips. She called to Plu. Gercomo trod around in circles, his tail scratching the earth. With is head cocked to the sky, he backed away. A guttural cry spat from his mouth. Perhaps it was a dragon curse. Garan realized that Gercomo could hear what Salinda was saying, and it was possible the stunted beast understood. While Gercomo backed away, his attention fixed on Salinda.

Overhead the beat of wings disturbed the air. Plu roared, his rage rippling over them as he swooped low. With his claws outstretched, Plu aimed for Gercomo. Gercomo made a run for it. But Plu was too quick, and struck a glancing blow across the head with his foreleg. The stunted dragon reeled, momentarily stunned.

Plu landed between Salinda and Gercomo and, with resolute steps, stalked toward the man-beast while blowing out fire. Recoiling, Gercomo backed up and screeched only to lunge and hiss threateningly. The fight between the dragons began.

Pity stirred in Garan for the man-beast. Wings stroked the air. Fire bloomed where Gercomo was. Then he burst through the smoke to strike at Plu. Salinda's dragon ducked and bit. Seeing Gercomo was distracted, Garan darted to Laidan's inert form.

When he reached Laidan and saw what had been done to her, he could no longer hold back a cry. "Oh, Laidan!" Brokenly he cried as he knelt at her side. He drew off his jerkin and tried to slow the bleeding at her neck. He grabbed the strips of her torn robe and made wadding to staunch the blood flow from her other wounds and tied them to her body as bandages. Then gently, he cradled her in his arms and stood up. Keeping his eyes on the dueling dragons, he made his way back to the rock face, hoping that he would be able to climb with his sad burden. A moan escaped Laidan's torn mouth. That gave Garan some small hope. But how would this girl live with knowing what had been done to her?

Salinda was intent on the dragons. The air was full of the stench of sulfur and soot. When Garan neared, Salinda turned to him. Dark rings like bruises shadowed her eyes, revealing her pain and loss. She looked down at Laidan's inert form in his arms. "Magol curse me for a fool!" Her hand shot to her mouth, her dark eyes wet with grief.

"Go quickly. Nils is at the Way Gate. I will follow. Tell him to send you on if he wishes to wait for me. I must be here to help Plu if he needs me."

The guttural dragon cries washed over them, making Garan's heart thump. "Come now, Salinda. There is nothing you can do here. Plu is giving you an opportunity to escape."

"But..."

"We have what we came for," he snapped. "Our power is useless against him. Gercomo cannot follow us into the Ways. You must hurry now." Tears ran unchecked down his cheeks.

Salinda looked away from him, lips clenched. She stood staring at her dragon, watching him send another mouthful of flame at Gercomo. The stunted dragon clung to its perch on the rock face, ready to lunge for Plu. Garan couldn't wait for Salinda to decide. He hurried off, climbing the rocks as best he could with his arms full. The smell of blood and fear and shit permeated Laidan. Garan hoped he was not smelling death.

The sound of rock fall echoed behind him. He paused to look over his shoulder and relief flooded him. Salinda was following. He lifted his head and saw that Plu still held Gercomo at bay, but there was blood on Plu's right thigh. If Plu fell they would be vulnerable once more. Garan faced forward and focused all his attention on getting them to the Way Gate. Salinda joined him and steadied him as they climbed higher. Laidan's bloodied hand fell by her side, brushing against Garan's thigh. Blood dripped onto his clothes. Another sob rose in his chest. Were they too late? "Is she...?"

"No. Not yet!" Salinda touched Laidan's bloody cheek. "But we're running out of time." Salinda wiped at her own tears.

Nils lurked in the shadows of the crevice where the Way Gate was situated. When he saw them, he pulled back. Garan reached the entry first. He handed Laidan's sagging form to Nils through the gap. Nils took her easily and laid her down on the inside of the gate, his expression aghast. Garan watched the Hiem's every movement while he squeezed himself through the opening, Salinda close behind. Nils inspected Laidan, his thin hands brushing against her skin. The sound of the dragon fight reached a crescendo of screeches and roars behind them. Nils's eyes appeared to glow silvery white.

Nils shut the Way Gate after Salinda, and the noise cut down to Garan's labored breathing. "Nils! Laidan is dying," Salinda said in a tear-clogged voice.

Nils looked up from his examination. "I will take her. I can travel faster than either of you and give her aid. Follow on behind. I will come back for you when I can."

"Take her?" Garan rose, about to grab for the girl. "But…"

Salinda put a hand on his forearm. "He will take care of her, Garan."

Nils eased Laidan's inert form into his embrace as he stood. His thin frame belied his apparent strength.

Salinda stepped forward. "Go quickly, Nils. I can find the way back. I pray the healing tray can save her."

"It can only heal her, not bring her back from death. I will do my best, but even I can see that she clings to life by a thin thread." He engaged his shroud. "I must hurry," he said and disappeared from view. The shroud covered Laidan, too, and Garan could no longer see her.

Before Garan could gain his breath to offer a comment, Nils had whisked Laidan away. He blinked as the gray nothingness swallowed them, staring at where they had been. Nils had stepped through the wall of nothingness that framed the Ways. Unable to digest it, Garan let the fear and the grief flow up and out of him and fell to his knees, a sob erupting from him. They had been defeated. There was no way to hide from that. They had attacked but had not vanquished. If anything, Gercomo was stronger as a result of their confrontation. And Laidan. *Oh, Laidan!*

Sinking to the ground, Garan buried his head in his hands and gave himself up to grief. It was as if his life had been cut out of him. Too much had happened. Laidan would die with his anger and abuse in her ears. He thought Salinda would take him to task for his weakness, yet she sank to her knees beside him and rested her head on his back. He could feel her weeping, too. Somehow that show of emotion bound him to her more strongly than any vow could.

Chapter Four

BOUND IN HATRED

Toola sat in her bathwater, commanding that more scented hot water be poured over her. She enjoyed the sting as the water struck, exciting the blood within her. Danton's desertion had hit her hard. She had no doubt he had left the woman behind as a bond for his return. She knew him too well. Her guess was that he wouldn't come back for that country tart. Despite his feigned lover status, if he really cared then he wouldn't have risked her. Besides, Mandin belonged to her now—signed, sealed and delivered. For the boy, Brill, she thought he would have come back. They had a strong relationship and Danton couldn't hide that from her. But as Brill was safely with Danton, she did not have the option to use him as bait. Not without some effort.

She lathered up her long hair, inhaling the spice and perfume in the soap. Then after rinsing, she clicked her fingers and one of the bath attendants came over to massage her scalp. She lay back against the end of the bath, enjoying the release of tension. But then she thought about her appointment and her anxiety grew.

She waved off the bath attendant and then grabbed her hair and squeezed out the excess water. A loud scream echoed through the baths. Toola grinned. Mandin was proving her worth in the bar. A public beating and public humiliation always made the patrons drink more and tip well. Toola found Mandin entertaining, particularly her vow to save her daughter. The woman had no finesse. Mandin was too open by far. If it had been Toola in that situation she would have schemed to get her daughter back, not sold herself for nothing.

Another scream echoed and Toola's grin widened. Linel would want her. He always did after a beating. She might let him have a taste of Mandin. He'd do anything for Toola and she liked to reward him now and then for his intense devotion.

Mandin's punishment would continue in private in Toola's room after Toola returned from her appointment. The anticipation made her moisten. Pity she didn't have the privacy or the time to deal with her arousal. Attendants dried her and then dressed her. While she sat in her chair, her makeup artist arrived to paint her face.

Toola had a parcel of information carefully gathered and refined, which she could trade for more information and possible favors. Commissioner of Police Narin was working with someone and she wanted to know who and what that cagey bastard was up to. For that she had to go to the baron—the former Baron of Sartell. The man was as frightening as he had ever been, and though not in office was tenacious enough to cling to power behind the scenes. In secret, he still pulled the strings. He had fornicated with half the government officials and knew damning secrets about the rest. His evil permeated everything and everyone. He knew no mercy, and understood weakness and fear so that his mastery was total.

The baron tolerated her presence on the fringes. If he had liked women at all, she could have worked her way to the center of Sartell's power by bedding him or controlling others who did. Unfortunately, his preference for torturing young boys and handsome men made even her squirm. Such a perversion. Such a waste of beauty and innocence.

A long piercing scream sent another shiver of desire through Toola. The makeup artist's hands trembled. "Concentrate, you oaf! You stuff up my face and it will be you in there taking the punishment."

The artist apologized and put on the final layer of powder. The reflection in the mirror showed a young, handsome face. The girl had done well.

"Do better than this tonight and you will be rewarded. I want those girls prettied up and readied by sunset."

"Yes, mistress." Placing the makeup carefully into her carry case, the girl then groveled at Toola's painted feet. Kicking her out of the way, Toola went to meet her escort.

☙☙☙☙☙

The baron's house looked deceptively run-down from the outside. The squat building with a single frontage disguised how far back the property went. It was situated in an exclusive part of town, yet the paint peeled around the windows and parts of the walls had cracked, revealing the stone underneath.

Within, richly decorated walls covered with expensive paintings offset the well-crafted, carved wooden furniture—a display that confirmed the baron's hold on power. The façade led the world to believe that the baron was down on his luck. Only those privileged to enter discovered the truth. Rumor had it that he owned more than half the city. The interior of his house proved the rumors true.

Toola was left waiting a long time in the darkened hallway. It was warm, too, and she had to loosen her wrap. Her eyes lingered on a group of statues in the corner, which showed young boys' bodies bent at unnatural angles, with their agony reflected in their facial features.

Toola looked away. Even her taste for pain curdled at the sight. That wasn't her scene.

How was she going to lure the baron to her special party? He already had the top-class boys in his possession. Even if she raided the boys from the other brothel, it wouldn't be enough. Lowering her exquisitely shaped eyebrows over heavily painted eyes, she realized he was not likely to accept the invitation in the first place. Yet, him attending her function would give her cachet, a possible in. The only thing she thought might be worth offering was some very old, very potent fortified dragon wine. It was said to thrill the senses, alter the mind, invigorate the sexual organs. She had one small bottle of it. A onetime offering. The only other angle she could think of that might work to get him in the door was torture. He liked watching pain being inflicted on others. Generally, Narin found it hard to restrain himself with Lexia. If she allowed Narin to go beyond his normal sampling, would that be sufficient to sate the baron's taste? No; even Narin's deprivations were too vanilla for a man like the baron. Besides, Lexia had her uses. There was no point in despoiling her and reducing her future profitability.

There was something more to her manipulations, though. Something that obtaining this girl Eneit would reveal. The good slave stock was going somewhere, along with the dragon wine and the food and the highly placed people. She would find out. Had to. She had a bad feeling about the situation and needed to know, needed to protect herself.

A servant finally came down the hall, nose in the air as if he held some position of importance. Toola glared at him, unwilling to be looked down upon.

A slight inclination of the head was all the deference she was going to get. Toola pushed in front of him and preceded him down the hall to the reception room. The baron was reclining on a large bed, draped in a very expensive-looking embroidered gown that appeared to have five layers of fabric. She had known him in his younger days, when he had been at the height of his power and was at his peak physically. Now, he looked smaller and older. She had held her age better than he had.

The gilt wrappings did not hide the fact that he was an old lecher of boys and an adept torturer. That he had married a succession of sisters was a mystery to her; she'd bet they'd died virgins. She was also willing to bet that his dick was a shriveled little morsel. Perhaps that was why he was the way he was. Nature had been unkind to him. That thought gave her the mental superiority to smile at the old bugger and slide gracefully into the proffered chair.

The baron smoked a large pipe. The smoke filled the room with a woody fragrance that was appealing to the senses. Her head began to spin. Immediately, she slowed her breathing, making it shallow so that the drug's hallucinatory effects would not hamper her dealings with the baron.

"Baron. How good of you to see me. I hope I will have the honor of your company this evening? I have something special to entice you. A rare bottle of fortified Blush dragon wine."

The baron's eyes narrowed and he sniffed. Toola couldn't interpret that reaction and did her best to keep her own disappointment in check. She waited a beat.

"Narin tells me you have been sniffing around, nosing into things that don't concern you. I warn you to stop now."

"Me? Sniff?" she responded, indignant. "I make discreet inquiries, usually on behalf of other people. You have benefited from my information more than once. Fair is fair."

The baron gave the pipe stem to a servant, who stepped up from where he had been hidden in the corner. This servant was a young man, dressed in tight string arranged in an intricate pattern around his flesh. His skin bulged against the twine. Toola's nose twitched. It must be painful. When he turned away to withdraw, Toola saw the scars across his back, buttocks and legs.

Another young man plumped the pillows and then withdrew when the baron had rearranged himself. His robe opened, letting his limp dick sit on his thigh. Toola repressed a smile. It did look rather tired. Archly she thought it probably never functioned properly anymore— if it ever had.

The darkened hollows where his eyes dwelled were directed at her. She repressed a shiver, glad he could not read her mind.

"Yet you were asking about things that stray into my business concerns. I do not like that."

Toola waved her hand nonchalantly, although a dagger of sharp fear pressed against her gut. "I'm not interested in what you are up to, baron. I know better than to interfere in what doesn't concern me. It is just that I have come across a little bit of news that I thought might interest you in some small…way."

He laid back against the pillows, feigning boredom. Yet she felt he was watching her and knew he was interested.

"What would you like in return for this information? You see, I know you too well, Toola, my ugly old slut. You'd sell your asshole if it was profitable. Luckily, your well-used orifice holds no appeal to me."

Toola ignored the insult. It made her angry, of course, but she could not allow that to show. She would take it out on Mandin later. "A girl. A certain girl that came downriver with a shipment of wine."

The baron said nothing for a moment. "I know nothing of such a girl. Girls do not interest me." His eyes flicked to the servant bound in string and lingered there. The flesh on the young man was an angry red along the binding marks.

Toola waited, knowing the baron was just playing with her, trying to make her feel insignificant. Toola would not have dared to ask for the girl if she didn't have something worthwhile to offer. They were both well versed in the game.

"I did not suggest that you were interested in girls. Yet, with your connections, your vast network of resources, it is in your power to get me this girl. I have heard rumors, unsubstantiated, of course, that there is to be an auction of six girls."

Toola was not sure about the number. It was a figure she had deduced from speaking with Mandin and Narin, combined with other sources. "Young, tender and untouched girls are rare these days. The bidding will be intense, the prices will be high. Although I did hear, through my sources, that there were ten of them originally. But I believe the men in charge of the goods overstepped the boundaries a little, sullied the merchandise during transport...even killed one or two of them with their zeal. Such a meager crop from a potentially larger and more profitable one."

The baron did not speak but Toola saw the sharp rise of his chest when she laid out the details. Her deductions had been right on the money. There was no arguing against a good brain. Narin had only guided her in the right direction; she had figured out the rest herself. Mandin had been pliant and willing to divulge more details about her daughter's capture than she should have, with the help of the right amount of dragon wine, laced with a useful drug and some well-applied sex. Yes, she knew that woman inside and out. She could barely repress a grin at the thought.

"If I did manage to stumble across any information about this particular shipment or the alleged auction I would need to know a name, if I am to secure the girl."

"Eneit. Her name is Eneit. Daughter of Mandin from the town of Vanden."

The baron inclined his head and the superior slave scribbled down some notes. Toola took that as a good sign. "And?" the baron prompted.

Toola sat back in her chair. "I am rather thirsty—the heat, you understand. I was wondering if you could offer me some very good dragon wine?"

The baron did even blink. He just slightly shifted his eyes in the direction of one of the servants. Toola waited and presently a fine goblet filled to the brim with dark, red wine was in her hand. She took a long draft, gauged it, and knew it to be of the same batch that Narin had offered her.

Here was her connection to the wider web of intrigue. In that instant she knew that Danton was snared in it, and she had second thoughts about passing on what she knew. It would not go well for him.

Yet, the high price for the girl needed to be paid. And the position in which knowledge of such information would place her would reveal more of this strange intrigue. Besides, a glance at the baron under her lashes and it was obviously too late to back down. The word "suicide" came to mind as she placed the wine on the small table next to her. She valued her own life too much to put it at risk by backing away now.

"I have it on very good authority," she began, exulting in the way her heart thumped in her chest. Life was nothing if not exciting. The baron had all his attention locked on her, while at the same time pretending that he did not. Already she had surprised him with the amount of knowledge she had gleaned. "That one of your former wives, the first one, the rebel who embarrassed you..." She waved a hand vaguely. "...oh, so many years ago. Salinda, I believe her name is, was alive and well not these many months past."

The baron said nothing but sat unnaturally still for a moment, his features as impassive as stone. Toola listened and noted the shift in his breathing. She was sure she had delivered some useful and surprising information.

"Anything else?"

"She escaped from the prison in which she had managed to survive all these years and was last seen near a town upriver, near Vanden, I believe."

"You seem to have quite a lot of information on Salinda and an unhealthy interest in my affairs. I wonder, how did you come by it?"

Toola drank the remainder of the wine. "I have means." She wrapped her shawl around her shoulders in preparation for departure.

The supercilious slave took a step closer to her chair and then halted.

The baron rearranged himself on the bed, placing himself closer to her. "Really? You are not in the mood, I see, to divulge these means to me, are you? I will have to show up at this party of yours, watch Narin pound that brat of his, while you gloat about the social coup you have wrought by commanding my presence."

"There are some advantages accruing to me if you did deign to attend, baron."

The baron studied her with cool, dark eyes, and it was a scary thing. Toola found she did not like the expression on his face. It reminded her of an executioner, ready to lower the blade on an exposed neck.

"If I do come to this party, Toola, your information had better stand up to further scrutiny. Then I want the precise details and the source of it or you can kiss that girl goodbye. Meanwhile, if you value that old, haggard body of yours, never come back here...unless...invited."

The look in his dark, beady eyes chilled her. She lowered her eyelids, and rose out of the seat in the most dignified manner she could manage. Difficult when one's knees were trembling and one was about to let go of one's water. She curtsied before leaving the baron's presence. Not that he required such abeyances, but she threw it in for good measure. Such warnings had come her way in the past. This one was not to be ignored. However, the knowledge that she was finally going to get that girl helped her balance her fear.

The victory would cost her, though, she realized, her heart sinking slightly, cost her more than she was willing to pay. Perhaps she should have known. In front of the superior slave, she let none of her emotions show. All would be reported to the baron. So she strode down the hallway, exaggerating her walk, and slid through the open door without a backward glance.

The slave had the audacity to sniff before shutting the door. She would not let that pass, so she turned toward the closed door, letting her expression show her thoughts. The slave watched her, as she'd known he would. If that slave was ever in her power, she thought, she'd watch him eat shit. These vindictive thoughts cleared her head, made her smile, made her put that last fear-ridden chill out of her mind. Lifting her wrap and placing it over her head, she turned back to the street and walked confidently away. No doubt the baron had her followed.

When she returned to the brothel, there was much to do to prepare. She inspected the girls she had chosen for the party, paying particular attention to the choices of their clothes and the application of their makeup. With a few changes to colors and one change of girl, she was satisfied that all was proceeding nicely. Next, she went to the kitchens to talk to the chef and made sure the appropriate threats and bribes had been doled out to the various suppliers so that the food was the finest to be had in Sartell and in plentiful supply. The chef was not very optimistic, given the poor quality and quantity of the food he'd obtained, but he was talented, and, on the threat of losing his manhood, promised to make her a feast beyond compare, despite the scant ingredients.

When she retired to her tea room, her kettle was steaming so she pulled out a mug and her small teapot and made tea. Then she sat down and took a sip. She had been rattled by the baron and she didn't like that one bit. Also, she had had to make Danton part of her bargain.

Why had she done that? Eneit was a good excuse, of course. But was that it?

Another sip of tea did little to calm her mind. It did not rest easy with her to betray her cousin, but she needed to get into the baron's good books, needed to reach the upper level of control in the city. She had her contacts, her power to manipulate and coerce, but she had never been able to penetrate the baron's circle. The real power in Sartell. She was sure this elite group were behind the missing slaves and the disappearance of quality wine and food; unfortunately, she just didn't know why. They had been subtle about it at first, but in the last ten days, it had accelerated. Food was poor in quality and diminished in supply. The wine had been scarce for a while. Her spies informed her about the disappearances. Key people in government and noble families gone from their homes. Not murdered. Just gone. What were they up to?

Her cup was empty so she refilled it, inhaling the spice-infused blend. Then she took a large gulp and swallowed. She would have to find a way to lure Danton back or else the baron would be very disappointed in her, and it didn't pay to disappoint the baron. She might lose more than money. She might lose her life. She repressed a shiver. Normally risk excited her, but dealing with the baron cooled her blood, froze her heart. Maybe she had gone too far this time. She frowned as she considered her line of thought. She wasn't used to examining her motives. Her wiliness had served her well in the past.

A knock at the door disturbed her train of thought. Her mug was empty and the tea pot needed a refill. Her contemplation time was over. "Come!" she said.

Linel carried Mandin over his shoulder and dumped her unconscious on the floor. Her back sported lash marks and there were multiple abrasions on her limbs. Her face, though, while haggard, was untouched. She smiled to herself. Linel really did understand her ways. Her best slave retreated to the corner, waiting for her command.

"Well?" she said.

Linel stepped forward and handed her a note before retreating to the shadows. It was from the bartender. The morning's takings had doubled compared to the same day the previous week, and he noted that the bar whores had done a roaring trade as well. There was a postscript asking if another round of punishment could take place the next day as traditional trade was slow mid-week and the bartender wanted to please his mistress.

She put the note down on the tabletop and rotated it once or twice while slowly sifting her thoughts. She put the kettle on again and refreshed the tea in the pot while she considered the contents of the note. After pouring a fresh cup of tea, she stepped around Mandin's inert form, ensuring she had the right angle, before booting her in the ribs. Mandin grunted but did not get up. Toola kicked her again.

"Wake up, slut. Your mistress requires you."

Mandin shifted her body out of the way of the next kick, then lifted her head and shook it a few times. Mandin gaped at her, bleary-eyed. "Toola?"

"Yes. Mistress to you. Say it."

Mandin elbowed her way up to a sitting position and dragged her hair out of her face. "Mistress."

"I accept your service in my employment. Your salary will be used to offset your keep and the costs involved in searching for your daughter. As Danton and his young friend aren't here, you may work off their debts too. I apply interest to debts owing. Do you understand?"

Mandin was still groggy but mumbled acknowledgement. Toola squatted next to the woman, ensuring that she had eye contact. "Do you understand? You are mine. If that cousin of mine comes back, you will deny him. In front of me you will denigrate him, repudiate him. You will be mine in front of him. Agreed?"

"Yes."

"Moreover, you will not talk to him, fuck him or suck his ungrateful cock, unless I specifically order you to. Agreed?"

"Yes."

"These are the conditions of your service. Disobey me, thwart me, and you'll be my slave. Then you will have no say in anything concerning your life. I could sell you, kill you, and you would have no recourse."

"Yes."

Toola studied her face. "Why am I not convinced?"

Mandin shook her head. "I will not go near Danton. I swear."

"With regard to my cousin, you will do as I say. Swear it on the life of your daughter. On Eneit."

"I swear it on the life of my daughter, Eneit. I foreswear any loyalty to Danton. I will have no contact with him."

"Good."

Chapter Five

MYSTERIOUS HIEM

Lifting her head and wiping away tears of frustration, Salinda stared at the spot in the wall of the Way were Nils had taken Laidan. Surprise shook her and then lifted her spirits. Nils had taken her through the Ways, not along the path. She'd not seen him do that before, nor had she heard him speak of traversing the Ways like that. It was extraordinary and her mind found it hard to comprehend. It must be faster. She looked up and around, narrowing her eyelids as she tried to understand the how, and hope grew in her heart. If Nils could get Laidan to the healing tray quickly, it was possible she might be saved. Even such a small hope was better than the despair she experienced when they'd fled from Gercomo with Laidan's ravaged body. Not much life remained in the girl and, without the healing tray to aid her recovery, Laidan would die.

Salinda had failed Laidan and that failure was hard to bear. Her knowledge was limited, even though she carried a cadre: it knew not of the Ways and how they worked. In this the minds that made up the cadre were equally in awe of what Nils had done. Her limited view of the world didn't let her see that there was more to Nils and to the Hiem than she realized. But then she was an ignorant former prisoner, who had little understanding of alien technology.

Nils had told her the Ways were different, that in them time and distance were distorted. Fully covered in his shroud, he seemed to have accessed the very substance that supported the Ways. How much faster could he travel like that? As she had only trod the paths, she had not known there were other means to move about.

With her fingers outstretched, she touched the wall. It was strangely malleable to her touch. Not quite a wall, not quite air. Yet, the moment when Nils had pierced it, it had seemed like it was flesh. Was this how Nils could sense when people traversed the Ways: because it was somehow alive?

Stepping back, Salinda glanced at Garan. The young man's face showed all his feelings and grief. Responsibility weighed heavy on her. The full might of what had transpired hit her. Laidan's fate rested in her own inaction, her own inability to predict the simplest thing—how a young man would react to a betrayal and a broken heart, and how a guilt-ridden Laidan would try to flee to avoid facing him. When had life got so complicated? She was kidding herself. Life had never been simple—hadn't been for her since she was born.

Now, as the consequences of her actions unfolded, she was truly humbled. She had been angry at the observatory because its inhabitants had relied on her for direction. Yet with Garan and Laidan she'd thought she known it all. There was some blindness in her that had made her overlook Laidan's weaknesses and Garan's blind devotion. Kneeling down, she laid her head on Garan's back and patted him gently. "I'm so sorry, Garan. It is all my fault."

Garan sobbed loudly, letting out his grief. Between sobs, he said, "No...'tis my doing. Laidan was never responsible for how I felt...about her...I was wrong...wrong to judge her..."

A tear slid down her cheek. When had she last cried, truly? It seemed so long ago. She let tears flow out of her now. After a while she said quietly, "I feel the blame rests heavily on me. This whole debacle could have been prevented if I had had more foresight. Even coming to the surface here I endangered her. Plu can sense when I'm near. So can Gercomo. I wasn't certain before, but now I am. It was a stupid, stupid mistake on my part."

Garan threw his head back and wiped his face with the back of his hand. Tears still streaked his face, yet he appeared more in control. "How could he find you so quickly? He must have been near. You could not have known."

"Maybe...but I should have figured it out all the same. Nils tells me I have a brain, though I am beginning to think he has imagined it. We should move away now. If we get lost Nils will find us. No point in lingering here."

Garan let his chin rest on his chest for a moment longer. "Do you think he could find his way in here?"

"The Inspector? Gercomo?" She shuddered at the thought. "As a dragon I expect he is physically too large to get near the entrance. Magol curse me if he figures out that we aren't just hiding in among the rocks."

"But you said he can sense you; can you sense him? Does Plu sense you in here?"

Salinda stood and looked back at the Way Gate, an innocuous door on this side, and cocked her head. Garan's question was a valid one and she considered it. She reached out with her mind, the part of it that could call to Plu, and there was nothing. She wasn't game enough to try to seek Gercomo.

Taking his elbow, she hauled Garan to his feet and said, "No, I don't think he can sense me once I am concealed within the Ways. But I say that because I can't sense him from here. There is no way of knowing for certain, and I would not like to test the theory."

"Then how does the Inspector have a link with you?" Garan asked, straightening his clothes, picking at the edges of his tunic that were darkened with blood, and frowning.

"The Inspector fed me tainted dragon essence, something that he had been distilling and refining over the years. Since then I've noticed something different in my relationship with dragons. When I open my mind to them, I can sense them, feel where they are, touch their minds. My bond with Plu has strengthened. I do not know if he can sense me here, although he always seems to be close by when I come to the surface."

Garan wiped his face and grimaced. His posture stooped, he stared at the wall through which Nils had departed. "That must be a very strange sensation. You must tell me what it is like one day. I am not sure this is similar to what you experience, but sometimes in Barrahiem I sense something—not a living thing, though...at least, I think 'tis not living, but 'tis a presence."

Salinda's heart leaped. "Something in Barrahiem?" She eyed him closely, trying to see the unseen in him. "Is it the cadre that senses this?"

Garan shook his head. "No, I sensed it before I acquired the cadre."

"Oh? We should investigate that. It may be important. Come along now." Salinda held Garan companionably by the elbow and led him along the Way. "We'd have to ask Nils about it first, though. It may save time."

Salinda indicated the direction they should take. "Ask Nils what?" Garan asked as he moved ahead of her to descend the first set of stairs. Walls of grayness surrounded them, quiet and eerie.

Salinda patted him on the forearm when she caught up with him. "Ask him to help us look for this thing you can sense. He would not like us traipsing about unescorted, and who knows what danger we may stumble into. The vaults are full of ancient things, things even the Hiem did not understand."

They walked along arm in arm. "I cannot really comprehend something so old. 'Tis hard to adjust to Nils's presence and his history. His talk of Moon Binders. I wish I had time to learn about them. We could learn so much about astronomy from the Hiem records and what they wrote about the Moon Binders who came from beyond this world."

Salinda considered Garan's words and remembered her first encounters with Nils and his legacy. "As did our forefathers, remember? Magol was a first comer."

Garan glanced at her. Of his expression she caught only the glitter of his eyes. "Yes, on an intellectual level I understand that we are aliens here, but I was born here. I can conceive of no other home."

"Yes, I love Margra too. Yet there is so much we don't know about this place. Nils says the dragons were new to the world. He categorically states that they weren't here before Ruel split. It is why they fascinate him so. And the Moon Binders are just as strange and unknowable to him as they are to us. Who knows what lies beneath the surface of our world?"

They separated to take another set of stairs. "You know, this thing I sense," Garan said cautiously, "seems to be very far below the city."

Salinda tried to keep her voice calm, but she was excited enough to shout with glee. After all her mistakes with Laidan and the Inspector, to see her intuition about Garan bear fruit was amazing. She had been right to bring Garan to Barrahiem. So right. "I see. Can you sense it now?" Salinda made the base of the stair and looked up as Garan took the steps to meet her. Then she cast around, trying to recall the direction they'd come from when they had used this intersection. There were three branch Ways.

Garan pointed to the right and she waited for him to catch up. "No. 'Tis strange, but I cannot sense anything within these walls; it's as though they muffle things. Even your voice takes on a different quality because there is no echo. This way," prompted Garan.

Once again she took his arm. "Was there anything else strange that you noticed today? The cadre?" she asked him, eager to see if the cadre was providing him with any insights.

Garan walked in silence, turning his head periodically to stare at the gray walls, sometimes trailing a finger along the surface as if he couldn't believe what Nils had done. "I had a strange feeling..." he said after a time. Salinda had begun to think he hadn't heard her.

"A feeling...what was it?"

"I suspected, or had the strongest feeling, premonition even, that Gercomo could now change his shape at will. As my power was hitting him, he seemed to absorb it, took it within and channeled it. I saw him shrug as if it did not matter that he was turning back into a dragon. He accepted the shape, wanted it."

"All that in a feeling? Wing dust, Garan! You will give me nightmares. That is a frightening thought..." Salinda was inclined to trust this feeling of Garan's. It would be wise to heed it and use the idea in future plans.

Her conviction that things had grown immeasurably worse when the Inspector had transformed, strengthened. What other proof did she need? And he knew about the cadre. Could he have learned that Laidan no longer carried it? Could he tell that it was in Garan now? Garan had thrown power at him and that had to have drawn his attention to the young man.

With pride she had demonstrated her power, hers and Garan's, and at the same time revealed a most treasured secret. The power Gercomo so lusted after resided in them; he was no fool, he would certainly work it out. He would hunt them down, and if he did indeed have the power to transform at will, he had the power to rally his allies to himself, because he could once again communicate with humans. And it was to be expected that he could communicate with dragons too. By the source, the world had become an even more dangerous place.

Gercomo also knew about the observatory. It would not be safe for long. With a shiver of fear and foreboding, she hugged her arms to herself as she hurried through the Ways. Gercomo could rally dragons to attack, or humans, or both. *No!*

As if sensing her fear, Garan lifted a shoulder and let it drop. "You did ask. I'm sorry."

Salinda tried to smile. "It will be fine. It must be."

"I think we should examine more deeply the nature of the power we have. The cadre needs to help us understand."

"That is true. We will. As soon as we get back…"

They continued to walk and Salinda found that Garan had a good memory for direction for he guided them skillfully. The closer they drew to the city, the more the tension in him increased. His footsteps were quick and he grew silent and thoughtful. Salinda was comfortable being alone with her thoughts: hers and the cadre's.

After a long silence, Garan spoke. "Do you think he was able to save her?"

He had broached the subject that had weighed heavy on both their minds. Laidan. Salinda urged Garan to a halt, and faced him in the dull, muted light of the Ways.

"Nils brought me back from near death. He put me in the healing tray, a wondrous machine. It took time: a month, he told me, maybe more. But it restored me. Not only my health, but it erased the traces of years of toil and the sun's blight from my skin. I was healed and renewed."

Her fingers brushed against her cheek in memory of that moment when she'd awoken alone in the chamber. She remembered when she first beheld herself in the mirror and the overwhelming feeling of bittersweet joy.

"If she had life in her when he reached Barrahiem, she will be well."

Garan sucked in a breath, and his expression softened with relief. "Thank you. I did wonder. Her injuries were so terrible. He tore her apart, ate parts of her flesh. How could she cope with the memory of that?"

Salinda gasped, experiencing a painful tug on her bond with Nils. Then she stumbled, suddenly weak.

"Salinda?"

Doing her best to cover the sudden weakness, she squeezed Garan's forearm. "I'm well." Nils had done something strange to their bond; or was it something else, something dire?

"Are you sure? You feel strange, like you are suddenly weak. Is it Nils?"

Salinda leaned against him for support. "Let us keep moving. We are nearly home thanks to you."

"Salinda?"

"It is Nils, but I do not know what."

"He told me of your bond."

Salinda gave him a sideways look. "Really? He must trust you if he was willing to talk about that."

"I like him. He is strange but he is good."

Salinda patted Garan's hand. "Yes, he is. Now let me see. Which way? Down, I think."

"Yes, down. This is the last stair." They took the stairs together, slowly. "You were saying about Laidan?"

Salinda concentrated on her footing. She was immensely tired all of a sudden. "The healing tray can bring her body back. I'm not sure if it will help her mind. The Inspector's attack was meant to scare her, meant to destroy her mentally...He is good at that."

Garan screwed up his face in puzzlement. "Why her?"

"Besides her being there in the dragon hatcheries? He was looking for the cadre. He knew she was a carrier of power, remember?"

"He was going to rip it out of her mind."

Salinda bit her lip as she considered her next words. "He would have destroyed it if she had still been a carrier. Killing the host kills the cadre."

Garan's step faltered. "She suffered because of me, because I have the cadre now. And maybe she'll never be the same again. By the source! How can I bear it?"

"You will bear it, Garan, because you must. Just as I bear the things I don't want to bear but have to. You told me not to blame myself about Laidan running away, well, it goes double for you. The Inspector's actions are not your own. Only he can own them. You should be happy as I am that she no longer had the cadre."

"Yes. Although Laidan might be dead."

Salinda shook her head. "There was so much chance involved in that encounter. What if this, what if that. We don't know. We only know what happened. If Gercomo were smarter, he would try to find out how to transfer the cadre to himself at the moment of death. Or maybe the cadre would want to survive and prompt the dying mind to transfer the cadre to him. Think, Garan. If Laidan had the cadre, he might have gained possession of it. Think of the consequences of that."

Garan shook his head slowly, remembering the cadre's importance and Salinda's devotion to its survival. "I did think," he said, as they changed direction yet again, "that someone like him could change the cadre for the worse. But now that I understand him better, now that I have tasted the evil he emanates, I know the cadre would not survive."

"Not survive? That would be terrible. Yet it would be worse if he gained possession of it and used that knowledge and power to his own ends. Then none could stand against him. We would be powerless to save Margra and have no means to divert that rogue asteroid that is crashing into the Wing and set to bring about final moon fall."

"Then you have found a way to use this power against the asteroid?" His expression lightened as hope radiated from him. "You can save us all?"

Salinda tugged at her hair and creased her forehead. "Not exactly. But there are hints there. We can do it, I'm certain. Ah, here we are. I think this is the final Way Gate."

Garan looked up to the roof and ran his fingers through his hair. "I hope you are right," he said like a sigh and then followed her through into the city.

They had made the journey before Nils had come back for them. Salinda wasn't heartened by this. Perhaps the situation with Laidan was worse than she had believed.

☙☙☙☙

Nils fought his way through the Ways. The shroud offered them some protection, but without the living energy of his people it was hard to move between the Ways the way he'd once been able to. Once thrumming with the life force of his people, now there was but an echo, and his lone life force was not enough. With the power level of his shroud weakening, he had to work harder and harder to battle through the Ways' substance. It was as if he was giving up part of himself to the Ways as he sped back to Barrahiem.

The Way was hungry for life. He was a spark in a dark tunnel and it was going to swallow him up. Yet he had to fight against that, hold on. This precious life he held in his arms could not be made to suffer. Only a breath was left in her body. He had to win through. He had to save her.

Laidan's heartbeat lurched and then stilled. She was suspended between moments, as he was suspended between the Ways. Soon, very soon, he would be there. Just a little more of a push, a little more of his life force expended. When the Ways shifted around him and his body reoriented itself, he knew it was time to push back out, to break through the substance yet again.

With one final heave, he clutched the injured girl to his chest and shoved against the inside of the Way. At first resistant, it finally yielded to him when he shoved hard and let him pass through.

Staggering out the other side, he tottered but still maintained his hold on the girl. Her heart limped slowly through the next beat. Soon it would stop, just as her breath was growing shallow. He had managed to exit close to where he needed to go, but there was no time to waste. Down through ornate passages he strode, as fast as his burden allowed. His breath was burning in his throat, and his chest was tight. He could not give in to his weakness. He must not falter.

Another corner and he was there. The lid of the healing tray lifted as he approached. He placed Laidan's bloody body on the tray and hurriedly stripped the remaining clothing from her. As he went to the controls the lid came down. The lights winked into existence. Already he could see the healing mist oozing out over her body, clothing her in healing webs. For a long time he looked at the panel, watching the lights to ensure they indicated healing. When the lights remained steady, he allowed himself to sag against the wall. If she was dead, the tray would have re-opened by itself, rejecting a patient who could not be saved.

With his head resting on the cabinet, he breathed slowly for what seemed like a long time. He needed to rest. The mad dash through the city had drained him further. It had taken what was left of his stamina, the remnant of his life force that the substance of the Ways had spared.

Using his bond with Salinda and his connection to the Ways, he saw that she and Garan were making progress and were in no immediate danger. Slowly, he lowered himself to sprawl on the ground, and passed out.

Sometime later he came to, but remained with his eyes closed on the floor where he had fallen. The effort to save Laidan had been greater than he had estimated; the depletion of his life force was more than he could manage in so short a time. He needed time to recover his strength, such as it was.

A short sojourn in the healing tray would not have gone astray. Yet, when would he have time for that? He was too busy. And Salinda needed him.

This thought gave him pause. Inexplicably, she had drawn him into her life and involved him, made him care. When he reflected on how morose he had been when he had awoken from his prison of sleep, he could see the gradual change in his outlook. Yet at the same time, he could extrapolate events into the future and see his own doom. There was no escaping it. But at least there was enjoyment and purpose in the present.

Sleep overtook him. He was not sure how long he had slept when a sound emitting from the machine woke him. As he adjusted his eyes to the light, he saw there was a report in the wall slot. Curious, he leaned forward and tugged it free. What he saw written there amazed him. Laidan had Hiem blood too. According to the report she had a greater proportion of Hiem blood than Salinda. That was extraordinary. That had far-reaching ramifications.

Climbing wearily to his feet, he went to study the girl shrouded in mist and healing webs. Long-limbed, fine blonde hair that was almost white, and fair skin. Pondering these physical attributes and the similarities to his own kind, he let his mind contemplate where she had come from, and very soon after he was thinking through the possibilities once again that some of his kind had survived. The evidence could not be disputed. Salinda had some Hiem blood. Laidan had more. She was almost a half blood. That meant that there had been some full-blooded Hiem living in recent years. The thought staggered him. His knees weakened and he slid once again to the floor. He may not be alone after all.

The other possibility was that there were many part bloods out there resulting from the Hiem interbreeding with the remnants of Sundwellers. In that case, he may still be alone but the legacy of his people lingered still, diluted but still there. He climbed to his feet, fighting the dizziness that threatened to topple him. Clinging to the edge of the healing tray, he stared down at her, trying to see her features through the healing web. Memory was used to fill in the gaps. A very human girl, he thought, graceful and silly too. He would have to remedy that. Nils would undertake to teach her, train her in the Hiem lore. Very soon she would lose her infantile ways and take her place as part of the Hiem.

He remembered the injuries. He thought them severe. Salinda would have to explain them to him. All Nils knew was that there had been a battle of some kind, and great fear had leaked through his bond with Salinda. Her fear had almost crippled him.

He sank to his knees and rested his head on the lip of the healing tray. He reached out to the Ways, detected the presence of Garan and Salinda and knew they were on their way home. He need not move to fetch them; they were on course. He could cease worrying. Just as well, for Nils didn't have the strength to seek them out in any case. He closed his eyes and let his body recover some of its strength.

Chapter Six

A SPECIAL PARTY WITH GIFTS

Toola thought the party was going along nicely. The baron had not yet deigned to arrive, but she had hopes he would. Lexia had been sitting in her father's lap. She was getting way too old now to play the child, and Toola sensed the onlookers were bored with the usual scenario. When she got hold of Eneit, she would regain their interest. Good stock had been hard to find for a while now. Obtaining that young girl would be a coup, and one that would keep on giving.

Behind the curtains, Mandin looked on, gagged and tied to a pole. *Let her see what will become of her daughter*, Toola thought savagely. Let her see where the child's innocence would take her.

Enormous platters of fresh seafood made their way around the room. Caught far out to sea, the fish was free of contamination from the city's sewage. It had cost her a small fortune to have a fisherman fetch it for her. Nothing like this was available from the markets in Sartell.

Clean-skinned teenaged boys, hired from the men's club across the lane, knelt on the floor, waiting to be summoned by her special guest. As much as it turned her stomach, she had relented and brought them in for the baron. She hoped that he wouldn't maim them, as the owner of the men's club said that boys were hard to replace these days. He would extract a heavy price for any damage. If the baron was a no-show they would return to their master untouched and the bond she'd paid would be refunded.

Lexia squirmed on Narin's lap. It was nearly time for him to say she was a naughty girl and punish her. The man had no imagination. "Fetch some wine for Daddy, Lexia, quickly now."

Narin pushed the girl off his lap. Lexia bent over the low table to pour wine, her short skirt lifting high to flash him with her nakedness beneath. How sick Toola was of that man.

Narin bumped the girl and the wine splashed across the table. "You spilled the wine, you naughty girl. Daddy must punish you."

Lexia let out a cry. "No, Daddy. Please. I will be good."

A slap and the girl was stunned. Narin grabbed her and arranged her for punishment. Turning her attention away, Toola decided to go and check to see if the baron had turned up. Perhaps she should greet him personally.

Before heading downstairs, Toola slipped behind the translucent curtains and paid a visit to Mandin's trussed form. Mandin sweated as she struggled against her bonds. Toola stood before her, eyebrows arched. "Only now do you see what I am, what power I have," she whispered with false sweetness. "You will die in my service, Mandy." Linel had tied her tightly, and Mandin struggled uselessly against the bonds. Toola's voice grew harder. "No one spurns me as you did. No one betrays my kindness." Then a smile grew on her face and she waited while Mandin took it in. Lexia's punishment was drawing to a close. Weeping, the girl did everything her father instructed her to, although Lexia knew the drill. "Picture your daughter in there, Mandy. Virginal Eneit would fetch a lot of money for her first trick. I'll teach her to be a naughty thing, playing the little girl to Narin like Lexia, or maybe to one of my other guests. They all have the taste for young girls, virgins in particular."

Mandin could barely make a sound as her gag was stuffed so far down her throat. Her eyes rolled up. Toola slapped her face to keep her focused.

"I'm not done yet. Lexia is past it now, don't you see? I'll be sending her to work the bar after I paint her red. When I get Eneit she will be my special one. I'll be like a mother to her."

Mandin's eyes shifted to hers, undisguised hatred in her eyes. Toola flicked open the curtain, and her smile swept the room and then grew wider as she looked down the stairwell. The baron had just walked through the entry that was reserved for special guests, his chief servant following behind.

Finally, she thought as she took her leave of the little gathering upstairs. Toola swept to the floor below in time to grace the baron with an elaborate curtsey, eager to reward the great honor he did her. "Just in time, baron. Narin is just getting into his stride."

"I'm not here to see Narin mauling his daughter," the baron said tersely.

Toola's eyes widened slightly as she fought for calm.

"I came to see you. Where can we talk privately?"

"Follow me." Toola led the way to a small, vacant chamber, trying to keep her trembling under control.

The chamber was bare, used for only one thing normally. Not the sumptuous reception she had prepared upstairs, but useful for private conversations. The baron was here, but clearly not in his capacity to boost her social standing.

The baron looked around. "I have what you want."

Toola sucked in a breath, surprised by how quickly he had come through with the goods. "How much will she cost me?" she asked lightly.

The baron named an exorbitant price for the girl. Toola blanched, failing to disguise her alarm. There must have been heavy competition for her for the price to be so high. Then the image of Mandin came to mind, along with memories of her sickly betrayal. Toola calculated the return she would get on the girl. A year and she would have earned the money back. It was still a bargain as far as Toola was concerned, just not as great a bargain as it could have been. As the baron stood staring at her, she realized that the money was not going to be the whole of it. Details, she remembered, he wanted details and a source. She would fabricate both, but not yet.

However, his next words made her start. "I want him."

"Him?" Toola feigned innocence. Looking around for a chair, she found that there were none. The baron's chief servant studied her. She could almost taste his satisfaction, his enjoyment of her discomfort.

"The one you have been harboring. Salinda's lover."

Toola swallowed. "I don't know who you mean. I am not currently harboring any men."

The baron's eyelids narrowed and he took a step toward her. "Don't play games with me, Toola. You won't like the result if you do. I have my own spies. I want him."

Toola smiled and tried to turn away to hide her disquiet. "If you mean my cousin, he has gone."

"Not gone, just absent for a few days, if my spies are worth their bribes."

"But there is no evidence that he was her lover."

The baron's eyes were hard glints and Toola had to stop herself from babbling. A chill cut into her innards. This was not how she had imagined the negotiations would go. If she sold out Danton, it was to be on her terms. Now things were out of control. "I will do my best," she said mildly.

"You most definitely will." The baron continued to track her with his steely eyes.

Toola fought for calm. She had to let him know it wasn't going to be easy. "He has killed three of my best men. Narin's police guards are searching for him now. I don't think he'll be back despite what your spies say."

The baron turned to the door and then paused, inclining his body toward her. "Yet you will surrender him when he comes. The girl will be delivered to your private residence tomorrow at noon. Be there to take receipt personally or the deal is off. I expect the rest of the payment by the end of the week. If not, your life and the girl's will be forfeit."

He spoke matter-of-factly and Toola had no doubt he meant every word of his threat. "Of course, I have it in hand," Toola said coolly, although her hand strayed to her hair, tucking away an imaginary strand.

He paused at the doorway and lifted an eyebrow. Toola was at a loss. "There is something more?"

The baron grinned. "You offered me a rare Blish liqueur. I will take it with me."

Toola bit the inside of her cheek. Now he was rubbing her nose in it. "Give me a moment." She ducked into her private room and retrieved the bottle from a secret floor safe. "Damn him to all hells. This deal has gone from bad to awful." She was alone in the room. After wiping the dust from the small bottle, she tied a ribbon around it. Then she checked her reflection in the mirror. She did not look rattled. She did not!

His uppity servant took the expensive liqueur from her hand. The baron had already left. The servant had the audacity to smirk at her as he followed his master. When they had departed, a growl escaped her throat and she punched the wall. "Fornication!" That had definitely not gone the way she had hoped.

The deal was bad. But she was committed now. No turning back. The kudos of having the baron as her guest was gone, so all she had was unimaginative Narin doing his daughter while his lecherous friends looked on. Well, at least she was going to get the girl.

Maybe this Eneit would have some information that would help unravel this picture. What was the baron up to? Why did he want Danton? Could she pass Brill off as Salinda's lover? Brill would be easier to snare. He was easy to manipulate. She shook her head. The baron spoke of spies. He would know whether it was Danton or not. There was no way around it.

In giving the baron the information about his former wife she had not intended to sell him her cousin. Now she was caught. Danton and she went way back. She would play games with Danton, thwart his plans, but she would not intentionally sell him out so completely to a monster like the baron. Somehow she had slipped up. She had not bargained on the extent of the baron's intelligence network or his desire to get back at Salinda. Someone on her own staff must have sold her out: sold Danton out. Right then she wanted to punish all of them, but she knew it would achieve little.

If she was going to sell Danton out, she wanted to do it on her own terms and to her benefit. But she feared it was too late. *Forget it*, she thought. *You played the game and lost.*

Eneit had better be worth it. Toola was committed whether she wanted to be or not. To back out now would see her head on a stick in a stinking bog somewhere. She shuddered and rubbed her arms. This was worse than being shat on by a fucking herd of dragons. *Wing dust!*

It was with mixed feelings that Toola left the brothel to return to her private residence—a small, unassuming house, where no one really lived. Her rooms were in the basement, with a narrow staircase leading to a small doorway giving access onto the street. For protection and ease of escape, another staircase was hidden behind a cupboard door and exited to the rear lane. It was disturbing to her to know that the baron knew where her private residence was. Not many knew she lived outside the brothel at times.

It was there she trained the special girls. Lexia had spent six months there, learning to be the little whore while feigning innocence. She was the best she had trained so far.

Lexia could get the cock out of the pants of a celibate follower of Magol and in her before the man knew that the sun was up. Talented and beautiful and obedient to Toola. It was part of the training; she taught each girl to love her as a mother, brainwashed them even.

When she'd used Lexia on Brill, she had brought out her big guns. Lexia may not have liked her father doing her, but she didn't mind the money he showered on her. His remorse benefited the girl and Toola both. But sadly, the girl was getting older and her usefulness was waning. She'd still earn for a while yet, but not in the same capacity.

That would be where this Eneit would come in. Pity, she would have less time to train Eneit. She needed the girl's virginity sold to the highest bidder as quickly as possible to recoup the funds she had to lay out. That wouldn't take much training at all. It was the teaching the girl to love her like a mother that would take time, and while it was important, there was no time. Toola had to be strategic. There was not only the money to be recouped; the girl's value had to be depleted quickly to reduce the risk of the baron stealing her back. That girl had been destined to go somewhere. Toola wanted to know where.

The expense of the purchase would stretch Toola to her limit and she would need to pay back the loans and favors before everything folded like a house of cards. Then there was Danton. Could she warn him? Dare she? If the baron found out, she'd be dead. She couldn't risk it.

It was a pity Mandin was so useless she was fit only for servicing the street scum for a pittance. Although, watching her daughter pleasure old men who had a thing for young girls would teach Mandin futility. Toola licked her lips. That was her divine revenge. The very thing Mandin wanted to save Eneit from and couldn't.

As she made tea and prepared a small meal, she added the idea of subverting the girl, making her transfer her affection for her mother to Toola herself. It was easy enough to do. Seduce the girl. Make her grateful. Make her love Toola. Make her hate her mother who was now a whore, make her think her mother had sold her out. *Oh so much to look forward to—a new, untouched virgin to exploit.*

A banging on the door had her leaping out of her seat to open it. A baker's cart stood on the curb, carrying various crates with bread and buns in them and sacks spilling over the sides. The local baker handed her a heavy cloth bag. "Your order, ma'am?"

The bag squirmed. "Why yes, thank you." Toola handed over a folded note with all the information she had on Danton and his associates and his suspected whereabouts. The baker put the sack on the ground and took the notes. Then he picked up his cart and continued his round.

Toola checked the street and then carefully drew the sack inside the door.

Her heart hammered when she thought of the note. She had sold Danton out. She'd actually done it. She had not mentioned Brill. If they caught him then that was bad luck. It wasn't out of friendship or concern that she kept the information about Brill back. She was saving Brill for later. She wanted to sell him out too, but to the right person and for the right price. She didn't want the baron getting more than his due. Prince Brilliant of Duval required careful research before his betrayal. Something she didn't have time for at the moment.

To shut the door, Toola had to drag the sack further in. It began moving on the floor where it had been placed and small mewling sounds emitted from it. Toola opened the bag and let the girl out. Mandin had said her daughter was around ten years old, but Toola estimated the girl was closer to eleven years old, and well under way into puberty. Her dark hair was in disarray and she was dirty and smelly. In her breath, Toola detected a trace of a sedative. She had a slight build, with little rounded breasts. This was something she could disguise or enhance as required. Of her figure there was not much to see as Eneit was wearing the ragged remains of a shift. While the girl fumbled about, trying to get her bearings, Toola gave her a quick once over. The girl was healthy, but unkempt.

"Come, my child, don't be afraid. I have saved you from those awful men."

The girl didn't move, just stared at her with eyes that had seen too much. Her irises were pretty if you ignored the expression of horror in them: brown with flecks of yellow. Toola knew that look, had seen it many times, and thus knew what to do.

She put her arm around the girl. "First I will give you a bath. I bet that is what you want most. Then some food. I have saved you, my dear. I always wanted a girl like you. So pretty and sweet."

"I want my mother," the girl whispered, as if she'd lost her voice. Probably from screaming too much.

"I'm your mother now. Understand? I am your mother and I will look after you always and keep you safe."

The girl shook with unexpressed sobs and her large eyes brimmed with tears. "I want to go home."

"Your home is with me now. Come downstairs and I will bathe you and feed you and put you in a clean bed."

The girl's gaze leaped to the corners of the stairwell, eyes widening at the shadows there.

"Come on. You are safe, truly."

The girl said nothing more and let herself be led down the stairs into Toola's apartment. There she stood stock-still, eyes darting about as if expecting someone to jump out at her.

Toola knelt on the floor next to her. "There is no one here but me, child," she said in her sweetest, calmest voice. "Come, embrace me. You will see that I do not hurt you."

The girl did not move. Toola brushed her fingers against the girl's hair. Still she did not pull away. That was a good sign. Too frightened and she would flinch away. Her young mind was intact. Toola wanted to check if the girl had been used but had to do that carefully. While bathing the child was the best time. If Eneit had survived the ordeal of being kidnapped and dragged to Sartell from backcountry Vanden, then she would cope well as a little whore.

Gradually, Toola expanded the caress, moving from her hair to touch the girl's cheek and shoulder. Inch by inch she moved closer until they were side by side, then carefully and slowly she encircled the girl in her arms.

Small shudders in the little body indicated that Toola was having an effect. Then the sobbing began. The girl buried her face in Toola's shoulder. Toola let Eneit cry without any exhortation to stop. The girl had been on edge for a while, had seen other girls raped and murdered if Mandin's story had any truth to it. She nestled the girl against her breast and stroked her head. When she had cried herself out and was placid and biddable, Toola undressed her then bathed her, being careful to check for previous usage. She had to be sure. She would lose more than money if she put up a virgin for sale and she wasn't one. She would lose her reputation and that was worth more than mere money.

Duly satisfied with the girl's condition, she fed her dragon wine and a meal of meat and bread. Just a small amount, for the girl needed careful handling so as not to gorge. Then Toola tucked her into bed. It was early afternoon by then, but in the basement one could not tell the time of day. Toola liked it that way, for often after an all-nighter she'd want to catch up on sleep. Watching the girl's somnolent form, she stripped off her clothes and slipped into bed beside her, ensuring that the girl was nestled skin on skin with her.

♋♋♋♋

Later, when the girl woke, Toola cuddled her some more, telling her how special she was and how safe she was in her arms. The girl acquiesced as Toola held her to her breasts.

"Are you hungry, child?"

"Yes," Eneit said, staring up with wide eyes.

Carefully, Toola extracted herself and strode to her small kitchen. "Would you like some spiced tea?"

"Yes, please," the girl said. "Anything."

Toola smiled. "I have some sweet cake here too. Would you like that?"

"Yes, please," Eneit replied.

"Ah, so you can talk. That is good to know."

Toola made the tea and sliced the cake and came back to the bed. "First you should have some dragon wine. It will fortify you."

Eneit drank the small portion of wine, then sipped the tea and hungrily ate the cake. Toola smoothed her hair. "Such a pretty girl. I love you like a daughter already."

Eneit smiled tentatively. "Thank you for the food." Her attention shifted to the corner of the room, probably checking to see if her captors were hiding there.

"I will look after you now. I'm your new mother."

Eneit's head lifted, her eyes flashing. "I have a mother. She will be looking for me."

Toola shook her head. "No, she isn't looking for you, dear."

Eneit's eyebrows lowered. "How do you know?"

"When I found you, I looked for your mother."

"And?"

"She left Vanden and she became a whore and maybe she's dead now."

Eneit's mouth dropped open. She shook her head. "Not my mother. She would never do that. She'd come for me."

"Tell me her name, dear child. I will look for her again. But you must call me Mother. You are mine now. My beautiful Eneit. Can you do that?"

"Yes, Mmmmother."

"You must rest here for the moment. Here is some more food." She gave the girl another slice of cake. "I must send a message. Stay there. All right?"

"Yes," Eneit replied, then catching Toola's look, added, "Mother."

Toola threw on a robe, scribbled out a note and raced up the stairs. On the street, she snagged one of the local urchins. "Take this message to Lexia at my place. You know it?"

"Yes, Mistress," the boy said, ducking his head.

"Good. Bring her here right away."

Lexia knew the score and would know how to treat the girl. Toola didn't have much time. There were things to do and she couldn't spend every minute with Eneit. While she waited, she went back to the bed and asked Eneit to sit on her lap. "Now, what lovely skin you have, dear, but so exposed to the sun of late. Let me rub this oil on you and that will make you beautiful again."

Eneit shook her head dully.

"What? Are you saying 'no' to your mother? That cannot be good, can it?"

Again the girl shook her head. "No," she whispered in reply.

She held up the tub of oil. "You see, it is only oil that is good for your skin. That can't be bad, can it?"

The girl shook her head.

"Then be a good girl and lie down so I can begin to make you beautiful again."

The girl studied Toola for a moment as she seemed to consider the request and then with a slight shrug turned and spread herself on the sheets.

Toola positioned Eneit's arms over her head. Then, pouring a large portion of scented oil into her palm, she began to rub it into the girl's back and buttocks, extending the strokes to her legs and feet and then to her arms and hands and fingers. The girl coped well with Toola touching her, and then relaxed and was soon lulled to sleep. Toola kept on rubbing the oil into her skin, noting that it was a pity that she did not have time to work on the girl longer. So much potential there.

She turned the drowsy girl over and rubbed the oil on her front, starting at the throat and working down the chest, all the while assessing her. Such a promising figure, she thought. She would earn her keep and more in the years to come. The girl slept on.

There was a knock at the door. Toola wiped the oil onto a towel and placed a sheet over Eneit. Then she ducked upstairs and let Lexia in. "Come in, we must talk."

On a small settee, she filled Lexia in on what she wanted her to do with Eneit until her return. Basically a year's worth of training had to be fitted into a day, maybe two. That was all she could afford.

Lexia bit her lip. "That's not possible. I will fail and you will punish me."

"No, you will not fail and I will not punish you."

"You will. I know you will."

"I won't. You love me, don't you? I am your mother."

Lexia's eyes widened. "Of course, I love you and I want to help you, but I will fail. I don't want you to give me to Linel again or beat me."

Toola bit her lip. She needed Lexia right now but the girl wasn't so important in the future if Eneit worked out as she was sure she would. "If you do this for me," Toola took Lexia's hand and squeezed it, "I will give you your freedom."

Lexia's eyes widened. "My freedom? You mean I could go home to my mother?"

Toola smiled, knowing that Lexia's mother would never even

see her let alone allow her daughter to return to her house. Lexia's mother held to the fantasy that her daughter wanted to be a whore. And privately Toola suspected that she knew what her husband did to his daughter on a regular basis. "If your mother asked for you, I'd give you to her tomorrow."

Lexia smiled tentatively. "Thank you. I will do my best."

Toola stood. "Help me to dress, will you? I have to go out."

Lexia did as she was bid. Once Toola was dressed, she smiled at the girl. "Now then, kiss me before I go."

Lexia embraced Toola and kissed her in the manner she had been taught.

Toola hid her smile as she left her private residence. Lexia was going nowhere. She had nowhere to go, except to the bar to service the riffraff that frequented the place.

Chapter Seven

A DRAGON FRIEND OR TWO

A sudden pain in her chest made Salinda cry out and fall to her knees.

"What is it?" Garan asked, peering at her with his bright eyes shining beneath a concerned brow.

Panting, Salinda tried to speak. "Something...is...is wrong." She tried to stand and Garan put his hand under her elbow so she could climb to her feet. "We must hurry. Nils—"

It was as if the tether that bound her to Nils had drawn tight and then broken. It was bad. Whatever it was, it was beyond Salinda's experience. Now she knew why he hadn't come to guide them back to the city. He couldn't.

They quickened their pace and gradually Salinda's strength returned. The tether was still there but thin, like the edge of a knife.

"Laidan?" Garan said between breaths. "Is she...?"

Salinda spared him a glance and then shook her head. "I don't know...I can't say..."

"...perhaps she did not..." Garan's voice was threaded with fear.

She squeezed his hand. "There is no point worrying now. I just sense something is not right. Soon we will find out."

Garan's expression lost some of its tension. She was grateful for the lad's support. His lips widened in an almost smile. "All right. Let us move."

After descending into the city, hastening up and down stairways, and hurrying through corridors, Salinda burst into a sprint when they came to the Hall of Elders near to the room where the healing tray was housed. When she rounded the corner and glanced across the hall, she caught sight of Nils sprawled on the ground next to the tray, a puddle of blue and white robes and the muted gray of his shroud. She threw herself to the floor besides her husband. She checked his pulse. It was faint, but there. She closed her eyes in thanks to the source. Then she set about examining him.

Nils was naturally pale and thin. But something had altered his complexion to a pasty gray and his cheeks were sunken, making him look more like a corpse. His breathing was shallow and when she ran her hands down his arms she found his skin cold to the touch. This was why the bond was weak: Nils was near death. A lump of emotion clogged her throat. She did not know what to do or why he was in such a state.

Garan hovered by the tray, trying to see Laidan inside. There was one healing tray and it was occupied. Salinda would have to think of another way to save Nils.

"Garan, there is nothing else to do for Laidan for the moment. She is in the tray and she is healing. That will take a few weeks at least. Please help me carry Nils back to our abode."

Garan did not appear to hear her. She glanced at him and saw his tortured look. "Garan, you will have time for recriminations later. I need your help now or Nils will die. Can't you see? Something has happened to him."

"Yes, I see," Garan replied. Together they eased Nils out of his shroud. Salinda realized that it had totally discharged, as the cloth was almost black instead of dull gray. When she touched it, the texture was different too. It was more like normal cloth than the vibrating material of a fully charged shroud. What could cause that?

On the way back to the abode, they had to pause several times because of Nils's dead weight and the climb. Salinda fretted silently. She had to hope that rest and care would help Nils recover. There was nothing else she could do. Garan took over and lifted Nils into his arms. "'Tis all right. I can manage. He is tall but he is light."

"If you are sure."

Garan climbed the stairs with his burden. Salinda followed along, guarding against overbalancing or when necessary placing Nils's hand back across his body when it flopped down.

After Garan had helped her to arrange Nils in their bed, she sent the lad off while she undressed her husband and washed him. Bathing him allowed her to check for any obvious injuries, of which there were none.

Then when he was swathed in blankets, Salinda went to the kitchen to prepare tea. Normally she would have given him dragon wine and a herb soup. But she wasn't sure if Nils would respond to dragon wine as he had never tasted it. He did not seem to depend on it as the rest of Margra did. In fact, deep in the ground, in this underground city, Salinda had survived well without it. The same could be said for Garan and Laidan. So there must be something else at work here preserving them. She wondered what that was.

But could the wine hurt Nils? Surely not. It was worth a try. She had a flask or two with her. Rummaging around, she pulled out one of them and stared at it, weighing up the risks. She had no clue if it would help him recover. It might make him worse. The idea needed to be considered further. What did the cadre think? It was silent. *Typical*, she thought in frustration.

Leaving the flask on the table, she brought the tea into the bedroom. Pulling Nils into a sitting position, she lodged pillows behind him and then laid him back. She tried to ply him with the tea, but he would not drink; the fluid just spilled out of the side of his mouth. Then, closing her eyes, she reached out, seeking their bond, and tugged on the tendril that remained, willing Nils to wake, if only for a moment.

Drink, Nils!

Nothing happened at first, so she tried again. The second time, his eyelids fluttered. As quickly and as carefully as she could, she made him drink the tea. He was not really conscious, but he swallowed when she put spoonfuls of the tea in his mouth.

When she laid him back down, he had gone into a stupor again. His breathing was shallow and his skin continued to have a grayish cast. Next, Salinda prepared a rub, something to stimulate the circulation, and as she massaged it into his limbs and then his torso she detected a slight improvement.

The tension she had been holding tight inside of her came out in a flood. She wept over him and a wave of tiredness overwhelmed her too. She felt sick for the first time since she'd woken from the healing tray. Placing her hand on her forehead, she tried to feel if she had a fever. If anything, she was cool and clammy.

Too much had happened. Gercomo. Laidan, and now Nils. It was as if all her hard work had crumbled around her. She thought when she'd discovered and explored the layers of the cadre that all would be well, that there would be clarity, and yet there was not. All she had achieved was the transfer of the cadre from Laidan to Garan. Everything else was broken.

Looking down at Nils, she wiped at her useless tears. What was this strange ailment that had sapped Nils's energy? How could she deal with it? Garan knocked on the door and squeezed his way into the living area. "Salinda?"

Drained, Salinda pushed herself up from the bed and made her way out to greet him.

His face dropped when he caught sight of her and he came up to her quickly, grasped her by the upper arms and sat her down on the sofa. "What is it? You look as bad as Nils."

She shook her head. "I don't know. Could it be some kind of flux, a contagion? I feel unwell."

"Not good," Garan said and went to the flask of dragon wine. He found a cup and poured some out. Then, bringing it to her, he made her take small sips until she had finished it. Immediately, she experienced a rush of energy and an overwhelming sensation of wellbeing. The dragon wine still had the power to heal her. She had wondered if it would after living so long without it. Yet, its potency seemed undiminished.

Garan smiled at her. "You look better already."

"I feel it also. You, too, must take a draft and go and rest. It has been a difficult day. I may need your help over the next few days while I nurse Nils back to health, so you must take care of yourself also." Just then the baby kicked and decided to rearrange its position inside her. At least the baby appeared unaffected by what was troubling her.

Garan did as she said and went away. Salinda sat quietly on the sofa for a while and then attempted to feed Nils some soup. After using her bond to prod him to some form of wakefulness so that he could eat, she felt drained again.

Staggering out to the living area once more, she took another draft of dragon wine and then went to bed. Somehow her connection to Nils was also weakening her. By morning she should have it figured out. As she put her head on the pillow and curled up next to the cool body of her husband, the cadre bombarded her mind with images.

Much had happened that day that needed to be analyzed, but she had no strength to focus, so she gave herself up to the flood of pictures. Throughout the night, she garnered a few small pieces of knowledge. The cadre was excited by the dragon wine and Nils's healing.

In the morning, Nils had two spots of pale pink on his high cheekbones. Salinda, though, was hardly able to get out of bed. Her feet felt like slabs of dead meat and her knees barely bent. She staggered out to the living area and drank dragon wine straight from the flask. Then, wiping her mouth with the back of her hand, she eyed it. The dragon wine was restoring her and the bond with Nils was taking her energy. That meant the dragon wine was working on Nils, although not directly.

Perhaps, if she added a small portion of wine to the soup... Salinda set to work, her body once again rejuvenated by the dragon wine. Nils took the fortified soup. She watched him for a reaction but there was none. Next dose, she increased the amount of dragon wine and took more herself, for her energy was easily and quickly depleted. That evening, Nils's cheeks were less sunken although he was still unconscious.

Seven days later, Nils could sit up in bed and eat real food. This was lucky because Salinda had run out of dragon wine. She had not drunk it all by herself. Garan had also shared it, along with Nils, who tolerated it diluted. This bond she had with Nils was surprising. She hadn't realized that it could draw on her life force, perhaps even to death.

With a jolt, she saw the drawback. There had to be a way of blocking the connection, for if anything happened to Nils, she was in danger too. She rubbed at the lump where her baby grew. Endangering the child was out of the question.

While she had been caring for Nils, Garan had been busy repairing the streetlamps. That morning he had reported that the sacred lamp was all that remained to be repaired. Salinda suspected that when not working on the lamps he had spent a lot of his energy gazing at Laidan in the healing tray close by.

It was a waste of his time. Who knew what impact the Inspector's dreadful attack had had on the girl? What physical and mental wounding of the mind there had been. There was no guarantee that the girl would want to see Garan, let alone talk to him, when she woke.

From the living area, Salinda heard Nils call out in a weak voice. Lifting her head, and pushing her unbrushed hair out of her face, she sat there thinking she had imagined it, then he called again. She hastened into the bedroom to see him.

A pale, long-fingered hand lay against bedcovers and his once bright silver eyes were dim when they looked up at her entry. A smile lifted the corners of his mouth. It was hard to keep the joy and the concern from her face when she regarded him. His complexion still had a grayish tinge and his frame was terribly thin. He reached out cold fingers to her, and she tenderly kissed them. The frail smile faltered with the effort and then Salinda fed more of herself into their bond.

She told him about the dragon wine to explain his healing. She couldn't tell him that he had sucked it from her without him realizing it; he would be appalled, she was sure. But she'd explained how she'd been adding it to his food to strengthen him. Letting go of his hand now, she bid him to rest some more. It was pleasing to see that he acknowledged her with a slight tilt of his head and then closed his eyes.

It was time that she checked on Laidan. Even though the girl was perfectly safe in the tray and it would be some time before the contraption released her, Salinda needed to assure herself that all was well. Nils would want to know, and going to see for herself and bring tidings was the only way to keep him in bed.

On the way down the long corridor she munched on a lairn apple and fingered another in her pocket. There was no more dragon wine to renew her vigor, so everything she gave Nils through her bond came from her. Like Nils, she knew she must rest and let time heal. Eating healthy fresh food was the next best thing.

Dust still lingered and rolled in balls in her wake. While their own abodes were cleaned, there was no way they could care for the whole city. Echoes and shadows made her pause. If she was so inclined, she would have imagined ghosts. With a shrug, she cast off the dismal thoughts of the long departed Hiem and continued on.

Light festooned the hall of elders, a testament to Garan's work. They had to celebrate this achievement when Nils was able, she thought before entering the small room beyond.

The girl appeared to be healing well in the tray. Not that Salinda could actually read the display of lights on the wall. At least they were on and winking, which she knew to be a good sign. Laidan was covered in fine webs and bathed in mist so that the extent of repair could not be seen. Yet, it was working. Nils had been in time and his sacrifice had not been in vain. Salinda would have been dead without the tray's healing abilities. Nils would be, too, and also Laidan. What a wonder! *Thank you*, she said by way of prayer to the long-departed Hiem.

After two weeks Nils was able to get out of bed and to begin to actively participate in his recovery process. He undertook small tasks around the abode but as expected became fractious as boredom set in. He ached to be among the archives and most importantly he wanted to see how Laidan was progressing. Unfortunately, while he was on the mend, tackling the city steps to go to either place was beyond him. He had to take it slowly.

Garan was able to keep him informed of Laidan's healing and did so three times a day in great detail. Garan had developed a fascination for the healing machine. It was during one of these conversations that Nils told them about Laidan's Hiem blood and his renewed interest in the existence of his kin.

"But Laidan was Thurdon's daughter," Garan said. "To have that much Hiem blood her mother would have to have been a full blood, wouldn't she? Surely Thurdon would have noticed that she was different."

"Not necessarily," Nils said between sips of tea. "The mother need not be a full-blood Hiem. The effect can be cumulative. Thurdon may also have had Hiem blood."

"The machine?" Salinda queried. "Is it possible that it uses Hiem blood in its repairs?"

Nils shook his head slightly. "There is a slight possibility of that, but this reading was taken at the beginning of the procedure, before healing had actively begun. Sort of a report on the status of the patient, if you know what I mean."

Salinda could see that he had begun to hope again. She hated to quash that so she stopped trying to throw rational explanations in his way. Perhaps there was a chance that some Hiem existed, either as Hiem or as mixed race. Until they found evidence of his people living they could not be certain. Laidan's blood could be a clue.

Nils was able to walk the steps within a few days, much to Salinda's relief. Although he was still paler than normal she was no longer anxious about his health. Her stamina had returned also. Caring for Nils had delayed a trip she needed to take. She felt compelled to return to the hatcheries and see how Plu had fared. He had been injured too. More importantly, though, she wanted to communicate to him the danger that the Inspector posed and wanted to try to counteract it if she could. Broaching the subject of a trip into the Ways without Nils was the largest hurdle. Yet he could not accompany her. Laidan could awake at any time, and besides, Nils did not have the stamina for the trip.

"Nils," she asked him before they fell asleep that night. "Do you know what happened to you? I thought perhaps you'd caught an illness of some kind, but it seems to have been something else."

"I cannot say," he replied, and drew his arm around her.

"Can't or won't? Nils, I need to know this. I nearly lost you and I have to make sure it doesn't happen again."

"There is nothing to fear."

She sat up and tried to meet him eye to eye in the dimness of their bed. "I have everything to fear. Your healing had something to do with me and our bond, didn't it?"

"Yes."

"So will you explain?"

"I will try." But he said nothing more.

"Nils...your shroud was totally discharged when I found you, and the way you went into the substance of the Ways was something I have not seen before. Are the two connected?"

There was a pause. Had he gone to sleep? "Yes," he said eventually.

"Nils...a little more information would be useful. I will not betray your secrets. I am your bond mate, your wife. There are some things I should know. Even you said I had some Hiem blood in me. Is it then not my birthright to know these things?"

"It is difficult to speak of. For with the knowledge comes the remembrance of loss. I almost died using the Ways as I did, because my kin are dead. Their energy—their life force, you might call it—was intimately linked to the Ways. Because they are gone, the in-between was hard to traverse. I could not have done it without the shroud for protection, but even that did not suffice. The Ways are hungry for life. When I went in, the substance of the Ways itself began to take mine."

"Oh, Nils. I see why what you did was difficult. You knew beforehand that it would be so, didn't you? You risked your life for the girl—that troublesome girl. I must confess, if I had known the risks, I would have let her die. You are too important in the scheme of things...and I...I love you. I came so close to losing you."

"An innocent harmed by malice. I could not let it stand, despite that she has been troublesome. I thought she had some importance, too, even before I knew of her Hiem blood."

"Oh, Nils, you amaze me."

He drew her to him and nuzzled her neck. Her stomach was rounder now as the baby grew. He caressed it and the child moved in reaction. "I must confess I did not wish to die. I enjoy being with you."

The breath rushed out of her. Nils actually wanted to live? Light flooded her mind. Happiness rolled over her. "That is the most beautiful thing you have ever said."

Salinda rolled over and brushed a fingertip down his chin. "Nils. I have to go back to that place. Tomorrow I am going to see Plu."

"But—"

She pressed her fingertips against his lips and smiled sadly. "I will be careful. You will be able to feel me, feel that I am well. Don't worry. Plu will protect me."

Although he was not happy about the short separation, he acquiesced. "I understand your concern for your dragon. It is an amazing beast. I wish I was well enough to come with you."

"I know, Nils."

⊙⊙⊙⊙⊙

Before leaving to visit Plu, Salinda called Garan to discuss the lighting of the sacred lamp.

"Best to do it now before you leave. It will lift his spirits and aid his healing," Garan said as he explained how he would light the lamp.

Salinda cocked her head. "Do I detect some complaint in your tone?"

Garan's head shot up and his cheeks reddened. "No. But..." He shrugged. "Nils's mood might be better if you do it now. I fear he does not like the fact that you are leaving while he is unable to come to your aid."

Salinda grinned and studied Garan. "You think the sacred lamp would distract him?"

Garan rubbed his lips with his right hand. "Yes. For a short time at least. I have to admit that I am looking forward to it too. It will mean my task here is done."

Salinda pursed her lips. "We have other work, Garan, and I feel that you have learned a lot while repairing the lamps."

Garan's eyes widened. "Yes, more than I can say. I learned a lot about myself and the city too."

"Very well then. Do you think you could carry Nils down here?"

Garan grinned. "I would but try. It is more likely that I will provide him with an elbow."

Salinda chuckled. "He is not a good patient. Very well. I will see what I can prepare by way of celebration. I fear this will be our last chance."

His forehead creased with a frown, Garan replied. "Very well then. I will prepare myself and fetch Nils."

☙☙☙☙☙

Nils was tired, oh so tired as he sat in a chair in the hall of elders. He longed to check on Laidan in the healing tray but he did not move, he could not move. Salinda rested her hand on his shoulder and he drew comfort from her presence. Being here like this in the hall of elders was confronting. It was a reminder of all he had lost.

"Are there any words you want to say before the lamp is lit, Nils?" she asked.

Nils climbed to his feet, reaching out to the chair arm to steady himself. "I had never seen it unlit in the past so there are no words for the lighting, but I would share some words of my people with you."

Salinda lips widened in an almost smile. Her eyes were dark with concern. Nils did not know how to convince her that he was recovering, that he was not mortally injured by his escapade in the in-between. If his mood was somber it was the occasion rather than illness.

"Then we will hear your words, Nils of Barr," Salinda said.

Nils looked to Garan and then to Salinda. "Very well, then. What I will say comes from the gatherings, when my people came together here to welcome their kin, or celebrate an occasion—a new year, the birth of a child, a change in seasons."

Nils swallowed and drew in a breath, bringing forth the words from his memory. Words that had not been spoken here in more than a thousand years. "Come gather at the heart, at the flame of the center, and be welcome among kindred Hiem. Come closer and see the essence of home, whether you travel to the world above, whether you toil in the world below, whether you hail from afar. The sacred lamp burns for you everlasting. Come gather at the sacred heart, and experience the sacred flame. Within blazes the soul of the kindred Hiem, those that are past and those who are yet to be…"

The flame erupted from the lamp. Garan edged away, his mouth open in wonder.

Nils sat down suddenly, as if there had been strings holding him up and they had snapped. Tears slid down his cheeks. The sacred lamp was lit and his heart broke at the memories it evoked in him. Salinda stood back, her expression uncertain.

"Nils?"

It took a moment from him to control himself. "It is good. Thank… thank you both."

They sat and stood there watching the flame as the echo of his words spread through the city as faint whispers. Soon, Garan slipped away to check on the girl. Salinda kept her distance and Nils appreciated her restraint. Nils studied the flames and both mourned and rejoiced.

☙☙☙☙☙

Salinda eased herself through the crack in the rock that hid the Way Gate and slid her pack through the gap behind her. She had no idea how long she would be away from Nils so she had packed some supplies. Her strength was still easily taxed. Nils would need to know what his exploits did to her—maybe he could teach her how to shield herself from it.

The sun was not too far above the horizon. The rocks were still damp from rain. Morning light painted the landscape mauve and amber and Salinda took a moment to experience the wider world. Everything looked so vibrant and full of life. Such a vast difference to the world beneath the surface. Barrahiem was beautiful, too, in its way, but her heart responded to the world above, with its stark and ravaged beauty and the perilous wonder of the sky.

She inhaled deeply, taking in the familiar scent of sulfur and dragon sign. She waited there, hoping that Plu would come to her. She was close to his nest and did not need to call him.

After waiting for half an hour and feeling the wonderful rays of the sun on her skin, she heard the scraping of claws on rocks and the fall of loose pebbles. Reaching out with her senses, she detected the familiar touch of Plu's mind.

Turning around, she saw him approach from the ridge to her left. Plu looked healthy as he let out a roar of welcome. Her smile became a laugh when she went to stroke his tongue and greet him properly. She ran her hands over the lower half of his body, finding the scar from Gercomo's attack. She rested her head against it, feeling a sudden and intense sorrow. Why did that man's malice extend to these creatures? Why had Plu been hurt by him? Twisted within this emotion was guilt. Unwitting it may have been, but her actions, her articulation of power, had caused this harm, and potentially greater harm to come.

The dragon speak allowed her to communicate her thoughts to Plu. She had to be calm and use her new, expanded awareness of dragons to understand him. Plu was excited by something and used his snout to urge her up the ridge where he had come from. Puzzled, yet willing to be led, Salinda climbed up the ridge after him. When she reached the top, she realized that she was on the outer rim of a large dragon hatchery. Below that spot were many dragons: bulls, cows and hatchlings. Their calls and groans swept over her, as did a very strong smell. It was like dragon sign but a hundred times more intense, and there was an overarching bitterness in the smell too. Salinda stumbled as the full force of it hit her, yet controlled her mental reaction. Plu scrambled over the ridge further to her right, so Salinda angled in that direction. It took ten minutes or so to reach the place where Plu had landed, his final leap sending up a spray of dirt and loose rocks.

Mindful of the other dragons, she carefully made her way to Plu's nest, settling her pack between her shoulder blades and wondering why he was bringing her there. When he moved his bulk out of the way, she saw the reason at once. In reaction, she pulled back. There were three new hatchlings in the nest, climbing over one another. With one glance at her dragon, Salinda realized that she had been wrong about Plu's sex his whole life. He was a she, and a mother.

Plu roared at her and Salinda wasn't sure what she wanted.

Then she remembered how she had greeted Plu as a newly hatched dragon. How the bond had been formed between them. Slowly she edged forward. The hatchlings stopped wrestling with each other at her approach. Their snouts arrowed back and forth and they made squeaky sounds. Remembering that she had given Plu food, she unslung her pack and fished around in her supplies. She had no meat to give them, but she did have bread. Garan had picked up useful bread-making skills when rostered in the kitchen in his youth. When Salinda and Nils had been recuperating, he'd baked some for them with grain he had found in the gardens.

Salinda broke the loaf into three portions and fed one to each of the hatchlings. Then she stroked them along the snout, careful to dodge the others as they vied for her attention. She had only two hands, and three snouts that needed stroking. With a quick glance at Plu she realized that she had done the right thing. Plu was content.

A bellow behind them gave her a start. Plu returned the call and stepped forward to meet the other dragon. This dragon was a huge bull. Salinda instinctively recoiled.

Would this strange dragon, one she had no tie to, let her live?

She did not want Plu to have to fight to protect her. Her visit was to check on the dragon and her injuries, not to endanger her further.

With her pulse thumping in her neck, she backed away from the hatchlings. Plu had reached the male and was nuzzling him. This had to be her mate. It made Salinda relax for about two seconds, and then the bull nudged Plu out of the way and took another step toward her. His screech was deafening. Salinda had to hold herself very still in order not to flinch. The huge head came close to her, the mouth, large enough to swallow her whole, showing an array of enormous, sharp fangs. If the beast chose he could kill her. Yet when she looked into the large dark eye that hovered near her, she felt something—a presence, large, powerful and very aware.

Salinda spoke soft words to the dragon, keeping her tone soothing and unthreatening. Then she switched to dragon tongue, forming thought patterns that the dragon could understand. She found he knew most of which she spoke. Plu had relayed their story and more.

The bull was not overly friendly, but there was no malice in him. It was more like protectiveness mixed with indifference. What did she matter to him?

Then she sent thought words about Gercomo. *The beast that attacked your mate*, she articulated to him. That got a reaction. This was his herd. Plu was one of the alpha male's mates. A favorite too, from what she could discern. He did not like the invasion of his territory. He did not like the attack on his mate. When she detailed what he was and what she thought he was doing, living with another herd of dragons, the bull let out a bellow of outrage that left her ears ringing.

Plu emitted a low-pitched growl, which her mate answered in kind. Salinda was not quite sure of the interchange between them. But when the bull opened his large mouth and flopped out its tongue, Salinda thought she understood. Surely Plu wasn't serious. Did she really expect that she would pet this bull by stroking its tongue? Yet even as she recoiled from the idea she saw the benefits—if she survived the encounter.

Plu would not let the bull eat her, of that she was fairly confident. So with a deep breath to shore up her courage, Salinda reached into the dragon's mouth and ran her relatively small hand along the dragon's huge tongue. She had to use her whole forearm for him to feel her touch. As he moved his head backward, she hastily withdrew her arm. Turning his large form around, he nuzzled Plu before he ambled off into the inner reaches of the hatchery.

With his departure and her survival, Salinda thought it a good time to leave, as she did not want to spend her time stroking the tongue of every dragon in this particular nest. She examined her arm, not quite believing it was still attached to her. While Plu had been a pet since her youth, placing her hand in the mouth of a large, dominant bull was probably the scariest action she had taken in her life.

Her heart rate started to return to normal as she made her way back to the cleft in the rock, with Plu following at a distance. Plu knew that Salinda was leaving her, again. But now Salinda knew that the young dragon had a family, a mate and hatchlings apparently bonded to her, she was relaxed. Gercomo could not influence all dragons. Salinda had been there first. Plu may not be able to fight for her, but her bull might.

Despite the fear she'd felt when she had stroked the bull's tongue, she knew it had been worth it. After opening the Way Gate she stepped inside, quietly confident that her ability to fight the Inspector in his dragon form had markedly increased. While she trod the silent path back to Barrahiem, she found that the cadre agreed with her, and was glowing with satisfaction. Its pleasure tasted like sweet fruit on her tongue.

Chapter Eight

A LITTLE RESPECT

Gercomo liked his new position in the herd, a position of trust. The bull did not defer to him at all, but at least he treated Gercomo with disinterest. This was better than being brutalized by the alpha and his subordinates on a daily basis. He could come and go as he pleased. So far, so good. Also, he had a new proficiency at keeping his thoughts to himself.

After his fight with Salinda, being able to hide his injuries was useful. What an encounter that had been, what a revelation! He could transform back to human form.

Not a pristine human form, because the dragon essence had bonded too deep within, but close enough to allow him to communicate. He could not see this new development in a bad light. It had the potential to give him the best of both worlds.

While he needed to recuperate, he was happy to remain here in dragon form, but he planned and he planned. How to trigger the transformation, though? Could he do it under his own power? He would have to bide his time. It was possible, and he would find a way. He couldn't test this until he was safe and on his own. Reverting to human form among a herd of hungry dragons would merely make him a tasty meal.

The herd was hungry and so was Gercomo. The girl's blood and flesh had been a mere nibble and not enough to sustain him. Her fear had been exhilarating, though. He had savored it until it evaporated when she completely withdrew into herself. There had been no power in her after all. It had been with Salinda...and the other...the boy.

This power could move around. Gercomo licked his lips and belched. If they could do it, then so could he. He could take this power. He didn't need the vessels. A snort alerted him to the bull lifting his head, eyes focused on Gercomo. He was thinking too loudly, too excitedly. He buried the thought deep, lest the herd detect it, lest they try to drag it out of him.

With minimal exertion, Gercomo had been able to steal eggs and eat his fellow dragon's young to keep up his strength while he healed. They were rather tasty. No other dragon appeared to eat the young as he did. Or if they did, they hid it well, like he did.

His female liked to rut. Once he was able, he accommodated her and habitually chewed on her neck wound, sucking the rich blood. It was heady and went to his head.

The effects of the dragon blood were potent. He had grown, not that he would ever be normal-sized. His mind, though, was altered, less alert as if the dragon's blood blunted his mind. Yet, there were other changes too subtle for him to name. While he enjoyed his increased proportions he worried what the end point would be. He did not want to lose the sense of himself.

Half-buried in sand, feeling the warmth of the sun and the afterglow of a successful mating, Gercomo considered the world.

Now that he was healed and he knew he could change back to human form, he could not simply sit idle. It was time he approached the alpha and communicated his ideas. How was he to induce them to do his bidding? What was in it for them?

Shielding his thoughts, he pictured the violet energy that humans emitted. Sartell would have many of those. Easy pickings too. Not like the observatory. That would require more effort and planning. There were too many holes for the humans to hide in in that place. But the existence of food, of humans, of tasty, violet lights? That would be easy enough to communicate.

There was little point biding his time here any further, as the encounter with that human bitch had proved. She had grown in power, too, and could control dragons. Gercomo had grown in power and had the potential to control dragons. In that they were matched.

Gercomo knew he must do more and do it soon. He had to act before she did. If only he could transform again and contact his former allies.. Would they recognize him? Would they kill him for his deformity before hearing what he had to say? Or should he do without them altogether? If he could bridge that gap between human and beast, he would be in a stronger position than ever. He would be one of both kinds. He would be all-powerful.

As the sun lowered behind the hills, Gercomo shook off the cooling sand. The bulls had returned from the hunt and the ripple of ill feeling that passed through the herd meant they had returned empty-handed. He wasn't quite healed yet, but he supposed he could manage a hunt. Should he go hunting first or would the bull be more amenable to ideas on an empty stomach?

The alpha bull roared his displeasure at the returning bulls. When Gercomo caught his eye, he thought that his timing was wrong. The bull lashed out at him, knocking him to the ground. Gercomo climbed to his feet and shook his head. That had been a savage blow, but he had weathered it better than any of the previous attacks. His female's blood was good for something. Gercomo defied the bull with a threatening hiss and an ear-piercing screech. Behind him he sensed his female. She had come to defend him. Gercomo smiled in his mind. He could feel the allegiances within the herd shifting.

With a grin full of broken fangs, Gercomo thought of food, lots of food. He thought of the city were the humans dwelled. Lots of delicious meat. Lots of delicious violet energy.

The bull roared. *Danger. Weapons. Hurt. Kill. Death.*

Gercomo stretched his neck, eased some tension. His mate stepped up closer, drawn by the images in his mind. Gercomo knew a way to get food from there, a path that did not involve the harpoons of men.

The bull understood, but was not convinced.

Gercomo would lead the way on the condition that he was accompanied. His confidence grew. They were hungry. They were desperate, and Gercomo had already influenced them, could direct them. He had edged into their minds through their hunger. Now he added malice and greed.

The bull growled a low rumble that vibrated off Gercomo's hide. He twitched his tail as if contemplating a strike. He circled Gercomo, issuing warnings with hisses and the swing of his snout. The thought-emotions Gercomo could understand were jumbled bits of fear and need. He stood his ground and kept sending out the word pictures of food and violet lights and images of the city. Other dragons moved in, heads tilted as if listening.

Then Gercomo sensed the alpha's acquiescence, the backing down, the wait-and-see attitude dulling the bull's mind. Gercomo was free to hunt, to bring back food. Prove himself. The texture of the thought was layered. In it he sensed the consequences of failure for both him and his mate.

At his flank, his mate hissed, her thoughts layered with anger, some fear, but with an edge of defiance and something unexpected: pride. She was proud of her runt of a mate. He was clever, she thought. Clever and sneaky.

Gercomo accepted the challenge and in return he allowed the idea, the mind picture of the humans as food, of the city full of humans and eating, to grow. The bull's attention was caught, yet he held back in seeking more.

Gercomo staggered under the force of bull's communication. A blunt force of picture and alien emotion. The alpha pictured the runt—him—and his mind filled with derision. A cough-like grunt was the equivalent of a laugh in the massive dragon's mouth.

Gercomo turned away. *You will see*, thought Gercomo as he stretched out his wings to take flight. *You will see and you will be sorry for your skepticism.*

Gercomo's mate joined him in the hunt. As they headed east, Gercomo changed his mind and banked left. They would head west. Initially, he had been thinking of striking one of the larger cities, but that was too far. There would be no benefit in striking a city now. Not without a large force to overwhelm the defense and eat the spoils.

Besides, there was too much food to transport and the kill would lose its significance. Tales of food did not equal food. Instead, he would head for a town. There they could gather food with far less risk and much greater impact. His human knowledge would allow him to select well, locate and avoid defenses such as harpoons and decide the best place to attack. Beyond the Fire Ranges there had to be a town ripe for slaughter.

He only had to seek the river to find what he was looking for. There were towns all along it, and some smaller settlements inland. Vanden was useless, gutted as it was; Gunner too well defended; but there was Misery and its sister town Bliss. A bit of a stretch, but if they flew across the land the towns were reachable. Maybe they were too close to Sartell...and yet...

Both he and his mate were tiring. Gercomo left the curving course of the river and flew across the plains. Then it was in sight. A small town, surrounded by brown fields and irrigation trenches. Both the town and fields were full of people. Those funneling water, those planting, those lumbering along with carts. As Gercomo came into his dive, he saw the walls of the town. From this side there were no harpoons. Screams reached his ears and he saw people pointing and running, dropping their tools.

The first mouthful was delicious. His mate roared when she ate her second. Her pleasure vibrated in his mind.

Gercomo grabbed a man, bit off his head and dropped him. Then he reached for another, a female who screamed and wailed until he ate her head too. He placed her with the other body. They had to take food home to prove their worth. His mate followed his example. Her bites were not so neat; sometimes she took half the torso and left only the limbs.

The pickings had been so easy, Gercomo didn't try for a larger town. Not that there had been any defense mounted to deflect their attack. Next time would be different. But there were other towns with ample food, and humans were the best fodder, after all. And when he returned and the bull's belly was full, the alpha would listen to Gercomo and then he could begin...again.

With their claws full of the dead, Gercomo and his mate made the journey back to the hatchery.

Gercomo couldn't stop smiling.

Chapter Nine

TO BAIT A TRAP

Danton and Brill made their way to the rendezvous point, not far from the wharves where the bulk of his men and been stationed. Squab had organized it and Danton and Brill had laid low until the appointed time. With the local constabulary looking for him, Danton hadn't dared show his face in public, so now he was itching to do something. Anything.

The brown murk that passed for a river oozed past, spreading its stench into the buildings. Filled with sewage and garbage from the city and further upstream, the river was a cesspit of human making. Belle moon in half phase spread dim light over the wharves, barely breaking through the miasma of city smoke and river mist.

Danton and Brill took up a position among an array of broken carts. The scavengers had already been through there, picking over the spillages, and there was nothing but grain dust and filth left behind.

"Why does it always have to smell bad?" Brill commented from beside him.

"Must be your nature to attract bad smells. I don't see Squab."

"That's a good thing, isn't it? If you can't see her maybe no one else can. Do you want me to scout around a bit, make sure we are in the clear?"

"Wouldn't hurt."

Brill ducked behind the remaining sloping side of a container and disappeared. Danton scanned the wharf, looking for signs that they had been followed or that Squab had made the rendezvous.

Water lapped against boats, rocking them against the timber of the wharf. For a time it sounded like someone was swimming in there. Danton wrinkled his nose. To swim in that was certain death.

A quiet whistle indicated the all-clear. That was Brill. Next Danton heard the counter call—Squab indicating that all was clear. After a few minutes the sound of Brill's boots in the grit signaled his return.

"Where to now?" Brill whispered.

"That abandoned warehouse." Danton pointed to a tall building wedged between two others, all three looking vacant and dilapidated. That didn't mean they weren't in use, though. "Not all the men will be there, but enough for them to see me and pass on word that all is well. Perhaps we can pick up some intelligence, too."

Once inside the warehouse, Danton could see shadows darting out of corners and looming behind storage crates, few though there were. There was enough debris to help disguise the number of his men. Squab still hadn't shown herself. Danton wasn't too concerned; he knew her signal anywhere. He should—he'd taught it to her.

Danton placed himself in plain view but gestured to Brill to stay hidden. Bits of broken wooden palings cracked under his boots and grit ground into the dry, packed-earth floor.

Movement up ahead revealed Squab walking toward him, a smile lurking on her scarred face. "Well met," she said.

Then other familiar faces hove into view. Brill jogged up to them and Squab belted him on the shoulder and sent the lad reeling. Danton's men laughed and then quieted.

"This is all I have left with me." Danton pointed to Brill, who dipped his chin in acknowledgement. "We lost the men who stayed with me but I sent men on in two groups. Any of you heard news of Merl?" Blank faces and a few shaking heads. "What about you, Squab? You were looking around. Did you find anything?"

Squab shook her head and ran a forefinger along her scar, her eyelids lowered as if remembering the moment she'd earned it. "Only rumors about that wine, though some new stock has found its way into the more elite bars—watered down, of course. There's a whisper of it being newly arrived. The price is rather steep, too. It's not the only thing that has come to my notice. Food is scare. And the slave market has dried up."

Danton covered his mouth with a hand while he thought. "There should be more than just a little wine. It's strange that no word of that shipment has spread through the city. That must mean it's not here. It must be somewhere else."

"I agree. There is something going on," Squab said brusquely.

Danton's head shot up. "What do you know?"

Squab shrugged. "I don't know for sure, but I suspect something big is afoot. Two of our men, Toots and Rael, who infiltrated a work gang that was sent to a job out of town, haven't been heard from since."

Danton lowered his eyebrows in thought. "Out of town? There's not much out of town that I know about. Just swamp, delta. It would have to be way out of town. Direction?"

"That's what I thought—I wanted to find out what was going on, so I let them go. They went north. That's all I know. I thought they might bring word back, but there's been no contact." She bit her lip and ran her fingers through her short-cropped hair. "I did the wrong thing. They could be dead."

"Maybe not. If this job is out of town, then whoever is responsible would have had to import labor. Perhaps there's just been no way for the men to send word. There's not much up north, though. We might have to investigate."

Squab screwed up her face and shook her head. "All the men were told was to meet the work gang on the North Road." She knelt and drew some lines in the dirt. "About here, a few clicks out of town. I don't know what's outside Sartell myself, but that's where I handed over the men. Could be the gang backtracked and went somewhere else." Squab looked up into Danton's face and shrugged.

"These men you met, who took the work gang. Did they say anything? Anything at all?"

Squab stood up and rubbed her chin, eyes half-closed. "Mmm. There was something. One of the men mentioned 'eternity' or the 'eternity project' or something like that."

Brill and Danton shared a look. "Eternity? Are you sure that is what it was called?"

Squab shrugged her thick shoulders, making her neck disappear completely. "As sure as I can be. Made no sense to me."

"Do you have any idea where this place is?" Danton pressed. No matter what she said, Squab wouldn't have let her charges go off into the unknown. She was holding back. He cast a look around at the rest of his men. If she wasn't telling him, there was a reason.

Squab shifted on her feet, casting her eyes around the gathered men. Danton surveyed them too. All of them were familiar. She couldn't suspect them of spying, so it was something else.

"Can you give us a bit of space?" he said to his men. Some touched their foreheads in salute and moved away. Others just rejoined the shadows. Danton shared a look with Brill. "Keep alert," he whispered as he led Squab away.

"Will do," he said, keeping watch while listening in on the conversation.

Squab licked her lips and lowered her head. "I had the boys followed. They were loaded up in a wagon full of recently purchased slaves and they headed north-west on the main Lukton Road. After tracking them for another day my men came back."

Danton studied her, not liking the sick feeling in his stomach. "Why did they come back so soon?"

Squab looked down and kicked the floor with the toe of her boot. "They saw something." She looked Danton in the eye, daring him to disparage her or his men.

"Tell me."

"The first morning after the night on the road, Toots and Rael were bound and gagged before they woke up. Then the bastards branded them as slaves and chained them up with the rest of them. My boys had to leave them—they figured I'd want to know about that and they said there was nothing they could do to help."

Danton lifted an eyebrow. Squab saw it. "Yes, they were panicked too. Branding is a painful business and they wanted to get away from the smell of burned flesh. Besides, there really was nothing they could do about it. The convoy was swarming with police guards and customs officials."

Danton scratched at his beard as he considered the information. Police and customs officers. So this Eternity had government sanction. What were they doing? "They did the right thing," he said to Squab. "You did the right thing." Squab bit her lower lip and acknowledged the compliment silently. Danton figured she'd not accept this comment at face value. She took her job too seriously. Losing those men in that way wounded her pride.

"This information is important, Squab. You did right to keep this for my ears only. If they hadn't come back with this news then we'd still be groping around in the dark. It gives us a clue, don't you see? It could explain why there is no word of the abducted girls or the wine in Sartell. It's not here. It's gone to this Eternity place."

"Bisma and his clue," Brill added, rubbing his chin as he considered.

Danton put his hand on Squab's shoulder and squeezed. "You did great, Squab. There is nothing you can do here in Sartell now. Get supplies and take everyone you can find and make north, see if you can find this Eternity. Be ready, and if you see a chance, then go in, get the wine, free the slaves, cause mayhem. I may not be able to get word to you beforehand, so any action will be at your discretion. Understand?"

Squab ducked her head like a salute. "We'll be there."

They ventured back closer to his men and Danton beckoned them forward. "Come on. Let's get busy."

As his men ranged around him and Brill held a light, Danton drew a map in the dust on the floor. "This is Sartell and this is Lukton. This is where I think Eternity might be. Follow the road the work gang took. You know what to look for: signs of passage and so on. When you find it, and I think you will, pull back and wait for word or an opportunity. Leave messengers to get word to you on the road and around this Eternity place. Dig in. Make camp. Be careful. We may still get that wine." He passed over some sizeable coin that Toola had loaned him when he'd first arrived. "Best you purchase provisions discreetly. The situation is a little hot in Sartell at the moment so this will be the last time we can meet for the foreseeable future."

"Toola?" murmured Squab.

Danton inclined his head. "Brill and I will catch up with you as soon as we can. But first we must investigate this Eternity project further, see what we can find out."

"You might need us," Squab said, and a few of his men ducked their heads in agreement. One added, "Don't send us away just yet; we could be useful."

Danton swung around and peered at his gathered troop, the sad remains of his fighting force. "You have a choice, lads. Go your own way now, or make this one last attempt to retrieve that wine. Remember what you are here for, what we've been fighting for all this time. Freedom, survival and justice. Now you have your chance." He drew his fingers through his hair and toyed with his eye patch. "I won't think less of you for leaving. But I'd be damn proud if you stayed."

"What, you think we want to disband?" said one of the men.

"No," Danton replied, eyeing them. "We've fought well together over the years. Squab here has taken good care of you. You deserve to be able to choose to walk away if you so desire. This could be a deadly fight. But if you are willing we can make this last attempt to do what we set out to do. This is why I'm leaving it up to you." He cast his gaze over them. "There is no shame in walking away now and staying in the city in the jobs Squab got for you. Or you can choose to go after the wine. It may be the last battle for us all."

A few men looked between themselves, frowning and shaking their heads. "Not me. I'm fighting to the end," said a voice from the shadows.

"Me too," another said. A murmur of agreement spread among them. "My brother has joined up too."

"Well, then. If we are all still in, then let's get on. My guess is that the wine is at the Eternity place, which is why the trail is dry here. And if my guess is right, that is where Merl and the others are, too. They could already be dead. We may be too late to save them. We may have no hope of succeeding. But the future is not yet written. We will need a really good plan and Magol's own luck, but the outcome is yet to be decided."

Squab scowled, not liking Danton's tactic. He knew she'd rather commit all his forces one way or another. "Let me organize it, Danton, why don't you? You'll have this lot pensioned off before I can sneeze."

Danton laughed and his mirth was shared by a few of his men. Not only had Squab looked after the men, she had grown their number, winning back comrades that had returned to Sartell years ago and recuriting new ones.

Squab appeared to relent. "I'll send a contingent to scout around and set up a preliminary camp. Leave the rest to me."

"Okay. We will rendezvous there at your camp." He pointed to a spot on the map. "Remember, take precautions. If you don't hear from Brill or me, you're in charge, Squab." Danton brushed the dirt with his boot to erase the map.

Squab signaled the men to disperse. She waited until the last one had left before she spoke again. "I don't like this, Danton. Sending us there without sufficient information places all of us in jeopardy. What do you think this Eternity is?"

"I can't say for sure, but I have a feeling. It doesn't make sense to me yet, but could this place be a stockpile of some kind?"

Squab squinted. "Like for a select few?"

Danton shrugged. "I suppose. You will know more once you scout it out. You'll be in a better position than me because I'm too well known and hot property. I'll get there when I can."

"Has your cousin betrayed you?"

Danton glared at her. "I've left Mandin behind as insurance, but still we were attacked by what I suspect were her men. The police are looking for me too. So, yes, I guess you could say pretty close to being betrayed but not one hundred percent sold down the river...yet."

"Yet?" Squab said gratingly. "And Mandin? You left her there?"

Danton squirmed. "It wasn't my choice. It was hers."

Squab snorted.

"I know. I know," Danton said. " I'm not sure I can get her out of there again if I go back, but I have to try."

"I think Toola knows something important," Brill said. "That slaver tried to tell us and was killed for it. If something is going down, then either she knows or she is in a position to find out."

Danton agreed. "Mandin thought Toola could get Eneit, Mandin's daughter. She bet her life on that. Eneit is tied to the wine. There's a connection. I'm sure of it."

Brill edged closer. "Toola is heavily involved in the politics of the city. She has the Commissioner of Police under her control, and who knows who else."

Squab glared at Brill. "It took you that long to figure it out? I could smell deceit on her the first moment I looked at her." Then she graced Danton with a look that women had been giving men for thousands of years, scorn-laced with copious amounts of pity.

"Thanks," Danton replied drily, giving her a friendly shove. "Get going. Head north and make your camp. I will get there as soon as I can."

Squab's eyes glistened. "I'll not leave you behind..."

"If we don't get the wine, it doesn't matter what happens. We will die. We will all die."

Squab stood up taller and jerked her head up and down like a salute. "I will wait for word, Danton. Then we will do as you ask in the north. I will make plans for an assault on this place. We'll be ready when the opportunity arises or a signal comes. It looks like it's all or nothing."

Danton hugged her briefly with a heavy slap on the back. Brill acknowledged her with a dip of his chin followed by a careful smile.

Wearing their Hiem shrouds, Brill led the way out of the warehouse district and back into the main streets. There they found a bar and squeezed themselves into a corner. With their shrouds disengaged they looked like they were wearing normal hooded cloaks. "Mandin?" Brill asked as Danton sipped some ale. "What will we do?"

"Can't leave her there. Have to go back, damn it."

Danton pulled out a note and unfolded it.

"Mandin?" Brill asked.

"Yes," Danton replied as he fingered it.

Brill put his elbows on the table. "You care about her. It's only natural. I like her too, but I'm not sure she'll come with us, not if Toola waves Eneit in front of her."

"I know, but in this note Mandin begs me to come back for her."

Brill screwed up his face. "Mandin begs? That sounds odd."

"It is," Danton agreed. "It could be a set-up. My gut tells me it is."

"Why don't you let me go back for Mandin?" Brill suggested. "Toola has no grudge against me."

"No. Can't risk you. If she wants me, she'll keep you. Then she'll have both of you and I'd have to go in there with my hands in the air and my pants around my ankles. I'd have nothing to bargain but my life. Understand?"

Brill lowered his head. "I see."

"Mandin is my responsibility. I left her there, knowing what I was doing. Getting her out of there...well, it is my job. But first we should do some scouting around, see what we can pick up in the bars around here. Someone may give us some more clues about this Eternity. I'll make for Toola's tomorrow before sunset."

"I'll come with you, then."

"Nah..." Danton saw the boy's determined look and changed his response. "Okay, you can watch my back, but you must stay well clear. If I go down, then rendezvous with Squab and get word to Salinda. She needs to know about this Eternity place, whatever it is. I have a feeling that it is something big."

Brill scratched behind one ear. "The slave trader, the scarcity of quality slaves, our two men forcibly enslaved, the wine…they are connected."

"Yes, and I'm not sure in what way, but it bodes ill. That much is certain. If some kind of stockpile is being collected, then why and by whom?"

"When do we move?" Brill yawned.

"After another ale. I find that I have a big thirst at the moment and a lot of thinking to do." They'd been sleeping rough in separate alleys. It was the safest way. If one was taken then the other was free. Why Brill was keen to return to his pile of rags, Danton didn't know.

Brill picked up his ale again and continued to sip. Danton sat back and watched the clientele and listened to the various conversations around them, hoping to hear something of interest. The ale felt heavy in his gut, or was it the feeling of pending disaster looming large?

When they finished the next round of drinks they parted ways in the street, Brill heading to the south side of the city and Danton to the north.

ဢဢဢ

All looked peaceful in the vicinity of the brothel during Danton's first pass the next day. Wearing the Hiem shroud, he passed unnoticed and saw nothing to concern him. The sun was casting vermilion light over the city, the shadows spilling dark blood. Clients came and went. Nothing was unusual. All seemed normal but Danton's gut twisted with unease. He reversed his steps and caught up with Brill, who was keeping out of sight in an alley.

They crouched together behind some packing crates near the rear door of a restaurant. It smelt of piss and rotting food. Danton grinned as Brill wiped the tip of his nose.

Their eyes met. "Why does it always smell bad?"

Danton's grin widened and then he sobered. "It looks clear, but I have a feeling…"

"Me too," Brill said. " Yet there's nothing out of the ordinary. Trap?"

91

Danton powered off his shroud and flicked back the hood. "Yes. Maybe."

"Toola?"

Danton frowned and rubbed at his beard. "Not her style. Well, not the Toola I knew. Maybe she'd yell at me, throw things and she'd give Mandin a hard time, particularly if I was going to take her with me."

Brill let out a sigh. "I don't understand your cousin. I don't know how you can. Or trust her either."

Danton groaned. "I used to understand her. But something is twisted here." He tapped his head.

"What's your plan?"

Danton rubbed at his beard again and stared at the ground. "I've got a problem, a dilemma you might say." He plucked the collar of the Heim shroud. "If I wear this and something happens then I risk the technology falling into the wrong hands. If I don't wear it, I have to brazen it out, either just walk in there or sneak in there."

Brill frowned and considered him for some minutes. Danton began to fidget when Brill took so long. "Wear the shroud," Brill said at last. "At least until you know the lay of the land. When the power winds down it will look like a normal cloak and, besides, if Toola has Mandin, I bet it is somewhere secure. The shroud may be the only way."

"Right, then." Danton stood up and flicked the hood over his head. "You stay here. If there is trouble run…in the other direction."

Brill lifted his head. "But?"

'No buts. Toola has powerful friends and if there is trouble it could be bad for you. Toola knows too much. Besides, you can help by staying here and keeping watch. If I make it out we can escape together with Mandin."

Brill looked down at his feet, his shroud sweeping his boots. "I don't like it." Then he looked up at Danton and they hugged fiercely.

"I know," Danton said. "But this way is better."

Brill acknowledged the point with a dip of his head and Danton thought he saw water filling the boy's eyes. There was nothing Danton could do about that. He had to go in there.

Danton strolled behind three youths who looked to be entering the brothel. Unfortunately, they decided Toola's establishment was beyond their means and redirected their amorous intentions to a smaller establishment further down the road. Danton changed direction and followed another pair of men, hoping to get through the doors in their wake. Once through the entrance, he stepped into a darkened corner. Still everything seemed normal. The noise from the bar was raucous. Servers and girls walked the corridors. Danton clung to shadows and no one noticed him.

In the corridor leading to his room, he paused to check that no one was there to see him open the door. Once inside the room he had shared with Mandin, he was surprised to find his weapons and other personal items where he had left them. He picked up his pack and shoved the items inside, disregarding heavier items that wouldn't fit into his pack and that would hinder him in a fight. The pouch with hurling blades he tied to his belt. His gaze traveled around the room, noting the absence of Mandin. The bed had been made and her things were nowhere to be seen. The room had an unused, stale smell.

His clandestine exploration of Toola's brothel continued without incident. Toola's private tea room was empty but by the time he discovered that he had grown uneasy. There were fewer people in this part of the establishment than he expected. And the tension in the air was almost palpable. It was a bad sign. There was always someone in the corridors in this place, even in the small hours. Danton had a feeling that even the usual spies had fled. The shroud rendered him near invisible, but at that moment that gave him no comfort. Where was Mandin?

⊙⊙⊙⊙⊙

Brill watched Toola's brothel from the corner of the alley. Peeping around the front of the restaurant gave him a clear view of Toola's front door. There were other entry points but he couldn't cover them all at the same time.

Danton had been gone for about ten minutes when Brill heard something that nearly made him piss himself. Troops came pounding down the street. Brill squinted as he tried to see any identifying marks. They were uniformed and well equipped but weren't city officials like the customs guards. It was some kind of private militia.

As the troops were deployed, Brill drew back and engaged his shroud. A detachment of uniformed soldiers ran up to the alley, then formed a cordon. Brill was stuck where he was. He could not help Danton, just when Danton needed help. Brill's shroud would hide him from their eyes while the power lasted. However, to see what was going on would cause him to be seen. The alley was a dead end. Brill could leave, if he was careful.

He huddled in the shadows while he thought things through. It was definitely a trap but sitting here in an alley wasn't helping things. He imagined the street layout. It should be easy for him to avoid the cordon by going up the street and then taking the next right turn to travel full circle back to within sight of the brothel. Eventually he would be close to the rear exit, the secret one that Danton had shown him.

Moving quietly, Brill slipped out of the alleyway, cast a look behind only to see the stern faces of the guards. Clinging to the shadows along the walls, he crept away, hoping to be there when Danton needed him.

ᏽᏽᏽᏽᏽ

A thump overhead sent Danton's heart lurching uncomfortably. Retreating out into the corridor he caught sight of a door shutting above stairs. It was the room in which he and Brill had had the punch-up over Mandin: Toola's party room. Danton stayed in the corner, shrouded in shadows, and waited. Still there was no one around. He'd never smelled anything that ponged so strongly of a trap. But how had they known he was coming; how did they know he was here? Were they expecting him or someone else? Mandin's note? *Damn Toola and her machinations.* He bet Toola made Mandin write it.

The shroud tingled against his skin, reminding him that he was invisible in the shadows. If someone was looking they might detect a ripple in the air. He climbed slowly and carefully up the stairs. To remain undetected he needed someone to open the door. He did not have Nils's knack of slipping into the spaces between the walls or whatever it was that he did. Taking a moment to look behind him, he saw someone dart down the corridor, then after some whispering it was silent once more. Not good.

The door to the party room was ajar. Interesting, he thought, and convenient. He angled around to peer through the crack. He saw no one. Wafting curtains impaired his vision somewhat. Waiting was difficult, but it was all he could do while he listened in the unnatural quiet that had fallen on the brothel. He swore he could hear water dripping from the baths at the rear. Then he heard it: a faint whimper of pain from inside the room. Mandin. It had to be. What other way could Toola bait the trap?

The door whined as he pushed it gently open, making it look like a draft was blowing it wide. There were no sudden moves from within. Carefully, he stepped onto the carpet, keeping to the shadows and hoping that the curtains wouldn't billow in his direction to reveal his form to onlookers, for onlookers there surely were.

Circling a pillar, he saw Mandin and his breath caught in his throat. She was dressed in tattered underclothes, gagged and bound to another fake pillar. The sheer curtains blew in and around her in front of an open window. Shadowed shapes moved stealthily in the corners. She couldn't see him, but she must have known he was there. She was shaking her head, whimpering. Trust her to try to warn him off. He was in too far now so he may as well do what he came to do: free her.

Danton eased around her in a wide circle. She had been badly treated, that much was evident. There were bruises on her thighs in the shape of handprints and welts along her back where she had been lashed. The bindings were so tight he could see blood along her wrists and her stomach where the ties cut through. It was the eyes that squeezed his balls, though—full of fear and pain and hope. He could not leave her to her fate.

Standing still, he tried to pick out where his attackers were. There were at least two in the corner behind Mandin, three behind the door he had entered through. The curtains hindered his assessment. He guessed too that the landing outside was now full of men. In fact, he could feel the vibrations of feet through the floor boards.

Out of the shadows, Linel appeared. Mandin struggled against her bonds as perspiration began to trickle between her breasts.

Danton backtracked to the door, darted into the shadows and flicked a hurling blade toward one of the shapes hiding in the curtain. A grunt told him that his aim was true. He dived for another shadow to keep them guessing where he was.

With a ripple of shroud, he threw two more hurling blades into the guards in the corner. Their bodies thudded to the floor.

Linel reached Mandin. Danton breathed through his mouth. Mandin's moan as Linel twisted the skin of her belly made Danton see red. His next hurling blade missed.

The curtains erupted with the movement of four more men, accompanied by the sound of their swords being drawn.

"There he is," one of them shouted.

Danton froze. Could they see him?

A sword thrust passed close to him and only a quick side step avoided certain death. Danton swirled curtains in his wake and retreated to the shadows. The man who had spotted him wore something over his eyes and his gaze never left Danton. He directed two men forward. Danton was cornered.

"I don't see nuthin'," one of his attackers exclaimed.

"He's there, I see his outline."

No! The chill in Danton's gut was like the thin edge of a cold blade. Somehow that man could see him.

Only one of the men had the glasses that could see him and he directed the others. This worked somewhat in Danton's favor as the fighters were clumsy and the instructions were imprecise. Danton sprang forward and rolled. He kicked out at one of his attackers, enjoying the crunch of kneecap as his boot connected. The man rolled into a ball and wailed. The other took a long slice that caught the shroud. There was a sound of a tear and the tingling sensation stopped.

Danton was fully visible. "Shit!"

He parried a sword thrust and flicked his assailant's blade out of his hand. Another attacker ran at him. Danton swiveled to meet him but the man dropped to the ground and kicked Danton's feet out from under him. Winded, Danton still managed to roll away from the blade that poked at him from above.

Linel stood stock-still, keeping guard over Mandin, not participating in the fight—for the moment, at least. Linel would be hard to beat. Linel had stopped torturing her, which was a relief. There was something unnatural about the man. Danton realized he had little chance of freeing Mandin. Linel's presence ensured that.

Perhaps he should have listened to Brill after all. He would be lucky to get out of there alive. Darting behind Mandin, Danton used the dagger drawn from his boot to sever a few of Mandin's bonds. She did not move an inch. Danton then rolled toward the downed guards to retrieve a hurling blade. He was able to free it and take aim. Another went down with a strangled cry. All the curtains had been torn down in the scuffle and the three remaining guards stood in a fighting stance with unobstructed access to him.

Out of the corner of his eye, Danton saw Mandin moving her ankles, working the bindings free. Hopefully she would keep Linel busy. Now that the curtains were down he saw they didn't cover windows at all but bare wall. The billowing had been the movement of the hidden guards. The window behind Mandin could take his size, but movement drew his eye. More guards arrived. Two of them crossed their spears, barring window; six more held their spears forward ready to skewer Danton if he drew close. That meant his only escape was through the door he had come through, unless he could break through the fabric of the walls.

Two guards inched forward, swords at the ready. Another went to bar the door. Danton thought a lit explosive would have come in handy right about then. He feinted right, and both men followed. Ducking and rolling, Danton lifted up a fallen curtain and swirled it around, entangling their swords. Then he rammed their heads together. The bodies slumped within their fabric shrouds.

The guard on the door stood firm. Danton darted toward him. He was ready and quick. A slash high was met and deflected, as was a cut low. Danton stumbled as the man drove him back. This wasn't going well. The other men groaned and fought their way free of the curtain. He had to move quickly. He lowered his sword and the door guard took the bait. Danton stepped in close and stabbed him in the ribs with his dagger.

Then he swung around, and felled one of the other men with a hurling blade. His last one. As the man fell sideways, Danton darted for the door. He snapped it open and paused.

More guards waited on the landing, but he had taken them by surprise. Danton took a leap for the railing. The guard positioned there lost a second recalibrating the situation and died. Pain shot through his knees as Danton landed on the floor below. The yells from upstairs and the stamp of feet told him his pursuers were only moments behind him.

Down the corridor was the escape hatch. Danton sweated, annoyed at his defeat. He had not saved Mandin and he was almost snared. From a run, he slid along the hall to the cupboard hiding the door to the secret tunnel. The cupboard door opened. A quick look up the corridor. Legs running, boots pounding. They were nearly on him. He reached for the hatch and it didn't move. He pushed at it but it stayed still. Turning, he used his feet to kick it. It wouldn't budge. It was blocked. "Damn you, Toola!"

That left the back entrance, through the baths. The shorter route was the front entrance, but it was likely both ways were covered.

The men behind him rounded the corridor and sprinted. That decided him: the baths at the rear. He bolted down the corridor and turned the corner. Something heavy hit his head. His legs turned to water and crumpled beneath him. Linel's vacant face was the last thing he saw. *How?* he thought, when he looked up that ugly scarred face.

Then he remembered the servant stairs and then his vision went white.

ᏋᏋᏋᏋᏋ

Brill drew back to hide in the shadows. By the time he had made his way close to Toola's place again, the trap had well and truly been sprung. He was close enough to aid Danton if he made it through the secret tunnel, but no matter how much he wished it, no matter how much he stared, Danton did not emerge.

A commotion in the street drew him to look. The troops that had been deployed were regrouping. Brill squeezed his hands into fists. Their mission was complete. From his vantage point he saw the lifeless form of Danton being dragged into the street. A lump in his throat made it hard to swallow. *Danton!*

Brill's heart beat on, even though he was shocked, heartbroken and afraid. Then one of the guards dropped to his knees and bound Danton's hands and feet. While Danton captured was a disaster, it gave Brill hope. They wouldn't bother tying a dead man. Danton's shroud was in another guard's hand and the man was eyeing it with some glasses. "This must go directly to the baron," he said and then pushed it into a bag and handed it to a courier. The younger man took off at a swift pace. Brill bit his lip as he considered what this meant. They knew about the shroud and now they had the technology. Nils was going to be very unhappy about this.

Still, if Brill attacked now, without them expecting it, he might have a chance. Linel hove into view and Brill recoiled. Linel sniffed once and then his head turned to exactly where Brill stood. Heart thumping, Brill stayed perfectly still, hoping that if Linel did sense him somehow that he wouldn't betray him.

Danton was dragged away. Brill itched to follow but stayed where he was, not moving a muscle. Linel stared for a long time, until all the troops had marched off, taking Danton and Brill's hope with them. Linel then turned and reentered the brothel.

There was the proof he needed. Linel was Toola's creature. Toola had definitely betrayed her cousin. Mandin was still inside the brothel in Toola's clutches. It was up to Brill to set her free. That is what Danton would have wanted.

Brill's gaze traveled along the street where Danton had been taken. Now, he must follow if only to bring word of where Danton was being held.

Chapter Ten

BLOOD BONDS

When Salinda returned to the city after her visit with Plu, she found that Nils was not in the abode. There was, however, a pile of freshly made clothes on the table. She fingered them, realizing that Nils must have prepared them for Laidan. It seemed he expected the girl to be released soon, as he had prepared new clothes for her in much the same way as he had for Salinda. Even the soft slippers had been exquisitely crafted. A surge of love for her mate enveloped her. How fortunate she had been to find him. An image of Danton's handsome face arose too. With a tinge of regret she put thoughts of the rebel away. Her life was with Nils now, and with him her duty lay. Nils was important to her task, important to the cadre, and important for the survival of Margra.

After refreshing herself with tea, she frowned. The Barr family node was unnaturally quiet. No Nils. No Garan. Where had Nils got to? Could he have made it as far as the archives in his condition? Garan? As she had passed through the city she hadn't noticed the young man lingering in the streets and thoroughfares as he was wont to do of late. Now that the actual work was done and the sacred flame lit, the boy had nothing to do but admire his handiwork.

The boy was restless and worried, though. Salinda was just as conscious as the young Skywatcher about the passage of time. The threat from the sky could only be drawing closer, and still they were none the wiser about how to deal with it. But without Nils, and with

Laidan's life in the balance, there was little they could do to speed things up.

Nils's illness had caused a few unavoidable delays. They had not been able to explore this "thing" Garan could sense in the vaults beneath the city, and Salinda sensed it was important. She had hoped that by bringing Garan, Nils and the archives in Barrahiem together, some solution would spring out at them. Sadly this had not been the case. Even the cadres were lacking in help. Yet, there was a thread of something there. She put a fist to her head and tapped, willing the answer to reveal itself. There in the visions the cadre had given her was something. A machine. People entering a machine. Salinda growled in frustration as the kernel of the idea dissipated instead of coalescing.

It was time to reassess the situation and visit the observatory. She needed an update on the timing of the final moonfall. She had no doubt that was what was coming. The movement of a large fragment of Ruel moon heading into the wing was the beginning of the end. The baby kicked once and she repressed the sudden need to weep. Her child—Nils's child—would die along with everything else. She couldn't let that happen.

Salinda descended through the city toward the room where Laidan lay in the healing tray, in the hope of finding the others there. As she crossed the Hall of Elders, bathed in the flickering light of the sacred lamp, she saw them. Nils turned at her approach, looking like his old self. He was still thin and pale but the grayness of death was gone from his gaunt features. Whatever the Ways had taken out of him, he appeared to be fully recovered.

Garan came around from the other side of the tray and greeted her with a smile. "You are back again. So quickly too. How did you go? Was your dragon healed?"

"Yes, Plu's injury is much better. He had something else to show me while I was there."

Both Garan and Nils turned to her, eyes bright with questions.

She grinned at them. "He is a she. Plu is a mother now."

"And you did not know this before?" Nils asked.

Salinda shook her head. "No. I thought Plu was merely small."

"Interesting. I will note this in my account. Can you write down all that you saw, felt, smelled? I will find it useful."

Salinda tilted her head and smiled at him. "I most certainly will."

Nils turned back to the healing tray. Garan joined him. Salinda put her hands on her hips, amused at their distractedness. "Does that mean you two didn't miss me at all?"

A grunt greeted her inquiry.

She shook her head. "Never mind. How is Laidan?"

Salinda didn't wait for an answer; instead she peered around Garan to see into the healing tray. The mist had cleared and the fine healing webs were almost gone. Laidan in all her beauty lay there as naked as the day she was born. All trace of her injuries had been erased. Had Nils stared at Salinda too, while she lay there naked? Until now she had not thought about it. What was such a sight doing to Garan? Laidan was unlikely to change for the better. Or was such a nasty thought unworthy of her?

Salinda was secretly afraid of what Laidan would be like once free of the contraption. The girl had power and knew how to use it, to bend men to her ways. It was something that Salinda didn't understand, had never tried. Her life had formed her in a different mold. The men she had known had been the enemy. The exceptions were Mez and Danton, and now she could add Nils and Garan and some of the men in the observatory to the list. Now that she thought about it, maybe she was being unfair to men.

Salinda shivered when she recollected what Laidan had endured at the hands of Gercomo. She didn't think she could have faced him the way the girl had, or endured what the girl had endured and stayed sane. She let out a sigh at the thought. Poor child. What if her mind had been destroyed in the attack? Her physical damage had been great— her body and mind wounded. Salinda let out a breath she hadn't realized she'd been holding.

She looked from Garan to Nils, noting how enraptured they were with Laidan. "I think we should cover her now," she said to Nils. "It does not seem right to leave her so exposed."

Nils looked up at her and inclined his head. "There will be time when she wakes. It is too soon to disturb the tray." He looked at Garan as if finally catching Salinda's meaning. "We should leave her now. All is prepared. Come, Garan."

Nils held out a hand to Salinda and they started to walk away.

Garan fell into step with them as they strode through the now well-lit halls. The carvings and murals were well served by the addition of light. Salinda was moved by their beauty and detail. The Hiem appeared ready to step out of those paintings and walk with them. She paused in front of one mural, in the hall before the main thoroughfare that led to the balconies that looked out over the lesser city of N'Barek. A light haloed the figure of a young Hiem woman, tall, willowy and with fine strands of white-blonde hair. Salinda was tempted to touch the face, because the complexion was so well captured, it looked real. But she held back as she didn't want to damage the picture, or sully it.

"Can you see the similarities to Laidan in this picture?" Nils asked.

"What?" Salinda blinked and then frowned as she re-focused on the painting. She did not want to get his hopes up. The Hiem woman had the distinctive bony brow of her race and her chin was rather thin and pointed. She was not what Salinda would call pretty, but Salinda acknowledged that she was no beauty herself. She tried to superimpose Laidan's features on the woman's. If you erased the brow, brought more color to the hair and rounded the face, she supposed there was a slight resemblance. She said as much to Nils, who merely paused before continuing walking.

As they passed along the balconies that overlooked the dark lake, thoughts of Laidan and Nils's new obsession about finding his kin alive worried her. He couldn't cope with further disappointment. On the other hand, the thought that some of his kin were alive had re-energized him and would make him more likely to help in their endeavor to save everyone on Margra. Yet, such a hope was a two-edged sword. Surely if his kind existed they would have shown themselves by now. It was entirely possible that the remaining Hiem had interbred with humans, just as he had done with her. But she feared it was no more than that. If Laidan had a lot of Hiem blood in her, then it was a fluke.

They ate a meal together, a spicy stew, which Garan had prepared all on his own. Salinda found she enjoyed the food, more so than Nils, who preferred very plain food: broths, vegetables and fruit. Somehow Garan had turned ingredients from the gardens into something resembling the thick stews and bread from the observatory. Perhaps the lad was homesick for familiar fare.

"Nils, do you think you have the strength to take Garan and me into the vaults below the city tomorrow? Garan has sensed something, he isn't sure what, but I think we should investigate it."

"Sensed? What do you mean?" Nils placed his bowl on the table, the contents only partially eaten.

Garan swallowed a mouthful of food. "I cannot say...exactly. I can feel it there in my mind. I am thinking it could be a mechanism similar to the lights."

"What makes you say that?" Nils asked pleasantly.

"I do not know. The lights are the only thing I am familiar with. I find it hard to describe. It reaches out to me in some way."

Nils continued to stare at Garan, until the young man raised an eyebrow at Salinda. Then, when Salinda appeared ready to ask again, Nils finally spoke. "I will take you on two conditions."

"Oh, Nils, when will you trust us?" Salinda said, putting down her teacup.

"Two conditions," Nils said again, raising two thin, bony fingers. "That you do not stray away from me, and obey my commands without question. If I say we leave, we do and no arguments. There is much in the vaults, much that I do not know about. Even when this place was full of my kin, there were many restrictions on access to the vaults. Some had not been opened in hundreds, maybe thousands of years. There are things hidden below that were not put there by the Hiem, things from a race that had died out before we came to Margra. Even I do not know what the Hiem have added over the years. You must recall that I am a reluctant historian and archivist."

Salinda let out a sigh. "That makes perfect sense. I agree. Garan?"

Garan poured the remaining stew from the pot on the table into his bowl. "Can we start now? There is no point in waiting." He shoveled more food into his mouth as if it was to be his last meal.

Salinda's eyebrows rose. He was right. None of them were tired and whether it was night or day mattered not in the subterranean city. "You think it will be easy then to track this thing?" Salinda asked Garan.

Garan shrugged, then stood and collected their bowls to take them for washing. "I am hopeful. I can feel it now, and maybe when we are closer I will be able to feel more, sense more. And I want it done and over with so I can be there when Laidan wakes up. So the sooner we start, the sooner we will come back."

Nils frowned. "I have no objection to starting this search now, but

I must tell you, Garan, it may not be wise to—" He broke off, his gaze anchoring on Salinda. She shook her head, not quite sure what Nils wanted from her. "To be there when Laidan wakes up."

Garan half-choked. "What? Why?" He dropped to his knees and placed the bowls on the table again.

Nils continued. "I think it is best that I care for her at first. I was not involved in the attack that earned her injuries. It is I who will bring her back to the fold. In this you must trust me too. I have prepared a room for this, near the healing tray itself."

Garan looked down at the pile of bowls, then wordlessly gathered them up again and took them into the alcove. Nils and Salinda sat there while Garan finished the cleaning and then he came back, and his eyes flicked to Salinda with a pleading look in them. "Salinda...?"

She smiled gently at Garan. "Nils knows best in this, Garan."

"But..."

"It is wise to provide a cushion between Laidan and us. We don't know what seeing us will do to her fragile mind. She may associate us with the attack, as we were present when it occurred. Nils is willing to bring her slowly and gently back to us. He can tell us how she is without harming Laidan's recovery."

Garan swallowed as his gaze swept Nils and then centered back on Salinda. He ran his hands through his curls. "I understand. You know I care for her...I do not expect her to care for me...not after..."

A silence fell over them once more. After they had drunk the Pardu tea Nils prepared, he led them down to the archives. He took them past his office, past the manufacturing vault that Garan had frequented while repairing the lamps, down and down even further where the passageways were more like tunnels, less ornate and not lit at all.

In a dark tunnel Nils said, "Wait here. I will bring light."

So Garan and Salinda stood together in the cool darkness and waited. "Anything?"

"'Tis still there. No closer. No farther."

Nils had retreated up the passageway to the previous intersection. He was gone a few minutes and then his robes made swishing sounds as he returned, a lamp swinging from his hands.

Salinda suggested that Nils guide them at a slower pace so that Garan had time to adjust to each level. At the next level, Salinda noticed a change in the air straight away. The atmosphere was damp and smelled slightly musty after the dry, odor-free levels above. After walking along for a few minutes they paused, letting Garan use his other sense to detect the mind or machine that had so tantalized him. The floor of the passageway was uneven. Then Garan breathed quietly while they waited. "No change," he said.

Nils led them on. The passageways became narrower, with many branches leading off them. The one they were in had a low roof. Nils hesitated. "Are you any closer to it?" he asked, holding up the light to peer at the young Skywatcher. The tall Hiem was hunched over so that he could walk in this tunnel.

Garan turned his head. "No. I do not think so."

"Can you feel it at all, Garan?" Salinda asked. She was beginning to feel uneasy this far below ground in these roughly hewn spaces where no one had trod for countless years. It sparked some deep fear in her, a fear of being buried, trapped.

"Yes, it is still there."

Nils lifted the light higher. The passage they were in terminated in smooth rock. "There is nothing here beyond that wall. Let us return to the city. We will have to try again tomorrow perhaps. There are many passageways. If Garan could better refine his sense of direction..."

Garan put his arm out, halting Nils as he turned to leave. "Are you sure there is nothing beyond there?"

Nils studied the rock face. "I do not know. It is possible it is sealed and the evidence of that closure disguised or erased on purpose or by the passage of time."

Garan stared at the blank wall of rock for a moment and then went over to it, running his hands down the smooth surface. He leaned against it with both hands and then put his forehead on it. "Could you find your way here again, Nils?"

Salinda stepped into the light. "What is it, Garan? What is it you sense?"

"I cannot describe it. It is like it is pretending not to be there. It is being nothing."

"Nothing. But that makes no sense. You detected it before. Now you don't?"

"Yes, it was there. Now it is nothing."

Salinda narrowed her gaze, at a loss. "That...I don't understand. Has it moved?"

Garan looked up, shadows almost obscuring his eyes. "Moved? Turned off?"

"Nils?"

"I do not know, but I can find my way back here. Quickly, too, now we know the destination."

Salinda indicated to Nils to precede them and he led them out of the passageway and up to the city.

⊙⊙⊙⊙

The next time they searched it took hours. The evening meal time had come and gone. Garan's stomach growled noisily. "Do you want to go back now?" Salinda asked. She could see the signs of fatigue in his eyes and in his step.

"A little bit longer, please," Garan replied, running his hands over a wall. "There is something in here. Not the presence I felt before, but something else."

Salinda let out an explosive sound. "Something else? Are you dust mad? We are looking for this thing you can sense, not something else."

"I am sorry. I cannot help it. There is something hidden here. I cannot explain it, I just know it."

Nils shook out the map and studied it, rubbing his chin occasionally. He lifted his head, his silver eyes glowing in the dim light. "We will continue then. Follow me." Nils turned on his heel and climbed up the stair back to the main intersection.

The next few doorways opened into rooms no larger than cupboards, one of which they had to crawl into. Garan ventured into another and backed out again, saying that it contained carvings and other strange artifacts. They were no closer to finding this thing that had touched Garan and his power.

Finally Nils slowed. "If we do not turn back we will have to sleep down here. Not a comfortable place, I assure you."

"I am willing," Garan said. "It is here somewhere. The more we look the more I need to find it."

"Nils, before you brought me here, I had not slept in a bed for more than ten years. A night down here on a stone floor is no hardship to me."

"Then I am outvoted. We will find a place to rest."

Huddled together in the hallway was how they passed the night. Garan moaned often in his sleep and Salinda wondered whether it was caused by his proximity to the thing he could sense. She worried about what might live down here: crawling, creepy insects. It was odd. Such fears hadn't bothered her at the vineyard. Perhaps that had been because there were other, larger concerns in her life at the time.

Waking early due to discomfort and hunger, they set off again, moving ever lower. Nils gave them small bars of food and a drink of water from a flask he carried. It wasn't much but it was enough to get them by. Garan's eyes looked haunted but he didn't talk about his disturbed night.

Nils directed them down a hallway. Salinda followed his lead but she noticed that Garan delayed, his gaze drifting down another corridor. She reached for Nils, putting her hand on his arm, and when he turned toward her, she directed his gaze to the lad. Without a word, he doubled back and led them where Garan seemed to want to go. At the end of a corridor was a large door, the largest she had seen in this warren of tunnels. Garan stood and gaped at it, until Nils nudged him away in order to examine it. It was locked. That was not surprising; most of the doors had been, but Nils had been able to open them. He gestured and manipulated levers and the door did not budge. This lock was beyond Nils.

"What do you feel, Garan?" Salinda asked while Nils worked on the door. "Can you describe it?"

It took a while for Garan to answer, as if his mind was otherwise occupied, but then he said, "Nothing—it feels like nothing and yet something. Like 'tis sucking me into it, absorbing me...It is the absence of something."

Salinda scratched her head and turned to Nils. What Garan described gave her an uneasy feeling. She knew Nils had heard, but he had not deigned to respond. She had no idea what Garan was talking about, and she wondered if Nils did. But the absence of something tasted of hunger to her.

Nils tried another way to open the door, a series of incantations and hand movements.

"Can you open it, Nils?" she asked eventually.

"I am working on it, Salinda. Be patient. This door has not been opened for more than a thousand years."

"Or longer," she added, pre-empting a lecture about how old the vaults actually were. Salinda had heard that too often.

Nils worked on opening the door for another hour, always with a new set of incantations and hand movements. Garan had sunk to the floor, sitting on his haunches with his back to the wall and his head resting on his knees. Salinda had been tempted to take the opportunity to rest, too, but found pacing in the corridor helped her work off her nervous tension.

What was this thing Garan sensed? Would it be useful to them or were they wasting their time down here in this unpleasant, ill-lit place? No, she assured herself, whatever it was, it had to be useful. Garan was special. His power was special and the Hiem machines responded to him and a machine was in that vision the cadre had given her.

Another hour passed and still Nils had not succeeded in opening the door. Salinda sank to the ground, feeling weary, cranky and hungry. Finally she said, "Nils, why don't you let Garan have a go and take a break?"

Nils swung around, surprise and alarm on his face. "Salinda, I do not think..."

Salinda climbed to her feet, nestling her arms across her extended abdomen. "It can't hurt for him to try. Otherwise we may as well head back now. I need to eat sometime soon and rest. I'm exhausted."

Nils stared at her, the light from the shuwai highlighting the silver glow in his eyes. His gaze shifted to Garan, who had lifted his head, eyes heavy with sleep.

"You are right. I am here to assist. Please try it. I will help you."

Salinda listened for sarcasm in Nils's tone but found none.

Garan swayed on his feet and walked to the door. He touched the panel and swung the lever as Nils had done at least a hundred times before, and straight away the door split in half, and two vertical sections withdrew into the rock face overhead and into the ground.

Nils jumped back, saying something she didn't quite understand, possibly a curse word. Her own cry of "Wing dust!" overrode whatever he had said. Nils did nothing more than glance at her because his attention was riveted on Garan and what lay inside the room.

As Salinda drew near, disappointment grew. The room held a large, black box, featureless and dull. There did not appear to be anything else in the room, nor room to fit anything else. It was as though it had been custom built. All three gaped at the contraption before them. Then, unbidden and without Nils's permission, Garan knelt down in front of it and touched his finger to the surface. The machine leaped to life. Sound and light filled the space. Nils gasped, dragging Garan and Salinda out of the room with him. The door slid shut and they stood in the corridor, stunned.

"I told you not to touch anything," hissed Nils, clearly rattled.

"What was is it?" Salinda asked.

"I do not know," Nils snapped at her. "It was not any technology I am familiar with. I have no idea if it is an old or new construct."

Garan had not responded to Nils's chiding. Turning toward the youth in unison, she and Nils saw why. Garan appeared to be in a daze. His eyes were open but his mouth was slack.

"Garan?" Salinda asked. There was no response.

Nils tried too, but Garan remained impervious. "I told you it could be dangerous. Now look at what has happened."

Salinda frowned at Nils while grabbing Garan by the elbow. "There is no point in berating either of us now. We should get him out of here."

"But he said he would obey..."

"Nils, really...come on."

Garan moved where directed, and she intended to head back to the city. As they walked, she said over her shoulder to Nils, "I don't think it was him touching the machine that's done this. He's been acting strangely since last night."

"I do not agree. The machine is now active and I have no idea what it does."

"But it is not his fault. He could feel the machine before he touched it. Therefore it must have been active already. You saw how the door opened for him just like that."

Nils fell into a troubled silence but assisted her to bring Garan back to the city. All the while, Salinda's fears for Garan grew. How could it be that he was able to walk under his own steam and respond to commands, and yet not be fully aware? What had happened when the machine had been activated? Garan volunteered nothing when she tried to communicate with him.

When they reached his abode, Nils and Salinda assisted Garan to lie down. To her immense relief, the boy appeared to rally a little at this, and was able to take food and drink before drifting off to sleep.

Before she could discuss the incident further with Nils, he left carrying the clothing he had prepared, saying he was heading to the Hall of Elders and the healing tray. He was worried that Laidan might have awoken while they were away. Remembering her own awakening from the healing tray, she understood Nils's concern and his short temper. Their foray into the vaults had turned into an ordeal. Salinda tended to the most important things of all: using the privy, eating a meal and having a long nap. She hoped that Garan could explain what had happened when he recovered himself.

Chapter Eleven

TO FREE OR FLEE

As soon as Danton was trussed up, bagged and in the baron's custody, Toola made her way to her other residence. It had been a nasty business. Her team was working hard to remove the bodies and the bloodstains so that they could reopen for business. If there was a hitch in her step, then she put it down to regret. Danton and she had meant something to each other once. She wondered why he meant less to her now.

Her best tracker was following the baron. Then she'd learn more about what was going on. She just had to bide her time. But for Eneit, time had run out. If she didn't auction the girl's virginity soon her finances would be dealt a serious blow. Even worse, if she didn't get her gainfully whoring, the baron would steal her back. He knew where Toola kept the girl. He knew more than he should about a lot of things. That he had sent his men into her escape tunnel to seal it up from the other side without any information from her was sobering. It had helped her catch Danton, right enough, but it meant he knew way too much about Toola's operations. If there was going to be a double cross, she was not going to get caught in it. Poor Danton! She had hoped he would escape the baron's noose, but it was not to be. It was his fate.

She unlocked the door to her private residence and as soon as she was in the basement, she called for Lexia.

"Start getting her things ready. We're leaving."

Lexia bowed her head and set to work. Toola could hear Eneit crying from the bedroom. Lexia had obviously informed her of the gritty details. Now it was time for Toola to play the comforting mother.

There were some things that could make life more comfortable for a whore, but these did involve some pain. Eneit was tied up as Toola had instructed Lexia to do.

She raced over to the bed and stroked the girl's hair. "There, there, my sweet child. What has happened here? Is this some game you have been playing with Lexia?"

Toola unbound the child and made her more comfortable. Eneit threw herself into Toola's arms and sobbed. "Oh, my dear, it is all right now."

Between sobs, Eneit regaled her with the last twenty-four hours of Lexia's instruction. Toola soothed her. "What a nasty girl. Never mind, I will not let her near you again. But you must be good and listen to your mother now."

"Yes, Mother."

"We are going to take a little rest together and I will soothe you with a bath and some oils. Later we will go for a quick trip. There are some nice people I want you to meet."

Eneit sniffed and nodded.

"So that you can look your best I'm going to dress you in a very pretty dress which will be yours forever. And if you behave correctly and do as you are told, you will get a very pleasant surprise."

Again the girl nodded. Toola liked her compliance. How unlike her mother! After bathing the girl and oiling her all over, Toola served her some dragon wine laced with a small amount of sedative. Before she could bring the child to the brothel, she needed to make arrangements and deal with Mandin.

♋♋♋♋♋

Mandin limped down the corridor after Linel let her leave his room, and she saw Lexia come through the front door. Mandin suspected something was up as the girl had been missing for more than a day. The talk from the other girls suggested that Toola had sent her somewhere. Putting the clues together, she suspected Toola had another place. As the girl went to pass her, Mandin touched her arm. "Are you well, child?" Mandin asked.

"I am very well. Thank you."

"But I thought…the other night…you were in so much pain."

Lexia frowned. "Oh, you were there behind the curtains," she said and looked to the ground. "I forgot. I try not to think on it. Toola doesn't let him hurt me badly. She is nice to me afterwards and, well, that helps…And he…well, he is so sorry afterwards that he gives me presents."

"Presents?" Mandin replied with a sick stomach.

"Yes." The girl flashed a grin that quickly faded. "See?" The girl held up a wrist with a shiny new bracelet on it. But her eyes held dark despair and were swollen with unshed tears.

Mandin's gut churned. What kind of warping had this girl endured? That man had been her father. But he…and the rest, well…Eneit? This is what she was destined for. "That is a lovely bracelet," Mandin said softly, not quite sure she wasn't about to burst into tears herself. This is what her daughter was destined for. Mandin had to act, had to save her. Yet looking at this broken child, she mourned that she could not save them all. Swallowing the lump in her throat, she asked, "You've been away?"

Lexia's eyes widened. "Oh yes. I've been at Toola's private place."

Mandin couldn't hide her involuntary reaction. Her eyes widened. *A private place?* "Did you go there for a rest?"

Lexia screwed up her mouth. "I wish. No, she has a new recruit she wants me to train. A little scrawny thing, if you ask me. Doesn't have any curves like mine."

Mandin's heart thumped. *Eneit!* It had to be Eneit. The sound of someone treading down the corridor made her turn her head. Linel trod heavily as he approached. Mandin moved past Lexia, hoping he hadn't overheard their exchange.

"Toola said you are to go to the bar," Linel commanded.

Mandin limped toward the bar, hoping that what Toola intended was not a repeat of her previous experience. The bar was half-full of hopeful onlookers, each with full glasses. As she entered they began to cheer. Word had obviously spread. Mandin lifted her chin. She could take whatever Linel and Toola dished out. After all, she had no choice. Danton was taken. Brill missing. But Eneit. Eneit was close. Soon she would set her daughter free.

Later, as she held herself very still in a dark corner so as not to make her aches and pains worse, she knew it was time to act. She feared she would not survive another public beating. She needed to talk to Toola. The woman had betrayed Danton and assisted in his capture; all pretense between them was at an end. Mandin had to hope that she could reason with the brothel madam, and at least be close when Eneit was brought there.

Toola clearly had no qualms about selling people out. Danton was gone to who knew what bidder, and yet Danton was Toola's own flesh and blood. Mandin didn't really understand it. She'd not encountered anyone like Toola before. But Mandin didn't care about understanding the woman, she just wanted to get her daughter back and save her from the slave life of a whore that was all mapped out for her.

After a bath Mandin dressed in a robe. She negotiated with the guard who had been set to watch her to escort her to Toola's tea room. When she knocked on Toola's door, Linel opened it.

"May I see her?"

Linel's face had no expression. It rarely did. The door closed in her face. Mandin waited. Five minutes later the door opened and she was shown in. Toola was drinking tea at her little table, a few scraps of paper at her desk.

"What do you want?" Toola snapped distractedly as she placed one piece of paper over another.

Mandin opened her mouth but there was a sharp rap on the door. It burst open before Linel could reach it. Toola's eyes widened and Mandin backed up to the wall. A man in a city police uniform burst in. The sounds of booted feet echoed up the corridor. He hadn't come alone.

Startled cries from other parts of the brothel could be heard in her small room. Toola's mouth pursed and her dark eyes flashed. She stood regally, exuding authority.

"What is the meaning of this outrage?"

"Your premises are being searched."

"Searched? Preposterous."

The sounds of search continued.

Toola's hands curled into fists at her side. "Leave now, sergeant.

Take your men with you. Your presence is upsetting my clients."

"I have orders."

Toola scoffed. "I'm giving you new ones. Leave now. I handle my own security. I'll speak to Narin about your attitude."

"Commissioner Narin was found dead in the street near here this morning."

Mandin saw Toola pale, but the woman recovered quickly.

"That has nothing to do with me!"

"Then he wasn't visiting your establishment last night?"

Toola frowned. "No. Of course not. How dare you question me!"

The sergeant smiled. "I have the authority to ask anyone questions."

"I know nothing. Now get out. I'll speak to your new superior about this affront."

A police officer came in and whispered to the sergeant. His eyes flicked up to Toola. "Very well, madam. I will leave you to your business." He bowed slightly and went to the door. Linel waited for an all clear from Toola before opening it.

When the sergeant had gone, Toola sat back in her seat. Still obviously shaken by the news, Toola seemed to forget that Mandin was in the room. Head gripped between her hands, her eyes glazed, she muttered, "The baron! That bastard! It has to be a warning." Then, after almost tearing the hair from her head, Toola's eyes focused and she glared at Mandin.

A chill cut through Mandin's gut when she saw the rage in Toola's face. Toola was not happy and she would no doubt make Mandin pay, because she had witnessed Toola's moment of weakness and because that was the way she operated.

Mandin cast a glance at Linel, but there was little point appealing to that subhuman creature. The man was Toola's obedient dog. Mandin now had to rethink her strategy. Gloating at Toola, enjoying her moment of weakness, was a luxury she could not afford. If Toola went down, so too did all of Mandin's hopes of getting her daughter back. With Danton captured, there wasn't even the rebel path to follow. She was on her own, more than she had ever been.

Toola raised an eyebrow, letting her rage simmer. "You asked to see me?"

Mandin bobbed her head "Yes, forgive me. I have come to ask a favor."

"A favor?" Toola stood up swiftly, knocking her chair over so it hit the floor with a loud bang. Mandin flinched involuntarily and eyed the other woman. She thought Toola might rage at her, but instead she slowly turned around, hooked a stray strand of hair behind her ear and stretched her mouth into a grim smile. "You are in no position to ask for favors. I should have handed you over to the customs officials for processing."

Mandin chose a passive approach. Toola was disconcerted; perhaps Mandin could get under her guard. "I am most grateful that you didn't."

Toola huffed and acknowledged with a tilt of her head for Linel to right her chair. "So what do you want?" Toola said, seating herself again slowly while arranging her clothes. She picked up her cup of tea and sipped.

Mandin fell to her knees, and placed her hands together in supplication. "To see my daughter. Please."

Toola lowered her cup and shook her head. "Still harping on about that brat of yours, are you?"

"Yes," Mandin replied simply. She kept her gaze on Toola.

"Why do you ask me about it? I've done all that I can to help you. As you see, one of my powerful friends has been killed because I asked questions."

"I don't believe that."

"Don't believe what? That Narin is dead?"

"No, I believe you have my daughter." Mandin stared at a point on the floor.

"Believe what you will," Toola hissed, and then the room grew quiet. A quick glance revealed that Toola was sipping her tea. Her hands trembled slightly. Mandin found that unnerving. Toola was her protection from the city outside. Without Danton and Brill, Mandin was truly alone. Linel had told her what happened to people who were unprotected. What if she got Eneit back and then they both fell prey to slavers or worse?

Mandin shook her head, letting her attention slide to Linel again.

"I can't keep quiet about this." She climbed to her feet, shrugging off the air of supplication. "You have done your best to keep her from me. I know you have her at your other house. I know you are training her, corrupting her to serve you."

Toola's eyebrow rose again, then lowered slightly. "You presume a lot to accuse me. You have seen my reaction to the news of Narin's death, heard that upstart lackey of his threaten me in my own establishment. Are you witless? Have you no idea of the danger I face, of what danger we all face?"

Mandin stared at Toola, swallowing spit while she weighed up the woman's words.

"I believe nothing you say. You betrayed your own blood when you gave them Danton."

Toola flinched and lowered her head. Mandin was surprised by that. "I don't have your daughter."

Mandin let out a slow breath and studied the woman. There was truth mixed with the lie. That had to be it. Mandin followed her gut feeling. "You do have her, don't you?" she said quietly.

Toola looked away and tut-tutted. "And if I do, what does it have to do with you? You are nothing but a worn-out servant. Good for nothing. If I put you out in the bar, the clientele are more likely to use you as a spittoon than a whore. What does it feel like to be too old and ugly and useless to sell yourself?"

Mandin swayed. In among the insult was an admission of guilt. Toola would have killed her outright if she was no use to her. Mandin had some value, either because Toola wanted to hurt her more, exact further revenge for her perceived betrayal, or because she was useful in some way that was beyond Mandin's limited imaginings. Perhaps that sexual encounter, the game of seduction and surrender, had been more than just a conquest for this hardened brothel madam. Could Mandin risk assuming that Toola had a softer side? No. Toola was more complex than that. She thrived on demanding devotion and having power over others. A desperate cry launching from her lips, Mandin threw herself dramatically to the floor.

"Please, Toola, I swear to serve you without question. Please let me see her."

Toola stood and walked around Mandin, who lay prostrate on the ground. She nudged Mandin in the ribs with her toes. "Now you are trying to play me. I can taste your lack of sincerity. Aren't you loyal to Danton, his unpaid whore? Did you not throw your affair with him in my face?"

Mandin pushed herself into a kneeling position and turned her head to the side to meet Toola's regard face on. There in the space of a heartbeat she concocted the biggest set of lies to pass her lips in her life. "He abandoned me. He left me here with you, knowing what you are capable of. When he did come back he ran at the first sign of trouble. I owe him nothing. You have protected me, punished me as I deserved."

"Yes, I did. But you're only saying this for your own ends. Nothing you can say will convince me otherwise." Toola walked back to her table and sat on the edge of it. She studied her fingernails.

Mandin thought hard before responding. "My life was for my daughter, and now I give it to you."

"Really?" Toola smiled. "Prove it! Invoke the slave clause in your contract."

Mandin's heart thudded as she held her breath. This was the price she had to pay. She had to trust that she could save Eneit even if she had to surrender her freedom. "Yes. I invoke the slave clause willingly."

Mandin's response made Toola freeze for a minute, then, tapping her cheek thoughtfully with her forefinger, she asked, "You surrender all your rights in front of witnesses?"

"Yes," Mandin said again, her voice catching. She was allowing hope to rise in her chest. It was going to work.

"Very well. Linel, bring Mandin's contract here."

Linel slid open a drawer and pulled out the document. The contract was stretched out on the table. Toola pointed to where Mandin had to request the surrender of her rights as an employee. Linel signed as witness and then rolled the document up.

Mandin straightened up. Toola's slap sent her reeling. Mandin rubbed her cheek.

"You deserved that."

Toola grinned but it wasn't a pretty sight. "I'll let you see Eneit. In fact, I was going to make sure that you did, whether you wanted to or not, as tonight is her big night, her pivotal moment. Eneit is to be auctioned, as my best clients will vie to take her virginity. By morning she'll be a used commodity, but still merchandisable enough to make a reasonable return on my investment, you understand." Toola watched her, waiting for some reaction. Mandin was breathing hard but not for the reason Toola expected. It was not rage but hope that made her heart sing. All she could think of was that it wasn't too late. She hadn't failed but succeeded. Toola kept on talking, reveling in her supposed moment of victory.

"I didn't want you to miss that moment when Eneit gives up the fateful cry as she is breached. I wanted to feel the moment when you realized the futility of your actions. Yes, your ineptitude is laughable. You stumbled through each incompetent attempt to rescue the most precious thing in the world and failed."

Mandin could not control her intake of breath, but it was hope, excitement and vexation combined. Tears rolled down her cheeks and she sniffed noisily.

Toola smiled. "Yes, it is true. The rebels did not rape her. Four girls made it to Sartell unscathed. Eneit is the prize, though. Ripe for plucking, provided the price is right."

Mandin closed her eyes, silently offering up gratitude. She had pledged her life for her daughter's and she knew now that it would end soon. That much was inevitable. "Thank you," she said, unashamed, as she sobbed.

To Linel Toola said, "Get her out of here. Dress her in something appropriate for an old whore."

A few hours later, Mandin was in a carriage with Toola and her loyal bodyguard, heading to the madam's private residence. Mandin kept her eyes down as ordered and followed the others out of the carriage to the front door. Mandin felt ridiculous in the clothes she was wearing, particularly as she was out in public. Of course the clothes were meant to humiliate her, particularly in front of Eneit. Mandin's breasts were pushed up high and spilled out of a gaudy red bodice, exposing her nipples. The skirt she wore hung low under her stomach, emphasizing her plumpness. The skirt was made of strips of fabric that left her buttocks exposed as she walked. To Mandin's relief, there were no passers-by when they stepped up to Toola's door.

Linel's slack-faced stare disconcerted her, though. It reminded her of his rutting and the total lack of expression that accompanied it. When he had lashed her, the vacant look was the same. The only emotion he ever exhibited was that of devotion toward Toola. One thing Mandin had to do before she died was rid the world of Linel.

Once inside the house, Toola descended a narrow, dark staircase, which led to a disguised door. Mandin and then Linel followed. Toola operated a panel and the door slid sideways. Behind it was the basement room. Mandin's excitement rose. *Please let this be real, let her be here. Let this not be another of Toola's games.* Linel slunk close behind, never straying far from Mandin. In the enclosed space she could smell him, the underlying reek of disease that had filled her nostrils more than once. Would she ever be rid of the memory?

As the flicker of lamplight reflected on the walls, Mandin had a terrible thought. What if one day Eneit was given to him? That thought made her quash her excitement and focus her mind on their predicament. There was no way she could attack Toola and make a run for it, not with her loyal bodyguard there. Any plan she made had to include eradicating him.

Mandin could not stop the fluttering in her stomach as Toola slowly entered the room that held her daughter. Hesitating on the threshold, Toola turned to Mandin and beckoned her to follow.

For a split second Mandin suspected a trap, but by then it didn't matter. She had gone too far to worry now. Once through, it took a moment for her to adjust to her surroundings. There was a large bed covered in purple coverings and in the middle of it was her daughter.

"Eneit?" Her voice caught in her throat. Toola stood back, letting her go to the bed.

Her daughter had started awake. "Ma?" Her eyes were wide and staring and it took a while for her to focus.

"Yes, dearest. It is me. May I hold you?" Mandin sat on the bed, hesitant and uncertain. What things had her child seen? What horrors and cruelties? The girl was as naked as the day she was born, scented and oiled like the best of the girls in Toola's house. Mandin's clothing also confused the girl. Mandin could see the girl struggle to recognize her.

"Oh, Ma," Eneit said as she buried herself in Mandin's embrace. Sobs racked them both as Mandin smoothed her daughter's hair. Then, grasping Eneit's face, she scrutinized her closely. Eneit was thinner than she remembered but looked older, especially around the eyes.

Then an unwelcome voice intruded. "Enough of that crying. You both have important things to attend to."

Eneit sniffed and wiped her eyes with the backs of her hands. The girl looked between Mandin and Toola, confusion crinkling her forehead. "Er...yes, Mother," she replied to Toola. Mandin froze and tried to hide the hurt. If she didn't succeed she would lose her daughter to this woman. Somehow she had to save her daughter from her fate.

Toola sat on the bed beside them. "Tell her, Mandin. Tell her what you are."

Mandin swallowed, tried to mentally signal to Eneit. Clutching the bedcover tight she spoke. "I am Toola's slave and one of her lowliest whores. I belong to her. I am no longer...no longer free."

Eneit recoiled and gave a small cry. "No." She looked between them again, lips trembling.

Toola smiled and reached out to caress Eneit's cheek lovingly. "You will be an obedient child, yes?"

Eneit gawped at her and then wiped at her tears with the backs of her hands.

"Good girl. Don't cry. I will make sure you are rewarded. Make me happy and I will be nice to Mandin."

Eneit shared a look with her mother before turning back to Toola.

"Give Mother a kiss, Eneit."

Eneit crawled over to Toola. There she lifted her face to the woman and kissed her full on the lips. Toola smiled and smoothed Eneit's hair away from her forehead. "Good, precious girl. Go with my slave here and get dressed."

Eneit frowned. Mandin slid off the bed. She hoped her eyes would tell the story her voice could not. "Come, Eneit."

"Then you..." She shook her head and then slid off the bed. "I'm ready."

Mandin was ready to cry all over again. Her daughter did not have to speak; her expression showed quite clearly that hope had been replaced with resignation. Yet Mandin could not afford to reveal her plans, not with her captors in the room.

Toola stood too and addressed Mandin. "Take her to the dressing room and prepare her. I have laid out the clothes she is to wear. It is only my tender heart that allows you to have this one last moment together."

"Thank you, Mother," Eneit replied, leading Mandin by the hand to the curtained alcove.

"Good child. You will understand in time that it is not good for business to have you together."

Mandin looked back, a question in her expression.

Toola relaxed back into a cushioned chair, Linel standing ramrod straight behind her. She waved her hand, apparently talking to herself. "Pampering the child, interfering with my orders..."

"I would not," Mandin protested, dropping the curtain behind her, removing them both from Toola's sight. There she hugged Eneit to her again. She heard movement and released her daughter. A shadow was visible through the curtains. Toola's voice whispered, "Tonight, you will give the order at Eneit's inauguration into her profession. You will witness all that transpires. If she doesn't do as she is told, you will suffer for it, do you understand?"

Mandin gulped, sparing Eneit a glance. "Yes, mistress. I thank you."

"Carry on."

Alone together, Mandin wept as she dressed her daughter in a child's party dress. No underwear was provided. The short white dress was embroidered with flowers and had a large bright red bow around the waist. Eneit hardly spoke to her, just stared at her with an expression of disgust.

"I am so happy to find you at last," Mandin said softly as she smoothed the folds of the dress and eased Eneit's foot into one of the sandals provided.

Eneit sat on a stool so she could put on the other one.

"Will you not talk to me?" Mandin asked in hushed tones, sparing a glance over her shoulder to the curtain. Toola was not listening in as far as she could tell. She was talking to Linel and pacing around the room.

Eneit's expression mirrored her own. "I thought you came to save me. I thought you came to take me away," she whispered in a tear-laden voice.

"I did come to save you. I've given everything to save you."

"But you failed," Eneit said and covered her mouth to stifle a sob. After she controlled herself, she continued. "Do you think I don't know what I am to do tonight? The other girl told me. Don't you know what that woman does to girls like me?" Eneit grasped her by the shoulder and leaned in close to her ear. "She has been training me as a whore." Eneit hissed the last at her, blaming her.

"I know, darling. I tried, but she is very cunning. I'll get you out of here. I promise you."

"How? You are helping prepare me. That is what it will be. And I will have to let all them have me for whatever they are willing to pay without a word or protest, unless they pay to hear me scream. Even then I may only do so if Toola commands it. Lexia told me about the punishments—told me in great detail about that man out there with her."

"I'm so sorry. I am trying. Please try to be patient."

"Patient? You don't know what those rebels did, Ma. How they kept us in line." Eneit put her hand to her mouth to stop herself from talking.

A tear trickled down Mandin's cheek but she did not wipe it away. Her hands were clasped in Eneit's as the story was forced out. Mandin wished with her life's blood she could save her daughter right then.

Dropping her hand, Eneit continued. "One by one they had at the others. I saw six girls beaten and cut and the men on top of them... Six. All of them girls I have known my whole life." Her tears were falling freely now. Mandin could barely breathe. She had imagined the horrors but now she would hear them from her own child's lips.

"They forced us to watch them. Then we all had to promise to be good. One night, they said it was my turn. I begged them not to take me so they asked me to choose one of my friends—a substitute. I chose, Ma. I chose someone else to take my place. I watched them rape and then kill her. Do you know what that makes me? Do you?"

"Hush, now. You survived. You will go home. You will be safe."

"Safe? Home? Ma, there is no place I can call home now. I can never be safe again. I will always remember. Always remember that it should have been me. Maybe this is what I deserve..."

Another slave brushed the curtain aside. Mandin started. She hadn't realized there was someone else there. Of course, Toola would not have left Eneit alone. "The mistress says to hurry. She wants you ready to leave in two minutes and she wants to inspect the girl before you leave."

Mandin shared a look with the other slave. "Yes. We are ready." Turning back to Eneit she handed her a cool, damp cloth. "Come now, wipe your eyes. You don't want them bloodshot."

"Let them be bloodshot. It won't make any difference."

When she had finishing brushing out Eneit's hair, there was nothing else to delay them. Her makeup was minimal as Toola's plan was to make Eneit appear younger than her years. The loss of weight only added to the illusion of youth.

A kind of calm appeared to settle over Eneit as she preceded Mandin out of the dressing room. Toola turned as they entered, her smile as wide as Mandin had ever seen it.

Mandin was full of cold, hard rage. Linel stepped up close to her, blocking her view as Toola drew Eneit out of the door. Her eyes flicked upward to his. "Time to go, I believe." Linel allowed her to pass. For a moment Mandin thought he'd been ordered to keep her there, contrary to Toola's threat. She let out a breath when she was free to follow.

Chapter Twelve

A LIFE RETURNED

The cool air brushed against Laidan's skin. Her eyes opened but she didn't comprehend where she was. She was naked and alone. There was a persistent hissing sound nearby and a transparent flap above her head. Her gaze flicked around the room, noting that it was large with shadows in the corners. Who was she? Where was she? Why was she here? All these questions bombarded her, frightened her, because she couldn't remember anything. Whimpers escaped her and she muffled them with a fist. *Must keep quiet.*

Tightening herself into a ball, she rolled onto her side, shutting her eyes because she was not willing to experience what she was seeing and feeling. After a few deep breaths, the panic subsided and she was prepared to open her eyes again and look out at the world. It was then she noticed the clothing in a pile on the edge of the tray she was lying on. Reaching for them, an image of a beast leaped into her mind. What was that? The stuff of nightmare. She pushed the image away. She didn't want to know. The image evoked fear, pain, loathing. She had to hide from it. Had to pretend it wasn't there. Whatever it was.

Intermittent sobs racked her as she dragged the robes over her head. The fear froze her and she dared not think upon the cause. How long she sat there partially dressed and confused, she didn't know, but soon she heard someone approach.

Peering out through the disarray of her clothes she saw a tall man with long white hair and strange silver eyes coming toward her. He seemed familiar but she didn't want to remember who he was. That memory was bound up with other, more troublesome memories. Memories where she was consumed and no longer existed.

Dumbly she sat there as he spoke to her, his tone quiet and gentle. She didn't want to see, didn't want to hear or understand the words. Very carefully, he walked up to her in gentle strides that barely disturbed the air, then he drew the robe from her hands and finished dressing her with a minimum of fuss, guiding her arms through the sleeves, fastening her tunic around her waist and covering her shoulders with the outer robe. Then he put the slippers on her feet and softly combed out her hair. All the while he exuded safety and calm. Safe was important. Safe was good. Laidan needed safe.

When he had finished caring for her, she buried her face in his robe, clinging to him as if letting go would be the end of her. The man let her hold him and tenderly stroked her hair. It was so good to be held, so good to feel safe. The image of a man with scales and a tail assailed her for an instant. She clung to the man, whimpering as she did so, fighting off that terrible image, that terrible nightmare. Then when her tears lessened, he put his arms underneath her knees and around her shoulders and lifted her from the tray. He carried her a short way and placed her on a bed, in a quiet, darkened room, talking to her softly, soothing her with words she really didn't understand, and then she closed her eyes and slept.

♋♋♋♋

The sound of screaming woke Laidan. Her throat was raw, and her ears rang with sound. Panting loudly, she looked about her in the dim light. She was in a small room. Someone was there. At first she panicked, and then that soothing voice came from the shadows and she relaxed. The man had a name. He called himself Nils.

Warm soup was pressed against her lips, spilling into her mouth, and she swallowed. The heated liquid soothed her throat like his words did her mind. Then he bid her to take water and she drank, and some of it spilled down her chin and onto her robe. She lay back down, wondering who had been screaming, and darkness closed over her once again.

Laidan lost track of how many days she passed in this way in that dark tunnel of confusion. Yet Nils was always with her, always talking in that low, calm voice. Now she could understand the words, now she could talk to him. The screaming had stopped after a while. Nils had told her it was she who had screamed, but she couldn't remember the dreams or why she had yelled in terror. She remembered the man who filled her with fear, but not the details of why and what.

Nils began to ask her questions. Questions about her mother, where she was born and about Thurdon, too. She could remember the answers to these questions easily. The memories appeared to be bright and happy, even the ones where she'd said goodbye to her mother.

"Do you know where that was, Laidan? Where did Thurdon say goodbye to your mother?"

"I remember snow and the ranges behind us. That is all."

"Do you remember what your mother looked like?"

"Not too well. Her hair was drab—dirty, I expect. She was tall and thin. She sold me to Thurdon. Well, I think she did. I remember him giving her money. I remember he was happy to have me finally. He said I was special."

"You are, Laidan. You are special. You are precious to me."

"Really? Where am I? Am I meant to be here?"

"You are with me, in a special place and, yes, you are meant to be here. Sleep now."

Laidan lay down and closed her eyes. She wasn't tired so she pretended to sleep. She wanted to know if he left the room. She decided she might even follow him, if he did. Just as she suspected, as she slowed her breathing to feign sleep, Nils got up from his chair and slipped out the door. A shaft of light broke into the room, making her squint.

After waiting for a few moments, she swung her legs off the bed and edged toward the door. Her legs were weak and her knees unsteady. Using the doorjamb to support herself, she peered out through the crack. The brightness made her eyes water, and for a few minutes she blinked and rubbed the tears away. Why was her room so dark, when it was so bright outside? There were paintings on the walls and carvings on the ceiling. The place was vaguely familiar. She had been here before. There was no sign of Nils so she slid through the doorway, stumbling at first, and then went in search of him. He could not have gone too far.

But Nils was not in the immediate vicinity. The room she was in was off a large hall with a round cup-like object at its center, which threw flame into the air. It was important, she thought, because it dominated the whole room. Out through a wide archway she followed a wide road. There was something in the back of her mind, niggling at her, something she should know about this place. It was there but she couldn't grasp the memory.

On reaching some balconies she stopped and stared. The walk had fatigued her and she rested against the balustrade, staring out over a lake with dark waters lapping the shore. Her attention was drawn upward to the roof. She was in a huge cavern. Light glowed from growths hanging from ceilings and when she turned she saw that the city was alight with lamps throwing off warm light.

The stairs leading from the balcony looked familiar, so she followed them. Wondering why she seemed to recognize this path, she kept on going up toward a particular grouping of houses. The closer she got, the faster her pace. When she reached the entranceway she broke into a run. She heard a voice calling her and thought it might be Nils, and then she plowed into someone, someone large and brown. Someone who grunted and then called her name loudly.

She fell backward and landed on her rear. Shaking her head, she opened her eyes and saw him. Saw him and screamed.

"Laidan! Hush! 'Tis all right. 'Tis only me."

Terror assailed Laidan and she screamed louder.

"Wing dust! Do not make such a fuss. You are safe."

Laidan beat at him, fought him.

"No, do not hit me, do not fight me," the pleading voice said. It sounded clogged with tears. Laidan understood tears. "I will not hurt you, Laidan!" The voice grew hoarse. She ceased hitting him and studied his face. Moisture trails glistened on his cheeks in the reflected light. "Please," he said. "You are breaking my heart."

Panic, nameless and strong, seized her. Frenzied, she continued to scream and thrash about until she heard Nils through the haze of her hysteria. He was coming for her, coming to make her safe. Then she recognized the sobbing and whimpering and knew it for her own voice, her own cries. All that screaming and crying over the days and nights in the dark tunnel of confusion had been her. Nils had spoken true.

Fragmented memories came crashing back, splintering her mind. A monster had hurt her, had tried to take something from her while he split her in two. Did that happen? Was it a dream? A nightmare? It was hard to decide. There had been violation, pain, absolute terror, and knowing she was going to die. It couldn't be real. Again she screamed, and then there was nothing, just a black wall falling down upon her head.

When she awoke this time, she was back in the room and Nils was there, holding her hand. She wondered whether it had been a dream, the walk through the city, the encountering of the one who had hurt her. Nils questioned her about her walk through the city and what she remembered. He asked her about the man she'd met, and then she told him what he had done. He had tried to destroy her, tear her apart. She did not want to see him again. He must be sent away. Nils had to get rid of him, had to, or she would never leave that room again.

Nils patted on the head. "It was not he. Garan saved you, carried you away from the one who hurt you. We will talk more of this tomorrow. More of what happened will become clearer."

"No. I'm telling you he did it. He hurt me. You must make him go away."

"And I am telling you, child, that it was another. But your memories are tangled. The harm to you was great. I do not know if you will ever remember what truly transpired and why. Sleep now. Stay in this room. I will return quickly. I will not leave you alone for long."

Laidan drifted off. Her dreams were vivid and full of blood. She woke often, and true to his word Nils was there, soothing her through it all. She loved him. Loved Nils and no other. He thought she was special. He cared for her. That was true and right. He was hers now and she was his.

༄༄༄༄

"I want to see her, Nils," Garan said for the tenth time.

Nils held him back. "You cannot see her now. Her memories are not complete. I warned you this might happen."

"You do not know what her screams did to me, Nils." He made a ripping gesture over his heart. Nils understood the feeling. Garan paced away and turned back again. "She reacted as if I was the Inspector, as if I had been the one to rip her apart."

Nils regarded him and then looked to the floor. He could not hurt Garan, not with his open face, his true heart. How could he confess to the boy what Laidan thought she remembered? While his strange encounter with the machine had left him near senseless, he was all to rights the next morning. Now the boy had to take another blow, also unearned.

"That is the issue, isn't it? She thinks I did it."

Nils did not want to answer. He found Laidan's twisted memories bitter too. He did not want to give them voice. "It is very close to what she remembers, Garan. Give her time and her memories will disentangle, and if that does not occur I can help her remember correctly. You must leave her to my care."

"No. Only by being with me, seeing me and knowing me again will she realize it wasn't me. Surely you can see that."

Salinda walked up and acknowledged Garan with a tilt of her head and listened to their conversation.

"I cannot allow it," Nils said, his attention shifting between them. "Not now. She is too fragile. We could risk losing what is left of her mind."

"Nils is right, Garan," Salinda said. "You must wait. There are other things we need to do."

Garan swung around to face Salinda. "Like what? Nils will not let us explore that machine until he finds out more about it, but he is tied up with Laidan and he cannot do that. You said there was little time. I feel that too."

"I know. I had hoped we would leave before this. I had packed some provisions for us. We will return to the observatory tomorrow. We will leave Nils and Laidan here for the moment."

Nils agreed, his silver eyes glistening in the light.

Garan frowned, looking between them both. "I thought you could not live without each other."

"I can bear it alone for a while," Nils replied. "Laidan is here. Her care is very time-consuming. But will you do me a favor while you are there?"

"What is that?" Garan asked.

"Look for a certain book for me in the ruins of the first observatory, if you are able. There must be some writings there from my grandsire.

Salinda will be able to show you the name and how it is written."

Garan was standing tall, anger filling out his frame. He wanted to stay with Laidan and yet he knew his duty lay elsewhere.

Salinda took the youth's hand and kissed it. "It will be well, Garan. You must trust Nils and leave Laidan to his care. You must understand that things cannot be what they once were between you. She is not the same as she was. Her brain was damaged and not all has been restored. You are not the same as you were either. Too much has happened to you, too. If your love is truly meant to be then it will be so in the fullness of time. You have to trust that. Right now, we need you—need you focused. We have to find out how the observatory is faring and how well they are coping with that asteroid."

Garan agreed reluctantly with a slow up and down movement of his head and chewed his lips. Compassion for the boy imbued Nils. He found it quite strange that he should feel such emotion. He liked Garan immensely; indeed, for a non-Hiem he was exceptional. Nils vowed to himself to thoroughly research that machine before they met again. Garan being able to open the door and enliven the machine had thrown Nils. He was caught between curiosity and fear. What if they unleashed something that destroyed Barrahiem? It would go against everything he stood for. That is why he wanted the book. It was the missing link. Trell had something to do with Moonfall and he had to have written about it.

"We will come back and Nils will know more about the machine," Salinda said. "It's a matter of priorities."

"There are so many artifacts down there in the vaults it is hard to distinguish what is attracting me. It could have been the machine I touched, but it might be another. We will have to try again. But you are right. The observatory is important right now. But I am coming back, and then I do want to see her, talk to her. I cannot live with the thought that she believes I harmed her, even though the fault of it is mine."

"Garan, don't," Salinda said as Garan slunk away to his abode, all his hurt radiating from his hunched shoulders.

A sigh escaped Salinda as she watched the lad walk away, then she stepped closer to Nils. He had hardly seen her since the girl had emerged from the healing tray. The task of tending the girl had taken nearly all his attention. He could not allow Laidan to wander through the city again, as it had set them back many days. As he tracked the flow of Salinda's long dark hair, he realized that they had not shared a bed since before Laidan's ordeal, and now he was allowing his mate to leave him and the city once again.

They stood close together, not touching but sharing silence. The baby inside her was growing steadily now. He wondered how long it would be before it was born. His feelings for the child were mixed. But finding that Laidan had Hiem blood had led him to hope that his child would not be alone in the world.

"I will return to Laidan now. And then if I can slip away I will come to you one last time before you leave."

Salinda smiled sadly. "Thank you for caring for her, Nils. You are doing more than I would find myself doing."

Nils traced the curve of Salinda's cheek with his forefinger. "I feel for her...her memories are incorrect about the attack. I can only hope for Garan's sake that she remembers it correctly in time. I tell her he did not do those things to her but she does not believe it. Yet the memories of her earlier years appear whole. More recent memories are patchy."

"Has she mentioned Brill?"

"No. Not once."

"You said that her head was bleeding when you put her in the tray; perhaps there was more damage than we expected. Might that not have changed her personality too?"

"I think so, yes. Her brain was injured, and along with it her mind. The healing tray heals the body...."

"But not the mind. So you said. It cannot erase the trauma. Does that mean people with head injuries were not healed by your people?"

"I am not an authority on the healing arts. I believe the clan responsible for healing would have assessed them and weighed up the options. It also depended on how important the person's memory was to their quality of life. In this case, I think Laidan will be able to function within a normally acceptable range."

"Oh, Nils. I don't think it is as straightforward as that. The whole situation is emotionally loaded for all of us. Have a care. She is vulnerable at present and ready to attach herself to you as her protector. Things could become awkward."

Nils hesitated before letting her go. "I am being careful and patient, much more so than I was with you when you first left the healing tray."

"I know you are being patient, Nils. But my mind was whole where hers appears fractured. I don't think I could have survived what she went through. I'll wait for you tonight." With that, she turned away and headed to their abode. Nils tried not to think about her leaving, and how desolate he would feel. Laidan was company, but she was not his mate. He would do his best to lie with Salinda before she left. Perhaps that would suffice for a time.

Part 2

Dragon wine teases the palate and kindles the heart

Chapter Thirteen

A WAY OUT

After Danton's capture, Brill ran through the back streets of Sartell, stopping first to alert Squab so she could go to ground immediately and direct the others to the same.

Brill was still reeling from the ambush and the loss of Danton. It had happened so quickly, there was nothing he could do. Danton had ordered him to watch his back in case men invaded the brothel in search of him, not realizing that the trap was inside. When they had carried Danton's inert form out of the brothel, surrounded by well-trained and uniformed guards, Brill knew it was futile to try anything. Hidden by the Hiem shroud, he had fled. He knew he had to warn the others and then decide his next steps.

Squab had reacted to the news calmly. She had been expecting Toola's betrayal for a long time and her plans to travel north to seek out the Eternity project were well advanced. Supplies were being stockpiled, and rebels had already been deployed to set up the advance camp. Squab had stayed behind waiting for word from Danton. Brill had to admire the canny rebel woman. He had never warmed to her but he respected her skill and her loyalty to Danton. The last thing she said before leaving the inn was, "Do your best for Danton."

Brill had nodded, knowing there was little hope. Danton had looked lifeless when they had taken him. They had known he was coming. There was no other way to see it, and Brill had only escaped because Danton had sacrificed himself and made Brill stay outside. Danton had sprung the trap for Mandin's sake. Brill had to ensure that the rebel leader's sacrifice was not for nothing. He would go back for Mandin.

Brill took a wrong turn after leaving Squab and found himself in a lane that sloped downward. Ahead the walkway descended into a round tunnel. As he continued along he saw that the tunnel was formed from the remains of an earlier part of the city. There was a junction, and the tunnel divided into two paths. One appeared to be heading in the direction of Toola's brothel, so he followed it.

The underground walkway terminated in a dead end. Hanging over the side of it was a rope ladder and various notches carved into the walls, which could serve as foot and handholds. In this section were stagnant pools of water and piles of rotting garbage. Climbing back up to street level, he found that houses backed onto this section of the lane. He skirted a broken wooden fence and found himself on the street. Ahead he recognized the corner where the rear of the brothel was situated.

Checking his surroundings so that he could find his way back, Brill walked cautiously along the road. As he passed the alley where the brothel was located, he saw there were now police guards swarming all over it. It was still too dangerous to enter.

Brill slunk back into the shadows and went exploring in the alleyways for another way around. Again he came upon an underground walkway, a kind of abandoned sewer tunnel that had been repurposed for foot traffic. In that section of the walkway parts of the older sewer construction were exposed and met with the normal pavement. Brill ran his hands along the grainy sandstone of the walls, looking at the cut of the blocks that comprised them. It looked very old to his eyes. Maybe it wasn't a sewer after all. It reminded him of the rock in the cave where they had found that first Way. Biting his lip, he inspected it closely. A Hiem Way Gate was a means of escape. If only there was one.

If this section was part of the original city, he mused, then traces of the pre-Shatterwing world could exist. Surely if there were Ways in the middle of nowhere, there could be one here in Sartell, and maybe even more than one. He just had to look for the signs.

Brill ran down the left-hand pathway that led back to the original tunnel, which also gouged its way under a series of old derelict houses. A few people and stray cats lingered in broken alcoves as he moved further in, and less light penetrated the gloom.

When he had walked in the tunnel previously he had not noticed the people. Danton's capture had been on his mind and had made him less attentive. Now he walked carefully and held his dagger close, sensing danger. There was water in here, oozing along the floor of the tunnel and dampening his boots. It smelled stagnant, with overtones of sewage. In heavy rains, the tunnel would act as a culvert, he surmised, taking the stormwater to the river and the ocean. That idea helped him to orient himself.

The darker it became in the tunnel, the warier he was. Something soft tripped him. He felt around and found it was a leg. By the feel and smell of it, the owner was dead. This wasn't a thoroughfare, then. He continued, feeling along the walls with his hands. The floor sloped down sharply, hopefully leading to an older and earlier level of the city. Here light filtered down through overhead ventilation holes. Judging by the noise seeping in from above, he was under the pavement. The light flickered as people and vehicles moved past the vents. As Brill grew accustomed to the poor visibility, he made out engravings on the walls: swirls and patterns that were familiar. His excitement rose. He had guessed right: this was a part of the old city, the pre-Shatterwing city, where the Hiem had roamed freely.

He patted his way along the wall, looking for the shape of a Way Gate. Then his heart leaped. There, in the shadows, was the tell-tale pattern. From what he could make out, the gate was undamaged. Relief flooded through him. Here, at least, was a chance of escape. Making sure he knew exactly where it was, he made his way out of the tunnel and up into the streets again.

Taking a circuitous route, he found his way back to Toola's. The rear was relatively unguarded now. Kitchen refuse was spilled in bins along with piles of broken furniture. Two house security guards stood by the back door. Brill considered the situation for a while, lurking in the shadows. There was no way around it. He would have to kill them.

Brill slunk from shadow to shadow, trying to decide how to take them as he approached. He wasn't certain his shroud had enough charge left to keep him invisible, since he'd used it extensively when out with Danton and when he'd fled after Danton's capture. He would have to risk it, though, as his choices were few. The thought of his friend made him wince. The loss was difficult to bear. Maybe Toola would know where they had taken him. Perhaps there was still a chance to save his friend. But first, he had to get Mandin out and away. The only person he could think of to assist in saving Danton was Salinda, and possibly Nils.

The shroud hummed as he spread it over his shoulders and lowered the cowl over his face. Then, as quietly as he was able, he slipped behind the first guard. The knife slid into the man's ribs easily and Brill eased him gently to the ground. The other guard called out when he saw his counterpart fall. "Hey?"

The guard turned his head left and right, hesitating between running to his comrade's aid or retreating inside and raising the alarm. Brill had no patience with such indecision and he threw his dagger, catching the man in the throat. The fallen man could not scream but he made one hell of a noise as he went down by pushing over metal bins. Brill stole the first guard's knife and slipped into the bathhouse. Disengaging and removing the shroud, he folded it carefully into his knapsack. He hoped its power would stretch to one more excursion.

♋♋♋♋

Mandin was still trying to come up with a plan when the carriage pulled up at the brothel. Eneit was tense, her eyes wide as they rolled to a stop. The burden beasts grunted and shat. A slave raced over with a spade and a bucket to clean up the mess. Her daughter's intent expression made Mandin curse inwardly. The opportunity to save her daughter was disappearing. She had to act.

Toola walked through the doorway first and Linel ensured that Mandin and Eneit followed close behind. He looked up and down the street before acknowledging the security guards with a slight dip of his head. On the threshold Mandin hesitated, not sure where she was to take Eneit as it was too early for the party. Her gaze lingered on the stairway to the upper room. The room where her daughter's deflowering would take place. She closed her eyes, trying to block out the memories of the atrocities she had witnessed there. That could not happen to her daughter. Narin was dead. That was a good thing. One less monster on the surface of the world.

A sudden yell when Toola opened the door to her tea room snapped Mandin out of her reverie. Linel burst past her, knocking her sideways. Eneit cried out, frightened by the commotion.

Toola was shouting. "What are you doing here?"

Alert for an opportunity, Mandin entered the room, keeping Eneit close behind her. There was Brill, keeping Linel at bay with a nasty-looking dagger. Toola was rummaging around her kitchen, searching for a weapon of some kind, Mandin guessed. Mandin pressed down her joy as she had to keep it hidden. Brill was here and whether he was the distraction she needed or the help she wanted, she didn't care. It was her moment.

"Mistress?" Mandin asked in a feigned servile voice.

Toola whirled around. "Get out of here, you fool. Take Eneit upstairs. Can't you see I'm busy?"

Brill extended a hand to halt her departure. "No. Wait. We are leaving. Are you ready?"

Mandin's attention shifted to Toola and then back to Brill. "I can't go with you."

Brill gaped at her, then said, "What?"

Mandin stood there calmly. "I gave my word. I am her slave now. I serve none but her." She hated how confused she made Brill, but the opening wasn't there yet. The pieces had not fallen into place.

Brill's surprise turned to anger. He picked up a chair and threw it at Linel. Toola's bodyguard dodged it but then stumbled and fell heavily. Mandin backed up, keeping Eneit behind her. A knife flew through the air, twanging against the wall near Mandin. Toola had thrown it and missed Brill. The boy jerked around, gaping at the near miss then back at Toola with a savage frown. Her aim had been very close. All Mandin had to do was grab the knife. Her chance had come. Darting forward, Mandin wrenched the large kitchen knife out of the wall.

"Brill!" she shouted at the young rebel. "Take Eneit with you. I'll cover for you."

Brill came forward, kicking Linel in the gut as he struggled to his feet. Toola screamed incoherently, for guards, for anyone. Brill headed for the door and Mandin pushed Eneit to him. "Take her, please!"

"Mandin. Come too." Brill grabbed her by the wrist. She was tempted, but she couldn't risk it. She had to stay, had to finish Linel and maybe Toola so her daughter could live free. "No, Brill. This is my time. Take my daughter and go."

Brill bit his lip, shook his head.

Linel was on his feet, shaking his head as if to clear it. "Hurry! Go before it's too late."

Brill hesitated only a moment. Then, sensing the danger, he wrenched open the door just as Linel charged. Mandin stepped in front of him, knife clenched in her hand and braced against her body. It slid in so easily. Linel's blood smelled as bad as he did, but to Mandin it could not have smelled sweeter. His hands grabbed her shoulders and his full weight made her knees buckle. Mandin was pulled to the floor.

"No!" Toola screeched, her fists clenched. "You'll ruin me, you stupid bitch. I have a full house tonight."

Mandin still grappled with Linel, trying to free her arms and legs. Blood covered her exposed breasts and hands. The knife slipped from her fingers. Turning her head, she saw Brill glance over his shoulder as he passed over the threshold to the tea room. "Bad luck, whore mistress," Brill said. "I'm taking the girl with me."

Eneit was with him, her eyes wide with fear. "He will care for you, sweet," Mandin said softly. "Go with him. Be a good girl."

Eneit gaped at her. "Ma! Come now, Ma." Tears flowed and she began to sob quietly.

Mandin shook her head. "I can't. Go now. Run. Don't look back."

Brill shut the door, and Eneit was gone.

☾☾☾☾

Toola ran at the closed door, yelling, "You won't get far. I'll kill you!"

Mandin threw herself in Toola's way, toppling the woman to the floor. There they rolled, each trying to get a grip on the knife sticking out of Linel's body. Mandin's hands were slick with blood and she missed the hilt.

Toola and Mandin grappled, rolling back and forth. They hit the table and teapots smashed to the floor beside them. Toola clawed at Mandin's face, ripped at her hair. Mandin didn't let it register. This was for Eneit. This was for her daughter's life. Toola didn't understand that. Mandin's life didn't matter anymore. She gave it freely for her daughter. She'd take Toola with her if she could.

Toola yelled for the guards. They both listened, still struggling with each other. The guards never came running. Then their eyes fell upon Linel, and his body jerked before his life light disappeared from his eyes. Toola began to scream in a demented fashion. "No! Don't leave me."

She thrust Mandin from her savagely and crawled to Linel, the struggle for the knife forgotten. Mandin could hardly credit it. The madam had loved her lapdog after all.

While Toola was distracted by her grief, Mandin crawled away. The door was so close. Freedom beckoned. Perhaps she could catch Eneit and Brill after all. Then Toola moved and Mandin grunted as the other woman kicked her in the ribs. Mandin rolled, lifting her folded arms protectively over her head.

Crazed, Toola kicked and kicked. "Fucking bitch! You have ruined me. I'm dead. Fuck you!" Mindlessly, Toola shrieked and kicked. No one came to investigate.

Mandin had no voice left to scream; her body was seized up with pain. She rolled onto her stomach and caught a glimpse of the other woman's mad expression. In Toola's hand, a long carving knife glinted with reflected light. Mandin lurched to her feet, using the wall to support herself. The door was so close now.

"You bitch. You fucking bitch!" Toola growled as she brought the knife down. Mandin was aware of voices behind her as Toola struck. The door was open. So close. Strange that she should notice that the staff of the brothel had come at last. Too late to be of use. The knife fell again and thumped into her as her knees folded and she slumped to the floor.

Hovering above her, Toola's red-painted mouth clenched in a hard line. With both hands she brought the knife down again. A fork of pain pierced Mandin's body and blood spilled into her mouth. It was over. Relief made her smile, and the blood seeped out onto her chin. Her only regret was that she hadn't managed to kill Toola.

As the blood welled up from her throat, one word bubbled up to spill out from between her lips—Eneit. Toola's frustrated scream filled her ears as the world darkened around her.

Chapter Fourteen

LOST THINGS

For all that Garan had yearned to return to Trithorn Peak, he had never thought he would do so with such a heavy heart. His mixed feelings did not help the cadre adjust to the change in its surroundings. If anything, it retreated from his conscious mind as if to avoid the maelstrom of emotions born of Garan's guilt. The city of the long-dead Hiem gave the cadre comfort. Garan tensed, wondering how the cadre's presence inside of him would affect his own perceptions of the observatory.

If not for Salinda he did not think he would have the heart to leave Laidan behind at all. Salinda was obviously comfortable about it, though, and exuded so much confidence that Garan had to accept the situation. Salinda was the leader, the one he admired, particularly where the cadre was concerned. She trusted the Hiem to do the right thing. As Nils's mate she had superior knowledge. Garan was less certain, less willing to leave one he held so dear behind, leave her to the unknown.

The cadre had remained mute on the subject of Laidan since it had revealed her seduction of Brill, and was subdued after the tumult caused by Garan's reaction to the news. Perhaps it was the strength of Garan's emotions that had tempered its power and presence. The minds must adjust to each other, he knew; his to the fused consciousness of the cadre, and it to him. The mental exercises Salinda put him through to improve his control of himself and the cadre were useful, comforting even. At the moment he did not need the glowing cadre, pulsing with thoughts and images, distracting him from his own inner torment. He knew he was yet to be tested. Salinda and he had failed in their attempt to vanquish Gercomo, so how were they going to defeat a rogue asteroid?

Both absorbed in their thoughts, he and Salinda passed through the Ways in silence. The substance of the Ways fascinated Garan, and often as he walked he felt that his ideas were being inhaled by it, or absorbed. Nils's ailment after rescuing Laidan had revealed a sinister side to the Ways. They were a boon, but also deadly if not traveled correctly. Not that Garan could attempt to traverse the "in-between", as Nils termed it. Nils said that it had taken his life force. Garan shook his head now at the thought, tempted to touch the seemingly hard surface of the gray wall around him. But he pulled back his hand. Having witnessed Salinda's concern for Nils, Garan knew that the Hiem had come close to giving his life to save Laidan—a terrible price, and one that Salinda would not have paid for the girl's sake if she had had a say.

As he looked out at the gray substance of the walls, he realized that he harbored some resentment about the change in the relationships between Laidan, Nils and himself. There was an empty space in him where Laidan once had been, where she may never be again.

The sound of Salinda's footfall made him look up and scrutinize his companion. Salinda, too, had a lot on her mind. With furrowed brow and unfocused stare, she walked distractedly. A slight zing in his own mind made him pay closer attention. There was a buzz about her, a hum in his own mind, and he supposed she was engaged with the cadre. Salinda was much more integrated with her cadre than he was. Then Salinda's expression changed and her step became swifter, more determined. She was present once again.

Garan chose to break the silence. "Brill and Danton have been gone for a while now. Do you ever wonder if they succeeded in finding the wine?"

Salinda slowed and let her gaze rest on him, eyelids half-lowered. "Yes. They should well and truly have reached Sartell by now. I fear for them. Sartell was always a dangerous place in my time. Now it could be much worse. I am hoping the observatory has word of them." She rested her hand on his forearm and they walked on.

"And if they do not? Is there anything we can do?"

Salinda lowered her head, slowing her pace once again. "I think our paths are separate for now. If Danton can achieve what he set out to do then he will let us know in his own way. Meanwhile, we must focus on the more important task. Even so, I would wish for some word from him."

"And the observatory?" Garan asked.

Salinda frowned. "Garan, there is little point in this idle speculation. We will know soon enough what has transpired in our absence. Why don't you practice that exercise I taught you yesterday? I can feel the cadre within you. You must do your best to engage with it, to learn how to temper it. Now that Gercomo can sense me, you need to make sure he has no opportunity to sense you. Understand? Meanwhile, I am working on a way to guard my thoughts from him. The cadre has shown me a barrier that I can build in my mind to shield it and me."

Garan considered this and scratched behind his right ear and tugged on the lobe. He did his best to imagine the cadre, which glowed in his mind like a campfire, as a tiny flicker of flame. By the time they reached the Way Gate exit he had made the fire smaller, but nowhere near as small as a candle flame.

Garan had to admit that the observatory, once his home, now held little appeal for him. Turnet was dead by Garan's own hand, the Master Elder was dead as well, and Thurdon would never again cross the threshold. Laidan was his only link to that past. The future was full of uncertainty. With this strange power he possessed he did not know where his path would lead. Salinda spoke of the end of the world, and of stopping it coming about. Brill spoke of a better human race. What did Garan desire? He hardly knew. Peace, life, love, everything? Was that too much to wish for?

It was dark outside the cave mouth when they exited. Salinda held a lamp. They had emerged during the night, but it mattered little as the observatory would be awake. His gaze roamed the sky, seeking a wayward meteorite or flash of purple light zeroing in on it, but the sky was cloudy so there was little to see. Once he'd thought that being a Skywatcher was the best thing in the world, the highest calling he could aspire to. Now, it was less so. Now he found himself in uncertain territory. He inhaled deeply of the outside air, but the aftertaste of rain was absent. He missed the rain.

Once inside the observatory, Salinda set about sending messages to the Master Elders so that she could catch up on how the new leadership had been working and the progress of the resettlement of the people of Vanden.

The rogue asteroid loomed large in Garan's thoughts, but he agreed with Salinda that the little details were just as important. Closer to the refectory, Garan smelled the enticing aroma of stew and fresh-baked bread. "Why not have a meal first?" he suggested to Salinda. "The elders will find you there easily enough. It has been a while since we ate."

"You go, Garan. I want to take a look around." Salinda smiled, patted his shoulder and then walked off in the direction of the schoolrooms. Garan shook his head. A meal would set him up nicely and Salinda would make her own assessment before talking to the elders. He had to hand it to her, she was very shrewd.

After a hearty meal and then a brief chat to Master Elder Wylie, Garan was left to himself. The observatory around him appeared the same as before, but he found it did not feel as it once had. It was rather disturbing, because his deepest wish was to feel its familiar walls and halls and particular rhythm, and that was denied him. Had he changed so much? Was it the cadre? Was it being in Barrahiem? He did not rightly know, yet he mourned that change.

He thought of Barrahiem and the machines there. The power that was within him. He thought of the crystals and went up to the gallery to where the Skywatchers scanned the heavens. There was idle chatter and a few nods to him. One of the elders waved a greeting and a kernel of joy and belonging grew within him. Garan shoved his hand into a basket of crystal shards to refill his pockets. It was then that he saw it. A crystal. It was large and faceted. It lay in the discard pile.

"Elder Newfen, do you mind if I take that crystal?" Garan asked, pointing.

The elder lifted his head. "Most certainly. It's too big for the scopes. I was going to send it back to be broken up, but if you want it for a souvenir, then by all means take it."

Garan darted over and picked it up. He'd need a dedicated bag for it. It was much too big for the scopes, but Garan had a feeling it might come in useful in the future. The Hiem machines seemed to run on power very similar to that of the crystals. Besides, such a large specimen was interesting. A part of home, a part of his own life that he could take back with him. He went in search of a bag and then came back to watch the Skywatchers at their work. It was familiar and strange at the same time. He was tempted to join them, to sight once again along the scope and focus his mind and voice on a crystal, but the night sky was quiet with not much activity at all. The basket boys talked softly among themselves and the Skywatchers joked with each other. With a sad twinge Garan knew he was dislocated from his former life. They did not need him anymore. Worst of all, he did not know if he belonged there anymore. With a farewell to his old friends and the elder, Garan left and headed down to the lower levels. As his sandals slapped the stone of the stairs, he recalled a conversation with Salinda where she had theorized that he could shoot down meteors without the scope and crystals.

Despite all he had done in the Hiem city repairing and energizing the lamps, Garan did not believe that. Even if he could generate power without the crystal, the scope focused the beam—or it had in the past. A meteor was so far away compared to where Gercomo had been when they had blasted him during the battle. Garan found he did not really know for sure. At least it didn't hurt to use the scope to focus the power.

Once again, like many nights in his past, he found himself walking the stone corridors of the observatory. Instead of making his way back to his room, which had been kept for him, he headed to the old Master Elder's room and adjoining small library. Titina and Elder Wylie did not use them and had set up in a larger meeting room, where they could sit together and share the work.

Garan sat there for a while, candlelight flickering over the desk and the piles of dusty books. Remembering Nils's request to search for Trell's writings, he flattened out the note with the title and the author name on it that Salinda had written out for him. After his first search revealed nothing new, he began to hunt in the not-so-obvious places.

On the third pass through the room he found two secret cupboards—one in the wall and one in the desk. Neither held the particular book Nils was searching for, but Garan put the books he did find in a sack ready to take back to Nils. No one at the observatory had the skill to read them, and they were very old. The cadre recognized the books, too, which was an even better reason to take them back to the Hiem. They belonged with the rest of the knowledge held in the archives. Perhaps these books were the ones that Thurdon had collected over the years and returned to the observatory.

Looking about the room, he ran his fingers along the desk and examined the dust. The Master Elder was well and truly gone. Garan shook his head, trying to fight the strange feeling of not belonging anymore. Perhaps a trip to the caves would invigorate his outlook. Peering through the window, he saw that it was nearly dawn. He had time to prepare.

Returning to his room, he recollected the conversation he'd had with Danton there—the one about taking life. *Danton*, he thought, *I miss your counsel*, and he closed the door behind him. After a quick trip to the refectory to pack some lunch things, he descended the path that would lead him to the caves.

Garan's mood began to lift, to find its old equilibrium, as he explored the familiar place and inhaled the musty smell. Finding a comfortable spot, he waited and watched while the faint shafts of light altered his surroundings. Shadows moved and changed. Light revealed details of rock formations and graduated color painted the scene in various shades. He had been there for a few hours, witnessing the scene around him grow and ebb, when he remembered the possibility of the ruins of the previous observatory. Nils had mentioned that Trell had visited it, or so the Master Elder had told him in his final moments. That particular cave was where the Way Gate was located. He checked his pocket for crystal shards and found he had plenty. The extra light would be useful as that cave was very dark. When he had traversed it in the past, there had been little time available to explore it. They were always on their way to or from the observatory.

Once past the section where the Way Gate was situated, Garan had to rely on the light emitting from the crystals to guide his path. His low hum reverberated around him as he ignited the power in the crystals, not to completely expend their energy but to excite illumination. The way ahead was difficult, with slabs of rock jutting up from the cave floor, some merging with the ceiling, leaving little space to squeeze through. Rocks rattled into crevices when dislodged by his sandals.

Assessing the climb ahead and planning his route took time, but it was necessary while he had light. About an hour further on, as he squeezed across a narrow shelf of rock, he saw what he thought were the remains of the observatory foundations. They appeared human-made in places, not natural formations or the result of the convulsing of the mountain range.

He set a crystal on a fallen pillar, putting enough power in it to keep it glowing, and moved off, pleased that it still threw out light even though he was no longer tending it. Then he drew out another and placed that too. By the time he had ignited eight crystals this way, he could make out the extent of the ruins and possible passageways through the rubble.

Garan tackled the ruin as he would an unexplored cave, checking methodically and charting the safest course, learning its particular peculiarities. There was little to be found in the way of artifacts in his first foray into the ruins. It was likely that any items near the outside would have been salvaged by the survivors, or those who came after.

When he thought this, the cadre nudged him forward, and he got the feeling that one of its previous owners had once traversed these passageways. To explore the cadre and garner this information would take some meditation and time. He ate lunch within the cocoon of light and planned a way in. Once he had it worked out and locked in memory, he brushed his hands free of crumbs and set to it. The first navigable way ended in a dead end. He was disappointed. It was getting late. He would have to do another assessment and start again. With a sigh, he decided to head back to the observatory and return the next day to continue the search.

☙☙☙☙☙

It was well after sunset when Garan found his way back to Trithorn Peak. He had managed to pass a whole day in the caves. He hoped Salinda had not needed him for anything. Belle moon was high and it bathed the pathway with mauve light. The sight lifted his spirit as it always did, and his chest filled with delight. At least he could still appreciate its beauty.

Salinda was in the refectory, apparently waiting for him. When her dark eyes met his, he smiled at the leap of relief in her eyes. Was she that worried about him and his mood?

"You went out," she commented after he sat down at her table with a tray of food. He found he liked the luxury of the observatory food. It was what he was used to. She pushed a large mug of mulled dragon wine, watered and spiced, in his direction. He took a long draft and smacked his lips together.

"Yes, I went into the caves and then decided to search for the ruins of the previous observatory."

"I take it you found nothing of importance."

"Not yet. But I think the cadre has been there before. I felt a nudge of some kind. What about your cadre?"

Salinda closed her eyes and pondered for a few moments. "Maybe… but I am not sure I wish to go climbing around the old ruins to satisfy the cadre, not unless it suggests there is some importance to it. Do you need help accessing the cadre? Is that why you have returned?"

Garan swallowed a mouthful of stew and dipped a piece of cacti bread into the gravy. "No. It was late and I was tired by the time I made some headway into the ruins. I will try accessing the cadre on my own first, before I go to sleep. I have to start sometime without assistance. If I have problems I will let you know. Do you think a former holder of the cadre was once at the old observatory itself, or the ruins?"

"Either is possible. The cadre goes back to before Ruel split, that much I glimpsed at its very core. It was strange, the impression I had of that time. It was almost as if there were distinct personalities at the same time, rather than a succession." She shook her head. "I think that is what I sensed, but I can't be sure."

"I have not delved into the cadre as you have, but I find I am curious that you think it was a group rather than a succession of carriers."

Salinda opened her mouth to reply but was interrupted by the entrance of Master Elders Titina and Wylie, and the rest of the elders.

"May we join you?" Wylie asked.

"Please do," Salinda replied with a genuine smile. She was obviously pleased with the observatory's progress. From listening in at the fringes while he finished his meal, Garan was able to garner that the harvest had been successfully brought in and divided amicably between Vanden and the observatory. Vanden's rebuilding was progressing and the refugees who had remained with the observatory were fitting in rather well, too. It was a tight fit, but some single men were very happy to have been selected by the Vanden women as husbands. Garan suppressed a touch of envy. Laidan would never choose him. But as the observatory's food stores were well stocked, Garan made a mental note to retrieve some cacti flour for bread-making back in Barrahiem. He had exhausted the supply he had originally brought with him.

Talk then turned to the training of children, the number that had been identified as being able to work the crystals, and those who would be trained for other tasks. As he swallowed the last of the bread and drank the last of the wine, Salinda raised the most important matter.

"The asteroid?" she asked, with a glance to him.

He leaned forward, catching a glimpse of some notes held tightly in Titina's hand. She laid them out on the table, smoothing them over and over again. Wylie said nothing, although his gaze was riveted on the notes. Garan could see they were calculations.

Titina faced them both. "We have three months and some ten days according to this. The skies have been quiet of late, but that is because of the previous close call. A large body swept the smaller debris clear. The next series of meteorite impacts will commence within about six weeks."

Garan thought that the next lot of activity would be the beginning of the end.

"And solutions?" Salinda asked gently.

Titina shook her head. "None so far. I have made plans. I hope you don't mind, but we have begun setting up refuges in some of the deeper caves. There is no certainty that they are safe, of course, but there is a chance that some will survive. We have stored some dried food there and laid down water. We need one more harvest to make it worthwhile, but I don't think we will get that." She ruffled the papers. "Not if these calculations are accurate."

"How will you decide who will enter the refuges?"

Titina shared a look with Wylie. "We thought the youngest and the fittest."

Salinda rubbed her chin. "Not the most learned among you?"

Titina reached over to clasp Elder Wylie's hand. They both shook their heads.

Garan sat back. "Not even a ballot to give everyone an equal chance?"

Titina met his gaze before answering. "What is the point of that? I am beyond child-bearing age. No future will spring from me. We will prepare instructions to assist those who may survive. We have to expect the worst, which is that none of us will make it."

Wylie said in his croaky voice, "We are agreed on this. We have to give our people some chance, even if the odds are very slim."

Salinda bobbed her head absently as she listened. Garan wondered what was on her mind. Was she thinking of Barrahiem? It was possible that they could weather the destruction there. It had, after all, survived Ruel's split, even if its people had not. Garan kept quiet. It was not his place to suggest it.

He was sad, though, that not even the greatest minds at the observatory had been able to think of a way to avert total annihilation. That put the burden squarely on Salinda and himself, now that he held the cadre, to find a solution. There had to be some means of averting the disaster.

Titina and Wylie stood up, and Wylie yawned loudly. "We must retire now. We have an early start tomorrow."

Titina paused. "I will have those items you asked for delivered to your room. Enjoy our hospitality and we are sorry our news is not better."

"Thank you both," Salinda replied, her smile faint. "You have done remarkable things together. It is not your fault that you have found no solution to the biggest problem of all. You must remember that the greatest minds of the pre-Shatterwing world could not prevent Ruel's demise. We are but a remnant of those people, with only a fraction of their knowledge, experience and technology."

Garan shook his head. If they had the technology, would they even recognize it? And if they did, would they know how to operate it?

ﭬﭬﭬﭬﭬ

In his room, Garan lay back on his bunk, trying to clear his mind of the night's conversation. He had to delve into the cadre, explore threads of experience that might lead him to Trell's writings in the old observatory. Had the Master Elder hidden it there? Had he actually seen it himself? He doubted the cadre would know. Garan waited for the mind chatter to ease off, then he called the cadre as Salinda had shown him. It pulsed and writhed in his mind, waiting for him to plunge in. It was almost eager, yet Garan hesitated.

Was he losing himself to this thing inside his head? Salinda was experienced with her own cadre, not this one. He did not want to change as she had. The power of her transformation echoed still. Yet he knew he was already changed by experiences. He was no longer the innocent lad who had left the observatory seeking to rescue a young girl. In the end, that was enough to convince him to enter the cadre. You could not avoid change. The world changed around you and you changed with it.

Inside the cadre his perceptions shifted. At once he was walking down a street. Then the image jerked to a passageway, dimly lit, clean. There was a window, a view to a mountain range and a sky with two moons. Garan's heartbeat thundered in his chest. He was at the old observatory. Immediately, he started searching for similarities in the surrounding mountains, but too much had changed during the cataclysm. It was alien and yet familiar, and the sensation was confusing. He had to remember he was enmeshed in the construct of multiple minds. A tendril of the cadre reached out and engaged with him, showing him the pathway to the library, but the journey continued to a small workroom. There people scribbled away, young people, people dressed strangely in clothes that were clearly manufactured in bulk. How did he know that? Again he let himself fall back into the mist of the cadre, allowing its currents to swirl around him, and then the scene changed. The cadre exuded familiar resonances. He saw a hand, old and gnarled, placing a book in a box, saw the hands shoving a stone over the hiding place. Now all he needed was the location. Where was the hiding place? And then he followed the cadre, retreating from the spot, noting the signposts, the small twists and turns in the ruinous passageways that would lead him back to that place. He rose up out of the cadre, feeling bereft and relieved at the same time. There was a secret hiding place, and Garan was certain he could find it. Filled with exhaustion, he fell into a deep sleep.

⠶⠶⠶⠶⠶

Laidan found that she liked walking through the streets past the empty houses. She liked it better when Nils accompanied her, telling her tales about his long-dead kin. The lessons in that strange script of his were boring, but she pretended to like them. She couldn't tell one from the other, but Nils showed nothing but patience. He cooked her meals and stayed with her in her abode until she went to sleep. He was a strange man, yet he was her own and so that didn't matter. No one would take him from her. That was important. She must not be alone anymore. There was no one else there in the whole city, except the two of them.

That woman and the horrible brown man had gone away, but

Nils had stayed. He spent all his time with her, assisting her to dress, to bathe, to eat. She remembered that it was his voice that she had woken to, his hand that assisted her, his body that comforted her in those early moments.

Caresses were important to her. She remembered them, the feel of hands running over her body, the pleasure that touch invoked. That must have been Nils, when she was not quite awake. He had not touched her like that since. Maybe he was waiting for her invitation.

At the top of the stairs, where they stood gazing upon the city wreathed in light and down to the dark waters of the lake, she reached out and grabbed his hand. Nils turned toward her.

"Laidan?" he said softly.

With that invitation, she wrapped herself around him, burying herself in his outer robe, trying to nuzzle close to his neck. Nils stepped away, deftly untangling himself. She stood there gaping at him. "What's wrong?"

Nils avoided her grasping hands and kept some distance between them. "There is something you must understand."

"What is to understand? You love me. I am special. You told me so. I love you too. I want to be with you always." She kept her gaze fixed on him, not understanding why he held himself apart from her.

"Laidan, you are special to me, but we cannot be together in the way you are thinking. You are not quite yourself."

"Why can't we be together? Am I not pleasing to you?"

"It is not so simple." Nils's eyes widened and he leaned away from her.

"I don't know what you mean. What have I done? Are you punishing me?"

"No, Laidan. Not at all. It would not be ethical even if I was free to take a mate."

"Ethical? Mate? I don't..."

Nils's silver eyes brightened for a moment. "You are not well yet. You have not healed completely. In your right mind, you would not even consider me in that way. Besides, I have a mate and cannot take another. Salinda and I are bound."

"Salinda?" she said, mouthing the word slowly. Why did she hate the sound of it?

"Yes, my mate...my wife...she is carrying my child."

Anger boiled up inside suddenly, surprising her. Laidan wanted to hit him in the face. She balled her hands into fists. He had tricked her, made her love him, and it was all a joke, a game...he hated her. "Why did you do it?" she yelled, tears starting from her eyes. "Why did you make me think you desired me, that you loved me, when you didn't?" A wail burst out of her and she rubbed at her eyes and felt quite at a loss. Emotions roiled and she could barely make sense of them, combined as they were with random images, some of which she shied away from.

Nils stepped forward but hesitated, not drawing any nearer, not offering physical comfort. "That was not my intention," he said in hushed tones, as if he was afraid of startling her. "I wished to care for you, to make you whole again."

It had to be lies. He couldn't even bring himself to touch her, to pat her on the back or smooth her hair. "What for? You don't want me... you have that horrible woman. There is nothing for me here." Laidan turned her back on him, thinking to flee but not sure which way to go.

"Please, Laidan, listen. You have to give yourself time to heal. Then you will see things differently. You have an unexplored heritage in me, in this city...and friends who care for you. Calm yourself now. You still have much healing to do."

"Healing?" She lifted her hands, and the sleeves of her robe fell back, revealing the smooth white skin of her arms. "There is nothing wrong with me. See?"

Nils gaped at her arm and shook his head, his silvery-white hair rippling with the movement.

"If you would disentangle your loyalty from that woman you could have this." She began to undress.

Nils turned his head away when Laidan threw off her outer robe and drew up her tunic, pulling it over her head and tossing it to the ground. Her body was beautiful, white, with fine legs and unblemished skin. She didn't understand about the healing he kept talking about. There was nothing wrong with her, not a blemish. While he looked away, shunning her beauty and her wholeness, she darted down the stairs, liking the texture of the air on her naked flesh. He followed and she kept on running, leaping the stairs two at a time. He followed her, but what good was that if he wasn't hers? Too late she realized that the lower stairs were damp from the lake. Her foot slipped and she tumbled. Perhaps she had been foolish after all. There was a sharp pain and then darkness swallowed her.

When next she woke she was in bed, wrapped in blankets and feeling quite sore. Nils sat in the chair beside her. He helped her sip some broth and stroked her brow. "So you love me again?" she asked.

"I care for you, Laidan. Can that not be enough?"

"No," she said before rolling onto her side to face the wall. "It's not enough for me. I need love. I need you to worship me."

☉☉☉☉☉

When Garan opened the gate to head back down to the cave, Salinda was waiting for him.

"I have taken leave of the Master Elders on behalf of us both. After you finish with the ruins we will return to Barrahiem. There's no point in doubling back, given that the Way Gate is so close and all."

"That is fine by me. But I have left a sack of books and a bag of supplies in my room. If you can fetch them for me I will meet you at the Way Gate when I'm done. I will mark the way for you with lights. I should not be too long after you."

Salinda lifted her own heavy bag, indicating that her hands were full. "Very well. It will not take me long. If you take this and leave it near the Way Gate, I will go back. Do not linger longer than you have to at the ruins. I am anxious to return to Nils."

His head jerked up. "Has something happened? Is it Laidan?" Garan sheltered his eyes from the morning glare with his hands as he studied Salinda.

She turned back toward him. "I'm not sure. Nils has a way of letting me know when he wants me back."

"I see. I will be as swift as I can."

Chapter Fifteen

INNOCENCE SAVED
AND INNOCENCE LOST

Congested blood in Danton's bound wrist caused him pain. Gingerly, he opened his eyes a fraction. Even the small amount of light lanced his brain. Overhead, shackles and a chain anchored him to the wall. Rope bound his ankles. He tried to focus, tried to remember what had happened. There had been a fight. He'd lost. Where was he now? In spite of the headache, he took in the darkened room that served for a cell, then he moved his head to the left. The stench of an unwashed body and shit washed over him. Screwing his eyes shut, he breathed through his mouth as he fought the urge to vomit. It was not good. Not good at all. That was all he could say. By the heavy, dull feel of his body he had been quite thoroughly beaten, too. He shifted to ease a pain in his shoulder and stifled a cry. Not good. Not good at all.

A dull ache in his jaw was evidence that he'd been knocked out. He had no memory of his capture and no idea of which faction had nabbed him. Whatever the means, it smacked of betrayal. He had been at the brothel. Only one person came to mind—bloody Toola, his dear cousin. It had to be one of her machinations. Squab had warned him and he had underestimated Toola's capacity for treachery. He could only hope that the others hadn't been snared as well. Brill must have gotten away. He hoped Brill had obeyed orders and stayed out of it. Danton grimaced and winced at the pain from a cut lip.

A wave of nausea and depression hit him. How had he gotten into this predicament? Thinking was too hard, so he tried to sleep for a bit, hoping a little rest would refresh him. He could only doze fitfully as no position was without pain. In the end he gave up and concentrated on easing the pressure in his wrist. His manacles were too tight. He tried to push himself up to standing, but darted up too quickly, and the resultant sudden burning sensation in his arms made him call out. His hands throbbed, and stabbing pains peppered his shoulders.

He breathed through it, trying to remain upright. He dry-retched, and then retched some more. Pain, nausea and the awful stench were too much.

The room was shrouded in gloom. A partially detached board high up on the window let in a gray sliver of light. Danton looked around but there was nothing but the dull, muted shapes of old furniture and piles of blankets. Nothing to account for that dreadful smell. It was as though something had died in there. He sniffed his own body but he was not the source. He passed his gaze around the room again and then whispered, "Anyone there?"

A pile of blankets near the window rippled. There was no sound, yet Danton had the distinct feeling that he wasn't alone. If the other prisoner had been dangerous, they would have attacked Danton by now, or reacted when Danton woke.

"You there. Where are we?"

Again the blanket twitched and there was a faint moan. Danton examined the chain anchoring him to the wall. In the dimness he saw that it had been looped around a large hook to restrict his movements. He used a nearby cabinet to lever himself higher so that he could unloop the chain. Each swing around the hook caused him to cringe as it jerked his wrists. Forehead against the wall, he breathed through the pain as the last of the chain came free, then he drew out sufficient length to allow him to get closer to the window

As he neared the mound, the smell grew stronger. This person was definitely the source of the stench. As carefully as he could, he peeled back the blanket and braced himself for the person to lash out. What the absence of the blanket revealed was an old gray face, unwashed, unshaven, and covered in sores. The old man was in a bad way—lips swollen and cracked, with grime thickly coating the neck so it was almost black. Danton did not move the blanket any further. He breathed through his mouth to prevent himself from gagging.

"Can you speak? Who are you?"

The eyes opened and straight away Danton could see that the man was partially blind, as one of his pale blue eyes had been so badly damaged. The good eye took a while to focus on him.

"Who is it?" croaked an old voice, barely a scratchy whisper.

"Name's Danton. Do you know how long I've been here?"

"Danton?" the old man repeated in a voice that hadn't been used in an age. Yet there was a hint of recognition there. The gaze faltered. Danton touched his shoulder gently, but the old man had slipped back into unconsciousness. Danton scrutinized the man's face, searching for some memory to account for the feeling that he had met this person before, but nothing came to him. He shook his head sadly. He'd never seen such a decrepit specimen, and he had seen some bad ones in his time.

He waited a few more minutes and tried to rouse the old man again, without success. Danton then turned his attention to food and water. He wouldn't last long without some sustenance. His captors had not finished with him yet, otherwise he'd be dead, so there was a chance that there was some food somewhere.

The chain gave him some freedom of movement in the room but he was still restricted to his immediate vicinity. He found a bucket of warm, stale water and took a long drink, without really contemplating the freshness of it. He did not have any choice. Further searching did not reveal any food.

He glanced at the old man, asleep with his mouth open, cheeks sunken. A piece of bread now would probably kill the old boy. It was clear his state was due to an extended period of privation. Danton wondered how long the old man had been there. Surely a long time. How long did it take someone to die who had been given just enough to survive a day at a time?

His thirst quenched, he felt revived enough to further explore the room. A foot poking out from a large pile of blankets was at an odd angle. Danton guessed that whoever it belonged to was already dead, but he carefully peeled the blankets back one by one to check. With a sad groan he saw it was his missing deputy. Merl's head was caved in on one side and his body was pockmarked with deep gashes that showed signs of charring, perhaps an attempt to cauterize the wounds. His deputy had been viciously and thoroughly tortured. Danton blinked. Now he knew what was in store for him.

Cursing, Danton replaced the blankets. Merl had been tortured for nothing, as he'd known nothing beyond the fact that Danton and his men were after the dragon wine. He wondered what had happened to the rest of the men with Merl. It was most likely they had been enslaved or killed outright. Danton spent a few minutes suppressing a sob and then cursed again, rubbing his hair against his chained hand. Of all the foolish idiots, he had to take the prize. He'd let Toola betray him. He'd known he shouldn't have trusted her and had acted too slowly. *Damn. Damn!*

Danton needed his strength. There was no use in expending it in grief, and as there was no food he thought it best to rest and think. He needed to plan, to be ready for what came next. Merl's death had hit him hard, harder than the betrayal that had led him to this place. Thinking about his man's injuries was not an option. That would lead him to give up hope and that was not something he was going to do. Not quickly, anyway. He'd suffered before and he could do it again.

Retreating to the spot where he had been placed, he squatted in the grime with the chain curled by his feet and rested the back of his head against the wall. It wasn't a good position for sleep but he was beyond caring. He closed his eyes and dived into the dark places of his mind—to escape this room.

ʚ ʚ ʚ ʚ ʚ

Nils sensed Salinda entering the Ways accompanied by Garan. The relief of her impending return made him sigh. He sat in the corner of Laidan's bedroom in her abode at a loss to know what to do. His motives had been good, but events had not transpired as he had hoped. Salinda had warned him, but in his pride he'd thought he was capable. He had not anticipated how Laidan would react to his ministrations. Now matters were worse and he could possibly have caused more damage to the vulnerable girl.

The problems with Laidan's mind were greater than he had first supposed. Her logic did not function as it should. Her long-term memories were twisted and inaccurate and her shorter-term memory was not working as it should either. This he knew from the lessons he'd tried to give her in language and writing. She retained nothing from one lesson to the next. Previously, though not a great scholar, she had demonstrated the ability to learn and had assisted Garan in the task of repairing the lamps. The ultimate mistake in his judgment was that she had formed an inappropriate attachment to him.

Now he could not leave her unsupervised in case she put herself in danger. She had relocated to their Barr family node when she was well enough. Once Salinda and Garan returned, Nils would have assistance in caring for the girl. Salinda had hinted that there may be an issue with him tending the girl on his own, and mentally he prepared a confession to her that she had been right. Laidan's actions on the stairs had taken him by surprise. The words he had uttered as comfort had been distorted in the girl's mind. Even now as he followed Salinda's approach through their tether, he dared not leave Laidan's side. He would have to seek the assistance of both Garan and Salinda to care for her.

Later, echoes of speech alerted him to Salinda and Garan's arrival. Through the small, round window, he detected movement at the entrance to the Barr family node. With a quick glance at the sleeping girl, he slipped out of Laidan's room and waited for his mate in Laidan's sitting room. Salinda bent and twisted to enter through the small doorway, her swollen abdomen hampering her movement. Behind her, Garan lingered uncertainly.

Salinda straightened and tugged her robe back into place. Nils stepped forward and took her hands in his. "I am glad you have returned," Nils said.

Salinda reached up and kissed his cheek, and then whispered, "Can Garan come in?"

Nils nodded and called out the door. "Please enter, Garan. We need to talk. All of us."

While Garan squeezed himself through the doorway, Nils poked his head though Laidan's bedroom door, checking that she still slept, then he quietly pulled it to.

"What is it, Nils?" Salinda asked as she arranged her robe around her legs and adjusted her position on the sofa. Her dark eyes looked bright.

Nils grimaced and wrung his hands. "I need your help with Laidan." He stood before her, shifting from foot to foot.

Salinda nodded slowly as her gaze traveled up his body. She pressed her lips together. "I see. Fixated on you, is she?"

"Yes." Nils collapsed onto the seat next to her. "How could you know?"

Salinda caressed his hand. "I know the heart of young girls, and Laidan in particular is very predicable in that way. She was vulnerable, alone; of course she would attach herself to you. But there can be no harm in it. As she recovers the intensity of her regard will lessen."

Nils removed his hand from hers and placed it on his knee, thinking deeply on Salinda's words. Sometimes she was very wise, even though what she said gave him little comfort, because he still had to be in close company with the girl and that had become uncomfortable in the extreme. He had no wish to make the girl suffer further or put himself in difficult situations. He let out a sigh, cleared his mind of his own concerns, and turned his attention to his mate and her mission.

"Did your trip to the observatory go well?" he asked politely, passing his gaze onto the young Skywatcher.

"They are managing surprisingly well. Titina is making preparations for final moonfall."

Nils swallowed. "She is?" Had Salinda accepted that they were all doomed? Looking at her expression, he did not think it the case. She smiled widely and her eyes twinkled.

"Yes. A very well-thought-out plan, too."

"Then they have given up hope of finding a way to stop the asteroid?"

Salinda shook her head. "No, not given up, but with no practical solutions at hand she is doing her best to save those she can. She plans to use the caves, deep ones, to shelter a few of the young people."

Nils's eyes widened. "Caves?"

"Yes. We have not given up, though." She stood up suddenly, gazing down into his face. "Nils, there has to be an answer in the archives. Some clue as to what we can do. Surely the great nations of old had some plan, some way to counter the moon's destruction. It may not have worked, but perhaps it is why there are people left. I remember long ago, when I was sixteen years old, Mez told me that people were alive by accident or design. At the time he could not say which. I believe that there was an intervention. If we could find out what it was, then maybe we can improve on it. And we have something they did not have then."

"We do?" asked Garan and Nils together.

"Yes, we have you, Garan, and we have the cadres, and we have you, Nils."

Nils frowned. "But you do not know for sure that they did not have similar resources. Trell certainly knew of Moonfall in plenty of time, and he left here." His gaze slid to Garan. "Did you search for the book?"

Garan glanced in the direction of the node entry and then bit his lip as he turned to study Nils. "Yes. I found a cache of books at Trithorn Peak and some that were well hidden in the ruins. I brought all that I could find. I figured that any book that was old was worth keeping with the rest of the knowledge in the archives. They are in a sack outside."

Nils's fingers itched to investigate Garan's haul and he turned to the door before being brought up short. "So, Nils," Salinda asked. "What do you propose to do about our young charge? Shifts?"

Nils turned back, frowning. "Oh?" He had forgotten for a moment. "Yes, that will work. I warn you, though, she will not adjust well."

Garan spoke. "I can help."

Nils considered this then ventured, "She may not react well to you, Garan."

"We may not have a choice in the matter." Salinda stood up and grimaced as she glanced between them.

Nils inclined his head. "True, I fear she cannot be left alone."

"I will make some tea and then take the first shift," Salinda said. "Garan, you take the second. I guess you will just have to cope with whatever Laidan gives out. She will have to adjust. We don't have time for anything else. Nils, it appears you have some free time and some books to read. Oh and that machine? Don't forget about it, Nils."

Nils did not hesitate. He exited Laidan's abode, grabbed the sack of books and retreated down to his office in the archives.

ᔕᔕᔕᔕᔕ

Garan was dozing in the chair when he heard movement from Laidan's

163

room. He snuck over to peek through the door. Laidan was standing in the room, naked. Swallowing uncomfortably, he entered the room. Laidan swung around and screamed. Even though he was backlit, she could obviously tell he was not Nils.

"Shush, shush," Garan said softly, using hand gestures to quiet and soothe. "You should put some clothes on."

His words had minimal effect. More screaming ensued. "Get. Away."

Garan shrugged. "No. I will not hurt you. Put some clothes on and come out here. There is food prepared for you." When she stood there gaping, he added, "Come on, you must be hungry by now."

He saw her reach down for her robe and attempt to don it. Stepping closer, he helped her tug it down over her body before she cringed away from him. "Where's Nils?" she hissed at him, facing him but keeping her distance. "I want him. Not you."

"He's busy," he said, watching her climb onto the bed and fold herself into a little ball. "Come on, time to eat."

"No. Leave my home. You hurt me."

Garan recoiled at her words. He knew from Salinda and Nils that her mind was addled, but still the unjust charge pained him. "No, I am not leaving." He bit his lips and eyed her with a great deal of pity. "I did hurt you once, but with words, not deeds. You have nothing to fear from me."

It was as if he had not spoken. "I want Nils." Her voice was harsh. "Give him back to me!" she yelled.

Garan stood his ground. To get through this they all had to share the burden of caring for Laidan. He was not going to fold, although he wanted to. It was hard to see what she had become, hard to bear her hatred when he cared so much. "He is not mine to give or take. He is a person and he is busy doing something else. Come and eat something. There is some cacti bread here. I brought it back from the observatory, especially for you."

Laidan blinked, her head cocked to one side. "Observatory...for me?"

Garan could not help the surge of joy. She remembered the observatory. All was not lost. "Yes." Garan pulled back, shut the door and retreated to the couch. He had already laid out the bread and some fruit in anticipation of Laidan being hungry.

After finishing the first shift, Salinda had left a few hours ago and was sleeping. He was not sure if Nils was with her or not. The empty city tended to amplify sounds. In the Barr family node noise carried so well that even whispers could be heard distinctly. It was a vain hope that Laidan's screaming had gone unnoticed.

Laidan's door opened suddenly and she darted past him, heading straight for the exit. Taken by surprise, Garan took a second to recover before he hurried after her. He hated to manhandle her, but he caught her around the waist and dragged her back. Clinging to the edges of the abode opening, her screaming was worse than before.

Garan shuddered and his stomach clenched in remembered fear. Her screams reminded him of the sounds she'd made when Gercomo attacked her.

Hands shaking, he buried his head in her hair and begged her to stop. "Please, Laidan. I love you. I would never harm you. Please, do not scream like that. Please."

The screaming stopped abruptly. Quaking, Laidan sobbed, sucking in huge breaths. She was trying to talk but her body was out of control, locked into a fear response. He soothed her, stroked her head, her back, her arms, trailing his fingers softly against her skin. "'Tis all right now. You are safe. I am with you now. No one can hurt you anymore."

The tension in her body drained away and she relaxed against him. She sniffed, her breathing becoming less labored. After a big exhalation, she spoke, turning her head to look into his face, her forehead wrinkled in puzzlement. "You…said…you loved…me?"

"Yes, I did. I have loved you since I can remember." Garan thought he was dust mad for admitting it, and knew he would regret it, but he was so moved by her distress that the confession had fallen out of his mouth unbidden.

"Really? But you hurt me. I remember that you hurt me…a lot."

He brushed his fingertips through her hair, moving it from her face. "I know…I said some horrible things, things that I had no right to say. But it was someone else who hurt you badly, who made you this way."

Her eyes unfocused and, as if a cord had snapped, her body lost all tension as she fainted. After carrying her to the couch, he caressed her face until she woke again. Sitting up on the sofa, she drew her legs up and hugged them, watching him with those pale blue eyes of hers. He broke off some bread and passed it to her. She took a tentative bite, chewed and swallowed. The rest of the food was passed to her in the same way. She said nothing, just watched him while he fed her.

When she'd had her fill, he sat by her, gazing into her perfect face and stroking her hair, like one did a baby. What else could he do? She was content to say nothing and let him stroke her. It had to be enough. She remembered the observatory and she was finally calm. Eventually her eyes closed and she slept. Garan kept studying her and stroking, a small smile creeping onto his face. She had tolerated his presence. His eyes watered and he sniffed. That was far more than he had hoped for.

Chapter Sixteen

REVELATIONS

Brill ran to the rear of the brothel, past the dead guards, while dragging Eneit by the hand. The girl squirmed and wailed her grief and he had to keep a tight hold in case he lost her. Mandin had given them time and he was not about to throw that away. There appeared to be no one pursuing them at the minute, but that was going to change.

Tears burned his eyes when he thought of Mandin's sacrifice. There was no chance she had survived the fight. He had come to respect her. He glanced down at the girl. Tears streamed down her face, though her wailing had quieted and now she appeared stunned and stricken. Eneit didn't ask to go back for her mother. Brill could see that she understood what Mandin had done. The mother had died to save her child. Now it was up to him to keep Eneit safe so that Mandin's sacrifice was not in vain.

The brothel madam, that traitorous woman, was most likely still at large. If she had no compunction betraying Danton, she'd not spare a thought before she sold out Brill as well. She was prepared to serve up this innocent child to lechers. Like Lexia, who was given to her father on a regular basis. Oh, how his innards had churned when the girl had revealed all to him. Both he and Eneit were in extreme danger. Toola would stop at nothing. The girl had cost her dear.

He tugged on Eneit's hand again. The child glanced up at him, looked him straight in the eyes, and squeezed his hand in return. Hers was an expression that had seen too much. His heart twisted with guilt. They had not been able to rescue the girl from the rebels. He could imagine too well what she and the others had been subjected to.

At the corner of the lane, he turned into the street that led to the tunnel he had scouted earlier. Very soon they were carefully making their way through the dilapidated fences and alleyways, trying not to be seen. Over the sound of his thumping heartbeat, he heard shouts and the beat of boots against the pavement. Eneit gaped over her shoulder and let out a cry. "It will be all right," he whispered and tugged her along by the hand.

Brill had no choice but to bring the girl into the Ways with him. It was the quickest and easiest means of escape. He doubted they'd make it out the usual way. The city gates would be watched and all other exits heavily guarded. In these extreme circumstances he thought Nils wouldn't mind that another person had been made aware of the existence of the Hiem, their city and their Travel Ways. If Salinda was with him, and when she found out what had happened to Danton, she would talk Nils around. Had to. It was an emergency.

While lowering Eneit into the underground walkway, Brill checked his surroundings. At the entrance to the alleyway he heard the rhythmic sound of marching feet approaching. A patrol, he guessed. He pulled back, flattening himself against the wall, with Eneit tucked up behind him. Cutting across the road, a band of men in the familiar colors of the customs militia jogged past.

They breathed hard as the men passed by, but none stopped to investigate their little alleyway. Brill closed his eyes and sighed with relief. The alarm had definitely been raised. He had to move quickly. He had no idea how far Toola's influence stretched, but he guessed her net was wide. Danton's capture loomed large in his mind again. It was a pity he had not had time to find out where Danton was being held. Toola would have known. She knew everything.

Finding the tunnel that resembled a sewer, he jumped down from the walkway and held his hand out to Eneit. She stood there, slack-faced. "Come on, Eneit, take my hand."

The girl blinked, looked around her and then shuddered, rubbing her upper arms with her hands. "Ma?"

Brill thought his heart would break at the desolate expression on her face. She began to cry afresh. It appeared the shock had set in. Brill stifled a groan. Although sympathetic, they had to move quickly or die. "Please hurry, Eneit!"

Her dark eyes focused on him and then she let out a scream, a high-pitched squeal that made his eardrums numb. "Shush," he said, making a grab for her. "Do you want your mother's sacrifice to be for nothing?"

That only made the child cry louder. Brill tried to muffle her cries by holding her face to his stomach, and forced himself to be patient. "Please stop it. We have to run now before they find us. Cry later when we are safe."

Frozen-faced, she glared up at him while she battled her emotions, then she stopped mid-cry and hiccupped.

"That's right. If you want to live, then be quiet and do what I say."

Nodding once, she put her trembling hand in his.

"Right then," he said, relief rippling through him. "Come on."

A ruckus coming from the direction of the brothel reached them. Holding Eneit tightly, Brill sprinted into the tunnel. The girl was light on her feet, but she was malnourished, and she had to take two steps for every one of Brill's. Already he could hear her sucking in breath with loud gasps.

Halfway through the tunnel, she slipped out of his grip and stumbled. Around them he could hear the murmur of voices and shapes shifting in the darkness. He ducked down and picked her up. "Can you stand? Walk?" he whispered.

"Yes. Sorry." Her voice sounded thin.

The voices drew closer. Brill picked the girl up, swung her over his shoulder and ran for it. No doubt the onlookers would give them up to their pursuers if asked. There was little time. Once clear of that section of tunnel, he lowered Eneit to the ground. In a shaft of sunlight, he could see she was red-cheeked. The ride had been rough.

"Sorry about that, but it wasn't safe. Can you manage another run now?"

With her wide, dark eyes staring, she put her hand in his. They continued on. Once in the dark of the second half of the tunnel, Brill had to slow down. He did not want to miss the door. He patted with his hands along the wall of the corridor, splashing the stagnant water in his haste. Eneit began to whimper again.

"It's all right. I know a way out of here. Just be quiet and calm, okay?"

"It's dark in here. It smells."

"I know, but we will be away from here soon."

His fingers found the edges of the Way Gate. Now he had to hope that the mechanism still worked. He had no means to blow the gate up and gain access that way. The sounds of pursuit grew closer, but overhead, not in the tunnel. He let out a breath, relieved. His thoughts went to the shroud. In a pinch he could use it to hide them, but for how long? It was at the end of its charge.

Shouts rang out, along with barked questions and mumbled answers. Brill's heart sank when he realized these were coming from the tunnel. Their time had run out. The sound of running feet echoed overhead as well.

"Eneit. In my backpack is a gray robe. Can you get it out for me?"

"Yes," she said in a quavering voice.

"Good. Hurry." He had no time to explain to the girl what use the shroud was or what he was doing with the Way Gate.

Blocking out the distractions of the pursuit, Brill replayed how the door had been opened previously in that little cave with Laidan and Garan. He ran his hand down the side of the door, feeling for an indentation. The rock molding was very worn, and he nearly missed it. Someone had entered the tunnel behind them. He could hear the splash of boots in water. He had to hurry. At last the door slid open. It hissed slightly then stopped. It was only open a quarter of the way. So be it. He shoved Eneit through, then picked up his knapsack and the pile of the shroud that Eneit had pulled out and pushed them into her arms. His sword, dagger and other tools came off his belt and followed. From down the tunnel, a gruff voice said, "They went that way."

Not a moment too soon, he rammed himself into the gap. Provided he could get his head through, the rest should follow. The shoulders were difficult: he had to contort himself, twist his body. Eneit desperately pulled on his clothing, dragging him with all her might. With a wrench, he came through the doorway and hastily keyed it shut. The door slid back and he rested his head against it, panting hard. His only hope was that no one had seen him. Or if they had, that they didn't have explosives.

Nils lifted his head from his desk, not realizing how exhausted he had been. The sack of books sat by him on his table. He felt rather guilty leaving Laidan with Salinda and Garan, after making so much ado about looking after her himself. But after her reaction, her fixations on him, Nils found that his interest in the girl had waned. He had been guilty of romanticizing the extent of her Hiem heritage, blinded by the hope that she was a link to his long-lost kin. What a fool he was. He could barely face Salinda. Indeed, he could still see her knowing expression in his mind.

He regarded the sack of books Garan had brought with him. The thought of locating Trell's writings in this stack made his hands shake. That the lad thought these aged tomes would be of interest and perhaps value to the Hiem archives touched him in a sentimental way. The young Skywatcher understood the power of knowledge.

Nils pulled the books out one by one, examining each carefully. Some of the books he recognized from the Master Elder Jalen's study, others he had not seen. Four were so badly damaged that they were illegible. He suspected these were from the ruins of the older observatory. These he placed on the floor, ready for disposal. The array of books interested him. One book had a cover that did not match the contents. It stated that it was a book documenting the mining activities of the first survivors of Moonfall, but it was in fact a later work that showed maps of the various watercourses in the Stoli continent. This work was of interest to him as it would put into context some of the later maps. He took another book out of the bag. The language of the title was pre-Shatterwing, but the content appeared to be a novel, a Sundweller romance of some kind.

He was about to draw out the last book when he felt something quite strange. His head jerked up, his breath hissed in.

ᏬᏇᏬᏇᏬ

Nils appeared at the doorway, leaning in.

"What is it?" Salinda asked, placing the bowl she was drying onto the table. She did not need to see him to know that he was greatly agitated.

"I am not sure. I felt something."

Her eyes narrowed. "I see. Come in. I have made some tea."

Nils hesitated and then inclined his head in a way that meant agreement. After he squeezed into their abode, he took a seat. Salinda passed him a bowl of the Pardu tea she had just prepared and Nils took a sip, then closed his eyes and swayed slightly.

Salinda put the teapot down and waited patiently before pouring her own tea. Her senses were on alert.

At last, after a sip of tea, he spoke. "I think I have I detected someone entering the Ways. It was distant."

"You think?" Salinda asked.

Nils cocked his head. "It is unexpected. Surprising." He drew his fingers through his long hair, his gaze fixed on a spot on the wall and after a few heartbeats he continued. "Yes, definitely someone is in the Ways."

"Can you tell who?" Salinda hoped it was Danton and Brill. There had been no news of them at the observatory. Sufficient time had passed for them to have found the wine, perhaps even to have retrieved it and sent a message.

"I...it is not easy...the vibrations are familiar. You forget that the Hiem traveled the Ways in great numbers. The general hum of their passing was a background noise that I filtered out. It is only because the Ways are empty now that I feel anything."

"Can you tell where?" Other people did not know of or use the Ways. If the vibrations were familiar then it had to be someone they knew. "It must be Danton and Brill. What about the map, can that help?"

"Yes, I believe so," he said, his silver eyes glowing in the light of the shuwai. Salinda went to fetch it.

Once she'd turned on the map, they examined it. She found it hard to read as the references were places she had not heard of before, even though Nils had taught her the Hiem script. Nils pointed. "I think it is this gate that has been used. It was once at the mouth of a river. It is a Way Gate that is very close to the township of Lassenail—Gateshead, in your language."

"Not another Hiem city?"

"Not a city. A township, a small place, a few thousand lived there.

Hiem went there to take the waters. There was an underground sea there."

Salinda swallowed the awe she felt. Even surrounded by the amazing artifacts and the city of Barrahiem, she was astounded when reminded how vast their civilization had been, how vast her own had been. "I see. Well, let's see where this gate is located nowadays."

With Nils's help Salinda worked out where the Way Gate was. Her heart began to pound. "I'm sure it is Sartell. Has to be. You must be detecting Brill and Danton. They wouldn't enter the Ways without good reason, though. They would not risk discovery."

"You think it is them?" Nils asked. "I am not so certain. There are two vibrations, it's true, but one of them is familiar while the other is not."

"They took a woman from Vanden with them—the one searching for her daughter. Perhaps it is her."

This wasn't part of the plan. Something must have gone wrong. Salinda did not waste any time. "We have to investigate, right away." She stood up from the table and began to gather the things she would need for a short journey. A flask of dragon wine, some bandages...

Nils regarded her. "You wish to go?"

"Yes, of course I do. Something must have happened. They might need help."

Nils raised his hand, gesturing for her to wait. "Then I will go. You must stay here with Laidan as she cannot remain alone."

"Garan can care for her. I'll come with you." Salinda closed her small sack and jiggled it in her hand.

"Is that wise? Laidan fears him."

Salinda cast him a fleeting smile. "He has made progress with her. We don't need to worry."

"If you come with me I will not be able to travel in-between. It is faster."

Salinda stilled and turned to face him. "I don't want you to travel in-between. If you try that again, it could kill you. I would not risk you. Promise me you won't travel in-between again."

"To travel so for any length of time would be at great personal cost, it is true. But your friends, you fear for them. Speed is important."

"Not that important. Not at the risk of your life."

"Very well then. We will travel together. I will prepare."

Salinda reached out and clasped his hand. "Thank you. I'll meet you at the north gate. I have to tell Garan what we are doing."

Nils crouched down to squeeze through the entrance to their abode. "Are you sure you should go? It is a long way. The child..." He nodded once, indicating her growing abdomen.

Salinda caressed her belly. "I'm sure, Nils. I am quite fit and healthy."

Once Nils had departed, Salinda went to find Garan. She found him sitting with Laidan and stroking her hair. That sight gave her a sense of wellbeing. She could be confident that Garan would take good care of her.

Chapter Seventeen

ETERNITY

Brill huddled close to Eneit on the inside of the Way Gate. The air was musty and cold and dust lay thick on the path in front of him. Even after he'd allowed time for his eyes to adjust, in the distance darkness still cloaked the Way ahead.

It was as if they were well and truly in the underworld. The Ways were quiet, dark and full of the unknown. Uncertainty racked him. They had to venture further into the Ways in the vague hope of locating Nils and Barrahiem city. There was no point in waiting. Thankfully there had been no sign of pursuit yet. Caution advised moving further into the Ways, away from the Way Gate in case they had been observed, in case their pursuers had explosives. Danger still awaited them on the outside, but there was no food or water to allow them to linger long on the inside.

Something else made him hesitate. He didn't want to leave Danton. He let out a breath slowly. Mandin was surely dead, but there was hope for his friend. If he fled into the Ways he would be abandoning him, and that was a hard decision to make.

He knew what Danton would say. He would order him to save the girl. He pictured the softness that had come over his friend's face when he had beheld Mandin in those last days, when they had played lovers. Brill knew that something real had sprung up between them. But that was over now, and there was only Eneit left to remind the world of Mandin from Vanden town.

He knew in his heart there was nothing he could have done for Mandin. The choice had been made and there was no going back. He was honor-bound to protect her daughter. Perhaps he had always known that it was the Vanden woman's fate to die to save Eneit. Had the woman not vowed it more than once? Wasn't that why Danton had brought her along? A smile lingered on his face as he thought of her, for the joy she had known as Danton's lover and the knowledge that she had traded her life for her daughter's. That was what he should remember, what should give him heart.

Danton was a different matter. He could be saved. Had to be saved. But for that Brill needed Salinda. It may have been a while, but Salinda knew the ways of Sartell and she had power. That had to be worth something. If only she could be convinced to bring it to bear to save Danton.

Brill shifted away from Eneit and squared his shoulders. "Come, I think we should head further in. There's no point in waiting here."

Eneit spoke in the darkness. "What is this place?"

Brill considered what to say. "I will try to explain later, but for now, the less you know the better. Here we are safe."

Eneit slipped her hand in his. "Where will we go now?"

"Eventually you'll go home, I think."

Eneit pulled back on his hand. "I have no home."

"Maybe...but you can make a new one. I know the perfect place." He was thinking of the observatory. Or maybe a future world where there would be goodness, peace, safety, and no moonfall looming.

As he moved off, feeling each step with the toe of his boot, she offered no further resistance. The Ways were too quiet and dismal for Brill's liking. He could not stop comparing this experience to when he was last in the Ways, with Garan, Laidan and Danton. They'd seemed so much more alive and exciting then.

Beneath his feet the path trembled. He hesitated. It felt like a distant explosion of some kind. His mind went back to when Danton had blown up the Way Gate entrance to prevent pursuit. The low rumble vibrated under his feet again, but the walls remained dull and dead. It was not someone trying to blow up the Way Gate. The vibration was not coming from the Hiem Travel Ways at all but from outside, and far off.

"What was that?" Eneit asked.

He smiled down at her, not that she could see it in the dimly lit Way.

"I don't know. Come on," he said to Eneit, squeezing her hand companionably, "let's keep moving." It was virtually impossible to see where they were heading. Brill had to feel every step, grope his way up or down every stairwell and comfort Eneit often as they inched their way along. The further they trod, the stronger the vibrations became. If he wasn't mistaken, there was some sort of excavation going on. Not in Sartell itself but north of the city. Could this be the "Eternity" Squab had spoken of?

Brill's uneasiness grew. Thoughts of the Infra-pact rebels finding the Ways and exploiting them curdled his stomach. He had to warn Nils. They had to take action.

"I'm hungry," Eneit said in a plaintive voice.

"I know." Brill kept on going. They stopped to sleep for an hour or so but woke hungry. Brill searched his pockets and his pack. There he touched on the shroud that Nils had given him. He didn't need the camouflage but he recalled with relief that there were some supplies within its deep pockets.

He pulled out the shroud and slipped it on, then searched in the pouches. Eneit moaned and he knelt down to give her a drink. Then he gave her some dried cacti bread. The girl ate hungrily. Brill had no idea how long they would remain in the Ways. Either they could wait for Nils to find them or Brill could try to find an exit, hopefully where it was safe and near to food and water.

He continued walking and kept an eye out for tell-tale signs of a gate, which he knew were usually preceded by a multiple staircases. With the light so poor, he knew it was unlikely that he'd spot one by sight alone.

It seemed they were on a straight section that went on indefinitely. Three days later—he thought it was three days; it was hard to tell in the dimness of the Ways—Eneit tired sooner than usual. Brill didn't think they had actually covered a great distance. Brill suggested they sit down and rest, and Eneit settled next to him. There was no more food but he offered her the last of the water. She shook her head.

"Come on, drink. There isn't any more after this."

Eneit lifted her head. "We're going to die in here, aren't we?"

"No, of course not."

Eneit took the water. "You don't have to lie. I don't mind. Being dead is better than being a slave or one of those—" She stopped abruptly.

Brill's throat closed up and he had to fight back the tears. After composing himself he said, "Your mother would have been very proud of you."

Eneit burst into tears and cried for her mother. Brill stroked her head. "She was a brave woman who gave her life so you could have a free one."

Eneit tried to talk but couldn't get the words out. Brill spoke to her soothingly until she quieted and then fell asleep. Brill wiped the tears off his own face. Mandin had deserved better. He tried not to think about her dying, and that left him thinking about Danton. Rubbing his forehead, he groaned. Later, he dozed for a while, and then jerked suddenly awake.

Eneit still appeared to be asleep so he stayed perfectly still, trying to discern what it was that had woken him. He could hear nothing. Eyes peeled, he searched for signs of movement. Was there something different about the Ways? Was the substance of the walls lightening to a dull gray?

Then a deep vibration rippled along the walls that he was leaning on, a movement so deep he could feel it reverberating in his lungs. Eneit must have sensed something too for she started awake and gasped, before she huddled into his side and hid her face. The timbre of this vibration was different: more in the air than underfoot.

Something was happening along the Way. It was lighter somehow and the walls had a luster of marble-like quality. Brill scrambled to his feet, pulling Eneit up and shoving her behind his body. A yell burst out of him and Eneit screamed in reaction to his fear.

Then, in the next moment he made out Nils walking toward him. After the darkness of the ways, it was Nils's passage that drew light.

"Nils!" Brill called excitedly. "Nils? Oh, Nils, thank the source you have come."

Nils straightened and appeared to frown, for his facial gestures were not easy to read, when his gaze rested on Eneit. Then he checked their surroundings. "Only two of you?" he said, turning back.

In the Hiem's presence, the walls of the ways lightened, casting a dull gloom onto them. Brill could see Eneit's wide staring eyes as she realized that Nils was not human. He squeezed her shoulder lightly. He did not want her running off.

"This is a friend. Eneit, meet Nils."

Nils bowed his head slightly. "Excuse me while I take rest. Salinda follows along behind and will be here shortly. I came ahead as I can walk faster than she."

Nils lowered himself to the ground and leaned his head back on the wall. Brill crouched down next to him, bringing Eneit with him. With eyes closed, Nils whispered, "Danton?"

"Captured." Brill found emotion ready to spill out of him.

"And the other who left with you?"

"She didn't make it." His voice was tight.

Nils's eyes opened and he turned them on Brill. "The toll has been heavy."

"Yes."

"Did you locate the wine?" His silvery eyes glowed eerily.

"Not precisely but we have strong suspicions..."

"I see." Nils shook his head. "We have our own bad tidings—" A faint tremor shook the ground. Nils's eyes opened suddenly and he shifted his head in the direction of the disturbance. "That is coming from the north of here."

Brill nodded. "I wanted to investigate but..." He shrugged. "I don't know how to navigate in here. Sounds like explosives, some kind of blasting."

"Explosives?" Nils struggled to stand.

"I suspect Danton is in the north too, along with the wine." Brill wondered if he should tell the Hiem about Eternity, whatever that was.

Nils gathered up his robes. "I will go and investigate." He dug into the pocket of his shroud and brought out some rations and a container of water. "This should tide you over until Salinda arrives. She brings supplies." Nils's lips compressed and he stared into the distance for a few moments. Then he turned back to Brill. "For the sound and vibrations to reach the Ways they must be either intersecting the Ways themselves or close to a Hiem construction. Wait here for my return." He took a few steps and paused. "If Salinda finds you before I come back, then ask her to wait. I will not be long."

"Are you sure?"

"Yes," he replied and strode away, his shroud billowing in his wake.

Brill turned to Eneit. "Make yourself comfortable, this could take a while."

"What was that?" She gripped his collar. "It's not a Lesseren, is it?"

Brill lowered himself to the ground, allowing Eneit to snuggle up next to him. "No, not a Lesseren, but someone different from us. He's also a good friend."

The girl made a soft "oh" of surprise and settled down again. Brill gave her a drink and some food and soon she was asleep, her breathing deep and even. Comforted by meeting Nils, Brill found it easy to doze off himself.

The sound of a female voice talking softly greeted him when he next opened his eyes. Bathed in the glow of a small light was Salinda, dressed in her white Hiem robe with flowing blue outer cloak. She knelt by Eneit and was engaged in talking to the girl. Brill rubbed his eyes and checked the path. Nils had not returned.

"Salinda!"

Salinda touched his arm softly and smiled. "You're awake. You must have been tired. Little Eneit here was alert to my presence before I had reached this place. I have been here quite some time. Did Danton go on with Nils?"

Brill narrowed his gaze, wondering how to break the news. "I'm sorry, Salinda. Nils went to investigate some explosions. Danton's been captured."

Salinda's eyes widened. "Tell me."

Brill told her what he had witnessed of Danton's capture. "There is something bigger than the theft of dragon wine going on," he said as he finished his tale.

"Do you know where he is being held? Is it possible that he is still alive?"

"I don't know. I hope so. I am not sure why he was captured, other than that his cousin betrayed him for some reason of her own. Why capture him only to kill him? I suspect he lives still. It makes no sense to me. If anything, I was more likely to be recognized and turned in for a bounty than he was. Danton said Toola had my pedigree worked out at first glance."

"Anything else that might shed light on why Danton was taken? Knowing the why would help us determine the where and the who."

"I do not know if there is any connection, but Toola did say that your mother was still alive."

Salinda's gaze narrowed. "My mother came up in conversation with a madam of a brothel?"

"It was my fault. Somehow I let it slip that we knew you. Toola was very clever and used information to get a hold on us. She told me that your mother was alive and a servant in someone's house. I don't remember if she told me whose house."

Salinda climbed to her feet slowly and took a few steps away from them, pondering, before turning back. "Did this Toola mention anyone called the baron?"

Brill shook his head. "Not to me. I did hear she was connected to the chief of police. Narin, his name was. She blackmailed him to do what she wanted."

"I met the baron," Eneit said in a clear voice.

Salinda leaned close to her. "You did? Can you tell me what he looked like, what you remember?"

Eneit began, twining her fingers through her dirtied, little-girl dress. "All of us Vanden girls were in a room. The bad men who had taken us from home had been sent away." Her voice was a hushed whisper, distinct in the quiet of the Ways. Brill leaned in closer too. "I was only there a short time when this baron came to talk to us."

"What do you remember about him?"

"Not very tall. He was sort of round, with dark little eyes. He wore a very pretty jacket and he was very scary."

Salinda bit her lip and nodded. "And then what happened?"

"He asked us all our names and then he asked me to come with him. He handed me a mug of wine and told me to drink it. I was very thirsty so I drank it all. I felt strange afterwards, like I had hit my head or something. Then I don't remember much until I woke up in a sack at Toola's house."

Brill rubbed her back as he spoke. "Your mother was searching for you, Eneit. She never gave up hope of finding you. Toola knew that, and used it against her."

Salinda waited until he had soothed Eneit. "Danton's cousin had the contacts and it seems that she made the right connections. If my former husband, the baron, suspected Danton's relationship with me, then it would be enough for him to hold Danton's life forfeit."

Brill gaped at Salinda. "The baron? Was he the man who put those marks on your back?"

"Yes," Salind said. "They are gone now thanks to Nils, but the memory remains. The baron does not forget betrayal. If he knows that I'm alive and free of the prison, he will come after me. He will abuse Danton until he can get the information about me he wants and then he will destroy him."

Brill felt wretched. "It is my fault entirely. Mandin tried to warn me, but the warning came too late. I had already blurted your name."

Salinda paced a bit, apparently deep in thought. "No use lamenting it now, Brill. There is a chance then that Danton still lives. But we must be prepared for the worst—that he has told them everything. Thank the source that he did not see Barrahiem—but he knows of its existence, and of the Hiem Travel Ways."

"Danton would never betray us." Brill's anger rose. Danton was very careful about who knew things. There were things that he'd never told Brill to protect him from revealing things under torture.

Salinda let out a sad-sounding sigh. "Of course, not willingly, Brill. But the baron is a master of torture. You know yourself what it is like. You know how it can loosen your tongue."

Brill did not like being reminded, but he knew Salinda was right. That was Danton's reason for keeping things to himself: to protect others and to keep information from being revealed. But who would protect Danton from revealing what he knew?

"We must move swiftly, but we need Garan for this. We cannot go alone and we cannot take this young girl into further peril. She has suffered enough." Salinda patted Eneit on the head. The girl took to her straight away, looking up with a kind of worship.

"What do you intend to do then?"

"Take you both back to Barrahiem. The girl can stay with Laidan."

"Laidan is still with you?"

"Yes, but there is a story in that." She held up her hand. "Nils approaches." The walls of the Way began to lighten again, signaling the appearance of Nils.

"What has happened to Laidan?"

"A lot, Brill. In short, be prepared. Laidan is not what she was. I am not sure she will even remember you."

Brill wanted to protest but Salinda warned him with a dart of her gaze. Then, when Nils joined them, she relaxed. Nils flicked off the hood of his shroud and regarded them all.

In readiness to depart, Brill stood and gathered up his things, then paused to hear the exchange between his rescuers.

Nils frowned in his particular way. Salinda commented first. "What is it? What did you find?"

"It was difficult to find my way back here. The conduits appear to be discontinuous."

"Which means?" Brill asked.

"There is some disruption to a major intersection. Not caused by the blasting, I think, but the passage of time and disuse. A sad thing. But we do have cause to fear. Gateshead has been discovered. It will not be long before they discover the Ways."

"Gateshead?" Brill asked, eyebrow raised. "What's that?"

"A small Hiem city," Salinda explained. "It is north of Sartell."

"North?" Brill blurted out. "But...could it be...? Mandin received a clue from a slaver, while we were searching for Eneit. There was something strange going on, a shortage of slaves. Anyway, we think Toola had him killed but before he was taken he slipped Mandin a note, with one word written on it—Eternity. We were able to deduce from this, and from snippets that Danton's deputy, Squab, told us, that it was a project of some kind underway north of Sartell. A—"

Nils was even more agitated when Brill related this news, interrupting him. "They have discovered a Hiem city."

"How do you know this, Nils?" Salinda's eyelids lowered as she studied her husband, giving every impression of not being pleased.

Nils inclined his head. "I confess I ventured out of the Way Gate and lurked there in the shadows. They are repairing sections of the city and appear to be adapting parts of it for other purposes. This puzzled me at first as they did not appear to be searching for knowledge, or technology. Nothing that was said in the conversations I overheard led me to believe they even knew the origins of the city.

"As I traversed the circumference of the city, I noted that there was a terrible smell and it did not take me long to discover its source. Many people are crammed into holding pens. Slaves, I expect. But they are not being used for labor or for long-term occupation."

"What did you see?" Salinda asked him.

"No bedding. No space for comfort. Whoever has possession of them cares little for their welfare or for keeping them alive for a longer period."

"Why do you think they are being gathered together, Nils?" Salinda touched his hand lightly. Her voice vibrated with repressed horror. Brill could see that she was trembling. Brill could not guess at the purpose of what Nils had discovered.

"It seemed to be that they are food. Just food."

"No!" Brill near yelled. "No, not that. They could not." Brill crushed his hands together. What Nils was speculating went against everything he believed in. Humans could not do that to each other. Not in such a calculated way. Yet the evidence was there, he could not ignore it. He could barely draw breath.

Nils waited until Brill had quieted before continuing. "Next to the holding pens I saw men stacking barrels."

"The wine," Salinda said in a whisper. "So this is where it all leads. Danton stumbled upon a web spun by the baron. The Inspector hinted that they knew each other. This is the powerful friend, the power behind the Infra-pact rebels."

Brill fought to calm himself, to let go of his horror and to question what he was hearing with logic. "I don't get it." He shifted his attention to each of them in turn. "Why would they be excavating this underground city and filling it with...with food and wine?"

"I am not sure why, but there has to be a good reason," Salinda said. She let go of Nils's hand. "Perhaps they know."

"Know what?" Brill was confused.

"Know that the end is near. It makes sense. The elite, those bastards," she added harshly. "They will have their own educated minds studying Shatterwing. Perhaps they have predicted when the rogue asteroid will fall. It makes sense."

"Some of the city roof has been exposed to the elements. How will that work?" Nils asked.

Salinda's eyes glowed momentarily. "Before Ruel fell there were many such things, bunkers, they were called. In these places below the surface of Margra, many hoped to survive the end. Some did. They can close themselves up again, don't you see?"

Nils shifted his scrutiny from Brill to Salinda. "I would have to see outside to see what they are doing. It is also possible that they are preparing to cover the city with more rock to secure it. It is possible that the work that I saw underway was to shore up the roof supports. Gateshead was near the surface, and it is possible that over the years and with the upheaval caused by Moonfall parts of the city were exposed, allowing the casual observer to find it."

"If they want to use the city," Brill asked, "why are they blowing it up?"

Nils nodded as if understanding something finally. "They are making a road to the edge of the city. They reinforce the city limits with rock blown from the mountain range nearby to better fortify it, I think, for it is near the sea—a wall, I think. They also widen the roof, which did at first puzzle me, but now I see that it is so they can bring in supplies along the road and then I expect they will cover it with more rock."

A deep rumble under their feet was unsettling. They eyed each other with alarm. "We had best return to Barrahiem. I fear we have little time to waste." Nils turned, his shroud swirling around his legs as he strode away and his silver hair glowing faintly in the pale light of the Ways.

Salinda shared a look with Brill and took Eneit's hand. The girl went with Salinda without hesitation. Brill guessed the girl had told her while he slept what had happened to her mother. At least Brill had been spared telling the story himself. After hearing what Nils and Salinda surmised about Eternity, he did not have the heart to utter one more word of bad news.

Brill took a glance behind him and joined them. In the dark of the Ways, his mind strayed to Laidan. What had happened to her that she could no longer remember him? That had to be impossible. She'd loved him, had given herself to him. How could she ever forget that? No, there had to be a mistake. It would all be sorted out later.

As they walked, Brill went over what Salinda had said about the baron having his own academics with knowledge of the sky. He shook his head. "I don't understand it," he said, catching up with Salinda. "There is no institution of learning in Sartell. My father was an educated man and he tried to teach the sciences in the confederacy but his school was put down. The old knowledge was forcibly destroyed. Along with anyone who had been taught it."

Salinda slowed and turned her head to study him. "I suggest to you that the knowledge was not destroyed but sequestered by those in power." Again he saw her eyes flash with unnatural light. It unnerved him. He had not noticed that in her before, not since that time in the vineyard. How young and naive he had been then. Only now did he realize how much he had grown. Danton had taught him a lot. Salinda's eyes now glowed in a similar way to Laidan's when he'd first encountered her with Garan. It made him shiver to think that Salinda had that thing inside her, something he could not see, feel or truly understand. Yet now, as she let signs of it escape, it brought home to him how little he understood of the world. It was a sobering thought.

Nils interrupted them. "Forgive me. We must travel faster to reach Barrahiem. There is no time to lose and a lot to prepare."

"Nils, you should take it slowly. You have not recovered your strength as yet," Salinda said.

Nils glanced back at them all, his silver eyes dimmed. "Do not worry for me. I am well." He faced forward and increased his pace. Salinda and Brill each took one of Eneit's hands to help her keep up with them.

As they hurried away from Sartell, Brill could not help but dwell on what he had left behind: Danton. Salinda's experiences with her former husband left little doubt in his mind that his friend was going to suffer horribly. His own torture was nothing to what was in store for Danton. Yet he had no choice but to leave his friend in the hands of that man, perhaps to die. Nothing that had been said so far had given him hope that Danton could or would be rescued.

Chapter Eighteen

GERCOMO TAKES WING

Flying through the air with his she-dragon mate, Gercomo rode thermals and set his keen eye on the landscape. It had taken him longer than expected to locate the main road to Sartell, but he had persisted, and on the fourth day of scouting he had spotted carts making their away along the rutted road where it skirted the foothills.

The first cart had yielded two men, who had satisfied his craving for human flesh. He'd let his mate take the bounty of the next. She could barely restrain her gratitude. Gercomo shoved her away, as he had more interesting things on his mind than her licking his genitals.

The next set of carts, they shared the contents. But the energy he had consumed did not allow him to transform. For that he needed dragon blood, and to get that he had to mount his mate and bite her neck during the act. Wounding her without mating would be construed as an attack, and as she was more than double his size, he could do without the complication. This time when she wanted to express her gratitude he let her fondle his oversized penis with her tongue. Her excitement grew along with his, and he mounted her, much to her delight. While she was in the throes of an orgasm he struck, tearing a sizable wound in her neck. Her appetite satiated, her blood was more potent than he had expected. As he glutted himself, the change kicked in and sent him writhing to the ground.

Pushing himself up, he staggered to the overturned cart and found a robe to cover himself. His human form was part dragon, as before. His hands were claw-like, his penis oversized, his mouth not fully functional. This did not concern him overmuch, as long as he could communicate. He needed to send a message.

His mate took his transformation well. Other than sniffing him, she didn't seem to mind. Together they hid the telltale signs of their attack. She used her snout to push the remains of the cart over the edge of the road and he picked up bits of wood and supplies and tossed them out of sight. He urged her to partially bury herself in sand behind the rocks. He hid himself and waited. As this was a trade route it wouldn't be long before someone came along.

He moved his shoulders, stretched his neck, experimenting with his human form. It would be interesting to see how long he could hold it and whether he could transform back to a dragon at will. He rubbed his clawed hands together in anticipation. The ability to choose his form would be a superb outcome. *Thank you, Salinda, for thinking of it.*

Dozing in the sunlight, he woke to the sound of wheels crunching over hard earth. The scrape of burden beast claws scratching a path along the dusty road drew closer. Standing up, he straightened his robe and hid his face in the hood.

A cart driven by a fat, bearded man rounded the curve. The man was wary, head jerking up at the first sight of Gercomo. The burden beast squealed and the man tried to stop it getting away from him.

Gercomo hadn't counted on the beast being able to smell dragon on him. Once the man had got his beast under control, he stopped the cart and covered the beast's nose with a cloth bag with some feed in it. The beast grew distracted and started to eat. Still the man was wary. His shoulders were hunched and he would not look Gercomo in the eye. He climbed back on board the cart and waited for Gercomo to approach. Gercomo tasted the tension in him. His dragon senses told him there were other humans on the cart. Gercomo strode up at an angle, catching sight of the blankets and clothes where these others were hidden. He inhaled and knew them to be a woman and a child. The cart man's, perhaps? Leverage was always a good thing to have.

Gercomo stepped forward and raised his hand. "Wellssmet," he said. His voice sounded muffled, unclear.

The man's face screwed up and he tilted his head, as if doing so would make his hearing better. "What ho?"

Gercomo drew closer. It would be difficult for this one to flee. Burden beasts had good stamina and not much else. With his mate close by to come in for the kill, this poor man didn't have a chance.

Gercomo repeated himself slowly. The man's eyebrows furrowed. "Afternoon," the man said. "Can I help ye?"

Gercomo spoke again. "Yesssth."

The man recoiled, not able to hide his shock. "Are you sick?"

If he only knew, Gercomo thought, and suppressed a laugh. Gercomo struggled to form the words. "No." The word came out throaty and cracked, but the man understood him.

"That'll be a good thing then. Don't wan' to be catchen nothin'."

Unseen by the cart man, Gercomo's mate emerged from cover on the other side of the road. Gercomo formed the thoughts that relayed his instructions and pushed them to his mate. Behind the man, a claw scraped the blankets and clothes away, revealing the woman and child. They screamed as his mate nudged them with her claws. She wanted to eat them. Human flesh was tasty, she sent at him.

Gercomo urged her to wait. Turning, the man yelled and fell backward off this bench in his haste to get away. His mouth opened and closed but only whimpers escaped.

"Helpsmme. Not hurtssthem," Gercomo said as clearly as he could. He waved his head around, annoyed at his lack of finesse. Damn Salinda. She'd left him half a man with her power.

The man gaped at him, not quite understanding that man and beast were working together. He shifted his attention between the she-dragon and Gercomo.

"Takes meessage. Yousth wriites?" Gercomo struggled to talk. "Understandsth?"

The man continued to gape at him but slowly lowered his head and lifted it again in a daze.

"Goodsth. Takes meessage andsth come back." Gercomo observed the man's wife and child. "Yesth?"

Again the man jerked his head up and down and inarticulate whimpers leaked out of his mouth.

"Nots comes back. Wees kill. Wees eat. Understandsth?"

Tears leaked down the man's face and his trousers grew a damp patch. Gercomo sniffed, liking the smell of the man's fear.

"Writesth?"

"Y-yes."

The man went to his cart and brought some writing cloth and ink. Gercomo dictated the message and gave him directions. It wasn't a long message, but it was to the point.

"Baaack tomorrowsth."

The man nodded vigorously.

"Don't," his wife cried at him. "Don't leave us."

The cart was empty of the man's family now, prodded out by the she-dragon. They stood together in a huddle, the boy child hidden within the mother's clothing, not that it was any real protection. The driver avoided looking at them as he went about his preparation. He removed the food sack from his burden beast's muzzle and then climbed into the cart. With his shoulders riding high, he goaded the burden beast into action with his whip. A growl and a screech, and the beast walked on.

🦀🦀🦀🦀

It was near sunset of the next day when the man returned. The cart rolled to a stop and Gercomo stepped from the shadows. His mate lay out of sight, finishing off her meal.

"Weell?" Gercomo found speech still came slowly but it was easier now that he had stayed in his human shape without incident for nearly two days. He had to concentrate, though.

The man peered over his shoulder at the road he'd come along. "He is coming."

Gercomo waited a while, staring at the man, ensuring he was discomforted. The man moved from foot to foot as if he wanted to urinate.

Then the sound of mounted men reached him. The jangle of gear, the scuff of many claws scratching a path on the road, voices. Gercomo lifted his head. There, coming up the road, was the baron, accompanied by some of his personal guard.

"Go. Join your familysth." Gercomo indicated the direction with his head. The man climbed off his seat and called out to his wife. She did not answer him. She couldn't. Bertha, the name Gercomo had given his she-dragon, had already bitten off the heads of wife and son and was currently munching on their limbs. The man disappeared behind the boulder and let out a throaty yell. A loud crunch echoed around Gercomo. Bertha would be very grateful and willing as a result of his feeding her three humans.

He was wrapped in blankets made to appear like a cassock, with a hood over his head.

The baron pulled up his burden beast and eyed the abandoned cart. He had obviously heard the man's final cry. He spared Gercomo a look that held surprisingly little curiosity. Gercomo let that pass. All would be revealed in good time.

"Good. I would have had to kill him myself. Can't have trash like that knowing where I live. How did he know where I lived?"

Gercomo shrugged, let the baron sweat it out. The baron dismounted from his burden beast. "Your message intrigued me. For the second time in a week I have heard the name Salinda."

Gercomo stepped forward and pulled back the hood. The baron's expression did not change.

When Gercomo did not speak, he lifted an eyebrow. "Who are you?" the baron drawled. His guards dismounted and readied weapons.

Gercomo wanted to laugh. The paltry humans had no chance. He took another step forward, concentrated on speaking the words. "Remeembeerr meee?" Gercomo said in hard, guttural voice. It took a lot of effort.

The baron's beady dark eyes assessed him. "You look like someone I knew once. Someone who recently sent me some wine. Could it be you?"

"Yeessth." Gercomo lost control in his excitement and he fought for its return. He could not appear weak in front of this man and live. His clawed hand gripped his covering and the baron's eyes rested there.

"I had heard the tale from one of your men about your transformation before I executed him. Now I owe him an apology. It seems he was not lying after all. So, Gercomo, half-man, half-beast, it seems. What is it about Salinda that you dragged me all the way out here to tell me?"

"Powersth."

The baron shrugged. "I know about her alleged power. Tell me something I don't know, like where she is and how I can get her."

"Cann...senses...her," Gercomo said. "Take...you."

"Good. Excellent. Where is she?"

"Nots nowsth. Caannnots. Sense. Her. Nowsth."

The baron turned his back on him and peered up at the sky. Night had fallen and Shatterwing glowed brightly. "You are not much use to me, Gercomo, if you cannot sense her at will. In fact, I can see little you are good for with your unfortunate handicap."

Gercomo grinned, exposing broken fangs. He would show the baron. He would like to see the old bastard lose his water, shit himself in fear.

Gercomo called to Bertha. A fierce growl made the baron's men jump and the baron himself jerked backward. The baron continued to back up as the vibrations of Bertha's stamping footfalls nearly knocked him from his feet and sent their mounts bucking and squealing.

Bertha lowered her neck to Gercomo, exposing the oozing bite mark. Gercomo licked and sucked, letting the blood fill his mouth, and the power entered him like acid in his veins. His senses whirled, then the transformation began. He screamed as bones bent, flesh stretched beyond breaking point and his brain knew once again the mind of a dragon.

The baron's men tripped and fell to the ground in their haste to flee, their mounts darting off and squealing in panic as they disappeared. Quickly, the baron backed down the road, the reins of his burden beast firmly clasped in his fist, as Gercomo took shape.

When Gercomo had completed the transformation, the baron stared, eyes wide, mouth open but silent. A few moments passed, then, with a shake, the baron recovered himself and he stepped forward. "Impressive."

Gercomo stood with Bertha just behind him, nudging his leg.

The baron grinned and nodded, altogether too composed. "One day you will have to show me how you did that. Now, I can see a use for you. Can you track me as I travel north?"

No longer able to speak, Gercomo nodded his reptilian head. He inhaled the scent of the baron, memorized it.

"Good."

Bertha screeched, almost sending out fire.

The baron blinked. "Perhaps you should feed your mate. Take four of my men."

Gercomo communicated this information to Bertha. She made short work of the baron's men, leaving nothing for Gercomo.

The baron laughed as she ate them. Then, with a flamboyant salute, the baron left, with his remaining guards escorting him. He was still laughing as he traveled out of sight down the road.

Chapter Nineteen

THE DARKNESS WITHIN

Danton jolted awake with a burst of pain. Judging by the abuse hurled at him, a guard had punched him. His gaze was full of red and confusion as he was unbolted from his chains and hauled from the room. He tried to get his bearings as he was half-dragged, half-carried down a decrepit hallway. Shaking his head to clear his vision, he saw the boots and the open door before he was thrown. "Wait! What do you want?"

After sprawling on the floor, he tried to push himself up. A punch to the mouth split his lip and he hit his head on the floor with the impact. "Shut up," the guard snarled. "You're to talk to the boss and no one else."

Weak and helpless, Danton could do nothing as they lifted him up to the tabletop. They arranged him face up with his head hanging down off one end and his legs spread and bound to the table supports at the other. He tried to move his arms, but they appeared to have been bound at the wrist by rope under the table. Escape was going to be difficult. In that position, his view of the room was upside down. He didn't recognize the lordling that walked in. He called him a lordling because of the clothes he was wearing: opulent, bright and completely impractical. More to the point, Sartell was full of petty princes and self-titled barons and he had no idea into whose clutches he'd fallen.

"Pleasant to see you again, Danton," the man said.

Danton blinked, trying to place the voice. Again? He had no

recollection of speaking to anyone. "Your information was very valuable to us. Unfortunately, your men and your second, Squab, had already fled their respective lodgings."

Danton jerked, unable to hide his mortification as sick fear built up inside his gut.

"I see you are surprised that I know so much about you. You were very forthcoming at our first meeting. I'm hoping that you will be again."

"Bastard liar. I wouldn't betray my men." Danton was sweating. He couldn't remember a previous interrogation. He'd been beaten, that much he knew. By the dragon's holy ass, he couldn't have betrayed his own. He breathed deeply, trying to calm himself and keep his mind under control. There was a smell in the room that was overly familiar and evoked memories that he shied away from. The lordling walked past his head, and Danton knew then that it was this man who was the source. Why would the scent of this man affect him so? Perhaps there was a reason he didn't remember what had happened. He didn't want to remember. That thought scared him.

Someone grabbed him by the hair and lifted his head so that he could see his interrogator. The lordling smiled, displaying a row of yellow teeth. He was an older man, bearing a slight paunch and a graying beard. He stroked his long fingers, which were covered in rings, along his bearded chin.

When he saw that he had Danton's attention, he lifted an eyebrow and then reached into a bucket. Danton squinted, not sure what was coming next. Making a show of it, the lordling pulled out pointed, rusty shears. "Such a shame to do this to you. I know how proud you are of your cock. Cut off his clothes."

Danton struggled as the guards dived onto him. One used a knife to cut away his trousers, the other tore his shirt off him in strips. The one with the knife was none too careful, and Danton could feel the cuts where he had been overeager. The situation was dire. He had to prepare himself. Death was his best option. Yet, there was a sliver of a chance that he could finagle his way out of there.

"You're rather hasty, old man," he said quickly, trying to act nonchalant. "You haven't even asked me a question. I won't talk much without my cock attached. That I can promise you. Best you kill me now and save time."

The lordling strode to the business end of the table and Danton strained his neck to follow him, keep him in sight. His stomach curdled when the old man took his cock in his hand and fondled his balls. Danton had locked away the memory of what the Inspector had done to him, what he'd made him do. If he didn't keep that memory repressed he would unravel. He swallowed a lump in his throat. He could do nothing to stop the unwelcome attention.

"I like my meat younger, you know. But you are quite right. You value your cock more than your life. But what use is it to you here, unless you like fucking corpses?" His eyebrows rose. Danton thought of Merl dead in the little locked room—deliberately left there for him to find. Of what importance was the other, older man? A spy? A more important prisoner?

He told himself the lordling's fondling didn't bother him. He was neither aroused nor repelled. The Inspector had made sure of that. He had no option other than to wait it out. He concentrated on his surroundings, noting that this room also had blacked-out windows. The light came from a lantern in the corner and from the open door behind. Suddenly the lordling turned his hand sharply still grasping Danton's genitals. Danton could barely breathe; the pain shooting through his body locked him up tight. The shears weren't necessary. His torturer already knew how to cause him excruciating pain.

"What's my name, Danton? Tell me."

Confused, Danton tried to think and came up empty. "I don't know," he said through clenched teeth.

"You do know my name. Only yesterday, you sucked my cock. Come on. Tell me. You were so sweet, surrendering to me in every way, words flowing out of your mouth as my seed went in."

Danton screamed as the lordling's grip tightened on his balls and twisted further. By the source, it hurt. He couldn't remember what the lordling described; he wouldn't remember. And then, something twisted inside of him, triggered by the pain racking his body, and the memories came flooding in as the drugged haze lifted—the torture, the abuse, the words falling out of his mouth as they held him while the baron almost choked the life out of him. He had betrayed his friends, all of them. "The baron!"

"Yes, that's better." The grip eased but the pain did not recede.

It pulsed in his groin like a beacon, stretching out with fingers that gripped even his toes and into his chest. "Now we will continue where we left off. You know a certain escaped prisoner, is that right?"

Danton threw his head from side to side, trying to hold back an answer. "I know many of them. Why?"

The baron leaned in close, mouth brushing against his ear. "I am interested in one of them, a certain woman, from a certain vineyard. My source tells me you are intimate with her and know her current whereabouts."

Danton mental anguish heightened: *Toola! No, Toola—not Salinda.* Danton knew this man, knew what he had been to Salinda, knew the extent of his cruelty. This was Toola's backer, the man who ran her like she ran her girls. What a fool he had been.

Danton thought fast. There was no point in denying it. "I met her once." His raspy voice sounded loud in his ears. "We were prisoners around the same time."

The baron leaned back slightly, excitement moistening his eyes, making them glint in the lamplight. "Yes," he said, and licked his lips. His dark, beady eyes glistened. "But you escaped. I heard that. She helped you, didn't she? How?"

Danton shook his head, trying to rearrange his thoughts. The Inspector had to have been reporting on her back to the baron, too. That figured, as the Inspector was cast in the same mold. "Maybe," he replied. "I don't remember clearly."

The baron picked up the shears and held them aloft. "You value your cock more than your life, but there are other parts of you that I can nip off that are less valuable. This finger, perhaps?"

Danton couldn't see which finger it was as it was tied below the table. He felt a burning sensation and screamed. His index finger. He even heard it plop to the floor. The baron moved to his other side.

"I..." Danton was going into shock. The room swirled around him; his stomach rebelled.

"Yes?" The baron paused. "You were saying?"

"It wasn't her that helped me. The old man, Mez, helped me escape. She wasn't involved."

"Cauterize the wound," the Baron said to one of his men. "There is blood dripping on the floor. I won't tolerate mess. Throw the digit in the fire, too."

Danton braced himself. Then he screamed until there was no breath inside of him as the stump was roughly burned. He dared not glance at the digit that was thrown into the fire. The smell of his burning flesh made him retch.

"Come now, don't be so queasy. We have only begun." The baron repositioned himself so his face was up close again. "You say she did not help you, but Merl mentioned you were searching for her. Gercomo Karonen had her, is that not so?"

"The Inspector? Yes, he…he…had her, took her away and we lost her."

"Where did you lose her?" Danton tried to turn away but the baron held his head by the hair. When Danton shut his eyes the baron shook him hard, almost breaking his neck. "Answer me."

"Gunner. That's right. A place called Gunner. She escaped, or so it was said. We gave up and went after the…ah…"

The baron let go of his head and stepped away. "The wine?" the baron finished for him, turning his body slightly toward the table. The baron stepped around and the two guards in the room edged out of the way as he passed them. Danton tracked him as he circled the table. "Tell me, why were you searching for Salinda?" The baron spoke without inflection, but Danton felt the power of the words, the importance of the answer. Death appeared to be unattainable at that moment. Oh, how he wanted to die, before he let any more information out.

Danton watched the baron, swallowed once and answered him truthfully. "I am in love with her."

"Salinda? How touching. Tell me, does she still bear the marks of my handiwork?"

Danton blinked some sweat from his eyes. He felt immeasurably dizzy. "Yes. I saw them once, caressed them. But that was so long ago now."

"Traitorous bitch!" the baron blurted in rage. Then, taking a deep breath, he calmed himself and once again presented a placid façade as he paced around the table. "I let her off too lightly then. She was not meant to survive. I will not make that mistake again." He paused, had Danton's head lifted to they could make eye contact. "There is something you are not saying. I heard that you have seen her more recently. Is that not so?"

"Not so recently." The baron reached for the shears again. Danton thought more lost fingers would render him unconscious. He'd welcome unconsciousness, anything to spare him more pain and betrayal.

"I heard tales of a monastery of some kind—a strange tale of Gercomo..."

The room spun for Danton as the depth of the baron's knowledge was revealed. With his mind addled by pain and deprivation, how was he going to navigate around the truth? The baron continued. "A story about Gercomo, the former Inspector of the prison vineyard, turning into a dragon with the help of a young man and a woman who sounded remarkably like Salinda. Would there be any truth to those stories?"

Danton realized that the rebels would have witnessed what happened at the observatory and brought their version of events back to Sartell. Was there any way to use this to his advantage? Yes! He and Brill had not been seen. The baron couldn't possibly know that they had been there helping the occupants.

"Monastery? What monastery? Don't know what you're talking about."

"I see." The baron moved quickly. Danton felt a burning sensation, a tug, and then mercifully he blacked out. When he came to again they were cauterizing the wound where his little finger had been.

The baron squatted by his head, which lolled freely, and grabbed him by the hair again. "No more passing out. I don't like your games, rebel. Now I'm going to give you something to loosen your tongue. Swallow it like a good boy."

A guard stepped into the space the baron had vacated and heaved Danton's head up so that his chin was resting on his chest. He saw his naked body and the pattern of bruises on his torso and thighs. No wonder his body ached; they had worked him over thoroughly. He had flashbacks to the previous interrogation session. He gulped once. No wonder he had blocked it out. Unfortunately, he had the sneaking suspicion that the baron was just warming up. The wounds on Merl's body had spoken volumes.

The guard forced a foul-smelling liquid between his teeth. Danton tried to fight it but his jaw was forced open and his head tilted back as the drug slid down his throat. It burned, scouring his insides on its way down. It worked quickly, too.

By the time the guard let Danton's head go, the room appeared distorted. Danton's muscles relaxed and there was a slight buzzing in his ears. They might have untied him then because he felt himself being turned over and rearranged. His legs were dangling off the edge of the table, and he felt the wood dig into his hips as pressure was brought to bear on him.

A question came out of the haze of his mind. Words fell out of his mouth unbidden. He heard the voice again, but couldn't quite catch the meaning. Yet he heard himself answer. What he said made no sense to him. Then someone barked orders at him. He was commanded and he obeyed, crawling like a dog, licking when asked, spreading himself when asked. All he could hear was the laughter. The humiliation went on and on.

ᏬᏬᏬᏬᏬ

Danton woke unbound this time, naked and dirty on the floor. It was hard to move as he was stiff, sore and in pain. It was the same room he'd been locked in before. The stench was stronger now, permeating the air without let-up. He squinted around the room. That sliver of light illuminated the spot where Merl had lain. There was nothing there now but a stain and a smear on the floor. The body had served its purpose. It had demoralized their captive.

Again Danton's memory was patchy. He recalled the fingers being lopped off but not much after that. The numb hand throbbed. A rough bandage covered the stumps. Shame coursed through him, staining his soul beyond measure. Death was too good for him.

He had betrayed his cause, his friends and worst of all, Salinda. Carefully, he edged himself onto his elbows and winced. His ass was burning, painfully sore. The baron and source knows who else had been at him. Perverted bastards. He'd cut their cocks off and feed them to them if he had a knife and half the chance.

The momentary flare of anger died, leaving him overwhelmingly feeling the hopelessness of his situation. No one knew where he was and even if they did, he was too far gone to be saved. He doubted there wasn't much else for the baron to get out of him. The next session the lordling would cut off Danton's cock and watch him bleed to death. A fitting end for a betrayer. There would be another session. Of that he was fairly certain. Why was he alive if the case was otherwise? Danton had something else to give up by way of knowledge. That kernel of knowledge, whatever it was, Danton wanted to hold onto.

The mound of blankets heaved suddenly, as if the old man had coughed. Danton crawled over to him. "Hey, old man. What's your name?"

The old man clawed the blanket down from his face with gnarled fingers, some twisted at unnatural angles. The good eye stared at him, suddenly alert. "Who are you?" the old man whispered harshly as if no longer able to talk normally. As the old man lifted his chin, Danton saw the scars. He had had been hung by the neck at one time.

Danton closed his eyes as weariness enfolded him. He had not eaten for days. "I told you before. Name's Danton." Danton cast his gaze around for the bucket of water. He was very thirsty.

The old man nodded slowly, drawing Danton's attention. "Danton de Lavental?"

Danton's surprise exploded out of him. "What?"

"Danton de Lavental."

Danton sucked in a breath. "Yes, that's me, but I haven't gone by that name for a very long time, not since the uprising."

The old man squinted at him, groping with his hand. "Can it be you?"

Danton edged closer, focusing on the face, looking for something that would give him a clue. "Yes. It's me. But I don't recall meeting you before."

The old man's face was attacked by spasms. "My name is...Hu...Hu..."

Danton stomach sank as the clues came together. His gaze ranged over the old man's ravaged face, trying to find a trace of the man he had known. "Hubert of Duval?"

The old man stared vacantly as if remembering something from the past. "You thought I was dead?"

Danton bowed his head, feeling the full impact of the horror of his discovery. "Yes. They displayed your body on Confederacy lands as a warning to any others. Damn, it must have been a decoy. I can't believe you've been a prisoner all this time. Ten years at least?"

Danton was appalled when the old man nodded because he knew then that he wasn't an old man at all. Hubert was barely ten years older than him. Yet the captivity had wrought irreversible damage to his body. He doubted that Hubert could walk out of there, even if the door was thrown open in the next minute. How could he have borne the long years of incarceration?

Danton brushed a chunk of dirty hair from the other man's forehead. "I've been with Brill. He was well last I saw him and he is just like you, full of ideals and ideas."

"Brilliant? My son?"

"Yes," Danton replied, patting Hubert gently on the shoulder. "He thinks you have been dead all these years."

The damaged eyes sought to focus. The cheeks sank as the memories set in. "I am dead. I know I will not leave here alive. Even though I am no longer of any use to them, they keep me here. The baron never forgets. He never forgives. Remember that."

"Do you know where we are? Is there a way out?"

Hubert shook his head feebly, not in the negative but back and forth like someone in pain. "Eternity. We are in Eternity. We will die in Eternity."

Danton mouthed the words. There was some memory, something important that he was searching for. "Eternity?" he whispered to himself. "I know that name." The vision of Mandin came to him and the note the slave trader had given her. "What is Eternity, Hubert?"

Hubert's eyes were closing. He was beginning to drift off. "A city, an underground city. It is being prepared for occupation by the chosen."

"The chosen?"

The eyes focused on him again. "Those who have been selected to live. Final moonfall is coming. They have scientists and consultants who advise them. Some, I think, are not even human."

Danton rocked back on his heels. All of his body radiated pain, yet this news startled him. *So this is where the wine is being stockpiled. For the chosen few, and the rest of us be damned!* "What do you mean, not human?"

But the old man had lapsed into unconscious. Danton tried to wake him but Hubert couldn't be roused. He crawled back to his spot and positioned himself in a way that hurt the least, resting his mutilated left hand on his right elbow. A smile found its way onto his face. Something had gone right. He had found the wine after all. But at what cost? The smile faded. *Wing dust! At what cost?*

๑๑๑๑๑

Danton limped across the floor of the small room, measuring its limits, which was both a painful and difficult task. He hurt in so many places he didn't even try to catalogue his injuries, nor did he try to work out what hurt more: the cut and burned fingers or the tears in his violated flesh. The furniture and other junk in the room made for painful obstacles. He bumped his hip and was cursing silently when Hubert spoke to him through the dimness.

"Danton?"

Danton rubbed his aching hip and rested his gaze on the other man. Pity for Hubert's predicament had him shaking his head. He still had to come to terms with the idea that Brill's father lived, had lived as a prisoner all these years, his dreadful fate unknown to all who cared for him. How would Brill react to knowing his father had lived this way while he had been ignorant? The boy would blame himself, even though he was blameless. A creeping feeling of horror came over Danton. What if such an end was planned for him, too? Source forbid that he would be forced to linger here for years.

"Danton?" the older man called again, sounding even feebler than before.

"I'm here," Danton said, lowering himself gingerly to the floor next to Hubert.

The blinded eye moved jerkily in its orbit; the other one focused on Danton. "Tell me about my son?"

Danton fingered his own empty eye socket, noting the similarities in their fates.

"Brill has taken up your values, Hubert. He fights for the rights of the innocent and the downtrodden. He strives for a better world and believes...believes as no one else does that we can be better than we are."

A sigh rattled in Hubert's throat and a smile creased the grime coating his cheeks. "For naught."

Danton leaned closer. "What did you say?"

"For naught…it is all for naught. There is no hope in the world. Gone…poof! I have seen what we are. You must stop them, Danton. You must destroy them. Kill them all."

Danton frowned. Had the old man lost his senses? He could understand disillusionment. Surely years of torture and deprivation engendered such feelings. But Hubert had heard that his son was alive and fighting for his cause. Danton had expected a better reaction than that. "I don't believe you, Hubert. You are alive for a reason."

"No…for no reason other than punishment. They force me to eat once a week to keep me alive. Enough to make me less of a man with every passing day. There is no reason I am alive…I just am. A devil's whim…that is all." Seized by a coughing fit, it was some time before Hubert was able to whisper, "Careful…they do not do the same…you."

Danton rubbed his chin with the edge of his hand. Clenching a fist was a bit difficult with the pain, but he wanted to punch something. Hubert was saying that they'd kept him alive for no reason, but that made no sense. In fact it scared Danton to his marrow, because it meant they could easily do the same to him, whether or not he had more information to give. That worried him because he was fairly certain, without actually knowing it, that he had given up every secret inside of him to the baron. He no longer knew what he had held back, if anything. By rights he should be dead. Yet, he wasn't. His hands shook, then his torso. Danton laid his head against the wall and shut his eye.

The Baron of Sartell, long deposed but still in power, kept people alive because it suited his sense of revenge. Hubert had defied him by proposing a better way to live and doing well at it. Danton had loved the baron's spurned, rebel wife. No, it was more than that. A kind of madness that had no meaning. It just was.

Salinda had been nothing but a possession, a thing to be abused and spurned. The baron did not love her, or want her, but he had never forgiven her for her role in the rebellion. Salinda had been convinced that the subsequent marriage and murder of her sisters was retribution. Hubert was right: the baron was a man who did not forget or forgive.

"Danton?" Hubert's thin thread of voice was barely audible.

"Yes?"

"Kill me…"

"What? No!"

"Please..." Hubert was no longer focused on him but on some distant spot on the far wall. "Please."

"Hubert, no. Don't ask that of me. How could I face your son knowing I'd delivered the final blow?"

Hubert lifted himself, pulling forward with the last of his strength. "Find something...anything...bludgeon me...choke me...while you still can. Soon he will incapacitate you and then you will not be able to help me or yourself." Hubert sobbed. The blind eye wept. The sighted eye tried to find Danton, tears trailing down the filthy leather of the older man's face. "Please," Hubert said, and then sucked in a breath, "for what we once were to each other, kill me, end my misery."

The old man's eyes closed. "For Brill," he whispered.

Danton gaped at him, filled with revulsion and pity and horror. Lifting his hands, he could see they were practically useless. But Hubert's plea had got to him. The old man had borne more than should be borne.

Danton could not refuse his request, but the immediate worry was how to do it. Carefully, he climbed to his feet, suppressing the groans that movement elicited from his throat. After studying the contents of the room, he came back to Hubert empty-handed. There did not appear to be anything he could use as a weapon.

Shamefaced, he lowered his gaze to the floor, ready to confess his inability to put Hubert out of his misery, and then he saw the tattered end of the blanket. He knelt down and examined it. There was a split in the fabric. It would be hard, but Danton could work the tear into a strip with his teeth. It was not the solution that Hubert hoped for but it would supply a means for him to kill himself.

On hands and knees, Danton worked, tearing the old blanket into a long strip. He had just completed it when there was a sound at the door. Danton spat the strip of blanket from his mouth and crawled backward as a key turned in the lock.

They were probably coming for him again. He was out of time. "Hubert," he hissed, leaning toward the old man. "Take this." He tossed the strip of material to Hubert. "Put it around your neck and pull with all your might." The old man remained motionless.

Danton edged away and climbed to a standing position near the spot where they had dumped him. The door swung open, revealing three guards: two who remained outside the door and one who came in to fetch him. Danton wanted to fight but knew the time was not right. He had no strength, no knowledge of a way out, no hope of rescue.

As the guard grabbed him around the throat and dragged him through the door, Danton thought he saw Hubert wrapping the strip of blanket around his neck like a scarf. As he was manhandled to the interrogation room, he caught the view out of an unboarded window. What he saw made him gasp. Unless his exhausted eyes deceived him, he was in an underground city. It was like no city he had ever seen. With a chill in his heart he realized it must have been built by Nils's people. It was concave with small white buildings climbing up the sides. Overhead, light speared through a huge, jagged opening. The rest of the roof was stone or something like that. Dust billowed over the opening. There was some blasting or construction going on up on the surface where he could not see.

The view was taken away as he was thrown to the floor of the interrogation room. He had time to think and calm himself. The building works had been in progress for some time, he calculated. This defilement of a Hiem city was not due to Danton or information extracted from him. He had not betrayed Nils's secrets yet. He hoped.

Chapter Twenty

NO LONGER ALONE

B rill held Eneit's hand as they followed close behind Nils and Salinda up the last stair. Standing in the middle of a group of three houses was Garan. His smile of welcome was genuine, yet something in the Skywatcher's expression told Brill that Garan knew about him and Laidan. Garan came forward to embrace him. "Brill! You are back. Where is Danton?" The tall Skywatcher looked behind him down the stairs, then his violet-colored gaze shifted once again to Brill, his forehead a ripple of puzzlement.

Their eyes met and Brill shook his head. "He was captured."

Garan's face fell and he nodded and caught sight of Eneit. "We will talk more later." Then Garan glanced down at Eneit.

The girl was staring up at him, wide-eyed. "You're a Skywatcher, aren't you?" she asked.

"Yes," Garan answered, emotion clogging his voice. "You must be Eneit."

Eneit nodded. "My brother is a Skywatcher. Do you know him? Turnet is his name."

Brill swallowed, knowing the history, knowing what it had cost the young Skywatcher.

Garan squatted down so that he was more or less at eye level with Eneit. "I did. I knew him well."

Brill saw the fleeting expression of pain in Garan's face, knew the grief he must feel to tell the sister of his best friend that her brother was dead.

Eneit turned to Brill, the question clear. "But...does that mean...?"

Brill lowered his head, a dip of the chin, letting her know it was true. Eneit burst into tears and buried her face in Garan's shoulder. He patted her back and stroked the back of her head. Garan's violet-colored eyes locked with Brill's and the expression in them spoke of his pain. How was he going to tell Eneit that it had been he who had killed her brother? After a while, the girl quieted and, hiccupping, pushed away from Garan's shoulder. "I have no one now."

Garan stroked her head. "We will take care of you. You have us."

There was movement behind Garan and Brill caught a glimpse of the flowing skirt of a white robe. He looked up. It was Laidan. Her smile was radiant and Brill could not resist returning the smile. And then he saw it—the total lack of recognition in her eyes. It was a punch in the gut. Brill fell back and tried not to gape or grab her and demand that she look at him. Salinda had warned him that all was not well with her. He stayed quiet and unassuming.

She walked up to Garan and stood a little behind him, like a child hiding behind its mother. Garan reached behind as he stood up, grabbing her hand and guiding her gently forward. "Laidan. I would like you to meet Brill and Eneit."

"Hello," Laidan replied, still smiling. Her gaze rested on Eneit. "Do you want to play?" Laidan asked the girl. "I know some games."

Eneit stared questioningly up at Brill. "Play?" she mouthed.

"Yes, Garan taught me a game called...er, well, you throw these five stones. Come on. I'll show you."

"Go on, it's okay," Brill suggested gently. Eneit allowed herself to be led off to one of the houses, casting a look over her shoulder at them as she went, her gaze dark and narrow.

Brill brooded as he watched them, until Garan clasped him on the shoulder. "She gets better every day. Feeding herself, dressing herself... one day I hope that she will be like she once was."

Brill faced the other man, his rival for Laidan's affections. "She doesn't remember me," he said as the two girls slipped through the small doorway.

"Nor me. Not from before, you understand," Garan said. "In my case, 'tis probably a good thing."

"What happened to her, Garan? I thought she was safe with you and Salinda."

Garan recounted what had led up to Laidan's flight and what happened after. Brill's cheeks heated when Garan described what he'd seen in the cadre. Tears leaked down his cheeks when Garan listed her injuries from the Inspector's attack. "By the source! It is too horrible." Brill let it sink in, then realized there was something even more horrible. "He can change from dragon to human and back again?"

Garan's pursed his lips. "I fear it is so, but not certain. Something to watch out for at least. As for Laidan, 'tis no wonder she does not remember it, nor the people associated with it. I hope you will be gentle with her."

Brill's head shot up. "Of course. What do you expect that I should do?"

"And you?" Garan said changing the topic. "What has happened to Danton?"

Brill filled Garan in on all that had taken place, quick, blunt and to the point. Garan recoiled when he spoke of Danton's capture and then he covered his mouth when Brill told him of the Hiem city being used by the baron's men.

"You think they know about moonfall?" Garan's mouth hung open, aghast.

Brill dipped his head up and down slowly. "Salinda thinks so and she knows more than I do. Nils saw the wine and Eneit confirmed that it was the baron who had her."

Garan shook his head and was distracted by Salinda and Nils entering the courtyard.

"Garan, come into our abode. We have to talk to you." She glanced at the doorway through which Laidan and Eneit had disappeared. "Do you think they will be all right in there alone?"

"Of course," Garan replied. This was seconded by Brill, who thought

Eneit would manage Laidan quite well. She was tough for a little girl; with all she had survived, it was no wonder.

Together Brill and Garan went into Nils and Salinda's abode.

Salinda's complexion was pale as she took a seat on the sofa. Nils's body appeared sunken in. The brisk pace of the return journey had taken it out of him. Brill, also fatigued, sat opposite Salinda. Garan studied each of them in turn.

"There's food and tea. I will bring it," Garan said finally, and slid into the food preparation area while Brill cast a glance around the room. Barrahiem was more than he'd expected. The roof was domed, giving the room a lofty feel. The abode itself was made of a kind of white stone, the kind he'd seen all through the city as they'd traversed the ancient pathways.

Garan carried in a large pot, wafting steam and intriguing aromas. Fungi stew by the look of it, and flat bread. Brill was suddenly aware that he'd been existing on field rations or nothing for nearly a week. He hoped Eneit was able to eat too. Next Garan brought some roast vegetables, and the sight of those roused Salinda, who sat forward eagerly and took a bowl.

"Thank you, Garan." She spooned some into a bowl and handed it to her mate.

Nils inclined his head and took the food. Brill detected the Hiem's trembling hands as he ate. Nils was not as hale as he professed to be.

Brill took a bowl in anticipation of his turn. Garan went out the door, taking a tray with him. Brill relaxed, realizing that the food was for the two young women.

Garan returned and joined them at the meal. "Where is Danton being held?" he asked. "Do you know?"

"We think we do," Salinda responded, with a glance at Brill. "But there is more. A small Hiem town has been discovered and is being converted to use for occupation. There is a risk to the Hiem Travel Ways and to Barrahiem being exposed if more of the relics of the Hiem are revealed."

Garan nodded, his gaze shifting between them. "You think Danton is there?"

Salinda bit her lip. Brill broke in. "I think it is highly likely. The hints about this place called Eternity, as well as what Nils saw, and the fact that the dragon wine and good slaves are being brought north. Whoever is doing this, has Danton."

"It's him. The baron." Salinda's voice was almost a sob. "Has to be." Her hands covered her mouth as she slowly shook her head.

Garan sat solemnly as Nils chimed in. "Then we must act."

Salinda focused her gaze on the table, no longer covering her mouth. In her eyes was a hard glint, one that Brill recognized.

Salinda spoke firmly now. "We must stop this exploration of Gateshead and prevent the Ways from being exposed, even if we must collapse them ourselves."

"What are they doing there?" Garan asked.

"We think they know about final moonfall," Brill said. "They are taking Sartell's elite and intend hiding away underground in the hope they will survive."

"Know about moonfall?" Garan spluttered.

"Yes, they must have their own astronomers." Salinda seemed quite sure. "Sartell used to be a place of learning. It is not implausible."

Garan's eyes shone. "Their information could be valuable to us, to the observatory."

Nils lowered his head and lifted it slowly.. "All knowledge is useful if you know how to apply it. Their observations of the heavens are from a different point on the surface of Margra, and that would add greatly to the observatory's information."

Brill hadn't considered that. He re-evaluated his opinion of Nils. Salinda went on to relate all that they knew, and what Nils had seen and surmised. Garan's mouth dropped open and his eyes were rounded with horror. "Are you saying that they are abandoning Sartell and leaving everyone else for dead?"

Brill nodded. "It looks that way. There's more to it, though. How did they know about Gateshead in the first place?"

Nils put down his empty bowl. "That is something I wish to find out."

Salinda sat forward and touched her husband's hand. "Nils. Not yet. You must rest first."

Nils opened his mouth but she put a finger to his lips. "No protests. You cannot hide your fatigue from me."

His eyes widened. "Yes, I did not tell you before. I didn't know how to, but when you drained your life force going through the in-between, you tapped into mine."

Nils did his impression of a frown. Hard to do with no eyebrows. "Not possible."

Salinda's lips widened in a smile. "Perhaps, but you can't fool me."

"Very well then, I shall go to bed."

Salinda turned her gaze on them. "Perhaps we should all rest and reconvene later. Nils will need to return to Gateshead to bring us more information. We haven't enough to plan."

Brill squeezed his fists in frustration, thinking of Danton and what was happening to him. "Surely we know enough to find Danton."

Salinda frowned as she faced him. "Danton is only one of our concerns, Brill. I suggest you take what time you can to rest and recuperate."

When faced with that expression, Brill lowered his head. "You can bunk in with me," Garan said.

᎒᎒᎒᎒

Brill took advantage of the free time to wash, dress in clean clothes and to sleep. Eneit seemed to be holding her own and Laidan had really taken to the young girl. Brill was able to let worry for the young girl and Laidan go. Garan took him on a tour of the city, showing him the work he had done in refreshing the lights, the fabled healing tray and the sacred lamp in the Hall of Elders. Truly, Barrahiem was a wonder, the stuff of myth and legend. "It was lucky that Nils was able to help Laidan with this," Brill said as he ran his hands along the smooth stone of the healing tray and studied the machine, green links winking on an off.

Garan turned away from the mural he was studying. "Yes. She would have surely died. Sometimes I think that maybe she has."

Brill's head jerked up, surprised. "I have heard of people recovering from brain injury. Give it time. You said yourself that she is learning to dress herself, eat by herself. There will be further improvement, I'm sure."

"Really? I did not dare to hope." Garan's attention was diverted.

Brill swung around. Nils was passing along the corridor. "He's back."

"Yes, we should head back."

༺༻༺༻༺༻

Salinda surveyed the group gathered in the living room of her and Nil's abode. Eneit was keeping Laidan occupied in her abode. Salinda was thankful for the young girl's initiative. By some instinct Eneit knew that Laidan was not quite right in the head and, despite the trauma of her kidnapping, was quite willing to stay quiet and keep Laidan company. *Poor child*, Salinda thought. Yet she was but one of many and Salinda had no time to dwell on the evils of the world, only to fight against them in the best way she knew.

Brill appeared rested and his face was less haggard. Garan's eyes were bright and his posture spoke of eagerness. Salinda smiled at them, feeling grateful from the heart for her wonderful companions. She poured Pardu tea and slid the small cups to them along the tabletop.

"Thank you for joining us so swiftly. As you may have guessed, Nils went back to Gateshead while you slept to gather information so we could make our plans. He drew a rough map for our purposes and we have discussed the finer points between us. Now we present this to you." She lifted her head and gestured to Nils.

Nils placed a drawing on the table. Brill leaned forward and studied it. "It looks quite similar in layout to Barrahiem." He picked up the map and showed it to Garan.

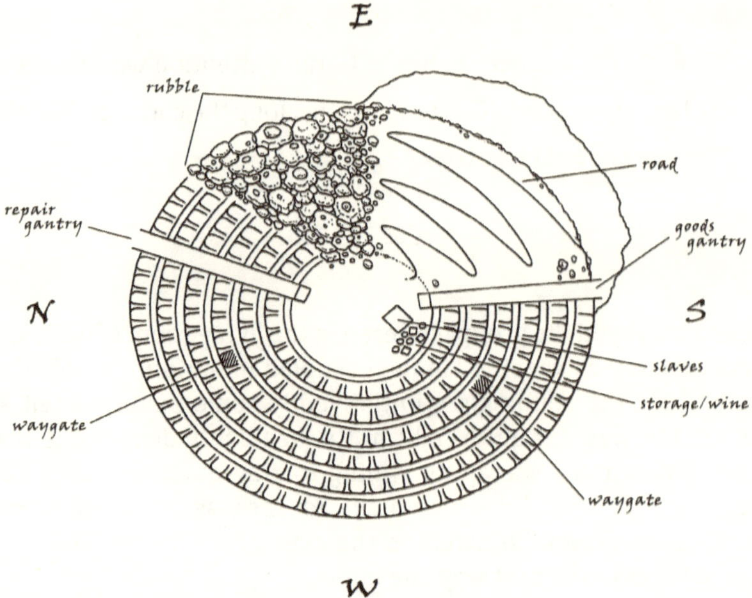

"Yes, are these balconies overlooking a lake?" Garan asked, his violet-colored eyes bright.

Nils tilted his head to the side and took the map from them. "Either you are very perceptive or my skill is better than I knew it to be. I am no cartographer. But yes." He used the tip of his finger to trace the lines of the five levels of galleries. "These are the balconies that look out on what was once a small lake. It is dried up now and is nothing but fallen masonry from the roof. It follows a similar design for most of the Hiem cities, just smaller in scale. I have not shown you the rooms and abodes beyond as they exist within the fabric of the earth. There are corridors and walkways beyond these galleries. I marked where I think the Hall of Elders should be. I did not go there as there was too much to do. I was able to mark the position of the Way Gates and give some indication of the breach in the roof. There was a cliff face looming above the hole. There were men working there. From what I could discern they were laying explosives."

Salinda studied the map. It was a better rendering than what she could do herself and valuable for them to start to plan their attack. To her it was useful to show where the cliff face was in relation to the opening in the city roof. The galleries and balconies spread around the sides of the city made them look like the inside of a cup. The Way Gates were marked with crosses. Indeed, it was a much smaller version of Barrahiem, for there were only a few abodes along the edges of the city, where Barrahiem had tiers full of them. Nils had told her this—they weren't marked on the map.

"So now we make plans. Brill, I expect you will join us," Salinda said.

"Of course," Brill replied, as it was never in question.

Salinda lifted her head and focused on Garan. "We need you to come with us, Garan."

The Skywatcher pulled back. "But what about Laidan? We cannot take her into danger. She has suffered enough."

Salinda turned to Brill. "Do you think if we left Eneit with Laidan that they would be safe alone? Eneit seems bright enough, sensible. Otherwise we would have to take them to the observatory, but with Danton captured I'm not sure that they would be safe there either, and we don't really have the time. We must consider all our plans and secrets as exposed. There is no way Danton could withstand the baron's torture."

Brill made to interrupt, to defend his friend, but Salinda continued, "Or any torture," overriding any comment he was going to make.

Brill rubbed his chin as he considered. "Eneit has been through a lot, survived a great deal. Provided we left sufficient food and instructions, she should be fine with Laidan. What are we talking about, a day, maybe two?"

"Yes, perhaps two." Salinda rubbed her chin. "The best-case scenario."

"Are we certain we are coming back?" Garan asked. "Because if we do not come back we are condemning them to death here."

Garan's comment sparked a hot argument between them all. Salinda settled it, raising her voice and then making a harrowing observation. "If we do not come back there is nothing to stand between Margra and final moonfall. All will be dead."

They fell silent at that. Salinda was not happy to bludgeon them with hard reality but they had to accept risks or there was no point in doing anything. Salinda had not expected to be leading this foray into enemy territory. She had thought Danton would handle it. But she'd led rebels in the past. Long ago now, but she found that the mantle of command came readily enough.

"So," Salinda said. "We agree there is danger. We here will go, leaving Laidan and Eneit behind. Brill will return when his task is done to protect the girls. Perhaps, if you return to the observatory, you can take refuge in the doomsday cave Titina has prepared. I will write a note for you to give her. I'm sure she will agree."

"The observatory has given up?" Brill gaped and then shut his mouth when he saw the truth reflected in Garan's eyes. Garan hung his head.

Salinda pursed her mouth, annoyed at the assumption and the diversion from their serious business. "They have not, but they are taking practical steps to save who they can in case we fail."

Brill gritted his teeth, but ducked his head quickly.. "Then I will return if and when it is decided I must."

"Good." Salinda tugged the map toward her. "Now, Brill," Salinda began, "do you know where your rebels are camped? You mentioned that they went north and are near Eternity. If you could make contact, we could use them as a diversion, and also to retrieve the wine."

Brill chewed his lip. "I should be able to find them. Do you have something to write on?"

Garan retrieved some paper and a pencil, sharpened to a point. Brill drew a rough map showing Sartell, the coastline and Gateshead/ Eternity and another city further north, Lukton.

Brill lifted his head and then pointed. "This is where Squab is supposed to be. But how do I get there? I could return to Sartell, but it would take time to travel there and there's the risk of discovery."

Nils drew the map toward him and made two crosses in Eternity itself. "These are the two Way Gates in the city." He studied the map further and added further crosses. "These are the gates in Sartell." He pointed to one. "This is the one that you used, Brill."

Brill nodded and studied the map. "Once I'm close by I will be able to confirm the rebels' position, as Squab will have left markers. Getting there?"

Nils studied the map, chewing his bottom lip. "If memory serves me, there is one Way Gate between what is now Sartell and Gateshead. There was once a trading town that shipped goods to the coast and to the cities of the Sundwellers. My people purchased supplies from them, and observed them, of course."

Nils marked another cross on the map. "You might have seen the stairwell leading to this exit when you were first in the Travel Ways."

Brill shook his head. "It was too dark to see anything much. Do you think it is still operational?"

Salinda inclined her head. "Next time you go there you will take a light and be better prepared. You will have to test it first. We can't take chances. Is that all right with you, Nils?"

"Yes, Garan should accompany him. He seems to be able to navigate the Ways well enough to get them there and back."

Salinda patted Nils's hand. "Yes, you need further rest before we attempt this."

"A few hours will be enough."

Brill studied their expectant faces. "I think I can manage this. I'll leave as soon as possible. If the Way isn't working I'll go to Sartell and head north from there."

"No," Salinda responded. "If it isn't working, come back here. It will be quicker to use one of the Gateshead Way Gates and a shroud to get you out. Risky, but better than diverting so far south."

Brill agreed. "We'll leave after we have finished discussing our plans."

Salinda inclined her head as she studied the map. "That works. We will be able to time our strike better knowing Brill has safely made contact."

"I will fight with them," Brill said.

"We need you with us," Salinda replied firmly.

"They stand a better chance of success if I can guide them, set them in motion. We have far more information than they do." He tapped the edge of the map. "We have this."

"All right then. Nils will make you a copy to give them, not with the Way Gates marked, though."

Nils agreed to this.

"I will let you work out with Squab how you will approach from the south road. These gantries Nils have marked must be used to haul goods. Nils, was there a roadway from the opening into the city?"

"Yes, the south road continues down a switchback road to the base of the city." He pointed to the map. "Slave pens are there and next to them the wine."

Brill frowned. "It must be a temporary position. If they plan to bring down that cliff face they will risk crushing the supplies."

"My thought exactly," Salinda said. "They have some time to deliver the supplies then sequester them elsewhere. Nils says they are working to reinforce the roof but that's on the other side, where this other gantry is. Can you describe this better, Nils?"

Nils narrowed his eyelids. "Yes, they use that to take men and stone and other construction material up to the roof."

"And what about getting up out of the city through the hole in the roof. We need to blow that cliff face before time."

Nils studied the map silently. "Near the gantry where they are making repairs there is lots of fallen stone. It reaches right up to the breach in the roof. It is possible you could climb up there and outside."

Salinda took the map and studied it. "Using the gantry is out of the question. Even shrouded, we would be noticed."

"Where do you think Danton is being held?" Brill asked, and Salinda's heart skipped a beat. She had been daring not to hope that Danton was alive, or able to be rescued.

"I saw no sign," Nils said. "There was evidence of restoration and conversion of abodes down here and along these areas. Gateshead does not have a vast archive so it does not have tunnels underneath as does Barrahiem."

Brill ran his finger along the lines where the balconies were drawn. "This section, though. Squab and me will be fighting here. Salinda and Garan will be here." Brill glanced up. "Nils?"

"Nils will be assessing the Ways to make sure when we blow the

Way Gate that it will hide all traces. He will also be scouting around for information."

Salinda dared Brill to contradict her. Nils was too precious to risk in a skirmish or by exposing him on a mission to blow up the cliff. His specialty was skulking in shadows and for backup if any of them needed rescuing.

"All right," Brill said. "So what next? We attack and start retrieving the wine."

"Yes. When you see that your rebels have the wine and are winning through, you will need to enter this Way Gate here and set off the explosives. Nils will cover the other gate and ensure it is ready to blow." Salinda indicated the two Gateshead Way Gates. "We will need to blow the final Way Gate as we leave. I don't want you to be left behind."

"I can come back via the other gate near Squab's camp," Brill suggested.

Nils and Salinda exchanged a look. Salinda spoke. "That would require backtracking and we do not know what forces will come in from Sartell way."

Nils faced him. "Once we blow these two Way Gates," he said pointing to Eternity, "I suspect that whole line of the Travel Ways will become unstable. They are already in poor condition. It is possible that when we blow these, that gate will no longer function. You must come through with us."

"What is my task?" Garan asked.

"You, young man," Salinda said, "will have the task of blowing up this cliff face. Of course, we need a way of delaying the explosion. Nils has put his mind to what he saw when he did his exploration of the city. Then he consulted his maps. Part of the mountain range that they have been using to build up a wall around the outside of the city, hangs over the roof, particularly the part that is open. We believe that they will bring down this stone structure to cover the opening to the city."

Nils pointed to the map. "This is why these people have been fortifying the roof underneath and have removed buildings from under the hole. It does not matter to them if the debris from the cliff face when it is blown fills up the gap between the floor of the city and the roof, it is all added protection from what will happen at moonfall."

"If that's part of their plan, then the explosives may already be in place," Brill added.

Salinda gave a short, sharp nod in acknowledgement. "Given what Nils discovered, that is a logical assumption. However, we will take our own explosives to make sure it does come down when we want it to."

"I can do that," Garan replied. "I helped blast in the mines. I will talk to Brill and Nils about ways to delay the explosion. We could adapt some Hiem technology, or I could find a way to use the crystals."

"I have timers," Brill said. "They are easy to rig." He shrugged. "Just not very reliable."

"I will find out what information the interlopers have uncovered and destroy it," Nils said. "It is important to find the source. They know too much about the town and that cannot have come from Danton. If possible I will see what happened to Danton, see if he lives."

"Agreed," Salinda said. "I think that Danton might be dead, but if you find trace of him, do what you can, Nils, but I don't want you taking any risks. You are too important." Salinda frowned as she voiced this last comment. It was hard to say that about Danton. As much as she cared for him, Nils was the key to the information in Barrahiem. "That leaves me," she continued. "I will assist Garan and find a spot to oversee the operation. I know this sounds a bit bloodthirsty, but I want to make sure the baron goes down."

Brill reached over and squeezed her hand. "What about Gercomo?"

Salinda snatched her hand back. "Gercomo?"

"Yes, didn't you say he can change back into human form? Isn't he linked to the baron?"

Salinda's face lost all color. "Gercomo in the mix? It doesn't bear thinking about."

"Perhaps we should consider the possibility."

Salinda licked her lips. "Very well. I will ask my dragon friends to search for him. I best do that now before tomorrow. Then, if he is close, I can counter him if need be." It was rather vague, but she found it hard to imagine Gercomo being involved with Eternity. Salinda leaned forward, elbow on her knee, hand rubbing her chin. "I will find a way to send orders. I'll be in command and if you receive an order from me, obey it. I will have the best position. Be on the lookout for our signals."

Brill studied her. "It's a good plan. You could be vulnerable, though, in plain sight."

"I will wear a shroud. Nils has started preparing one for all of us."

They discussed strategy for a while longer. Garan was assigned with providing food for the girls and for the trip, and Brill was to gather explosives. Fortunately, Salinda had taken a store from the observatory when she left, much to Nils's surprise.

"You brought explosives into Barrahiem?"

"I wasn't planning on using them here, Nils," Salinda responded mildly. Titina had supplied them and she hadn't had time to let Nils know or even to consult.

Nils stood up, arms waving as if he was about to begin a rant, but then apparently he was lost for words.

Garan let out a chortle, then Brill couldn't help himself and burst out laughing. It was a good way to defuse the tension. Luckily, Salinda saw the funny side and smiled. Nils narrowed his gaze, not quite getting it. That made it even funnier.

"Explain," he said.

Brill tried, but Garan interpolated. "It is funny to us that anything Salinda does is a surprise to you. Salinda bringing explosives with her seems so natural to us."

Nils's eyes narrowed further. "I see. You mock me."

They all went quiet. Then Nils grinned. Brill's jaw dropped open in surprise.

Salinda's smile widened. Nils was learning. "I meant no harm, but I thought it would be good to have some. Danton always had a supply..." Salinda's voice faded. How was she going to go on knowing that Danton was no longer in the world? She let out a sigh. Brill nodded and Garan placed his hand on her shoulder.

"I know..." he whispered. "I miss him too." Salinda took a minute to gather her thoughts and then stood up, sliding her arm through Nils's. "When you are done, get a good night's sleep. We start preparations in the morning, early." To Nils she said, "Come along. You shall go to bed. I need to vist Plu's mate."

Chapter Twenty-one

TRACES

It took Brill the better part of a day to locate Squab and the rebels. The sky was darkening, with big, roiling steel-gray clouds obscuring the sunset. Once out of the Ways he cloaked himself and headed in the direction Squab had agreed on, hunting for signs. He was about to give up when he saw the first marker, and then broke into a jog when he saw the second.

Squab had about fifty men assembled, double the number she had originally. Brill was impressed with how well she had hidden them, broken up into groups of ten. He stumbled into one band before he knew he'd found them.

Tori, one of the men, recognized him. "Brill!"

With a huge sigh of relief, Brill grasped his hand. "I never thought to see you out here," Tori said.

"It's good to be here. Squab?"

"I'll take you. She'll be pleased. She's been itching for a fight, what with Danton taken an' all."

Brill followed the man and was soon facing a cranky-looking Squab. "Danton?" she said by way of greeting.

Brill wiped sweat off his brow and scanned the men who had gathered in around them. There was no campfire and only the feeble light from a shuttered lamp helped him see who was there. "We think he's been taken to Eternity. I have confirmation that the wine is there.

That's the order: retrieve the wine."

"And?"

"Free the slaves too. They are meant for food."

A groan went up from one of the men. Squab's scar distorted her features. She spat onto the ground. "When?"

"First light."

"You staying?"

"Yes, I'll be with you for the first part. Once the operation is underway I have other tasks to attend to."

Squab's eyes glittered with reflected light. Brill shifted from foot to foot, uneasy under her scrutiny. "Good," she said finally, then turned away, yelling rapid-fire orders. "Salinda plans well."

Brill relaxed. Squab was Danton's deputy and Brill hadn't been sure the woman would regard him as Danton's stand-in or accept Salinda's orders. He was glad that she did.

☙☙☙☙

Nils skirted along the shadows, his fully charged shroud humming with power. He had to trust that the others were in position and attending to their various tasks. It was hard to trust others. He trusted Salinda, but sometimes she could be tricky, bending her notions of loyalty far from what he considered true.

From the shadows near a mid-level balcony in the township of Gateshead, he stared out over the concave city with its faded gray stonework, and experienced a pang of regret. These streets and abodes were not meant to see sun, wind and rain.

In the distance, where the construction works were in progress, he could see that the decay was even more advanced. What he had surmised appeared to be true. Gateshead had been exposed to the elements for some time, the far section's upper layers, at least. The humans had widened the hole in the cavern roof, expanding it so they could bring goods inside and shoring up the decaying roof. From the surface a road zigzagged to the base of the town and slave pens stood next to storage areas where once had been a lake.

A noise alerted him to someone moving furtively down the

corridor. Near invisible, Nils watched as whoever it was slipped into a room, a door closing behind him. The door was an addition, not part of the original architecture. A shabbily closed-in archway held the support for the door. The destruction of the original Hiem design wounded Nils to the heart. How could they destroy something they did not understand, mar such beauty?

Nils did not think he could bear to see more of what the invaders had done, but he knew he had to. Nothing could bring Gateshead back to its original glory, and it saddened him that there were none alive who would appreciate the aesthetics of Hiem architecture. What a fool he was still, worrying over inconsequential things. His kind were gone forever and when he died, living memory of the Hiem and all their deeds would die with him.

As he drew closer to what was once the Hall of Elders, he saw the ruins of intricate murals, chipped away and replaced with modern script. Rage, hot and strong, surged inside him. He almost lost himself to those darker feelings, when from behind him came other footsteps.

Survival instincts kicked in and he let go of his outrage and ducked into the shadows, where he waited and watched. There, passing just in front of him, was a tall, thin man, wrapped in a cloak with a hood lowered over his face. Something in the gait, and in the stoop of the shoulders, triggered recognition in Nils. The man paused, lifted his head and cocked it as if smelling something. Nils held his breath, hoping that he had not by some unknown means advertised his presence. In the next instant, the hooded figure moved on. A shiver ran up Nils's spine. *Who was that?*

Waiting to ensure that there was no one else traversing the walkway, Nils slid out of the shadows and ghosted the retreating figure, slipping from shadow to shadow. His shroud hid his presence as its substance fluttered around him, bending light, minimizing sound. Still, his innate caution made him careful. The right light, the right angle, and he could be seen.

The person he was following did not hesitate again but marched directly to a large door and opened it. It looked like it was a modern construction within Gateshead's former Hall of Elders. The edges of hastily erected walls cut into the fine scrollwork and paintings of the Hiem architecture.

Gritting his teeth at the desecration, Nils sped up, hoping to pass close behind the man to ensure that he was not left out in the hall and excluded from the room. As he crossed the threshold, Nils noted the empty alcoves that had once held the sculptured forms of notable Hiem. Had they been removed recently? He ached to know. It was a sick kind of fascination, which had the effect of weighing him down with depressed thoughts. A bad habit of his.

Gateshead was not an ancient city, like Barrahiem or Stregahiem, but had been in Nils's time a modern construct, built by his kin to provide a place of rest and reflection, and to assist with the transition of the chosen ones who were to dwell among the Sundwellers to serve as advisors or secret observers, noting down events for the archives. Yet those modern Hiem architects had replicated the traditional style so well that it was a home away from home for most. His quick study of the city in the archives the night before their departure had been brief, but to the point. He had what passed for a familiarity with the city that he had not had before. Before Ruel split apart, Nils had never visited this place; he knew of it by reputation only.

If a city of the Hiem was to be exposed to the world, Nils reasoned, Gateshead provided the least risk, except for the potential access to the Way Gates that its discovery offered. The existence of the Travel Ways, the other Hiem cities and their archives must remain hidden from the world. Brill had put down explosives to collapse the Ways behind them when they retreated. Given what Salinda had told Nils of this baron, there was no telling the danger he represented if he gained even one-tenth of the Hiem's treasure or infiltrated the Ways.

Once through the door, Nils slid sideways before it was shut and skimmed across to the dim patches along the wall created by the overhead light. What had once been the sacred lamp bathed a large table in flickering light. Its flame was tainted with the smell of animal fat. The cloaked figure threw back his cowl as he leaned over a large map.

Nils faltered as he saw what lay beneath the head covering. The figure was tall, his long hair falling past his shoulders, a layer of silvery-white over a darker layer. The hand that traced the roads drawn in the map was white-skinned, like Nils's own. The long fingers tapered to a fine point. Nils lifted his own fingers, touching them tip to tip and then lowering them once again. He stared at the man before him. His heart raced and his nostrils flared. *It could not be.*

Taking a wide circle around the map table, Nils sought a closer view. There, in the light of the sacred lamp smoking with foreign fuel, was a Hiem face. Bony brow, pale, not-quite-silver eyes, and a mouth pinched into a frown. Nils could hardly draw breath. The impulse to shout in surprise had to be overridden by the deepest caution.

The man lifted his head. "Why don't you come out of the shadows, friend?" he said, turning to face Nils's direction. "I will not harm you."

Nils stood stock-still. Could this part-Hiem actually sense him even though he was hidden in the shroud? There was something quite alien about this man. He was familiar but warped. Something warned Nils to stay hidden.

Behind him, Nils detected movement. He stepped aside to avoid the person walking toward the man leaning over the map. The other person had been stretched out on a bunk. Nils closed his eyes. He had not known there was another person. He could not afford to let his guard down again. That had been too close.

The other man walked forward to greet the man who so resembled the Hiem of old. The other man was human, dressed in clothes similar to Brill and Danton's usual garb. The man patted the part-Hiem on the back, a few loud thwacks. Nils recoiled in sympathy. To be touched in such a way was repulsive and smacked of disrespect. "Nakel, good to see you. What do you think of the baron's new intelligence?"

The taller man's hair flared out as he turned quickly. "Nonsense. There are no other cities like this. My people would know about them."

"The baron sounded pretty convinced." The human leaned over, running his fingers over the map as if he knew what he was doing.

"Perhaps the rebel was talking of Gateshead. What that man was reported to have described fits the description of this city and this city alone."

The man pulled a face. "And these Travel Ways he mentioned? Pathways through the world?" He shook his head.

Nakel shrugged. "Such information is clearly the product of a mind tormented, a mind that would do or say anything to stop the pain the baron was inflicting. I do not credit it."

"I never knew you for a cynic. Yet the baron says they are true mouthings and must be acted upon."

"Of course, I will do as instructed." Nakel returned to his study of the map.

The human glanced at him sideways, his eyes narrowed. "Where do you think these Way Gates are? I confess I see no sign of them, but I have no idea what they look like."

Nakel glanced at the man, his lips pulled tight. After a while he said, "If the baron is convinced these gates exist, then we have to produce these gates."

"'Fraid so. You know what the consequences are if you don't."

Nakel leaned both hands on the table and lowered his head. "I do indeed." His voice was a whisper and tinged with sorrow.

The human smirked, an expression that Nakel did not see. It chilled Nils to witness it. "Is it your wife he has, or your mother? I can never remember."

Nakel nodded slowly and lifted his head. "Your concern is touching. All my family is held captive," he said coldly. He turned to the human. "Does that satisfy your morbid curiosity? Does it whet your disgusting appetite for suffering?"

The man backed away, raising his hands in mock defense. "Don't get upset with me, now. I meant nothing by it. He has many of us by the short and curlies." The human must have seen something in Nakel's expression because he continued to back up, hands raised as if in surrender.

"I suggest you get out, then, before I rip your innards out and decorate my map with them."

The human's eyes widened and he nodded and backed away.

Nils tried not to breathe, in case he was discovered. The ferocity displayed by Nakel frightened him. It was so un-Hiem-like. Yet his anger at the human Nils could understand. One part of him wanted to leave, as he could not bear to see this corruption of the Hiem form, to hear the malice in his words, yet curiosity drove him and—though he hated to admit it—longing too. Yet, Nakel represented betrayal. He was actively involved in the defilement of this Hiem city. It was possible that Nakel was acting under duress, but Nils wasn't sure. A Hiem would never betray his people or their technology.

The human left the room, leaving the door ajar behind him. Nakel picked up an ornament and tossed it idly between his hands while he studied the map. Nils headed to the door.

"Please, don't leave just yet. I have something to say to you."

Nils paused and turned around. Nakel put the ornament he had been juggling on the edge of the map and began making his way to where Nils stood. "Don't think I don't know you are there. I've been expecting you, Nils."

Nils froze. His heart thudded and he was seized by fear. How had this Nakel known he was there? How did he know his name? Could it be that Danton had told them everything? Salinda had said it would be so. Danton would have had no choice. He would never willingly betray her, so if he had, it meant he'd been forced.

Nils needed to know. As much as he hated confrontation and feared exposure, he had to act now in order to know. He threw back the hood of the shroud, revealing his face, and then he parted the garment to allow his robes beneath to be visible.

Obviously surprised by the sight of him, Nakel recoiled before recovering himself and standing normally again. His gaze traveled over Nils in an insulting way. Normal for a human, but he lacked the subtlety of the Hiem.

"That is impressive," he said, meeting Nils's gaze. "Full blood, I suspect. Never seen a full blood before, except in pictures. How do you happen to be a full blood?"

Nils said nothing. Danton did not know all and, therefore, had not revealed all. This man did not know Nils's origins, even if he knew of his existence. Now that he was face to face with Nakel, he could see more signs of human in the other man. He was shorter and stockier than Nils. Up close Nils could see that his skin tone, while pale, was not as smooth and white as Nils's own.

Nils had wanted to see some evidence that his kin had survived, but he had not expected it here, amid this rape of his heritage.

"Come on, there has to be an explanation." Nakel began circling him, occasionally darting disconcertingly forward, possibly to test Nils's responses. Nils tilted his head while he studied the half-breed, his mind working to formulate a false history.

"Throwback," Nils said, following the other Hiem with his eyes and maintaining the distance between them.

Nakel chuckled. "Really? But all the others have been rounded up. I don't remember seeing you anywhere in the compound. How did you get out?"

Nils's heart fluttered. There were more of the part-Hiem in a compound somewhere? He had to interweave lie with truth if he was to learn more. "I'm not from around here," Nils said, preparing to move out the door, but Nakel got their first, blocking his way. He made to grab Nils, but Nils ducked beyond the other man's reach and back-stepped.

"How many are there of us part-Hiem?" Nils asked.

"About one hundred in the compound."

Nils's mouth dropped open. "One hundred? Where?"

"Not here."

Nakel made another feint, sending Nils back further in order to keep his distance. An odd smile played around the other man's mouth. Physical violence was not something Nils excelled at. But the need to survive drove Nils to move faster than he'd thought he could. There on the edge of the map was the ornament that Nakel had been juggling. Nils reached for it, found it heavy in his grasp.

Nakel smiled. "Yes, a useful piece of ornamentation, don't you think? Your arrival is quite timely. Your friend, Danton, has revealed the existence of the Ways. I am about to show the baron where the nearest gate is."

"No!" Nils surged forward and struck Nakel in the temple. The crunch made him cringe. Nakel's eyes glazed and he smiled oddly as his knees buckled. Puzzled, Nils leaned in closer over the felled man and heard the words leaking from Nakel's mouth. He said, "Thank you" in the Hiem tongue. "You have saved..."

When Nils checked for life signs he found that the Hiem was dead. It was strange, but he had the impression that Nakel had given him the victory. He had been willing to die. Nils was angry at himself. He had killed. That in itself was bad, but it was also a waste; the man had known things, he could have answered questions about matters that were dear to Nils's heart. There were part-Hiem alive somewhere. Nils thought back to the conversation he had overhead. This baron had

Nakel's family. Leverage, threat. Nils shook his head. That is why the man had wanted to die. To protect the Ways from exposure. He could not protect his family, but he could protect Hiem secrets.

Anxious not to be discovered, Nils dragged the body into the shadows, hoping to delay anyone stumbling across it, then he quickly checked the map Nakel had been studying.

The map showed the city of Gateshead, or Eternity as it was called now. It had been amended to show the modern changes, including living quarters, slave cages, food stores and a prison complex.

Nakel had left a marker on the prison section, a red chalk triangle. Nils was confused. It was clear Nakel had been helping the human invaders, but his actions were also contradictory. They smacked of coercion. He had spoken of a compound, but the map did not indicate such a place. More of his kind could be in the city or they could be held somewhere else. Nils had no time to think about it. His fingers traced the red triangle. Danton had to be there. He fed the map to the flames of the sacred lamp and fled the room.

❧❧❧❧

Brill thought that the edge of the city that had been exposed to the elements looked like a broken shell that had been pecked at the corner by a seabird. The road to the southern exit had been cleared of rubble and led to the lip of the city, a mound of earth that hid it from view. The city itself lay in a depression half in the shadow of its intact roof; the rest was now exposed to the elements. The intact sections of the roof were made of thick and solid layers of stone, although Brill caught sight of some scaffolding where reinforcement works were in progress just as Nils had said. At present, all was bathed in pre-dawn gray light. Around the edge of the city, boulders and sharp rocks thrust out of the ground. Stones and pebbles lay scattered ahead of them to the cliff that overhung the eastern side of the city. Brill inhaled traces of salty brine. The sea was just over a day's march away.

Guards patrolled the southern entrance to the city but they were few and far between. Some on duty appeared asleep, rolled in their capes and oblivious to their surroundings. Their complacency allowed Brill to crawl close enough to peer down into Gateshead. A roughly hewn switchback track led into the bowels of the city and its storage areas. Alongside the road was a gantry from which six ropes hung over the side to winch goods down into the city. On the other side of the city's basin, another gantry hung. It had flat platforms to move people and objects between sections of the city where the stairs had collapsed.

Brill sent a nod to Squab, who then dispatched a group of five men to start rappelling down into the city proper to secure the wine. They knew they were outnumbered by the baron's men, so they needed stealth at first to succeed, and then they needed chaos, because the odds would be against them if the baron's men got organized enough to mount any resistance.

It was clear to Brill that the perimeter guards were not expecting an attack. Rather, they seemed bent on preventing slaves from escaping. A hurling blade cut off the cry of alarm from one guard, who turned at the wrong time and caught Brill as he moved into the light. Squab slit the throat of another who was dozing on a stool and was in the middle of waking up. She ordered another five men to finish off the rest of the perimeter guards, and another five to take the switchback road, with instructions to disable the enemy quickly and quietly and then prepare their bows. They would be providing cover for those retrieving the wine.

Brill set about locating carts and found two. Four fellow rebels began harnessing the burden beasts who were quartered in a nearby yard. Another two were sent off to bring up the other carts that the rebels had commandeered in preparation for the fight. It wasn't going to be enough for all the wine, but it was better than nothing.

That left about thirty or so men to join them for the hand-to-hand combat. They just had to choose their position. With the perimeter guards accounted for, the southern entrance was the best place for the rebels to defend. However, they had to protect those recovering the wine. Arrows would help thin out the enemy attack, but once engaged, Squab and he would have to fight down below, leaving only a handful of men to guard their escape and provide an escort for the wine carts.

Dawn light filtered a mauve glow over the landscape. A shout from below made Brill twitch. He listened intently. Another shout. Then orders flew about. They had been discovered. Squab hove into view. "Ready?"

"Yes. Let's do it."

Squab gave the orders, and twenty-five men tramped down the

road into the depths of the city at double time. Brill and Squab chose the ropes. Descending into darkness, Brill kept his senses alert. The morning sun had not penetrated far into the city as yet. Firepot lamps containing yellow flames sent dirty smoke into the air. Sounds assaulted his ears—orders, cries, the clink and grate of swords clashing. Then the stench hit. Nearby slave pens bursting with the unwashed accounted for the smell. Brill made a mental note to free them no matter the outcome of the battle. It would cause chaos and some slaves might escape.

Brill dropped down from his rope and unsheathed his sword in time to deflect a blow coming from his right. He followed that up with a kick to his attacker's gut. The guard had expected his blade to chew flesh; instead he got a fist in the face when he doubled up from the kick. Brill finished him off with a thunk on the back of the head with his sword pommel. A hurling blade came in useful in cutting down the next man. A grunt behind him made him turn. Squab had walloped a would-be attacker with her axe. His smashed face disappeared from view when he fell. "Thanks," Brill said. The bloody mess of the man's face made his stomach clench.

Squab just grunted and grinned. That wasn't a pretty sight either. "I'm going for the pens."*

A spear cut the air between then. Squab hurled her axe and a scream advertised that she'd hit the mark. "Hurry."

The first wine barrel was being winched up. A cheer erupted from his men. Brill gritted his teeth. They would have to work hard to keep the wine at this rate. More guards came pouring into the place where they fought in front of the stacks of wine barrels and the rows of slave pens, which were gated with doors made of steel bars. Arrows thinned out the line that was charging them, and Brill darted for the first pen.

No amount of jiggling was going to open the lock. Brill searched for the guard who held the keys. He spotted him fighting young Tori, the bunch of keys knotted at his belt. With no time to spare, he plowed into the man, knocking him flat. Tori, readying to strike, gaped at him. "Sorry, Tori. This one's mine."

He clubbed the guard with his sword hilt and groped for the keys. Tori darted into a fight of three guards against one rebel and evened out the odds. Gripping the keys tightly, Brill sprinted to the first pen. He had to breathe through his mouth as he unlocked the gate. He'd never smelled anything so bad. The wave of humanity pushed the gate open and he backpedaled to get out of their way and moved to the next pen. As predicted, the chaos caused by the slaves escaping complicated the enemy's attack. Some slaves were attacking guards with their bare hands. Some were also attacking Brill's men, but he and Squab had anticipated this and considered it a risk worth taking. Brill went to open the last pen.

Squab yelled and Brill froze. A large phalanx of guards was pushing their way through the fighting men and the swarm of slaves. Armored and armed, they were intent on the rebels retrieving the wine. These were Infra-pact rebels, well trained and dangerous. Squab yelled a warning as she lobbed a lit explosive into their midst. The phalanx collapsed. Body parts flew up and out. Blood and gore rained down in a series of sequential splats. Smoke wafted filling the air with stench.

᎒Ꮽ Ꮽ Ꮽ Ꮽ

Nils slipped into the shadows and went deeper into the city. The corridors leading to the prison section were full of men. Sharp-eyed men, Nils amended, jumping whenever one turned his way or lifted an eyebrow when he passed by.

The level of traffic prevented him slipping through the crowd without brushing against anyone. He waited in the shadows, uncertain how to continue. He was not sure how long he had waited there before he heard shouting, then the report of an explosion. It was too soon for the Way Gates to blow. It had to be something else. Brill's attack, perhaps.

The guards shouted and ran for the nearest exit, leaving Nils alone. Scanning the exposed section of the city through a window, he saw men coming over the top of the hole in the roof. They rappelled down ropes, merging with the roiling dust created by the explosion below. A surge of pleasure rushed through him. Brill and his rebel friends were retrieving the wine. Nils wanted to investigate further but the sudden emptying out of the corridor ahead gave him access to the prison, and it was a chance he couldn't afford not to take. As he began to move toward the building, more guards from within came hurtling out into the corridor and took off toward the sounds of disturbance. *Even better*, thought Nils. Rescuing Danton had not been his specific mission, but Salinda had said that if he found a trace of Danton alive, and the opportunity arose, then he was to try. "Don't risk yourself," she had told him.

Nils was able to slip inside the prison section. The smell alone told him he was in the right place. It was dark but that did not hinder him; the shroud enhanced the light and his Hiem sight gave him an advantage.

The outer room was empty. It was clear the guards had been sitting there. One chair had been knocked over and wine dripped to the floor from an overturned mug. One solid, locked metal door was unguarded. Nils had to open this one and he hoped there were no guards on the other side to question who had opened it.

He searched around for a key, and saw it hanging from the wall. Another explosion shook the room as Nils inserted the key. He winced. That was flesh and blood that was being torn apart out there.

The rank smell within made him reel. The room was filled with the foulest of odors of death, decay and feces. Nils thought twice about entering, but at least his fears of guards hidden in the room were unfounded. None of them would have been able to bear the stench. Covering his nose, Nils edged into the room. It was hard to see, not only because it was dark but because the room was jammed full of old furniture and rubbish. Passing around one particularly large wardrobe, Nils caught a glimpse of a bloody leg. Then he came into full view of Danton, lying on the tattered remains of a sheet, naked and covered in old and fresh blood. Another dead body lay nearby, an emaciated old man.

Nils had to approach the rebel to see if he was alive. He detected a small rise in Danton's chest. The man still lived, but not for much longer without medical aid. Amputated fingers were infected, the sickly sweet smell an indication of deadly rot. The man's rib cage had been hacked into, the wounds roughly sewn together with ugly stitches. One testicle had suffered the same fate. Danton's eye patch had been removed, giving the world a view of his mangled face. So this was how humans extracted information from one another. There was no way for Danton to move himself. Nils would have to carry him to safety. It needed to be done now.

Maneuvering Danton into a sitting position, Nils levered him up so that he could carry him over his shoulder. It took a few tries, as Danton's inert form kept falling back to the ground. The sound of battle outside intensified. Nils knew he had to move quickly. He drew a second shroud from his satchel and threw it over Danton as he engaged it. Together they could navigate the treacherous pathways outside without drawing too much attention.

Nils hoped that the camouflage would work. He peered back and saw the tell-tale sign of blood drops. There was nothing he could do about that.

Just short of the door to the corridor, he heard boots tramping closer. He positioned himself by the opening, ready to step through when the door opened. Danton moaned suddenly. Nils shifted the weight slightly and Danton quieted. The door opened and a head popped through the gap. The head rotated left and right and then withdrew. Nils had no idea if it was a rebel or one of the guards stationed in the city. He took no chances. When the sound of feet receded, he edged the door open and saw that the corridor was empty. Then, when he was certain it was clear, he shouldered Danton a little higher to secure his hold on the man, one hand holding a draped arm, the other hooked around a leg, and then ducked into the corridor. He clung to the edges, keeping to the shadows. He had to move up three levels to get near the Way Gate.

One level short of the gate, Danton woke up. Before the rebel leader could raise a cry and expose them, Nils had him on the floor and was whispering hard. "Danton. It is Nils. We have come for you. Danton?"

"No...no," Danton moaned repeatedly.

"Be quiet, our lives are at stake, Danton, please." He covered Danton's mouth with his hand. "Keep quiet while I carry you to safety. We are nearly there. A few moments of discomfort, that is all it will take." He removed his hand.

Danton's good eye fluttered open. He began to struggle until Nils lowered his cowl. Danton stared at him wordlessly, a sign of recognition glinting in his bloodshot eye. Nils nodded, put the cowl back on and rewrapped Danton in the other shroud. Danton helped as much as he could but was so injured and weak he could only allow Nils to lift him. Nils thought he heard Danton weeping as he carried him up the last stairway. After seeing what had been done to the rebel, he could understand the other man's despair and relief. Surely Danton had expected to die. He might still.

Nils would never have survived such treatment. That Danton still lived was testament to the fact that he had not told them everything they wanted to hear. Salinda had warned him of that. If Danton was dead, then they knew it all. If he was alive, there was more to be forced out of the rebel. If he was alive, there was hope.

The corridor was still clear. Nils slipped behind the wall covering that hid the Way Gate and dragged the unconscious Danton after him to hide them from casual view. After propping the rebel against the wall, he opened the gate. Then he positioned himself to drag the rebel through the opening. Danton was flaccid and heavy, too. Once his legs passed the threshold, Nils shut the Way Gate, then rested his head on the cool stone and panted.

Nils then sagged to the floor, right next to an array of fully primed explosives that Brill had set up. He had further to go to reach safety but his exertions had taxed him. He needed time to rest, so he arranged Danton carefully on the ground and sprawled next to him. Nils's health and strength were not what they had been. A coughing fit seized him and left him wretched when it passed. He had been wrong to hide how much his last foray into the in-between had taxed him. Salinda would never forgive him.

Danton was in bad shape, close to death, infused with pain and infection. Without the healing tray there was little Nils could do for him, but Nils set about trying to make the rebel more comfortable before their final journey to Barrahiem.

From the pocket of his shroud, Nils took the flask of dragon wine that Salinda had pressed on him and held it to Danton's lips. How had Salinda known he would need it? She knew of his scorn for its reputed benefits. But any type of sustenance would help Danton. With encouragement, Danton swallowed some. It had to be enough.

Chapter Twenty-two

CHOICES

Once out of the Way Gate, Salinda's attention was drawn to the commotion to the south of the city, where it was open to the sky. Her hope soared when she saw that it was caused by Brill and the rest of Danton's rebel crew. Salinda intended to accompany Garan part of the way so she could keep track of Brill's attack and Garan's progress. From a good vantage point she should be able to monitor the situation and alert the others if they needed to retreat.

With her hand caressing her distended abdomen, she continued along the gallery. She knew she'd be a hindrance to Garan if she tried to climb over the rough terrain to the cliff face with him. Her gaze passed over the galleries and staircases they would need to access to reach the breach. Frowning, she realized Garan had to pass by where the fighting was strongest in order to climb up and out. Leaning over the balustrade, she saw that it was too dangerous for Garan to go up the switchback path and into the thick of battle even in a Hiem shroud. Although it was the quicker route, there was too much action and too many people. Another explosion destroyed a tight group of guards slicing through the fighting men. Screams and cries reached her. Her heart skipped a beat when she saw dark clumps on the ground when the smoke cleared. They were body parts.

Giving herself a shake, she peered along to the left of the galleries, hoping to find another way. The northern path was cut off as the galleries had collapsed when the roof had fallen in. A gantry with a movable platform was close to that collapsed section. That was where the new occupants of the city had been engaged in repairs. However, if she and Garan tried to use that movable platform it would advertise their presence.

No point in wearing Hiem shrouds if they were going to do that. Through her shroud she could see the outline of Garan as he strode along beside her, and then she gazed out to the concave remains of the city to her right and below and to the left again. They could go beyond the movable platform where the rock fall had created a stair up to the jagged edge of the breach in the city's roof. She had to remember that the baron was most likely here. And even if he wasn't, he would have put an equally ruthless person in charge and so they needed to be careful.

Garan was loaded down with explosives, which were strapped to his waist, his thighs and over his shoulder in a knapsack, which he wore under his shroud. They passed the gantry apparatus, then climbed along the rock fall, which was flat like a footpath and then rose in a stair. Around half way along the length of the breach, she saw a pile of debris that appeared steady and climbable. There was also a large slab of broken roof masonry that she could stand on, with a place to hide herself if needs be. She cast her gaze around and realized it was perfect. She could see the battle and keep an eye on the galleries that ringed the city.

"This way," she said to Garan. "Look! You will have to climb up but there are plenty of handholds."

He nodded and followed her.

Bringing the cliff down on top of the city would not only cut off the inhabitants from the outside world, it would seal them inside, because Salinda and Nils would ensure the Hiem Travel Ways were collapsed as well. If only she could be sure that the baron was imprisoned at the same time. He could rot in this tomb. Salinda fretted over how much the baron knew and how much other people knew of the previous inhabitants of the city. If word had got out, their mission, their very lives, would come under threat. She could all too easily imagine people swarming the ancient streets of Barrahiem, plundering its treasures and destroying its wealth of knowledge. Or worse still, taking away something that would help prevent moonfall, either deliberately or in ignorance.

Once the city was buried, she hoped the government in Sartell or whoever was backing this venture would decide that it would take too much time and effort to excavate and occupy the city a second time. Burying Gateshead would kill the baron's immediate plans for salvation for him and his cronies. Just the thought of what he had set up here made Salinda clench her jaw and her stomach turn. That he of all people should have a greater chance of survival than all others. Him! That foul beast of depravity? She would rather all humankind died than have the baron be the only one to live on. Knowing him, the baron would rather kill everyone if he couldn't survive.

They drew close to the end of the path where the crude rock stair angled up. Garan was already assessing the way up and nodding. Then he peered up through the breach. "I think I can manage this."

"Remember to check whether explosives have already been laid," Salinda said. "And that they are viable. They must be close to blowing it themselves if they are set already."

Garan turned to her, a slight furrow on his forehead. "Yes, Brill said the baron's people would had probably already laid them in preparation. In that case, I'm just to set the timer."

"Good. And if it is not complete or there are none, then you can lay ours." Another explosion from below made them both jump.

Garan bit his lip. "I best get a move on. Will you wait here? Will you be all right?"

"Yes, this is as good a spot as any." She could see into the sky and down into the city, and the galleries, the north ones quite closely, the west not as well and she could see south and the battle in progress there. A slight overhang would hide Garan for much of his climb.

As Garan climbed up, Salinda slid into the shadows and found a place to sit and watch over the city. Nils had prepared a shroud for her and now she was hidden from view she disengaged it. The sun lifted higher in the sky and sent a thick shaft of light through the hole in the city's roof. It illuminated the battle below and sent shadows scurrying on the far side. There she saw movement. The explosions had drawn more men to the battle. Someone shouted orders and gesticulated to others as they ran along the western gallery across from her on two separate levels. In the dark shadows she could not be seen, but she crouched down in any case, hand ready to engage the shroud.

Maintaining the cramped position was hard work. The baby kicked and squirmed.

While she was conserving the power of the shroud, she needed to get a better view so turned it on and leaned out. Above, Garan moved slowly. He still had his shroud engaged and was thus invisible to others. To her, though, he shone like a beacon with his inherent power and the steady pulse of the cadre. When she glanced away, she realized that it was the Hiem shroud that enhanced her vision, for she could make out more figures running along the galleries and others joining in the fight below.

♋♋♋♋♋

Garan pulled himself higher until the rim of the cavern was only a few handholds away. With the shroud and the explosives strapped to him, the climb was awkward. He could not move fast and had to be careful where he put his hands and feet, as well as avoiding snagging the cloth of the shroud. His life depended on it working.

Reaching up from the shadowed interior to the free air and light, Garan blinked at the brightness. At last, he scrambled over the crumbling edge, dislodging some rocks and dirt that hissed as they bled away below him. The cliff face loomed above. It was much more imposing than Nils's drawing had led him to imagine.

Down in the city, he saw that the rebels were fully engaged. A number of wine barrels were in ropes halfway to the top. Looking up and over he saw that one cart was already partly laden with the wine. He grinned, his heart lifting at the sight.

Garan focused on the path ahead. Boulders and uneven rock fragments blocked his path and he had to climb over them to reach the cliff, which was part of a long upthrust of land. Crevasses riddled the ground but Garan's keen eye kept him clear of them.

Now the sun was fully up, the sky above was clear, a pale pink with a clearer mauve above. Garan breathed in the air. It was good to be outside, even though the scent of smoke wafted around him and the screams of chaos filled the air.

Garan disengaged his shroud and took it off so that he could move faster. There was no one else around that he could see and the flowing length of it hindered his steps. Taking a moment to rest, Garan assessed the terrain. The trip back would be risky, particularly with the timer ticking away. He might need to adjust it, lengthen the time just a little bit. He thought of Brill and his rebels; they needed time to retreat to safety, too, and the wine was not all reclaimed as yet. Salinda was to give a signal so a slight adjustment in the scheduled detonation was allowable. The usual timers were unreliable mechanisms and could blow up well ahead of time or not at all. Garan and Brill had gone over some plans for improvements—Garan was sure the one he had would work as planned.

Trudging on, he had his head down and eyes on the obstacles. Then he stopped and shifted his gaze upward. The ridge ascended in front of him like a huge wedge, brown and red and orange. Garan gaped in awe. It was very impressive this close up. Surely it would crush rather than cover the city when it collapsed. Garan scrambled over to where fissures in the rock sprouted up from the ground and forked through the bluff. Garan examined the extensive net of explosives tucked into a crevice, clearly intended to shatter then collapse the overhang. The baron and his chosen elite were going to exploit a pre-existing fracture. Casting an appreciative eye over the array of explosives, Garan knew that whoever had laid them was an expert.

Garan used rope ladders already anchored to the rock face to climb up into the fracture, which narrowed the higher it went. There he checked all the connections between the sets of explosives. It took him some time. He drew out the timer he had created from a device that Nils had given him. Garan had charged it. In his hand was a small heater. Nils had said it could heat water very quickly. They'd tested it on fuses and had turned it into a timer. Now, Garan had to adjust it so it did not heat as fast as it normally would. It was not going to be precise, but it would give them more time—exactly how much more time Garan was not sure.

Higher up into the fracture, he could see that over time the weight of the overhang would increase the stress on the rock and separate it from the hill behind, bringing it down on the city below. But without intervention that could take hundreds, maybe thousands of years.

Timer set, Garan scurried back down the rock face, and at the base decided to lose the explosives he had tied to himself. As quickly as he could, he stuffed them into cracks near where the other explosives were set. It was better than being blown up himself and it would strengthen the blast that would bring the rock face down, and make it less controlled.

His return was easier without the encumbrance of the shroud and the bulk of the explosives. As Garan made his way across the terrain toward the breach, he saw that two more carts filled with wine barrels had begun their passage down the road, and another was nearly loaded. Slaves were filing out of the city, some assisted by the rebels. Hope began to grow in his chest. Finally they might have a win. He climbed back down to the ledge where Salinda waited.

"Brill needs more time, I think," Garan said as she stepped from the shadows.

"Brill or the rebels?" Salinda asked as her gaze swept the view below.

Garan ran his fingers through his hair, feeling a release of tension with the scrape of nails against his scalp. "Both. Three carts of wine are almost clear. Slaves are escaping as we speak. I lengthened the time to the blast." He hesitated when her eyes widened in alarm. "But not by very much."

Salinda's expression relaxed. "Give the signal that the timer is set."

Garan drew out a crystal, hummed and threw it into the air. It glowed hotly then exploded in a shower of sparks. Garan spied some rebels pointing at it. Good, they had seen it. Hopefully Brill had too.

Garan brushed off his hands, smiling. Then in the next heartbeat his face grew slack as his attention was drawn elsewhere. He felt a nasty prickle in his mind. Garan grabbed Salinda's hand and pulled her along.

"Garan, what is it?"

"No more time to waste," he growled at her.

"Garan, tell me!"

Garan faced the horizon and pointed. Salinda followed the line of his arm. "It is him."

⚋⚋⚋⚋⚋

Salinda's heart beat so fast and hard it hurt her chest. Breathing was suddenly difficult. Gercomo was coming. He could sense where she was. On the horizon a flock of dark figures approached: not just Gercomo, but a whole herd of dragons was heading in their direction. She could feel their minds, powerful beyond understanding and tinged with dark. She had known this was a possibility, but she had not truly been expecting it. Not expecting him.

"What should we do?" Garan asked. "We cannot escape into the city before they reach us."

Salinda reached for calm and found panic instead. "It is what I feared. He has corrupted the dragons and can direct them."

Garan's eyes widened. "And he can change form, which means he can communicate with the humans, too. We have to go. Now. He cannot follow us into the Ways."

"But they might already know about them. We will destroy them behind us. But think, Garan, we could finish it here, rid ourselves of him."

Already Salinda was searching with her dragon sense for Plu's bull, the dragon she had sent out to seek Gercomo. If the bull had done what she'd asked, he would be nearby. Closing her eyes and ignoring her body's panic mode, she stretched out, stretched far, and found the mind of the dragon. With him were others of his herd. Plu was not among them, but they had come anyway. Plu was minding her young. Salinda rubbed her abdomen full with her unborn child. What would she be like as a mother? Would she live long enough to know?

"Remember what happened last time, Salinda?" Garan pleaded. "We made things worse. We should leave now, take cover in the Ways where he cannot sense us."

"He has already sensed me—us. You detected him approaching before I did. He will destroy this place searching for us."

"What do you intend to do? Fight him?"

Salinda shook her head. "Not alone. I have you, and Plu's mate and his herd are close."

"A dragon battle?" he asked.

"Yes. I have no choice. I don't want to involve them. If fear it will change the dragons somehow."

"But Gercomo being a dragon has already done that. 'Tis not your doing."

Salinda's mouth widened in an attempt at a smile. Trust Garan to help her over her moral dilemma. He was right she had no choice to fight dragons with dragons. "I know I have little choice. Yet, I risk corrupting the dragons and making them more like us and killing their own kind. We barely register to them except as food. Changing that balance could change more than we can control." She watched as Gercomo approached and shook her head.

Garan pointed at the approaching dragons. "I think the balance is already changed."

Salinda pursed her lips. "We have to stop Gercomo here and now!"

Garan's eyes tracked the sky. The dragon shapes grew in size as they spoke. "This is going to slow things down. Should I go back and remove the timer?" Garan asked.

Salinda shook her head. "No. It can be our last resort. But keep reminding me. We still have to signal the retreat and make it back into the Ways before it goes off. Come, let's choose a better position, one where we are closer to the Way Gate. I will summon the dragons."

Salinda paused, then sent out her awareness as she put out the call. The bull was resistant at first so she sent out images of human food, and of the enemy dragons taking them all. It was a mean trick and she was ashamed of herself, but the bull responded with a resounding affirmative. Salinda reeled from the force of the contact.

A movement across the city caught Salinda's eye. People were on the western galleries across from them. Without actually being able to make out who they were, Salinda suspected the baron was among them. Garan was unshrouded. They'd been spotted.

Garan steadied her. "Are you all right?"

"Yes," she said, "it is done. They come. But we need to move. See there?"

Garan took her hand. "Come on, then." They ran along the path and reached the intact gallery. Garan dragged Salinda down a flight of stairs and they were on the level below. They passed by the gantry ropes. Salinda caught a glimpse of people running along the gallery above, heading for the gantry they had just passed. If Garan hadn't tugged her to this level they would have met face on.

Dragon roars vibrated in the air, and a flame lit the sky. The dragons came in to land on the outside of the city, peeling back the rim of the roof with their claws. Rock fell like rain and wing beats sent gusts of wind, stirring up smoke and fanning the many small fires. Screams of panic from the rebels and slaves added to the noises below. Slaves ran in all directions and the rebels faltered. A wine barrel hung motionless in its ropes. If Brill had followed the plan, he had already left his rebel band to make for the Way Gates. He had explosives to blow.

Salinda slipped into the shadows once more and Garan engaged his shroud. One level above the contingent of men who had run toward them stopped by the movable platform. Salinda had to look twice before she believed what she was seeing. Her former husband, the baron, was indeed there. He was ignoring the rebels and concentrating on the breach in the cave roof. It seemed as if he was trying to get up to the outside. Men quickly tugged on the ropes, bringing the platform up. Ropes slithered through pulleys and the square contraption reached the level where the baron stood. He stepped onto it and the men controlling it tugged, jerking it into motion. She gaped as he was winched up. He did not know that she was there. Thank the source! But if he talked with Gercomo he would find out exactly where she was. She needed to hide and silently chastised herself. She should have listened to Garan. Gercomo could talk to humans and dragons, making him doubly dangerous.

A screech of a dragon made her turn. Two rebels were scooped up into a dragon's mouth. A barrel of wine fell into the city and splattered on impact. There was little they could do now to save more wine. The dragons were a greater threat now and Plu's mate and his herd wouldn't know rebels from the baron's men.

"Garan, send the double signal. Get them to retreat."

Garan bit his lip and then gave a nod. He threw two crystals into the air. One went pop and fizz and split into glittering shards, while the other's hue was a darker purple and just exploded with a loud cough.

Salinda checked, and confirmed that the rebels had seen it. Shouts from above indicated that the signal had been seen by the baron's men, but for now at least, she and Garan were invisible. Was there anything she could do to help Squab and the rebels escape the dragons? Closing her eyes, she sensed that her force of dragons was moving closer. Soon they would be noticed.

Carefully, she placed herself where she could see what was going on. Only a thin trail of slaves were now making their way up the road and out of the city. Well defended, the rebels kept bringing up the wine that they had already started to haul up, but even they were withdrawing now, more men leaving with each barrel. Salinda's nails cut into the palms of her hands. *Leave the wine*, she thought at them. *Go now.*

A large male dragon, with orange and purple markings, landed near the rebel crew rolling a barrel of wine from along the road. It blew flame. A barrel of wine exploded, making the beast recoil. A rebel ducked out of the way. A slave did not and was captured and torn apart by the dragon's fangs. Blood sprayed in all directions, staining the dust on the road. Another beast landed, its feet thumping the ground as its head darted and dove, snatching at the fleeing slaves.

Turning back to the scene across from them, Salinda saw that the baron was waiting just below the tip of the breach, sheltered by the overhang from dragons. His foot tapped on the ground and he glanced around him as if there were no dragons savaging humans above his head.

Then she saw what had landed. The lead dragon was smaller than the others and it waddled forward, tail sliding awkwardly behind powerful rear legs. It was him—Gercomo. Yet as he stretched out his claws, he transformed. Dark purple scales rolled up and curled as they fell to the ground. An inhuman scream ripped out of his throat. Bones shifted. Muscles twisted. Then Gercomo shrugged. He was returning to human form.

Looking on, Salinda's heart thudded in her chest. Gercomo's human shape was still malformed, with clawed hands, a muzzle on his face, tattered wings and a tail. The dragon was part of him, yet he could speak. Gercomo jumped and landed across from the baron.

"She isth here."

Salinda froze. Even this far away, his grating voice penetrated, and fear trickled down her spine.

"Who?"

"Thsalinda."

The baron swung around one hundred and eighty degrees, his gaze raking the cityscape. "Where?"

Gercomo jabbed a claw in her direction. In spite of the shroud, Salinda recoiled at being identified.

At that moment a large female dragon lumbered up behind

Gercomo and Salinda could only gape. The dragon was huge. Salinda detected something from the she-dragon. Possession. She owned Gercomo. Salinda blinked away the shock. There was more. The she-dragon had a wound in her neck that seeped blood. Salinda narrowed her gaze. Something other than blood leaked out of the wound. Closing her eyes, she reached out with her senses. Her mind's eye could see a pale mauve-colored essence dissipating into the air. Was that the magic of dragons she could see? Before she could think more, Garan called her.

"Salinda," Garan said in a voice like a moan.

Salinda only gaped at him and shook her head.

The baron turned and frowned. "I see nothing. Is it this power you spoke of? The power she has that you can detect?"

"Yes."

"Then bring the power to me."

Gercomo shrugged and the guttural denial was swallowed by his transformation as he changed back into his dragon form. Human skin was swallowed by purple scales, his hind quarters surged up and out, his tail thickened, and his wings expanded. Then he was running, clawed feet scratching at the rocks. Behind him, the she-dragon leaped into the air with him. Salinda had thought she would have a chance to attack the baron, but the moment had passed. She was being attacked herself.

Out of the corner of her eye she saw the baron descend on the lowering platform, taking refuge once more in the city. Though she'd only been distracted for a second, Salinda was nearly caught in a ball of fire that erupted in front of her. The she-dragon, so large in the enclosed space, grasped at the walls and the galleries for purchase. She could not fly, thank the source for that. Gercomo could, being smaller. The floor shook and shattered beneath their feet as the gallery gave way. Salinda and Garan had to keep running. The she-dragon angled her head and blew more flame. It missed them, but halted them.

Loud bellows sounded, booming above their head. The other dragon herd had arrived.

Garan dragged Salinda back to safety, ripping her shroud in the process. It stopped working and she could be seen.

Breathing hard, Salinda asked, "What should we do? I don't think we can fight off all these dragons. Gercomo alone will be difficult enough."

The she-dragon climbed out of the hole in the city's roof to join the battle above. At once relieved that the large dragon was otherwise engaged, Salinda searched for Gercomo. His smaller stature meant he was not restricted within the city confines. As if in reply to her thoughts, a scream announced Gercomo's arrival as he swooped down on them. Praise the source that he could not blow flame as his mate had done. Yet his claws could rend.

Garan gathered up his strength and sent a line of power straight at Gercomo. The puny dragon was lithe and swerved around it. Salinda readied a ball of flame and threw it, only to see it dissipate harmlessly on Gercomo's hide.

More screams from above. The dragons were attacking the rebels. "No. No. No!" she cried out.

Garan dipped his head in acknowledgement. With the she-dragon no longer blocking the hole in the roof, Garan could send out power. A line of dark purple fire streaked up and ripped through the herd of dragons that were swooping in for the kill. Two veered off and one connected with the overhang with a wet thud and tumbled. Blood fountained out of its twisted neck, falling like rain down into the city. Eyebrows raised, Salinda realized that Garan's powers had grown since the attack on Laidan. From the wound of the dragon, she saw more of that strange light. It called to her senses, throbbed in her veins. Mauve light spilled out with the blood and bled up and away into the air and then faded from view.

Yet, as she felt the dragon die, she was saddened by the loss. It was not right to kill dragons. It was not their fault that they had been corralled into a coordinated attack; it was hers. Her thoughtless use of power had made Gercomo into a greater threat, and then she'd let him loose on the unsuspecting dragonkind.

A ripple of awareness filtered into her mind. She shook her head and gazed up to the sky. Her dragons were in sight, tiny specks growing larger as she watched. Another blast of flame curled close and Garan covered her with his body, smothering her and removing her view of the new dragons. The she-dragon was sly. She'd lowered her head through the roof hole and spewed liquid fire at them.

Gercomo was on the attack again.

Garan threw another line of violet fire upward as the she-dragon again stuck her nose through the hole above their heads. Garan was ready for her this time, and she backed off with a roar. Garan's power hurt but did not damage. Did not kill. Not like when they'd combined their power and struck together. Salinda's focus was on Gercomo, and her fireball hit him dead on. He fell and disappeared onto one of the balconies below, but he was not dead. No, he was climbing to his feet, getting ready to strike again. She had not harmed him. It was as if he'd taken the power in. It made no sense.

As she glanced down at her hand, at the flame she had conjured there, understanding dawned. Her power was transformative. It changed the nature of the object or persons it encountered. In her mind, her cadre agreed with her chain of thoughts. Finally, she understood the significance of that. Power like hers had been used to fight Moonfall. It was the power that had changed the mass of the broken pieces of Ruel as they had fallen to Margra's surface, thereby lessening their impact. The cadre had been part of the solution then and could be useful now. She just had to figure out how.

A yell from Garan drew her back to the moment. A swoop of wings and the screech of dragons overhead advertised the arrival of Plu's mate and his herd. Large, scaled bodies clashed and writhed in the air. Two bulls collided and tumbled down into the breach in the city's roof, temporarily plugging the hole. Scaled skin and rippling muscles were all they could see of the clash as gloomed cloaked the city. Rock rained down from the impact. Screeches and fire and the thump of huge bodies overhead sent Salinda backpedaling. "Careful, Garan. The ceiling."

The hole was uncovered again as the dragons fought and rolled away. Plu's mate's massive mouth struck at a smaller dragon's neck. Fangs ripped, and using a foreleg the bull ripped off a head. Blood gushed and spewed. The head dropped down, landing with a decisive thud on the floor of the city. Mauve-colored essence seeped from the dragon's headless neck and slowly evaporated. Flame rolling like thunder reached them. It was like the vineyard all over again. Sweat gathered in the small of her back and she found it hard to breathe.

In the light of the afternoon, two huge dragons faced off. Ducking and darting heads, claws ripping, rending. Screeches so loud, Salinda thought she'd go deaf. Higher in the sky another pair of dragons came together, twisting and turning as their wings struggled to keep them aloft. Salinda had to close out their mental traffic. It was too overwhelming to decipher, and she was having trouble thinking clearly. Garan dragged her backward. If any of those beasts fell they would land on top of them, bringing the roof with them.

A quick scan of where the rebels had done battle revealed that humans were scarce now. No slaves wandered about. The rebels were gone. Bodies lay like litter on the ground.

It was time that she and Garan also disappeared. Salinda leaned over the railing, searching. She called to Garan and pointed. "Strike at the baron."

Gercomo was still coming for her but their way was momentarily clear. She watched the line of purple light pierce the air in the baron's direction. In her hand she juggled balls of flame, ready to fire at Gercomo. Perhaps she should aim above him and dislodge some masonry from the ceiling to take him out, she thought, since the balls themselves were unable to harm him. Visions of Gercomo crushed by rubble came easily to mind. The baron too. Salinda licked her lips in anticipation. She had no scruple about erasing either presence from the world. The old rage came back to her easily. The baron was a dealer in so much unnecessary suffering and death, and he'd made Gercomo as if he had forged him from clay with his own hand. He was the core of evil in the world.

The baron dove to the ground to avoid the first volley. "Damn him! Why does he always get away!" Salinda grimaced when she saw him patting out the fire that had ignited the platform. Close, but not close enough. Out of range, he was able to reach the safety of a lower floor, and disappeared within the city.

With a savage yell, Garan covered her with his body again as another glob of flame exploded above them. Then Garan did something surprising, throwing up a shield woven from his power. She sensed it surround her, tingling and alive. Was that the cadre? Or just Garan evolving, learning to use the power that was naturally his?

Over the sound of the screeching of many dragons, she yelled, "Garan...how did you...?"

Garan shrugged and wiped at the dust on his clothes before offering her a hand up. "'Tis natural, I think. I have been experimenting when I have quiet time. The stream of power is but a thick thread; make them finer, weave them together and you have a shield."

Salinda gaped at him as she dusted off her own clothes. "I do not think I could do such a thing unless I had a long time to practice."

Then the ceiling cracked as two dragon bodies slammed against it. Salinda gulped nervously. If they didn't go now, they would die.

"We cannot stay here, Salinda. That cliff will blow and we will be caught if we do not retreat now. We must go."

He tugged on her shoulder and she faced him with wild eyes. She exhaled and said, "Yes, we must flee." But instead of moving to retreat, she sank to the ground.

"Salinda?"

Breathing proved difficult and she took her time to answer. Her body ached. It wasn't only her stiffened diaphragm and fatigued muscles. She hoped she wasn't in labor. It was too early and she had promised Nils she was hale. Garan knelt beside her and offered her a draft of dragon wine from his flask. She took one swallow and straight away the warmth of the wine spread through her body and out to her limbs. The pain in her back faded and did not recur. With Garan's help, she rolled onto all fours, ready to take the stairs down to the next level. "I am ready. Gercomo?"

"No sign at the moment. But he is still here somewhere."

They took the stairs hurriedly, feet barely touching each riser. Garan stopped suddenly and Salinda froze.

"'Tis him, hurry," he said urgently.

In her mind she could feel Gercomo, poised in dragon form ready to strike. However, she could not see him and could not therefore get a clear shot.

"We only have to go down one more level to reach the Way Gate."

Salinda glanced around her. "He is close."

"I know, but 'tis not far."

They rounded a corner and the way was clear.

"He is gone."

"No. He is hiding. Waiting for me."

Salinda's breaths were short as she edged around, leaning over the balustrade to pinpoint where Gercomo was. "There!"

Garan squinted in the direction she indicated. Then the top of Gercomo's dragon head and a section of wing became visible. "I see him," Garan replied.

Fortunately, Salinda detected the buildup of power in Garan and clamped a hold of her own cadre. For it suddenly wanted to leap out of her and join in. She just had time to duck down out of the line of fire. The blast Garan expended was even stronger than the last one, and her own cadre swelled suddenly as if it had absorbed some of the force.

Gercomo was hit head on. He leaped, clutching at the railing of the balcony he was on, and nearly fell. Salinda hoped that it would work, that he would fall to his doom into the city below. Garan kept sending his power strike and Gercomo dropped, falling backward. Like a cat, he twisted in the air to land, scraping boulders and tearing the rigging of one of the gantries. The structure shuddered once and then tumbled from the rim of the city to follow Gercomo. With a groan of frustration she saw Gercomo grab onto a something and halt his fall. He leaped to a gallery and was climbing up again.

Garan reached for Salinda and pulled her to her feet. "Are you all right?"

"Yes. We should go." Together they turned to run. Salinda held her side as a stitch caught her unawares as they went down the stairs to the next level. Garan ran forward when they reached the gallery and peered over the rail. "The baron."

Salinda glanced sideways and saw Gercomo had climbed back up to meet the baron. The baron was above and across from them. Salinda wondered how Gercomo had survived that fall. For a moment she thought that Gercomo would bite the baron's head off, but instead the dragon-man carefully bowed his head.

Salinda watched on, disbelieving. Gercomo had more power than the baron. He could control dragons, yet he genuflected before the other man. What had the baron done to him to make him act that way?

Then Gercomo's head jerked up and to the side, and their eyes met. Salinda and Garan were not far from Gercomo. He bunched his muscles, pushed off with his powerful hind legs and leaped across the gap separating them. Air filled his wings. He was after them again.

"Together," she shouted at Garan.

Carefully they separately aimed their blasts, but without volition their power twined. It joined together in front of them, growing larger, then, when it was big enough, Garan launched it like a ball. Gercomo recoiled as the power hit him.

Salinda did not see what happened next. Garan dragged her by the arm and kept on going until they had rounded the corner. They were off the gallery and into the bowels of the city. A couple of corridors and they would be home free. The entrance to the Way Gate was near. With her cumbersome weight, she hampered their progress.

"Run!" Garan cried. Salinda did her best. The surroundings were familiar. They were close. The baby was quiescent inside her. She did not think it had been harmed by all their exertions. A tearing sound made her steps falter and she stopped to peer back along the corridor. She could see straight across from where they had left the gallery.

On the other side of the city, Gercomo was climbing onto the balcony railings, snapping his head from side to side while he fought off the residual power from their strike. That must have been some blast, yet still not enough. The distance between them gave them some breathing space. Salinda clenched her fist, angry that she had not killed either the baron or Gercomo. And now she had run out of time. She had to escape and live to fight another day.

The Way Gate entrance was hidden by one of the newly constructed rooms. This was an advantage as it would disguise their exit. She wondered if the others were in place, and that when everything blew, it would go according to plan. If she stayed behind as bait for Gercomo, he might get caught up in the cliff fall. Her step slowed. The temptation was very great. Garan pulled up beside her. "Salinda?"

Salinda turned toward Gercomo, who was snarling and spitting at her as he clung to the gallery railing that was crumbling with his weight. He could not get to her. She sensed his thoughts. Anger laced everything in his mind. He could not blow flame. Rage! His dragons were caught fighting their enemies. Wrath! He had tasted her power and wanted it. Fury!

Salinda eased her mind out of his, trying to shrug off his feelings. Behind Gercomo she caught a glimpse of the baron as he withdrew into one of the access ways that led deeper into the city. Knowing him, the wily baron had another escape route and it was too much to hope that he would be caught up in the landfall from the detonation of the cliff.

Eyeing Gercomo again, she realized she had to go now. This fight was not won, but this could not be her last stand. There was no time to prepare for such an end, to transfer the cadre to another. There was no time for heroic acts. She had to survive this. The baby chose to kick, reminding her of its existence. Turning to face Garan, she said, "Let's go now."

Salinda reached out to Plu's mate. The bull was fighting hard. He had lost two of his herd, but had killed more. "Go now. Go!"

The bull's mind focused on hers and her knees buckled. Garan grabbed her by the elbow. She could not interpret the bull's emotions. They were too big and too complex. "Go," she repeated. "Danger comes."

The bull roared and leaped into the air. Salinda severed the mind contact, happy that the bull had understood. With a nod to Garan, they continued on and reached the room containing the Way Gate. Wrenching open the door, they paused on the threshold and exchanged looks. Sweat gathered on Garan's forehead and upper lip. He was splattered with blood, which glowed faintly. They were alive.

Behind the screen, Garan found the Way Gate and opened it. The interior of the Way was decorated with explosives, evidence of Brill's work. Further in they found Brill himself, carefully twisting the fuses together so that they could be lit. "Almost there," he said breathlessly. "You should retreat further into the Ways. No point in all of us being here to set them off."

Garan knelt down and began assisting Brill to tie the fuses.

Salinda glanced around and frowned. "Have you seen Nils?"

Brill paused. "No. I've been expecting him to help with this but he never showed up. Could he be at the other gate? I set the explosives there earlier. He might have confused the instructions."

Salinda shook her head. "Not likely. Nils has an excellent memory and he would not forget a thing like that."

Brill bit his lip and continued to work, his hands nimble.

Seeing that all was under control, Garan took the opportunity to check the sealed Way Gate entrance, squinting as he strained to listen for sounds on the other side.

"Brill, how soon will it be ready? We were seen coming in this direction and I'm afraid it will not take them long to locate us."

"I can be ready in two minutes. You go ahead and I'll catch up. The fuse won't take long to catch. Then the Way Gate will crumple."

"And the other gate?"

"It should blow too. Even if Nils doesn't set it off, this explosion will trigger that one."

Garan grabbed Salinda by the arm and urged her to move. With one final sweep of her gaze, she inclined her head to Brill and lurched after Garan.

They hadn't gone far when a low rumble shook the walls of the Travel Way. It grew in intensity, then peaked. Then the pressure wave from the blast hit them, and Salinda and Garan were thrown to the ground.

"That was the cliff face collapsing," Garan shouted. "I'm sure."

The rumbling and shaking went on and on. Garan pulled Salinda to her feet. "We've got to keep moving."

Dust rained down. The Travel Ways had been fragile, but now they were precarious. Salinda trudged wearily on. Pain was her steady companion. Every step she took she found a new source. Brill was finishing up behind them, stopping now and then to peer up as if he expected the roof to cave in. Soon he was out of sight.

Chapter Twenty-three

SALVAGE

Nils stirred when the rock face blew. Lying inside the Ways beside Danton, he realized he had passed out himself. The ground roiled beneath him, the Way severely compromised by the destruction of the rock face as it fell on Gateshead. Danton lay still, apparently unaware of the tremor shaking the ground beneath him.

Soon Brill would blow the Way Gate, which was the signal for Nils to do the same to this one. Yet Nils was curious. He had to know. Had the collapse of the rock face sealed Gateshead as they'd hoped it would? Leaving Danton where he lay, Nils slid open the Way Gate. There was less light now, and dust and grit billowed around him. Distant screams attested to the fact that there was still some life within the city. Engaging his shroud, he slipped down the corridor and hastened to the balcony that would give him a view of the city. It was dark, with only small fires giving off light. He adjusted his shroud and enhanced his vision.

There before him was a pile of rock, wide at the base in the center of the city and completely covering the breach. Nothing was going to uncover the city now. Not that way, at least.

Nils heard urgent voices and slunk back into the shadows. "We have to find a way out of here." A small old man passed him, followed by others. All were richly attired.

"Danton said there were secret ways. Search for them."

Nils's skin chilled. He had to leave now. They had to blow the Way Gates. Retreating, he skulked back to the gate, opened it and slid inside. He ran his hands over the fine sculpture in a gesture of farewell, and then closed the gate behind him.

Soon Brill would blow the first Way Gate. It was time to set off Brill's explosives at this one. Brill's calculations and their plans had not allowed for the discovery of Danton. It was only ever a vague possibility that he would be alive.

It was a blessed and difficult complication. Nils would not be able to get a safe distance away when he set the fuse. He should have moved Danton earlier instead of passing out himself.

A thumping made his head jerk up. It was coming from the other side of the Way Gate. It had been discovered. Sharp clangs sounded, as if the men were bringing a metal pike to bear. It would not be long before they tried to blow it up. Hands shaking, Nils double-checked the explosives. They had to work or they were all doomed; the Hiem legacy was doomed.

He tried now to revive Danton, but the rebel leader had not moved and would not be able to walk on his own. Nils could not leave him behind, but he doubted his ability to carry the man all the way to Barrahiem. There was no choice but to risk the in-between. Bending to light the fuse, Nils engaged his shroud, as he would need its power to survive the energy-draining substance that supported the Ways.

Once the fuse was lit, he engaged the rebel's shroud as well, and bent to lift Danton. He barely managed to pull the man over his shoulder, grabbing his arm and hooking his own around Danton's leg. Under the rebel's dead weight, he staggered. He knew he could not carry Danton far, even in the in-between.

Time had run out, and so had Nils's options. Gathering his strength, the Hiem steadied Danton on his shoulder and worked his way into the in-between.

Because the Ways were discontinuous in the area, it took a lot of effort to move away from the Way Gate that was going to explode. The impending destruction of the other gate would only increase the effect. Not ever having used the in-between for such a purpose, Nils was not at all certain how far he needed to go to reach safety. He did not know if he or Danton had enough life force left to survive in there for long. Yet he could not leave the rebel and save himself. He understood there was a bond between his mate and this man. Nils could not face her and admit he had abandoned Danton. He needed to exit the in-between before it was too late.

He was in the process of emerging when the substance of the Ways buckled around him. The Ways fought back instinctively, grasping onto the energy of Nils's shroud and not letting go. Tendrils of his life energy tore away. Nils's knees buckled at the sudden weakness. With the last of his strength, he threw Danton from him, hoping that his humanity made him immune to the life-draining in-between. He hoped rather then heard Danton's body land, and then Nils's perception darkened as he too fell out of the in-between.

೨೧೨೧

Salinda felt the Way Gates collapsing behind them. The Ways flexed and then vibrated violently. Holding her breath, Salinda hoped that they had put sufficient distance between them and the gate to keep them out of harm's way. Swift footsteps coming up behind them announced Brill's approach. When he caught up to them, all three of them sped to the main junction, where Nils had earlier calculated they would be safe. Rolls of thick dust and grit filled the Ways and coated the walls. Salinda nearly slipped on the stair leading to the junction but was steadied by Garan's hand.

"Thank you," she whispered to him, before inhaling a mouthful of dust and being seized by a fit of coughing. Brill and Garan linked arms behind her and supported her down the stairs. When they reached the junction, the trembling in the Ways stopped. Their gear was piled where they had left it, but was now covered in a thick layer of dust. As the air began to clear, Salinda saw with a heavy heart that Nils was nowhere to be seen.

Salinda could hardly speak for the dust. Her mind was harried by fear, and then she reached out through the bond, searching for the thread of Nils's life.

"No!" she hissed. The bond felt dead.

Brill grabbed her. "What is it? Is it the child?"

"No. Oh no!" Salinda crumpled to her knees, overwhelmed by the feeling of loss. Brill sank to the ground with her, clasping her hand. Numbly, she finally let go of the bond and focused on Brill. "Nils," she said, feeling hot tears on her dirt-caked face. "I can't feel him anymore."

Garan knelt beside her. "Wait here. We'll go to find him."

Both Garan and Brill stood up, peering into one passageway and the next and the next. The junction split in three ways. Salinda groped her way to her feet and swayed. "No. I will come with you, too."

Garan turned to her. "But what if he comes and we are not here?"

"I told you, I cannot sense him, and that means that he is not coming. He...might be dead."

Brill interrupted her. "You can't be certain. We have to check. You take that path, and we'll take these ones."

She nodded and made her way along the chosen path. Dust made her gag; many times she had to stop and cough up the muck that she was breathing. She went as far as she thought it was likely he might be before reluctantly returning to the junction. Given the condition of the Ways after the destruction of the gates, she did not think it was safe to linger. There was no sign of Nils anywhere.

When she reached the junction, the others had not returned. She began to worry. All the dire scenarios that had been passing through her head while she searched for Nils were renewed.

Again she reached out for her bond with Nils and felt nothing. The blow was heavy. Had she lost him? Alone in the empty Ways, her doubts amplified. Nils was not meant to be hurt, not meant to engage with anyone, not meant for danger. How had he gotten into this situation? She thought she had been clear with him about his role. She could not entertain the thought that he was gone. It was more than the loss of a mate, or a unique life; his demise had far-reaching consequences. No, she wouldn't let that thought take over. Too much depended on him. She needed him. Her child needed him. He must not be dead. She sat down and huddled in the lonely Way.

Brill came trotting down the other passageway, shaking his head at her unvoiced question. They both stared at the third path, where Garan had gone.

"Let's go," Brill said, picking up a bag of gear and tossing it over his shoulder. Salinda selected another bag to carry and Brill bent to collect the remaining one.

Together they jogged along the Way, Salinda feeling the weight of the child inside her with every step. She was so tired she could barely shoulder the bag of gear she carried. Yet she kept on, supposing that if Garan was delayed it would be for a reason. Hopefully that reason would be Nils.

Rocks and dirt made the going hard. This Way was severely compromised. Her ankle twisted when she misstepped on a chunk of rock, and Brill stopped to help her. As they straightened up, Salinda gasped. Ahead, amid the thick cloud of dust, was Garan, leaning over two bodies. So many thoughts went through Salinda's head—that Nils had been attacked, that he had been followed, or that some of his own kind lived in the city and had ambushed him. Yet when she drew nearer, she stopped suddenly.

The other body was hard to recognize at first, naked, dirtied and bloodied. *Danton! By the source, Danton!* How was he even alive with so many injuries? Next to her she heard Brill's sharp intake of breath before he darted forward to kneel by his rebel friend.

Salinda took another cautious breath, hardly believing what she was seeing. Brill was leaning over Danton, gently touching here and there. Danton made no sound, nor did he move. Garan hovered by Nils's inert form. The damage to both men was bad. Salinda's eyes kept returning to Danton. It was obvious the baron had been at him. The pattern was unmistakable. That made her shudder with revulsion. Her own memories assaulted her, so she forced herself to turn away. Her eyes returned to Nils.

Still and as pale as death, Nils lay next to Danton, arms spread, head thrown back at an angle. Salinda hesitated. She felt nothing in the bond. Garan peered up at her. "He lives...but barely. His body is warm and he breathes. But he will not wake."

A surge of hope raced through her. Not dead. Not yet. Salinda stood there gaping at the two casualties, indecisive. Both of them were severely wounded. Both of them. What was she to do?

"We have to bring them with us," Brill said to her. "Salinda?"

She hesitated. She would have to make an impossible decision.

"Salinda?" Brill repeated.

Brill took her by the shoulders and shook her gently. "Salinda, take our things and we will carry them. Garan, can you manage Nils?"

"Yes" Garan replied and began to lift Nils's unresponsive body. Salinda dropped her belongings and helped to secure her mate over Garan's shoulder. Brill was not so lucky with Danton, and the rebel's injuries complicated things. "I'll have to help you with him, Brill. He is too badly hurt," she said softly, hovering by Danton as Brill tried to pick him up.

Brill agreed. He positioned the shroud that Danton lay on under him and tugged the ends past his head and feet so they could use it as a stretcher. Salinda lifted one end. "I will help. We can leave our things behind." Brill took the other end, and they began the slow walk down the Way.

"How do we find our way home?" she asked.

"I can find it well enough." Garan took the lead, his step faster than theirs.

"Garan, go on ahead and put Nils in the healing tray. Then come back to help us."

Garan turned his eyes to Danton. "Surely Danton needs the tray more?"

"No." Salinda shook her head. It was a brutal decision to have to make, and one that could end Danton's life, but Nils was the more important. His life was more valuable. That was what the cadre told her, and that was what she knew in her heart. "Nils must go in the healing tray."

Garan shared a brief look with Brill. Salinda kept her gaze averted from Danton. She could see the despair writ large on his face. Her heart was breaking, but the choice was clear.

Then a great rumble rose up and the ground tilted. She lowered her end of the shroud and braced herself against the wall. More dust dislodged, and for a moment she thought the Way would collapse. The Way shook and groaned, and Nils stirred on Garan's shoulder. Yet the Ways held. "The explosions have destabilized the whole area," Salinda observed. "We must hurry."

When they had ascertained that they were all unharmed and the Ways were not set to collapse on them, Garan left them, taking long strides until he disappeared in the gloom ahead.

Brill and Salinda continued on alone, carrying their heavy burden. "Salinda?" Brill asked, facing forward.

Salinda knew what he was going to say. Was not the same idea in her head, was not her conscience struggling with the decisions she had made? "I'm sorry, Brill. I will not discuss it. I cannot discuss it. I have decided."

"But Danton seems to be the most in need. You told me the healing tray can restore the body. It regrew your finger after it was severed and removed the scars on your back. Danton has many injuries. He has lost bits of himself. Nils is whole."

Salinda tugged the stretcher higher and Brill slowed down to check her progress.

"What would you know?" she replied, close to tears. "I see Nils with more than my eyes. I have a bond with him and I can feel that he is nearly expired. I cannot delay putting him in the healing tray. I nearly lost him before when a similar thing happened and he was nowhere near as far gone as he is now. Dragon wine does not work on him, not as it does on us. I have tried it."

"But Danton...he cares for you. I thought you..."

"Can't you see that this isn't about me, or how I feel? It isn't about who I love more. It's about the future of the world." She stabbed a finger in the direction Garan and Nils had gone. "He can save this world. We need him, we need him desperately." She studied Danton, and her voice dropped to a whisper. "He can't save the world. The choice for me is clear."

Brill shook his head, tears glistening in his eyes. "But Danton's injuries?"

"If I can save Danton, I will. I promise you that. I will nurse him as best I can. If Nils heals quickly then we can put Danton in, if...if he survives that long."

"I don't doubt that. But what of the quality of his life? Look at him. See what has been done to him."

Salinda kept her head averted. The image of Danton's mangled body would be in her mind's eye forever. "I don't have to look, Brill. I know what was done to him. You forget that I was once at the mercy of the baron."

Brill lowered his gaze and said nothing more.

"Let's keep moving," she said finally, and quickened her pace. "We have a while to go."

"Wait a minute," Brill said and changed his grip on the shroud. Danton rolled but then steadied. Shoulders hunched, Brill led them along the Ways, voicing no further accusations. He didn't need to speak to them, as Salinda could feel the reproach emanating from him. It was no worse than the agony she felt herself. Once she had loved Danton dearly. Had despaired for what the Inspector had done to him. Now she must put Nils ahead of him, knowing that this decision put Danton's life in the balance. Yet, if she failed, if the world failed, then saving Danton would count for nothing.

♋♋♋♋

Salinda turned away from the healing tray, seeing that Nils was safely inside and the healing process had begun. With a heavy heart, she headed back to her abode. Danton was alive, but was in a very bad condition. Brill had tried to clean the wounds but had spent a lot of time sobbing over his friend. Guilt was a powerful enemy. Salinda knew her share where Danton was concerned. Her choices had never been favorable for Danton.

As she squeezed through the door of her abode, she saw that Danton lay on the low table. "You can go now, Brill. Rest awhile. I will tend him."

Brill spared her a resentful expression. He had not voiced it again, but she knew he was angry about her choice. Danton could have gone in the healing tray. The tray would have restored him. The fingers, the missing ribs, the savage mutilation of his sex, all of the damage. Salinda wasn't sure about the eye. Yet she had chosen Nils over Danton.

Brill hesitated, glancing between her and the rebel leader. Salinda didn't have time for recriminations. "Laidan is searching for you. I think they are about to eat."

He acknowledged her with a bob of his head and left. They had struggled in the Ways for most of a day before Garan had returned to help them. Salinda had been close to exhaustion and was glad to give up her burden to the young Skywatcher. Garan didn't judge her like Brill did. Garan understood the burden of the cadre, and what was at stake if Nils died.

While the battle in Gateshead seemed like a loss, a setback, she had learned much. Her power was to be used in saving Margra, she just had to find out how. The dragon's blood had something powerful in it.

Now that she recalled her past, her life in the vineyard, it made sense. If grapes grown in dragon dung were imbued with magical properties, then of course, the dragons themselves, their blood, was even more powerful. Whatever allowed her to sense dragons, allowed her to see the essence of dragons. Garan's power was growing and maturing and his skill was way ahead of her own. That had to count for something.

And despite having thought Danton was dead, they had him back. She had him back. She thought of Nils in the healing tray. They still had Nils and that was the most important thing, of that she was sure.

Salinda studied Danton's naked body and examined the bandages on his hands. The smell of decay was evident. Brill's ministrations had not stopped the infection. She traced a finger across Danton's brow and detected the fever there. She may have denied him the healing tray but she would do all in her power to save him, to heal him. "There may not be Hiem technology at my disposal," she said out loud to Danton, "but I have the traditional methods."

After brewing herbs, she immersed a cloth and cleaned Danton's body, carefully undoing the filthy bandages and the coverings over his wounds. Then she filled a shallow bowl with dragon wine and began to cleanse the wounds again. She started with the hands. Danton moaned and tried to pull away. Sensing that he was close to consciousness, she raised his head and tried to get him to swallow some of the wine. Talking to him eased him somewhat. He took a few sips. Then she began again, pouring the wine over the wound where his little finger had been.

His groin disconcerted her. It had been stitched but it wept pus. She would not attempt to tidy the surgery. That would cause unnecessary pain. Again Danton writhed when she applied the wine to his injuries, and so she tried to get him to drink a little more, hoping that the power of the dragons would work from the inside. She stroked his brow while he swallowed and laid his head gently down on the pillow.

Next were the wounds in his side. She felt carefully around the stitches and could feel where the bones had been cut. Danton flinched again. Here she felt more surgery was needed. It had been a hasty job, a patch to stop him bleeding out. Who knew what had been done internally. She had to check that they had not sentenced him to a long, slow death by removing something important. That would seriously shake her resolve.

As she prepared to open the wound, her tears flowed. Danton had suffered because of her, and continued to do so. From the day she had refused to leave the prison vineyard with him she had set them on a course. Some of her choices had been wrong, but she had hope that they would come out well in the end. Tears became sobbing. "Danton. Forgive me," she cried brokenly. "I love you but my love is a curse."

Then she wiped away the tears, washed her face and hands and inspected and re-stitched his wounds. He was lucky they had not punctured his lungs.

Later that night, Brill harangued her until she rested, taking over the nursing himself. Garan then relieved him and between them they shared Danton's care as his life hung precariously in the balance.

A few days later, she sat there, bathing his wounds, letting her tears flow, when he spoke suddenly.

"Salinda?" He lifted a bandaged hand to her face.

"I am sorry," she managed to say. "I chose Nils. I chose to heal him ahead of you. Oh, Danton!"

Danton lowered his head as if he understood. Then he drifted off to sleep. The next day he seemed stronger, though he was not conscious. His fingers were less inflamed. The wound on his ribs was tidier now. The baron or his men had cut out portions of three ribs. Danton's groin was a worry, though. The infection there would kill him quickly if she did not control it. Already his penis was misshapen and his remaining testicle swollen. There was nothing else for it. She would have to pour on some dragon wine and hope that the pain was worth it, that the wine would heal the wound. There wasn't much wine left now. The small supply they had had was dwindling. Lifting the sheet, she screwed up her face. There was a smell now, too. Danton's skin was flushed with fever. Salinda unpicked the infected stitches, fighting nausea as she drained the wound. Hot, wet cloths helped open and clean it. Then she took the last of the wine and poured it on.

She'd hoped the unconscious Danton would not feel it, but she was wrong. He sat bolt upright and roared and roared. Brill and Garan came at a run and Laidan's voiced carried. "What is it?"

The pain was too much. Danton stiffened and then fell back in a dead faint. His skin grew pinker by the minute.

Salinda felt shaken, but it was the best she could do. She stood up, reeled and used the wall for support. She was tired. Sleep didn't seem to help the fatigue. There was too much to think about. Garan helped her out of the abode. "I want to look in on Nils," she murmured. Garan put out his arm and lent her his support.

"When is the baby due, Salinda?" he asked suddenly.

"I am not sure. Soon. Too soon." She sent him a weary smile. "How is Laidan?"

"Improving," Garan replied. His violet eyes studied her, but she saw no judgment in them and for that she was grateful. "This morning Laidan spoke to Brill, like she remembered him, like her old self."

"Did she remember him?" Salinda asked.

Garan's expression fell. "No, not everything. But the spark was there. I think bit by bit she is coming back. Having Eneit there seems to help. Laidan tries to take care of her. They sleep together you know, cuddling."

Salinda focused on the healing tray when they entered the chamber. She had no idea how long Nils would take to mend, or even if he would. A thought came to her.

"Garan. Remember that box you found? The one you touched and the lights came on?"

"Yes."

"We have to find out more about it. It's important. What about that other thing you sensed? Is it still there?"

"Yes, it is still there."

"Good. We have to continue with our work, even if Nils is... indisposed."

ꞁꞁꞁꞁꞁ

The battle at Gateshead had been over for a week. Salinda walked through Barrahiem. Danton still lived and had passed through the worst of his fever. She'd left him asleep with Brill watching over him. She strode through the Hall of Elders, took heart in the still-flickering light of the sacred lamp and went to check on Nils. He lay in the healing tray covered in fine webs, still and somber. She caught a glimpse of his white hair flared out around his head. He was healing. Salinda hoped he wouldn't take too long.

Too restless to return to her abode, Salinda went walking, down into the depths of Barrahiem, down where Nils worked. She found the pile of books that Garan had brought him and tidied them on the desk, inspecting them with idle curiosity. She lifted the bag that Garan had carried them in off the floor and realized there was a book inside.

Drawing it out, she saw it was bound in hardened, black paper, but held no writing on the outside. She turned it over and then back again. Nils had been searching for writings of his grandsire: Trell of Barr.

Salinda went to place it on the top of the pile, but a sliver of interest prompted her to peek inside. She blinked a few times, screwed up her nose as she peered at the text. It was in the code that Nils had taught her long ago. She started to read. A few words in, her heart leaped. Her eyes darted to the bottom of the page where a name was written. She gasped. It was signed: Trell of Barr.

The End

Author's Note

What an amazing journey! The Dragon Wine series is so close to my heart. I can't really explain why I have so much emotion vested in this series, but I do. It's been a long journey and many things have happened in the real world that have shaped what goes on in the world of Margra. Scary as that seems.

Humankind is capable of many great things and many cruel things. My fantasy is that we will move beyond that.

After a bit of a gap in working on the series and not writing notes years ago, I now have heaps of ideas to help in the writing of the last two installments, *Skyfire* and *Moonfall*. Not that I didn't know what was going to happen, but the devil is in the details. A lot of this story was written by the seat of my pants, but that is going to change. For once in my life, I will need to plan before I write. There is a lot of ground to cover, threads to tie off and maybe a world to save.

Writing this series has helped me grow as an author. The more I write, the better I become. However, my editors tell me I have bad habits!

I wouldn't have made it this far without the amazing Brianne Collins, who has edited all the books and put in some very hard yards with this installment. She was very particular in telling me how much she liked the book and how awesome she thought it was. Then, of course, she edited the thing like she was filleting a fish with a very sharp knife. Ouch! But I think it was better for it. Jason Nahrung has been an excellent proofreader and provided much comfort to me, knowing that all the little things are correct.

I would also like to thank the guys from Momentum Books. Hayley Nash, Joel Naoum and Patrick Lenton in particular. While the imprint has gone, their support for me as a writer remains and has given me courage to keep at it.

I want to thank my partner, Matthew Farrer. He is a writer and he gets the absence of mind, the total immersion that happens when writing just has to be done, and he really understands the qualities of dragon blood. Thanks for the reminder!

If you liked this book or the series, please drop me a line and let me know. Encouragement is always welcome. If you care to leave a review that would be most welcome too. If you think it was awesome then tell your friends.

Donna Maree Hanson

June 2017

Coming your way in 2018/19 the stunning conclusion to the

Dragon Wine Series

Skyfire and *Moonfall*